ETHICAL
NECROMANCER

L. S. DAELY

Disclaimer:
This is a work of fiction. All characters, locations, and businesses are purely products of the author's imagination and are entirely fictitious. Any resemblance to actual people, living or dead, or to businesses, places, or events is completely coincidental.

ACKNOWLEDGEMENT

To Stacy,
You were the first to believe in my story. Without your mentoring, this would just be an unfinished pile of words in a document. It is because of you that this story has progressed.

Thank you.
To Bishops University,
Thank you for taking the chance of accepting me, helping me complete this book, and showing me that that my horizons are further away then I imagined.

Ethical Necromancer
Some want their heroes fast and strong and to always be straight out of a fight. Jennifer had a mop.

CHAPTER 1

JENNIFER BRUSHED HER LONG black hair out of her face, trying to remember what she was doing. Looking around to recollect her thoughts for why she was here. She realized whatever this was, it was not what she was expecting. The room was cold with rows of computer banks with wires coming in and out from one row to another. Jennifer looked at the mess of cables, they formed more of a spider web than what she thought a server room, she thought. A bottle filled with lightning was attached to the ceiling. She stopped, closed her eyes, and took in a deep breath. The smell of ozone tickled her nose. Mentally she tried to retrace her steps when she noticed footsteps.

"I was coming to campus to speak with someone. There were so many classes to choose from, and I didn't know where to start." She wanted to reinforce why she was here.

She understood that coming to university would be anxiety producing, beautifully exciting, and at times overwhelming. But she was not expecting to have all those feelings when looking for advice on choosing her classes. When she opened her eyes, a strange little man stood in front of her. He had a bushy brown beard and a hairline that had been in full retreat for some time. He wore a white lab coat over a button-down shirt.

"Oh bother, this is not going well. All so a youth could play a dinosaur." The little man ran between the high-tech machinery and monitors. Lines of worry creased his face as he looked at readouts. All the needles on every indicator mounted on pipes sprouting out from the walls were in the danger zone. The question of why pressure valves were in a computer room vanished as lightning cracked and rumbled, causing Jennifer to cover her ears.

The man turned and acknowledged her for the first time. "Oh good, you're here. There is not much time!"

She blinked in confusion. "I'm here to choose my classes, sir."

The lab coat man shouted over the noise in the room, shoving something into her hands. "Oh, what? Never mind. There is no time to explain. Take this. The system is going to reboot!"

This was all getting to be a bit much for her. "Is this where I choose my classes?" She tried to make sense of the scene before her.

"Save the town! Save the nation! Save the world!" The little lab coat man yelled over the increasing thunderclaps.

The volume of the thunder increased with each passing heartbeat. The sounds of the storm hurt her ears, and the flashes of lightning hurt her eyes. Feeling overwhelmed, she closed her eyes and sank to her knees, taking deep breaths to try and calm herself.

After a few heartbeats, the noise stopped as if someone had hit the mute button which caused her to hold her breath. Moments passed before she let out her breath. Jennifer opened her eyes, stood up, and took in the room around her. Everything had changed. The man in the lab coat was gone, the bottle on the ceiling was smashed, and the banks of computer equipment looked old and rusted. Just a moment ago they had been new and shiny. The urge to talk to someone about this had her pacing. She knew university could be hard, but this did not make any sense.

"I will find someone to talk to about this." She crossed her arms and glared at the state of the room. "Maybe even the Dean."

"Listen, kid, I don't know who this Dean is," said an unfamiliar voice, putting an emphasis on the word Dean. "But I'm betting he grabbed whatever wasn't nailed down and skipped town, never looking back."

Jennifer gasped as she realized that the thing the man had shoved into her hands was a rather large red egg, and the egg was talking. She held her arm out, freighting the egg as well as dropping it. She looked around for a place to sit down. Not seeing any chairs, she took a seat on the ground.

Jennifer had been a student at this university for at most a few hours. She was overwhelmed and confused. Jennifer came here looking for advice picking her classes, not to be given a mission to save a town, let alone the world. This was not at all going the way she thought it would. Her goal in coming to university was to learn how to help others, which did not sound too far off from trying to save the world.

"Okay, kid. The world is a strange new place, and you haven't been here long. So, before you get all panicky, let's talk." The red egg spoke in a firm voice. "Let's start with the basics. What's your name?"

"Jennifer." The wheels in her mind turned faster as she focused to answer the question.

"Do you have a last name?" Jennifer could feel a smirk in the eggs' voice.

Her mouth dropped open, her chin tilted up to the right, eyes darting left and right, before turning her head to glare at the large red egg. Of course, she had a last name. It was on the tip of her tongue. When she tried to say it, the memory slipped away, and she had no idea what her last name was.

"Listen, kid, I don't have eyes, yet." The egg sounded annoyed. "So, you're going to need to talk to me. I know the odds. You don't have a last name."

"My name is Jennifer," she said slowly, her voice raised, disturbed by the hollow feeling of loss at something she had her whole life, just forgotten. "How can someone forget their own name? This isn't like losing my keys. This is my name. It's important."

"I understand this is something you are not used to, kid. This is a step down, a path you probably did not ask for, and it is hard. I am here with you. I will help. What else do you remember?"

She searched her memory and remembered an older woman, telling a story as they picked berries when she was younger. The older woman was much taller than Jennifer at that time and she told her something important.

"I'm descended from giants." The older woman's words came out of Jennifer's mouth.

"That's new. But what you are now is, " the egg paused for a slight moment, "what we call a fragment. The reason we call you this is because you're an incomplete copy of your original self."

Jennifer's mind whirled, trying to make sense of the egg's words. She may have forgotten her last name, but she felt whole. "Why do you think I'm an incomplete copy?"

"Do you know Lord Dexx's theory of non-linear temporal interference with connection to the mainframe relativism?"

Jennifer thought that was a lot of made-up words and phrases. "I was going to major in sociology, not whatever that was," she replied defiantly.

"We all make mistakes, kid. Luckily, we got you before you fell down that rabbit hole." The egg sounded as if choosing sociology was a bad thing.

"Listen, I wanted to help people. Sociology would give me the education I need to be able to do that." She remembered having this argument before but not with whom. Jennifer let out huff of frustration at the incomplete memory.

"Okay, your major may have sounded like a good idea at the time, but, kid, that was a world or two ago." The egg sounded like it was trying to hold in a laugh at its own joke.

Listening as the egg began to lecture, "A man invents time travel by putting a message in a bottle and sending the bottle through time. When it's found, others learn this message-in-a-bottle time travel method and move it forward in time. The bottle could've been forwarded millions of times, affecting untold numbers of people, events, and objects. At some point, the message starts going backwards in time," the egg paused for effect, "with instructions on how to properly send the message in a bottle to any place and time. So, the message starts its return journey in a long line of return to sender steps. The message in the bottle arrives back to the original sender. That first sender realizes all he has to do is send the bottle, with all of the instructions back to himself, before he sends the first message. The one who sent the first bottle through time, creates a time loop. Then he breaks the time loop. Do you see where this is going, kid?"

With all the information being thrown at her, she had but one response. "No. Is this going to be on a test?"

The egg started up again as if Jennifer had not asked a question. "The bottle was sent, forwarded, and then returned. Now, the bottle is going to be returned then sent. Skipping the forwarded part. The forwarded part is what we call fragmented timelines. The system administrators take people, places, and things out of these fragmented timelines to make this world. Those people, places, and things are never whole, always missing something. In most people, what changes are only memories." The egg gave space for another moment, this allowed her to digest the information.

Jennifer was getting annoyed at how dramatic the egg was being.

"So, you're a fragment," the egg said.

"No. That doesn't make sense. I'm not a fragment. I'm a person! I have two feet and a heartbeat." She felt whole and knew her wants and desires. She may have forgotten a few things, but Jennifer was Jennifer. She felt whole no matter what anyone said.

"Well, you are. We think the fragments are put in places like this and studied, like how scientists study mice in a maze. The whole world is a system put in place, and people must navigate the system as if it was a maze. Or it could be just window dressing. This world may even be made up with parts of broken timelines, why some sayings get confused, or why some landmarks are different colors then they remember. Some call it the Mandela effect, people remember seeing him make a speech a week ago, then find out he died decades ago."

"Okay that makes less sense, red egg thing." She said, glaring at the egg.

"Well, kid, those are just theories." The egg went on half-heartedly, "Anyways, it's time to choose your classes."

For the first time today, things were going in the right direction. She had come looking for help with picking her classes, like introduction to sociology.

"Let me pull up your character sheet using the system interface."

The temperature of the egg rose to a pleasant warmth in her hand as it spoke. She realized at the mention of the word 'system', that she had no idea how to interpret what being 'in the system' was or how it worked. Her mind spun adding up what the egg lectured on. Red egg could have just said that she was put in a computer system. It must have been in a long-winded profession before it became an egg. If the egg was a professor, Jennifer was going to avoid his classes.

Black letters appeared in the air in front of Jennifer. Putting the egg in her pocket, she reached out to interact with what looked like an options menu. When her hand went through the screen, it dawned on her that it might react to her thoughts. She closed her eyes, focusing her mind on closing the menus. With a 'close command' thought, her menus obeyed. Happy she could interact with the menus at will, she opened the menu up again.

"Is this going to be the new normal?" she wondered aloud.

Name: Jennifer
Alignment: Neutral
Primary Class: None
Secondary Class: None
Role: None
Health: 100
Energy: 100
Powers: None
Abilities: None
Skills: None
Traits: Trait one > Error: Name not found. Trait two > Error: Name not found. Trait three > Error: Name not found. Trait four > Error: Name not found.

Seeing how little information was on her character sheet, she hoped that a lot of unused space on the page meant there was room to grow and improve. If she could look at her character sheet often that meant she would be able to choose her path forwards. Moving her hands to navigate through the pop-ups. She knew moving her hands was useless, but it did help her with aiming her intentions. She saw several potential role choices. After narrowing down the selection, her mind continued to make connections to how much like a video game this world was.

Buffer Classes: Will enable teammates to be stronger, faster, and better.

Debuffer Classes: Will disable enemies to make them weaker, slower, and worse.

Summoner Classes: Will enable you to bring more into the party.

Jennifer remembered playing some fantasy series that had summoners. In those games, the summoners always seemed overpowered. She willed the menus to bring up summoner options. Dozens of options popped up in front of her, like **Forest Guardian, City Rats, Wave Rider, Spirit Thrower**. All the options blurred, and she felt her will slipping. Panicking, she let out a squeak and selected a class.

An announcer's voice rang out from the menu in front of Jennifer. **"Congratulations, you're a necromancer. You can make new friends out of old enemies. As a necromancer, you can summon the dead to aid you in fights or everyday activities. The dark corners of the world will be your playground."**

"Necromancer, eh? Did not think you had it in you, kid," the red egg said.

"Umm, I didn't mean to do that. Can I choose again?" Jennifer spoke knowing there was little hope.

The egg laughed.

The choice was made, but there was still an option to pick: dirty-looking zombies or dirty-looking skeletons. The zombies looked to be in a state of decay. The thought of having the foul smell of rotting meat following her around made the decision simple. Jennifer chose the skeletons. The menu before her showed a list of powers that would unlock as she leveled up. Rather than summoning a skeleton, her first power was a dark pulse.

Dark Pulse: Basic energy attack. 10 energy. Quick cooldown. You can now hit with darkness.

Jennifer knew what she wanted to do next. She was going to choose some kind of healing power for her next set.

"Umm, Mister Egg, can you bring up just healer options? I don't want to make another mistake like choosing a necromancer." Jennifer hoped she would have more control over those windows.

The egg sighed. "I was hoping you'd choose something just as interesting as necromancer." By some unseen power, it brought up four options.

Cleric: Through the power of a patron deity, you are able to heal others.

Alchemist: Why waste energy when you can throw a potion to heal others?

White Mage: Through the purity of magic, you can heal others.

Bard: Oh the things you can do with a lute. Not well, but you can still do it!

Without hesitation and with more confidence than she had felt all day, she knew what to do. With a smile on her face, she closed the window for the bard.

With less confidence, she closed the cleric. Not only did it not seem like her style, but something felt wrong looking at the class.

The two remaining choices were white mage and alchemist. She wanted to be more careful with the next choice if for nothing else but to make up for becoming a necromancer. Reading further into white mage, Jennifer noticed a particular line of text. **White magic will also damage the undead.** She rolled her eyes and read the alchemist. **Potions must be ingested to take effect.** Skeletons do not drink, or did they? To her, this was far more guesswork than she would have liked.

"Umm, Mister Egg, what do you think I should choose?" Hoping the egg would have some insight that could help her pick her second class.

"Necromancer takes a lot of energy, and white mage too. The alchemist is more of a stamina drain. You do you, kid," the egg added, keeping his words tight. His words were not leaning either way.

Looking at the two choices before her, either was good. It seemed to Jennifer that it was easier for her to choose a university major than to choose her classes. In university, it was possible to switch majors, whereas this system appeared to lock her into the choices she made.

She thought on the idea of jobs she could take on as a white mage. Town healer maybe? Couldn't she do that as an alchemist as well? Join the town guard? End up just being another healer, city architect? No, that last one would just not work as a healer.

As a white mage, all she would be doing was healing, and she wanted more than that. The old saying, the spice of life is variety, flitted through her mind. As an alchemist, she might be able to make more than just healing potions. Maybe even have a little shop where she could sell her potions like some kind of old-school snake oil peddler. The difference being her potions would work. She chose the alchemist.

Level 1 skill unlocked. Craft Potion: Craft small healing potion 20 health recovery over 1 second. Energy cost 20. Moderate cooldown. Keep calm, drink this, and carry on.

Jennifer was unsure how she should feel about choosing alchemist. This was a lot of pressure for someone who was starting out.

A third class window popped up, accompanied with the announcer's voice: **Future Defence Tech, you have been granted lost tech as a third power pool.**

Force Field: Protective bubble. Energy cost 50. Long cooldown. User may cast force field on any target. The target is granted a shield worth 50 Health. Shield will take 100% of damage until it fails. A little protection can go a long way.

"Okay, Mister Egg. I have my three classes. Now what?" With a sense of accomplishment, she smiled.

"Three classes? That is uncommon these days." Doubt peppered the egg's words. "Let me take a look. Well, I'll be. Three classes! Did you get to pick the third or did the system add it? Oh never mind, the next part you're not going to like."

The smile left her face. A large red warning came up on the menu along with the return of the announcer's voice.

Prepare for symbolisation of classes. Warning! Some discomfort may occur.

A hum came from all around the room, growing louder as each moment passed. Jennifer felt herself being lifted off the ground. The disembodied voice turned to static. The static and humming grew in volume, as if in competition to be the loudest.

Error: Third class found > Gnome override found > Gnome

override accepted. Clause 114 in effect.

The announcer's voice faded as the static volume increased. She covered her ears, as her feet dangled in the air below her.

Even though she was inside, Jennifer felt the wind against her skin, creating a vortex around her. It stopped as if flipping a light switch from wind and noise from on to off. She did not fall back to the ground, but the weight of standing returned to her legs. She met a new perspective of the world and everything was just a bit shorter now.

Her eyes were closed, but she did not remember closing them. Opening them, she saw she was in the same room as before. It looked a bit off to her, but she could not tell why other than the dust covering the ground was gone, having been picked up by the wind. Her clothes had changed without her noticing, and Jennifer felt different as if someone re-wired her.

The menu before her now read, **Welcome to Bishop's University of Magic, Jennifer the Alchemical-Techno-Necromancer.** Beside the words, stood a purple and gold bishop chess piece.

"Umm, it's just Jennifer, thank you," she said to the system.

Welcome to Bishop's University, Just Jennifer.

She had chosen her classes but did not know what to do next.

"So, Mister Egg, now what?" Where her pants and shirt were supposed to be, were now dark robes and baggy pants. She guessed this was what people expected necromancers to wear in video games, but she did not like the outfit. Moving around a bit she had to admit that the robes were comfortable. Still, the first chance she got, she was going to need to find something more to her liking.

A dainty mew and something with little claws moved up her arm inside her sleeve. Jennifer shrieked, freezing in place at the thought of a mouse up her sleeve.

"Oh, for the love of the system, kid. I hatched."

The voice was that of the red egg. Her heart settled as the realization seeped in.

A tiny white and gray lynx, no bigger than a mouse, popped out of her sleeve, and looked at Jennifer. The lynx had long legs with oversized cat paws, pointed ears, and a broad but short pointy head. She let out an audible, "Aww," while looking over the cute but strange creature. It had a furry coat and a hairy shark-like fin on its back with a shark tail to match. The fur was cream colored with spots of brown and black. The tail and the ear tufts were tipped with black. On the sides of the back fin were rectangular prisms with intakes like a jet engine.

"According to the system rules, I can't tell you what to do." The lynx raised his voice to emphasize the words. "But you should just say yes to the next question."

Do you wish to accept a jet-powered lynx-shark as a familiar at this time: yes or no.

This was a no-brainer. This was an adorable creature who, so far, had been a big help. She willed the 'yes' option.

What do you want to name your familiar?

She glanced down at the face of the tiny lynx. "So, what do you want to be called?"

The lynx-shark deepened his voice for effect. "Destroyer Of Worlds. Bringer Of Doom. The One Who Is The Storm. Defeater Of The Moon. Slayer Of All Before Him. Something that would suit me."

She blinked. The names sounded like titles that a B-movie villain would pick. Not sure why she was choosing the name, Jennifer concentrated on a moniker that for some reason seemed to fit.

The lynx jumped out of the sleeve. To Jennifer's astonishment, it flew around the room using the jets on its back while showing off its shark tail, oversized paws, and dorsal fin. "Oh, kid, I don't know where you got your lucky, golden horseshoe, but this is the best body I've had in a long while."

The lynx-shark landed on his paws with what one could assume was grace if you squinted or were looking the wrong way. The small familiar stood on his hind legs looking at Jennifer. "So now move around a bit and get used to your new body. Move forward, move back, side to side. Yeah, that's right."

Jennifer did as he instructed. As she moved from side to side. Her robes caught on her back, she was unsure why but kept moving.

"So, now that I've proven I can walk and talk, can I explore the school now?" Not knowing why, she needed or wanted the permission of the small beast, but he seemed to know what he was doing.

"This is still just a starting area. Maybe look around before adventuring out there?"

"I came to Bishop's to become a student. New world, same goals. I'm the first in my family to ever go to university. So, I will be a student here, and I will graduate."

A pop-up appeared in her menus.

Do you wish to accept quests: 1) Become a student at Bishop's University; 2) Graduate from Bishop's University.

With a smile on her face, she gave a mental command, and accepted the quests.

Looking around the room again, nothing seemed to be of value, but her eye caught on something. Someone had left an old mop propped up in the corner of the room. Jennifer did not have anything beyond the clothes on her back. If this place was like a video game, she would end up having to fight, and she wanted to be able to protect people with something. Without a better option, Jennifer took the mop, straightened her back, and said, "I'm ready. Let's go."

CHAPTER 2

RANDOM ENCOUNTERS IN SCHOOL.

"YOU NAMED ME WOOZLE?" the lynx-shark asked for the fifth time. While he sat on her shoulder, Woozle gesticulated his front paws as he talked, and she grinned at the cuteness. "Now, kid, imagine sitting in your sedan chair, being carried by your undead minions, and looking out over your vast army as your enemies face your army of the unliving. You could have said, 'Go forth, Destroyer of Worlds, and bring my enemies to their knees.' What are you going to say now?"

While speaking to her new familiar, she was testing her force field ability. Casting was quick, but while using the power she sensed a minimum time required before activation. It was not the sense she could feel with things like taste or sound but closer to the sense of maintaining balance, or knowing where your hands are. The sense was there if she looked for it, just not something she could fully describe. To bring a protective field up, it required the use of mana before the power activation. After the power was mentally pressed, her mana required less than two heartbeats to fill up. Jennifer had no idea what mana was, but the bar it sat on was blue. To her it was much like moving her arm. She knew how to use it but had no idea of the mechanics of how it works.

"Since I don't want to take over the world but help it, I would ask you to deliver a message asking them if they would like to go apple picking or maybe some other group activity. You know, something where we don't try to kill each other." It seemed strange, but apple picking was a fun activity. "Apples even kept doctors away, so that would be an enjoyable pastime." She looked at the small jet engines on his back sag slightly, "I get you're not happy with your name, but it's a good name. You are who you are. What I call you isn't as important as what you do."

With a mental nod, she could see her health, stamina, and mana bars. As she used her abilities, she could see the mana bar lower before casting and raise after casting.

"But why the name, Woozle?" He was fidgeting on her shoulder, but he stopped. The front of his face moved down with a sigh, "There have been worse names. Why not move on to your health potions? Those kinds of powers can be tricky."

"Good idea." Jennifer took his advice with her next mental button press. After a few tests, she discovered that she could store up to four potions at the same time. This came with a small twist. Craft Potion did not need ingredients or a crafting station. Jennifer was able to activate the power the same way she activated the force field. Rather than using mana, the Craft Potion used stamina. After the ability was used, her stamina would recover one third of what had been drawn out. Mana recharged the fastest while appearing as a blue bar in her menus. Stamina was represented as a green bar. The red bar showed her health. The skills, powers or abilities would use those bars.

But her stamina was not recovering like her mana. After the initial recovery, her stamina did not go up again. While only one-tenth of her stamina was grayed out for each health potion crafted, each time she used the power, it was harder somehow. She felt weaker and drained like she walked up a flight of stairs. The first one was easy; the tenth was harder. The force field bubble was like lifting something heavy once, but the last lift was only as hard as the first. Not wanting to see what her dark pulse would do in this room, she opened the door. It was time to explore the school.

With four health potions in her pockets, a mop she used as a walking stick, and the young lynx-shark in force field bubble,

Jennifer walked down the long, unlit hall. Light fixtures were on the ceiling, but the bulbs were missing. The only sources of light came from the classroom windows on either side of the hall and the force fields that gave off a slight glow. With the bubbles having a light-blue glow, much like a single candle, there was no point in trying to be sneaky. She weighed her options of protection versus stealth, recognizing that both offered a level of safety. With stealth, she was only protecting herself. With Woozles' size maybe stealth would have been better for him, but the force field offered her and her familiar something beyond just hiding in the shadows.

Not long before she heard the sounds of voices. Jennifer could not understand what they were saying, but she could tell they were coming from down the hall. As she turned a corner, her eyes went wide seeing three green-skinned children were playing with something she could not see. As she moved closer to see them, she saw a spider toy the children were playing with. It looked cute, with long silver legs and a large white circle on its abdomen. The toy was about the size of her hand.

Something was off, but she could not put her finger on it. Woozle moved from her hood onto her shoulder. While he continued to be silent, her hair moved from his engines powering up, while never adding noise. The largest of the green children pulled off one of the spider's legs and laughed. Jennifer's hand flew to her mouth, and her eyes widened even more as the spider tried to pull away.

This was not a toy spider but a live spider! On instinct, Jennifer reached out with her energy and bubbled the hurt spider. What the children were doing was wrong. Something in the core of her being moved to anger knowing that they were causing undue harm to another living creature. Remembering that she was dealing with children, she used her best schoolteacher voice. "Stop that, this instant!"

The children jumped away from the spider. They looked startled, holding sticks, and were looking at Jennifer with oversized eyes.

"You were being mean to this little spider. You children were being naughty." Jennifer did her best to maintain her impression of a schoolteacher and picked up the spider. Woozle shifted on her shoulder and growled.

Jennifer took one of her health potions, popped the top off, and put the mouth of the bottle before the spider. She was not paying attention as the youths moved closer to her. They had, in fact, surrounded her. With some hesitation, the spider drank the potion in one go. "Oh, poor baby. Do you want to come with me?" she asked as it finished the potion. "It's okay. Come on. You can ride on my shoulder." The spider moved with grace and sped up her arm to sit on the unoccupied spot.

She did not like being surrounded by all three children and moved so she could face them. Looking the children up and down, she noticed that their proportions were off. Their legs were short, their arms too long, and all three children were bald. One of the green kids rushed at Jennifer. Grabbing her mop, she bopped him on the head. Not hard enough to hurt him, but hard enough to make him stop. "Stop. I know that hurts. Now think how that spider felt when you were playing with it."

The green child who rushed her hunched his shoulders. He turned to his companions, looking for support. One of the other green children shrugged and pointed at Jennifer.

Jennifer rested the mop at her side, trying not to be threatening to children.

The spider may as well have been made of air as it sat on her shoulder, in spite of its size weighed so little. She reached up to pet the spider on the head. "Now, you're a good spider. I'm sure the children will apologize." Turning back to the children, Jennifer said, "I would like you all to say 'I'm sorry' to the spider."

The children stared up at her with their mouths open before turning and speaking to each other in a tone too quiet for her to make out. While they talked, they took quick glances at her.

Annoyed, she pointed at the closest child then pointed at a spot in front of her. She made a petting motion over the spider, speaking the word, "Sorry," in a raised tone.

One green child took the hint and repeated the word in a strange guttural accent.

She motioned to the next child, who proceeded to pet the spider and apologize in the same accent, followed by the third child.

"Good children." She smiled as she addressed the children. They stood before her, looking down, unwilling to meet her eyes.

Continuing with her instructor voice, "Now, go home. And if I catch any of you being mean again, I will speak with your parents over this." She pointed down the hall. They took one look before running off down the hall at full speed.

Once the children left, the spider on Jennifer's shoulder lowered its body and stretched out its remaining legs. The lynx-shark relaxed on her other shoulder.

Feeling a little smug about this encounter, she said, "I have no idea if they learned their lessons or not, but I hope they don't do that again."

"Kid, I was expecting you to fight the goblins, not talk to them," Woozle said in the same tone Jennifer used on the children. "They were low level goblins, and you made them say sorry to an even lower-level spider."

With her brows coming together, she tilted her head. "What's a goblin?"

Once Woozle stopped laughing, he said, "Kid, goblins are one of the most basic monsters in this world. They're mean little guys that low level adventurers are able to easily beat."

Jennifer was not sure why he called these goblins monsters. They were a little mean, but they said sorry before they left. Her voice raised and she felt defensive. She searched her vocabulary for words to convey her feelings, "Well, I was able to stop them. I think they learned their lesson. They know better than to hurt a poor defenseless creature now, too!" She knew her own pouty voice was coming out.

"What about the goblin you hit on the head? And do you have any plans for the missing spider leg, kid?" Her familiar pointed out.

Woozle's words stung. "You're right, I shouldn't have used

violence. Next time I will do better." She turned her head to look Woozle in the eyes. "Violence is never the answer."

This seemed to take the steam out of the lynx. He slowly closed and opened his eyes a few times before he responded, "Okay kid," and added in a calm, non-patronising voice, "Well, what about the spider leg?"

There was no good answer for what to do with the spider. The healing potion restored the spider's health but not the limb. After petting the spider, she picked up her mop and walked down the hall. "I'm sure the village I'm supposed to save will have a veterinarian that will be able to help."

The hall ended in a T junction. On the wall hung a sign saying LIBRARY with an arrow pointing left. Someone had painted the word beware in red on the bottom. There was no sign for what was on the right. All she could see was more hallway.

"Woozle, what way do you think we should go?"

The lynx-shark yawned from Jennifer's shoulder. "Unmarked corridor in an abandoned university, or one that has beware on the sign? Neither looks like a good option." He then moved to be in the hood of her robe.

"Just because we haven't seen any teachers or students doesn't mean this place is abandoned." She ignored how much dust covered everything while looking around the hallway. "Besides, how dangerous could a library be?"

As they moved down the hall towards the library, she took her time and renewed the force field bubbles around herself, Woozle, and the spider. Each time she used the ability, it got a little easier. Soon the action would be as natural as if she had been doing it her whole life.

At the end of the hall were two large ornate doors in a stone wall. The word Library was carved in calligraphy in the stone above the door. After taking a deep breath and holding it for three heartbeats, she opened the doors.

Standing in the hallway, she gazed inside at the beautiful library. Her eyes passed over clean white marble floors, matching tables, along with high-back, black-leather rolling chairs. There was no sign of dust or age on the tables, chairs, or floors. Computer screens floated without support in front of keyboards. To Jennifer, the room looked like it belonged in some sci-fi future movie, technology she had never seen in her life. It was covered from floor to ceiling with bookshelves. This place offered both the new and the old in one place. The lights were bright, mimicking sunlight rather than white, fluorescent light. Compared to the room she started in, this was nice. With desks, tables, and reading alcoves, this is what Jennifer thought of when choosing her school. To Jennifer, this room was more modern, a fantastic place to read on a screen or study from a page. There was even a large turtle statue, which peered in her direction and was amazingly lifelike. It looked a bit like a box turtle standing on its hind legs and was at least six feet tall. Taking in every artistic detail of the statue from its black robe with gray lines on the side to its realistic eyes, she marveled at the sculptor's skill. Until the statue blinked.

"Goblins, then a sci-fi library with a robed turtle in it? What exactly is the theme of this world?" Jennifer asked aloud to no one in particular.

"The theme of this world is whatever the system had and the ones who made this system needed," Woozle responded in a hushed tone.

The turtle croaked.

Jennifer froze before replying in a natural way. "Hello, my name is Jennifer. This looks like a wonderful library. May we come in?"

The turtle stared at Jennifer and Woozle.

In a whisper Woozle said, "That's a level fifteen turtle master librarian. I think we should just close the door and look for another way."

Confused, she whispered back, "How can you tell the name and level?"

"Remind me to reset your interface with the system, but this could go really badly here."

Without missing a beat, Jennifer said, raising her voice, "I am new to this world, and would like to read some books on alchemy."

The large turtle librarian remained still and didn't reply.

Her heart quickened at the thought of not being able to use the resources of the library. She needed books to learn, and all professors would have assigned reading. Trial and error was a way to go, but books would have stories about other people's errors that she could learn from. She was very lucky libraries were a thing here, and that she had found one. This one had a lot of books. Not wanting to lose this chance, she took a step into the library.

The turtle's head turned, gazing at a section of books. Jennifer held her breath as several books moved off of the shelf under their own power, floating slowly at first but gaining speed once they were in the air. The books spread their covers like wings, but they looked like they were floating or gliding rather than flapping their covers to fly. Each tome slowly floated in directions on tasks known only to them. No two collections of bound pages moved in the same direction at the same speed.

Amazed at what she was seeing, she turned to turtle librarian. "Is this normal? Do books float on their own here?"

The turtle librarian snapped its jaws and hopped away from Jennifer. Hiding under a desk, it retracted its extremities into its shell.

She thought this was not a good sign.

"Hello books, my name is Jennifer, and this is Woozle." Jennifer tried to sound nice.

"Kid, I think it is time to start attacking." She heard the tension in Woozles' voice.

Jennifer did not want to fight these books. One of the larger leather-bound books with a very thick cover gained speed, charging at her. On instinct, Jennifer held the mop out in front of her as more of a shield then anything. She closed her eyes. The book hit Jennifer's mop hard, pushing her back and causing her to lose her balance. She was not hurt but surprised a book could hit that hard.

After opening her eyes, the world slowed down. Her body was

unable to keep up with her mind as events happened around her. Woozle leapt off her shoulder and charged at the book with teeth and claws extended. She was grateful that Woozle had a bubble shield on. But she didn't want the book to get hurt either. Something clicked in her mind. Hoping that it would work in time, Jennifer cast a force field around the old leather-bound book attacking her. Before her heart finished a beat, Woozle and the book collided, but the shields took the damage and only a little dust fell from the book.

"That book was attacking you, kid. If that's not an argument for self-defense, I don't know what would be!" The lynx-shark's concerned voice was loud and deep.

The book was now floating undamaged in a bubble shield. All the other books were floating around like a school of fish, but a few went to inspect the bubbled old leather-bound book.

Jennifer stayed still and Woozle remained on guard as one of the books, which had been inspecting the force field around its companion, turned and floated over to her. Time returned to normal, but her mind still raced on what to do next. Making no sudden or threatening movements, she allowed the floating book to approach her.

This new book was a much smaller paperback book that had a picture of a castle on the front cover. It had no words. The book, in spite of looking new with clean colors and white paper, was covered in dust. Jennifer took a moment to look around. All the books were in various states of dustiness and disrepair. She looked at the turtle still hiding in its shell and thought how hard it would be to clean, maintain, and repair books without thumbs. Jennifer reached out, causing some of the books to flutter faster, but the paperback novel landed in her hand.

While trying to maintain the calm in her voice, Jennifer asked, "Woozle, can you look around for some dust rags or something? We need to start cleaning these books."

"I'll get right on it, kid. For now, why not just use your mop on them." Showing no movement in looking for rags, Woozle went from a ready to attack posture to lying flat on the ground. She decided to call this the monorail pose.

Jennifer assumed Woozle would be happier if she used the mop to attack the books, not clean them. She did have a cleaning tool, so she used the dry mop head to dust off the book, and for safe measure, she put the book in a force field bubble.

All the books, as well as the turtle librarian, were watching her every action while she cleaned the young book. When she finished cleaning the book, the words Level Up in glowing golden light appeared before her.

The books opened and closed a few times, as if in applause, while floating faster before returning to their previous state.

Looking at her menus, she realized that there were leveling options to choose.

Level two came with one new power for each of her three power trees. Since she had her tech tree, alchemist tree, and necromancer tree, she would get three new powers. She also now had access to the generic power pools, which had thousands, if not tens of thousands to pick. Each power pool had between four to six powers. She also got to have two new perk points to enhance or add to a power or skill.

"Woozle, can you highlight any repair skills?" Jennifer asked wearily, not wanting a repeat of how she ended up as a necromancer.

Woozle waved a paw but did not disturb his monorail pose.

The **Tailor (Generic)** power set allowed repairs, which is what she wanted, but the rest of the power's levels mentioned alterations to suits. While that skill would be useful, she did not want to be fitting, altering, and enhancing people's clothes.

The second choice was **Mechanic (Generic)**, which fit Jennifer better. She could get Mend right now, then at level five she could use a power called Over Charge. It would make her powers stronger and faster at the cost of additional mana and stamina. At level twenty, the final power in the set was Rebuild. All three powers appealed to her.

Not wanting to choose the first one she liked, she reviewed the two remaining choices. Almost immediately, she dismissed **Field Medic (Generic)**. It could mend wounds, give out stimulants, and resuscitate, but she could already do that with her alchemical powers.

Crafter (Generic) offered Mend, Craft, Improve Craft, and the top tier ability was Scrapper. She would be able to scrap something for parts and build something else with the scrapped items. That would be a pretty useful skill to have.

Although she felt better having narrowed down her choices to **Mechanic** and **Crafter**, the pressure to choose quickly nagged at her. On the whole, all of the powers appeared nice. The difference between Mechanic and Field Medic seemed to be one repaired what was not alive, while the other healed what was alive. Crafter and Tailor both looked interesting. But they seemed more specialized than she would like and would not be helpful in this school or a dungeon.

Thinking for a moment, she decided to call this a school dungeon.

Another book moved towards her, the pressure continuing to build. The urge to pick a power, and then return to the book built up inside her. She knew this was just herself pushing, but she did not want to just sit and wait. Knowing she could heal others with her potions, she counted Mechanic as the logical choice. Something still caused her to hesitate. She was getting sick of making choices that would affect her entire future without knowing what was best in the long run.

She had Woozle, but she still felt isolated and alone and wished there were teachers or elders around to talk to and get advice from.

What choice did she really have? She did not know what would happen if she did not pick one, but she did not want this sitting over her head. She had to choose, and she had to choose with the best available information.

Jennifer chose the Mechanic power pool, taking the Repair power. She had two powers left to choose, so she decided to check out what generic powers might apply to the ones she already had. In

Future Defense Tech, there were two options. She could add more health to the bubble or add a chance to deflect damage. In Necromancer, she could Raise Undead. In Alchemist, she could add more health to health potion or generic alchemy craft. These choices seemed simple to her.

Jennifer made her mental selections.

Raise Undead: Skeleton can be put into attack or bodyguard mode, 25 mana per skeleton, Each skeleton will have 15 health, 0 mana, long cooldown. In attack mode, the skeleton will attack the enemy's user targets or closest enemy to the user. In bodyguard mode, the skeleton will attack the closest enemy to the user. You can now raise the dead. It is easier than raising a house.

Deflect: Force fields can now deflect damage. Cost and cool down are unchanged, forcefield will now have a 1 in 10 chance to deflect attacks. Who needs dodge when you can deflect.

A second book landed in Jennifer's open hand. This was all too much, she was going to find a way to simplify how the system displayed her powers in the future. Something simple like, add rainbows or something. The feeling of frustration left as she focused on the tense and stiff book. Moving her hand over the cover reminded her of petting a dog that had never felt the caress of a gentle hand. Taking a deep breath, she cleaned this new book. The book remained closed, its cover had some scratch marks. Running her hand over the side of the book, it had more than just superficial damages.

The way the book moved made more sense as the back cover flapped a bit. Jennifer smiled, taking this as a good sign that she had made the right choice when leveling up. She put her hand on the cover of the book and cast repair. A glow from her hand and the feeling of something moving, and a slight itch coming from her palm, told her it was working. She assumed it would be mana being used. With a quick look at her menus, she saw it was stamina draining.

Jennifer was confused. She was triggering repair through her interface, which was costing stamina rather than mana. After the power was ready to be used again, the book was whole. Once the force field was cast, the book floated away. It bobbed up and down as it went, which gave her the impression that it was happy, but she was not an expert on the emotions of books.

The other books floating around no longer felt menacing. Some of them had formed a line in front of her. They seemed eager for the cleaning, repairing, and force field bubble. Although Jennifer was happy to help, she did not want to spend the whole time on her feet, so she went to the nearest desk with a chair and sat down. "Okay, I'm ready. Next, please."

The next book in the line floated into Jennifer's hand.

After the fourth or fifth book, the head of the mop would need a good shaking out before it could be used again. The turtle librarian had come over with some dust rags in his claws.

"He's saying he found you some rags," Woozle said, having not moved from his chosen spot on the floor.

Jennifer thanked the turtle and gave a half-hearted glare at Woozle. After spending what felt like hours cleaning, mending, and adding protection to the books, she felt drained, but happy and a bit hungry. Her stamina was two-thirds grayed out.

Woozle wandered off to explore the library while Jennifer worked on the books, and he brought her a few non-floating books to look at.

Jennifer decided to take a break. When the next book approached, she put her hands out in front of her with her palms facing out, hoping this was the universal signal to stop.

The books left the line for cleaning, returning to their own business and floating around to do their unknown errands. Several floated from one section to another, while others rested on shelves or on top of other books.

This was the first time she was able to sit and relax. She found her mind wondering, as she watched the books for a bit. There was a combing feeling as the books would leave the spot they landed on and headed off to another section of the library. The books came in all sizes from small paperbacks to massive hardcover leather-bound books and everything in between. She even saw a comic book floating behind a shelf at one point, but she only saw that one out of the corner of her eye.

Making eye contact with the turtle, she put a smile on her face, hoping it would make it easier to approach the turtle. She hoped the turtle would be able to communicate with her more.

"Woozle, I think I remember hearing that a turtle holds up the world." Even to her own ears, it sounded more like a question than a statement, unsure of the memory.

Woozle returned and relaxed in a sunbeam on one of the desks. "At least your timeline got something right. The librarian's name is Wegeforth, and she's wondering if you're hungry."

With a small mental nudge, Jennifer brought up her status bars, which showed a larger section of her stamina bar that was grayed out. But she did not feel hungry or thirsty, even though she had not eaten or drank anything since she got to this new world. She could feel her body slowing, which she assumed was her body's way of telling her that she was tired. She figured this would be as good a time as any to have a snack.

"Please tell Wegeforth I am hungry, but I am not sure where to get food here." She hoped her familiar would relay the message. The turtle nodded and turned without a word from Woozle.

Stretching out his paws, and opening his mouth wide for a yawn, he said from his sunning spot, "Kid, the turtle understands Common, and she even offered you a common quest with a Speak Turtle ability as a reward."

She blinked several times, attempting to collect her stray thoughts. Jennifer had not realized she had been given a quest. Bringing up her full character sheet menu, she could not find where the quest was listed.

"Umm, can you help me find the quest in the menus?" Part of her wondered if she should already know these things. While she had not been in this world long, having to ask for help made her feel weak and useless.

Woozle left his spot in the sunbeam, walked over to Jennifer, rubbed his head on her arm, moved to her lap, curled up in a crescent shape, and purred. The whole set of actions took less than a handful of heartbeats, but it put a smile on her face.

Jennifer's menus came up without her mental command. Before, the menus were small tabs scattered throughout her menu scape. She could tell Woozle was somehow moving them around. Before, when she pulled up her character sheet, the menu just appeared in her vision without borders. Pulling up her menus now, there was a stark contrast. Now, at the bottom right of her vision was a space where her powers were placed in a neat row of circles. Casting Force Field on herself, the power's circle grayed out with white illumination moving in a clockwise direction around the power. When the illumination made a full circle, the power lit up again and was ready to be used.

On the top right, she could see her health, energy, and stamina bars. Her stamina was about two-thirds full with the last third being grayed out. The gray part of the bar was growing. About halfway between where her power sat at the bottom and the status bars at the top were three colored tabs with labels. Red showed Character sheet, blue indicated level up points and an achievement section, while green held quests. Both the blue and green tabs had stars on them.

"What does it mean if there is a star on one of the tabs?" She felt silly asking and understood that it was probably important, but not why it would be.

"Well kid, it means there is new information that you have not seen yet." Woozle moved from the sunbeam to Jennifer's lap.

On the top left of the menus was a mini map, showing where Jennifer had already been. The rest of the mini map was blacked out. On the bottom left was a transcript of her actions and dialog. "Is that better?" Woozle asked while purring in her lap.

Relief washed over her. This was getting better thanks to her little familiar. She snuggled Woozle. "Yes, that's much better. Thank you." When she picked up her familiar, he was no longer the size of a mouse. Woozle was the size of a kitten. Curious about the change in him, "Woozle, you are getting bigger."

"I'm miniature now. When you level up, I'll get bigger until I reach adult size. I'll also have the chance to be faster, stronger, and maybe jump higher every time you gain a level. I'm hoping that my adult size is as big as a massive shark." Woozle replied with some pride in his voice while wiggling his back fin.

"So, you're a miniature, giant, flying lynx-shark?" Jennifer eyed him for a minute and smirked. "Can I add space to your description?"

Woozle spoke slowly as if considering the question. "I think there is a rare quest line that would be able to do that. I have never done it. I wonder what kind of power or abilities that would come with."

The turtle returned with a plate of green bread and a square juice box.

"It is a cucumber sandwich," Woozle said, still curling up on her lap.

Accepting the plate with a polite nod, she asked, "Why is the bread green?"

"It's seaweed bread. I think this turtle is a vegetarian." Woozle stretched out his front paws, opened his jaws, and let his tongue curl in an enormous yawn.

It was the cutest thing she had seen in all of her time here, feeling the need to make a sound to accompany her feeling she let out an, "Awwww."

"Kid, you were going to accept the quest."

Jennifer could bring up the quests now and saw four available to her.

1) Save the town, Save the Nation, Save the World: 0 of 1 towns saved, 0 of 1 nations saved, 0 of 1 world saved. Town

not yet explored. Task extreme hard, reward proportional to experience, legendary loot.

2) Explore Bishop's University of Magic, Social Sciences, and Ninjas: 35 blocks of 155 blocks explored, experiment room explored. Task easy, reward acceptance into Bishop's University of Magic and Social Sciences.

3) Get into Bishop's University of Magic, partying, and brewery. Then finish education.

Pending

4) Clean books: Clean 10 books, task uncommon, reward library card, reward perk, unlock Speak Turtle language trait.

Jennifer mentally pushed the accept button for the last quest, and the text **0 out of 10 books cleaned** appeared. As she munched the sandwich, she noticed her stamina bar was filling with green. It had dropped to about two-thirds filled with gray, but now it was only one-tenth gray. She felt better. Her muscles no longer slowed.

After eating the sandwich, she stood up. In a loud clear voice, she said, "I can clean and repair the next ten floating books. Would you please line up." Jennifer returned to cleaning and casting Mend on the books.

She ended up cleaning closer to twenty and was happy to have something to focus on. She sat down and mentally brought up her menus. The Clean Books quest was listed as finished, and a library card was presented from a webbed turtle claw.

A ding from the menu rang out, when an alert came up.

You have been given a perk, speaking basic local turtle trait. If you wish to make this permanent, you can choose to use one of your available traits.

Jennifer double checked when she was leveling up. She chose

her powers but had not chosen any traits, stats, or anything else. Jennifer was unsure how to maximize herself or if she even wanted to. She did remember that librarians were either very helpful or an evil cult trying to take over the world.

She had one trait listed as Half-Giant and two slots listed as **EMPTY**. She decided to use one of her free traits, knowing she had one trait left she turned to the turtle. Believing that new students should be polite and professional, she said, "Hello. My name is Jennifer. I'll be one of the new students. Thank you for your help."

The turtle spoke with an experience that only came with age. "Hello, Jennifer. You are the first student I have seen in almost three hundred years, and you are the sole student to ever repair the books. As a functionary, I am impressed." The words were smooth and reminded Jennifer of what it was like speaking to her elders. The strange thing was that the turtle's mouth did not move when speaking.

"What is a functionary?" The words escaped Jennifer's mouth before she had time to think about how to ask the question more politely.

But the turtle seemed to not mind the question or how it was asked. "A functionary is placed with required tasks that need to be completed. Most functions do not speak, but important ones like myself do. My tasks are to maintain this library and to assist those who come here in the pursuit of knowledge. Guiding people tends to require more than just miming, after all."

"Woozle here - " she looked down at her lynx-shark for a moment, "said that I am a fragment, but I feel whole."

The turtle's head turned down facing the ground. "Oh, I was hoping you were a parallel and the system was starting the education sector again. I do miss when this school was fully powered and teaching." The turtle's voice held more than a bit of sadness.

Wanting to change the subject, Jennifer asked, "What is a parallel?"

Woozle spoke up, "We don't entirely know, kid. We think the parallels come from another system. Some seem to come for enjoyment because they go on adventures and rush into danger for fun, damn the consequences. They don't even die. If they get hurt or are near death, they're just teleported away to, respawn, as they call it."

The word respawn hurt Jennifer's ears. She heard the word, but it escaped her mind. She tried to say the word but couldn't.

Before Jennifer could ask, the librarian continued. "Respawn is a system word. They understand it. I can say it, but most fragments can't. Some of the parallels come here for training. You can normally tell parallels that come for training apart because they have a rank rather than a name followed by numbers. They barely interact and are always running around having mock battles or maneuvers or whatever they do." Woozle stood up and looked both Jennifer and the turtle in the eyes before adding. "The most important thing about the parallels is that they have the ability to log out and go back to their own worlds."

Time stretched in front of Jennifer and everything slowed down. She was holding her breath and released it. "I can go home?" With hope before her, she did not realize it was an option until now. There was no response from the others for a long time.

Arms wrapped around Jennifer in a comforting bear hug coming from a turtle woman. "I am sorry, Student Jennifer. This is your world now. There is no going home for any of us."

Dread filled Jennifer, and she tried to tramp down the rising fear. "My parents said when they were young, they were sent to school. Those schools taught them to walk the way of other people, to talk the way of other people. And in those teachings, they took something away from my people. My family could no longer speak our own language. They lost traditions and many of the youths at that time. Their graves were still being found when I got my acceptance letter to come here. When they were able to return, they were strangers to their own families. When I was born there were 17 of those schools still in operation."

Tears welled up at the memory. The few times her parents spoke of the reservation schools, it was accompanied with the pain of loss and shame. They could not even look at each other when speaking of those institutions. They had not wanted her to go to university for fear of losing her, and they were right.

"Well," Woozle clearly searched for something to say, "at least those schools taught something."

Jennifer's anger threatened the edge of her mind. "You don't understand," Jennifer yelled but trailed off not knowing how to explain it. "What do schools do here?" Jennifer looked at Woozle.

"Schools teach," the turtle said.

But such a simple explanation was not enough to satisfy her. "Do young children go to day schools here?" Jennifer asked, seeking common ground to start on.

"No, this is a university. We normally have young adults come here," said the turtle.

"No, I mean, do children in this world go to day school? Where do the children go when their parents are at work?"

The turtle's mouth opened with an unspoken 'oh', understanding the question. It seemed to think on the answer a bit before replying. "To answer the question, parallel children are given the same tasks and rewards as an adult parallel. They have the same level of commitments, jobs, adventure, and crafting. There are no child fragments. However, there are child functionaries. A child born from parallels, fragments, or a function is a function. They attend a storage area during the time the parents are occupied doing other things. The age of the child is equal to the level of the child. However, at level eighteen, the child is processed into an adult function and is given the tools to change classes or traits to better serve the function they are assigned to."

This felt like a lecture, but it gave Jennifer what she needed to explain the schools she was referring to. "That sounds more like a normal school, one I wouldn't have minded attending. The type I was talking about, the type my family was forced to attend, was more like a prison. Imagine living in a dungeon where you're trapped for years and are never allowed to see your family or friends. The guards are cruel and steal what few resources are supposed to be used to run the place. What few functions are taught are tasks no one else would want to do." Jennifer shuddered at the thought. "With no medicine and little food, only one in every four children survived those places. Some running the school took the money meant to provide necessities for themselves. They wanted the money more than they cared if the children lived or died."

Woozle questioned, "Well, if one in four made it out, that one person must have been very tough by the end, good enough to survive the world, probably going adventuring, right?"

Jennifer slowly shook her head. "What does not kill you does not always make you tougher, Woozle. These schools were brutal in more ways than one. Those places had survivors, not graduates. And not just for the children. Most parents never knew what happened to their child, even if they died." Jennifer let out a sob as the memories of her own childhood rolled over her. "When I was young, my parents made me run and hide every time there was a knock on the door for fear of me being taken away." Jennifer's voice rose with alarm as her situation dawned on her. "Now, now I've been taken away into this strange world."

Woozle paws patted her face. "But you're a fragment. That means the person you're copied from gets to return home,"

Jennifer calmed as Woozle's words sank in. Taking a deep breath, she counted to ten then exhaled. "But I can't go back."

"Sorry, kid."

"What makes people so cruel? Why destroy a culture's belief, language, and self-worth only to treat them like they were less than dirt? Even the adults weren't safe. Why did they want us to conform to their cookie cutter standards, knowing they would never accept us?"

Jennifer spoke slowly, fighting to get the words out, "My family gave me the ability to come to this school, to make myself better, and to make the world a better place. I didn't know the risks coming here, but I will not let it stop me." Jennifer could feel the anger well within her as her voice rose, and she held her mop with white-knuckled. Her voice continued on, unwilling to stop the words that pained her memory. "I came here to learn and to help improve things, not just for my people but for the world. If the world tries to stop or slow me down, I'll tear it down. I will not let the pain and suffering of my people be repeated."

"This is nice, deary. Would you like another sandwich before going back out to tear down the social barriers?" asked the turtle.

"Yes, please," Jennifer blinked, wiping away something in her eyes. "Why do I remember those res schools, and not my parents' faces?"

"Backstory," said Woozle. "Parallels get to pick their back stories, fragments get to live with their backstories, and functionaries get to know what to do. One of the gnomes told me that it helps the parallels, but I'm not sure how. Something about psychology or something." The words rolled off his tongue with such practiced ease, it was obvious this wasn't his first time in explaining the subject.

Jennifer blinked back the tears threatening to run down her cheeks. She looked at the turtle and attempted a smile. She was unsure if she had answered the librarian's last question, "Yes please, I very much liked the last one you made." She closed her eyes. "Time to make the world a better place." She said as she opened her eyes.

Woozle laughed. "Kid, you went from being the big scary necromancer bent on tearing down the world, back to being a kid." Woozle paused looking down for a moment, before he raised his head and made eye contact with Jennifer. "I've seen lesser people start out with more. I'm sure they achieved less than you will."

Thoughts and ideas clashed in Jennifer's mind as she fought to make sense of it all and corral it into a cohesive plan. Should she choose what she needed and what she wanted, or choose what she wanted, and then figure out later what she needed. Jennifer wanted to go to school to learn. She wanted to learn so that she could help people. While she worked out what to do next, she started cleaning the books again. The work became automatic.

"Okay, Woozle is with me," Jennifer spoke aloud without meaning to.

"With you till the end," Woozle replied while cleaning his paws.

She smiled at Woozle for the response. "I have a mop and what I'm wearing," She trailed off as a memory floated up. You can survive three minutes without air, three days without water, three weeks without food. But what was shelter? She could not remember how long someone could survive without shelter.

"How long can I survive without shelter?"

The librarian handed Jennifer a book. *An Outriders Field Guide* was the name of the book. On the cover, a young boy was smiling while wearing a beige button up shirt and a red sash with some badges on it. Behind the young boy was what looked like a lean-to. A poorly made lean-to. But the thing that caught her eye the most was not the title, the sash, or the lean-to. The boy had the head of an orca. It looked like an orca just replaced the boy's head on a human body with its own and said, "This is my body now."

Jennifer thanked the turtle and skimmed through the book. When she realized that there was still a queue of library books in front of her, she held her arm out with a single finger pointing up, indicating she was pausing for a moment. She was able to find what she wanted after reading a chapter on shelters as fast as she could. She realized a couple of things, the person who wrote the book thought children must be very slow, and she would need a shelter to stay in before tomorrow. It also dawned on her she was homeless, alone, and in a strange place. Taking in what she had, a smile broke her lips. She did have Woozle and a silent spider.

The library did not seem like a good place to sleep, but she needed to find somewhere to stay while going to school and adventuring. "Umm, are there still dorms on campus?" Jennifer asked the turtle librarian.

"I am sorry, I do not know. And the only active member of the administration core seems to be the dean. I can mark the dean's office on your map."

"Do you mean the dean is the only one left for admissions? He's the one that will let me sign up to be a student?"

"I believe so," the turtle said.

"Then I shall find the dean." With her course set, Jennifer grabbed her mop and took off in the direction of the dean's office marked on her map. A line of books followed Jennifer to the door. As she passed through the doors, most of the books trailed her when floated down to the ground. Woozle ran by Jennifer's side while she walked with her seven-legged spider on her shoulder.

After the third or fourth turn, she thought they built the school as a maze. At most, it was about one hundred steps before coming to a three-way intersection, and there were no signs anywhere. After opening another set of doors, Jennifer walked back into the library and realized this was the same door she left from. The shadows were getting larger.

With a huff, she set out again. After following one side of the wall, and seven left turns, Jennifer ended up back at the doors she had left from.

"Kid, maybe take a navigation trait?"

Jennifer let out a huff, letting her frustration show.

"My people were hunters and trackers." She tilted her head and added, "I think." She was sure she knew where she was going, but she seemed to bounce around on her mini map. It was almost as if the university was moving around, but that was crazy. Jennifer looked at her familiar. Lynx-sharks were pretty crazy. They did not exist in the real world. But then again, she no longer lived in the real world. She needed to readjust her idea on what was crazy and what wasn't.

Woozle looked up at her, waiting. Reviewing or her own recollections of her memory. She found she was able to easily navigate, helming her way and not finding the point of her travels was new to her existence . Trying to sound confident, she said, "One more try, and then I'll see about the navigating traits."

Jennifer stormed down the corridor again. Before the first turn, she spun around and did not see the doorway to the library. Groaning, she pulled up her menu and checked her mini map. The spot she was in was on the top left corner of the Bishop's map. While she could see the library and the dean's office on her map, she was in another building. There was no straight connection from where she had been before to where she was now.

"Shenanigans." Jennifer said as her fist met the palm of her other hand. "I'm calling shenanigans. Not only am I moving around, but the rooms are moving around."

"Kid, what are you going to do about it? With a navigation trait you'll be able to move around without being moved around," Woozle replied sagely.

The next hallway had a row of windows. With her shoulders squared, she stormed over to them. After pushing open a window, she jumped into a courtyard. Jennifer put her hands on her hips and looked out on the courtyard. It was a space with four sides. The school was made with red-brown bricks and green pointed roofs, with small towers jutting out, revealing its windows. The building was bright, pristine, and well maintained. The green in the courtyard looked like it did not have a single blade of grass that was too tall or too short. It had some benches for sitting in the area, a path leading through an arch, and a black and white cow wearing sunglasses with a cowbell around its neck.

There was an overpass she could go under to leave the courtyard and an enormous set of doors that were between her and the dean's office. After using the doors, she decided to check each room they passed rather than just head down the hallway. The first door Jennifer entered led to the most typical classroom ever. A blackboard hung on one side, tables and chairs lined the room, and large windows looked out onto a field. Beyond the field was a forest.

In front of the blackboard was a professor's desk. When she searched each drawer, she found that they were all empty except one. A small notepad with a grocery list lay in the bottom. She sighed, reading the list. She knew in her heart the professor forgot the list and probably forgot to bring home food.

Woozle also searched the room with his nose down on the ground. By the casual way her familiar was walking and sniffing, there was nothing of interest here.

Jennifer turned to leave the classroom, but something caught her eye. Walking next to the tree line across from the field, she saw four large deer-like creatures.

Although a window and a sports field separated her from the deer, she still whispered, "Woozle."

Woozle pried his nose from the ground and looked up at her. He turned his head, giving Jennifer a tilted head look. She patted her shoulder, inviting him to come and see the creatures. With a small burst from his engines, he was able to leap onto her shoulder.

The herd of slow-moving deer had compact torsos, long legs, small tails, and graceful necks. Their fur was dark blue, like a night sky with a full moon, with dark forest green swirls on their sides. All four deer had obsidian black antlers. The one leading the group was much larger. Its antlers had many more points than the three following.

The trio watched the deer walking along the tree line. A black and white cow in sunglasses followed the path of the deer.

Neither of the pair spoke until after the deer turned and walked back into the forest, on what she assumed was a path only the deer knew, with the cow following not far behind.

"Do you want to hunt them and use one as your skeleton?" asked Woozle.

Jennifer tilted her head. "I haven't thought about it, those were beautiful." They were magnificent beasts. Having one at her summons would be useful, but she was no hunter. She did not know how even if she wanted to. "Back on task," Jennifer stated, not letting herself get more distracted.

Two more turns and a few empty classrooms later, she knew she was letting herself get distracted. While exploring the school would be helpful and allow her to take classes in Magic and Ninjas, but now, she was just getting frustrated. This new classroom was different. There were large metal barrels with spouts and an area for a small fire under the barrels. It seemed that a small fire would be lit under one of these metal barrels, the vapor or gas would be pushed up to the spout, then condense back into liquid to be collected in another metal barrel.

She was staring wide eyed at the setup, remembering she needed to blink every once in a while, "Is this what I think it is?"

Woozle seemed to be as stunned as she was. She explored the setup and while moving behind one of the drums, "The sign reads, 'The end product cannot end up being collected in a bathtub. - Drew.'"

She decided to look around for any signs of what they could teach in this classroom. Finding nothing of interest and not knowing what else to do, she decided to open up her mini map and put a marker on this room. Turning to Woozle, it was clear he had found nothing either.

She brought up her mini map and looked to see where the dean's office was. It was forward and to the right. She was so close. Jennifer turned to the door that was between her and her desired destination. With a wide Cheshire smile across her face, she opened the door. And walked into the library.

"What the. How?" the words echoing the sentiment in her mind.

Woozle walked past her and plopped down in the center of a sunbeam. "That's what happens when you don't take a navigation trait."

Jennifer sat in a chair, feeling defeated as the turtle librarian handed her another cucumber and seaweed sandwich. Remembering her manners, she thanked the turtle.

She pulled up her menu. Looking through the traits, the options that came with them, it seemed simple. A trait was unlockable and she received one trait per level. She had a species trait that was currently unlocked. She had two race traits that were currently locked.

She found a list showing the effect that her traits had on her. Her size was listed as half giant and "descended from giants" with an illegible signature next to it.

With a quick search through the trait options, she found she had unlocked a few options. Due to getting lost, basic navigation was a selectable option for a trait. Focusing on the word trait, **"Most** traits have passive effectors that are always on." There was a list of attributes listed as standard. The list was uncountable to Jennifer, with a mental twist she was able to simplify it to the point where the list had three items, **Body, Mind, Spirit**. Focusing on each item she saw the words standard. Focusing more on **Body** came a large list of what that attribute affected, the first three on the list was **Strength, Health**, and **Endurance**. Seeing each line listed as Standard, made her lose interest in attributes and return to the traits section.

She selected navigation, not wanting to do any more reading in her menus. The bottom right of the menu screen in her trait options had a random button. Jennifer did not want to lose control of her mental landscape leading her to end up with something random, but seeing a button labeled Random made her curious. She pushed the random button just to see what would happen. Four traits came up.

Solar Powered, Advanced Ant Farming, Imperial Tea Tester, Tourism & Hospitality II.

Maybe she was just getting tired and grumpy, but none of those looked good. According to the trait descriptions, solar power had a tiny positive boost to her body and mind during the day, ant farming seemed completely useless, tea tester let her taste tea like an expert, and tourism helped her mind in making a good host or to get guests. The only one not useful was ant farming. After the explanations, there was the fine print.

You must choose a trait from this list, or the traits will be locked for the next five levels. You may hit random again, but by doing so, one trait will be assigned to you and other traits will remain unlocked and be available later.

Jennifer did not like any of the traits, so she decided to hit random.

Imperial Tea Tester. You now have the Imperial tea tester trait. Does this taste like poison?

Trait level 3: You have unlocked a free trait. "This does taste like poison." You can now ignore the first poisoning of each day. Note, this does not stack.

Knowing that the next trait would need to be, she mentally searched for navigation. A diagram with overlapping circles came up. In the center of each was Land, Air, and Sea. To the left of the diagram was other, however it was grayed out. No matter how much she focused on other, nothing came up. With a mental shrug she went to her choices. Thinking briefly on choosing Sea, she pictured herself on the deck of a ship. Of course the ship's flag had the jolliest of rogers. Dismissing the idea she went to the center of the diagram for general navigation.

General Navigation 1: Who needs a roadmap?

With her new traits chosen, Jennifer got up and headed for the dean's office. After walking outside, entering the next building over, going up some stairs, and turning left, she found herself knocking on the administrator's door. If she had known why it was important to take a navigating trait, she would have listened to Woozle sooner. He was right, but she did not want to admit it.

A moment after knocking, she heard something like a computer booting up. "Please come in, unless you are a vampire." Hesitating, she took a breath and went into the dean's office.

The dean's office was what she expected. The square room had bookshelves on every wall filled with books three layers thick, and piles of books scattered around. The desk, that was carved out of a single piece of dark wood. By the look of it, an elephant could step on it and the desk would not even creek. Under the desk was a vibrant red carpet. The dean, she noted, was glowing blue, and transparent.

Almost everything was what Jennifer was expecting.

"How can I be of assistance?" The dean's light faded out for a moment. When he returned, he was looking at his hand with his brows forming a glare. Looking back up at Jennifer he added, "Fragment?"

"I enrolled here before coming here. Now that I am here, I still want to be enrolled here. Can you let me be enrolled here again? I would be a good student if you let me in. You should let me in, can you let me in?" She wanted to keep talking but forced her mouth shut with a smile.

The hologram faded out again.

Jennifer was shifting her weight from one foot to another. It was taking longer than she expected.

After far too long for her liking, the dean appeared looking at his wiggling fingers, "You wish to re-enroll in Bishop's University, fragment?"

"Yes." The word came out loud and slow to make sure the dean understood.

"I will send you a quest to start off the entrance tests."

Three quest options appeared in her display. **Rich, Famous, and Standard**. Since she was not rich or famous, she focused on standard. The description explained that she would need a letter of recommendation from someone who held a public office, a business owner, and a parallel.

Seeing the list of things she would need, she realized it was going to take more than just asking to be let in. Her shoulder moved forward ever so much; her head turned to look out the window, the sky was entering twilight, a yawn escaped her mouth. It was time to find a place to sleep for the night. Just under the dean's window was a couch large enough for her to lie on.

"Mr. Dean, are you, or are there others, plugged in somewhere?" she asked as innocently as possible as a plan formed in her mind.

"Why yes, thank you for asking. The plug is right here under my desk. Do you need to charge a device?"

Jennifer made her way over to get a better view of the outlet. She stepped on a cord.

"While it does pow—"

She cut him off with an, "Oops," and accidentally knocked out the wire with her other foot. Roger jumped onto the Dean's desk. She gave him a few good pets, "why don't you find a nice place to sleep in this room?"

She turned back to look at the couch. Woozle was already curled up on the middle cushion. "I think we should all just sleep in this room." Jennifer walked over, picked up her small familiar, and moved herself into a sleeping position. She put the lynx shark on her chest. "This does seem like a good place to rest for the night. Too bad the dean got taken offline." But she was out before she could hear his response.

CHAPTER 3

ALONG CAME A SPIDER.

A COLOSSAL SPIDER WITH far too many eyes, legs as long as Jennifer was tall, and pincers the size of her hands stood over her. The spider's thick carapace looked to be made of black and gold metal like a tank. It was large enough to ride, or to eat her.

She fully awoke in an instant, frozen in terror. Woozle was still sleeping on her stomach, but she did not know where her little spider was. She contemplated if she could grab her familiar and run. Only moving her eyes, she was able to see the seven-legged spider walking around on the dean's desk. Beads of cold sweat formed on her skin and her heart pumped adrenaline through her body. Looking at the giant spider in front of her, she knew she had no chance in a fight.

Realizing she had been holding her breath, she focused on breathing out and in. The weird thing was, she smelled bacon and eggs. Woozle was waking up, stretching out his paws, and giving a big yawn. Although it was still one of the cutest things she had ever seen, she couldn't coo over him.

The titan of a spider transferred the weight of its bulk without a sound from one leg to another. It rotated in place. The silent predator's two front legs were holding a tray of food. She did not even look at the food as the giant spider moved.

The spider's legs were segmented and hairless. Every part of the arachnid was metallic ore, including its face, which came with six large black eyes that shined. Or maybe they glowed. Below the eyes were two mandibles that were as thick as her thigh, ending in pincers that would count as short swords. One bite from this spider would remove a limb, no question asked.

Jennifer whispered, "Woozle, is a massive metal spider serving me breakfast in bed?" Her voice cracked even though she did not want to show any fear.

Woozle blinked and turned his head, seeing the spider for the first time. All was silent for a few heart beats.

Too many heart beats passed, she was not being attacked by the massive metallic spider. Fearing the spider would attack her if she was not watching, she took a chance, taking her eyes away from the beast, and looked around. The spider Jennifer rescued yesterday was standing on the dean's desk manically moving around animatedly.

The door to the dean's office was closed. How did the immense spider even get into the room? She was not allowed to be in the dean's office, let alone sleeping in the room. In her mind, this could not end well.

Woozle went from unmoving cuddle buddy to full jet lynx mode and attempted to attack the metal spider. "Run, kid. I'll hold this thing off for as long as I can," Woozle shouted, sounding desperate. Woozle's claws could not do any damage to the spider, and his teeth could not bite into the spider's metal carapace. Jennifer knew that every second the lynx attacked would buy her time. Each heartbeat Woozle attacked faster, he had started with the part of the spider's head that connected to the front mandibles. Even here, his mouth was too small to get into the spider. He moved to the underside of the arachnid, his jets roaring with power while the arachnid was above him. His claws digging up. He was unable to even leave a mark. She remembered the saying, eat or be eaten.

"Is that breakfast for me?" Her words came out in a near whisper as she slowly sat up, never taking her eyes off the metallic spider.

The spider bobbed its body up and down, knocking Woozle to the ground. The familiar bounced and as he came up he moved to one of the legs of the spider. The giant spider slowly and gently handed Jennifer the tray with eggs, bacon, and home-style fries.

Jennifer took the tray that held her first real meal since coming to school. The sandwich from the turtle was just a snack. She had not realized just how much she wanted to eat. Woozle was pushing on one of the spider's legs. If he was able to move the much larger one it would have been away from Jennifer. Picking up the silverware, she went for the potatoes with a fork. Before taking the first bite of food, she remembered her manners. "Oh, right. Thank you for the food."

"Woozle, you can stop now. I don't think we're in danger." Jennifer still eyed the very scary spider.

With a huff, Woozle landed next to her, standing at attention on all four legs facing the giant spider. He reminded her more of a guard dog about to attack then the purring creature that had slept on her all night.

She was still not sure what was going on, but with slow deliberate care, she started eating and placed a piece of bacon down to Woozle. He did not move on the bit of meat. Woozle continued to watch the arachnid. Only after she gave Woozle a few head scratches did he pick off the bacon in his front paws and he sat on his haunches. When he did eat the food, it was while grumbling too low for her to hear.

After finishing the food, Jennifer looked around the room once more, this time with a much slower heart rate. There were small details in the room Jennifer had not noticed before. For one, the office was overall smaller than she had first thought. In front of one of the bookshelves was a table with many pictures on it. She didn't know who a hologram would have pictures of, but the people in the frames had smiles on their faces. All the other walls had either bookshelves or windows.

The spider she rescued was still dancing on the professor's desk. Jennifer guessed the little spider was attempting to mime or communicate with the larger spider. The motions were irregular but graceful in a way only a spider could be.

She felt the need to break the silence in the room, but did not know what to say. Though, she remembered she was not supposed to be in this room at all. "Hello, my name is Jennifer. I know I was not supposed to sleep here, but this seemed like a good spot." It was not a good explanation, but it was something. Hopefully, something would be better than nothing.

The spider did not seem to move or make any sounds in reply.

A notification came up in her menus, which she opened with a mental command.

New quest offer from Grandmother Spider: Accept Rover as a pet, reward perks, Pet Armored Colossal Trapdoor Spider, trait Speak With Spiders. Difficulty unknown. This quest line is not currently active. This quest has not been completed in {redacted}.

Jennifer looked over at the extremely animated spider she rescued yesterday. She would never have guessed his name was Rover. With a smile on her lips, she accepted the quest.

Congratulations, you have been given the free trait Speak With Spiders. No need to write on a web.

Congratulations, this is the first time this quest has been given and accepted in {redacted} time. The bonus trait Gathering has been added to the pet, Rover.

With a voice that did not come from her mouth, the giant spider said, "Are you sure about this, dearie? This one is just a fragment and seems kinda slow." The system had added a voice-over for the spider using **Speak With Spiders**, rather than downloading the information into her brain. The seven-legged spider appeared from a trapdoor beside Jennifer. Rover was gesticulating, so there was no voice over for her pet. The small spider was trying to communicate with her, but she did not understand what he was trying to communicate with her. She laid her hand flat before her new pet, and Rover did not hesitate to climb onto her hand. With her other hand, she gave a one finger petting to her now official pet spider.

Jennifer reviewed her situation. She now had a pet seven-legged **Colossal, Armored, Trapdoor, Gathering Spider**, as well as a **Miniature, Giant, Jet Powered, Lynx-shark**, a **Mop**, the clothes she was wearing, and a few quests. She felt the need to be doing something. Looking at her quests, she knew where she wanted to go.

Woozle went up to Jennifer's hand that was holding the spider, and he sniffed it. The spider turned to face the lynx continuing to wave his legs around.

She looked at the tiny armored spider, "Why can I understand you and not Rover?"

"He's too young. Probably only hatched a day or two ago. So, he's hard to understand. But in less than a month, he'll be fully comprehensible." The much larger spider spoke with obvious affection in her voice.

Jennifer appreciated the voice-over system's ability to add affection into the voice of a monstrous spider.

Taking a deep breath, she thought about all she needed to do. This was a strange place, but even here, there were things that needed to get done. She didn't want to spend another night in the dean's office, so she would need to find a place to stay for tonight. She also needed to get letters of recommendation from a parallel, the mayor of a nearby town, and a shop owner for her to be accepted into the university. This place of learning had been the only place she knew. She would need to leave. Feeling the pressure of her situation, Jennifer asked in a flat voice, "How do I get to town? There is a town nearby right?"

The massive spider said nothing but pointed. On her mini map, a spider graphic appeared with a note explaining that the town was ten kilometers away.

She thanked the giant armored spider and placed Rover on her right shoulder. The lynx landed on her left shoulder and climbed into the hood of her cloak. Jennifer brought up her traits again to make sure her navigation skill was active, waved goodbye to the much larger spider, and marched out of the dean's office as a woman with a quest.

CHAPTER 4

ON THE ROAD

THE FIRST HALF HOUR of the journey went pretty well, but after an hour and a half of walking down a dirt road, Jennifer grew bored. There were trees. The trees were green. Oh look, another tree! It had white bark, and so did the next one. The one after that was brown, much like the next ten. Or the next thousand. Either way, there were far too many trees and nothing to do but walk. She was getting thirsty and decided that the next time she was going on a quest, she would make sure to pack water and a snack. Maybe she would get a bag. Woozle had made her hood his spot, sometimes pointing out on her shoulder to look around. Rover either sat on her shoulder, or was nowhere to be seen. When the spider left her shoulder, it would be by way of a trap door that would appear next to him. She had no idea how the spider summoned the door, or where the door went.

A low-pitch, rumbling arrow shot past her. "Since when did arrows make noise?" she said aloud to no one in particular.

A man holding a bow with an arrow set to fire stood thirty to forty paces ahead of her on the trail. Time slowed for her as she took in the whole scene. The arrow looked odd, with an oversized arrowhead, a shaft thicker than her thumb, and no fetching or feather on the end. Automatically bringing up her mop in a defensive stance, she estimated that once the loud arrow was fired, she would have time to cast one of her abilities. "You're shooting at me." The shock of the situation made her shout far louder than she intended. Woozle moved around in her hood. She did not know what her spider could do, but Rover had come out of the trap door and was standing on her right shoulder.

"Stand and deliver," the man said.

Jennifer had been focused on the bow and arrow, but now she looked at the man dressed in a green and brown tunic with matching pants rather than just the weapon. The man had on a black mask that only covered part of his face.

A long moment passed.

After about ten heart beats, the man repeated in a loud clear voice, "I said stand and deliver!"

"Yeah, you said that before. But I don't know what you want me to deliver. And how can I deliver something if I am supposed to stand here?" she yelled.

Woozle leaped from Jennifer's hood and took an attack position beside her.

"Historically, when someone is being robbed, they drop their valuables and run," the masked man shouted back.

She eyed the man, looking for an opening or a way out. The man looked like some kind of game hunter, but something seemed off. He stood aiming the arrow at her. If he was a game hunter, he was not a good one. She did not see any kills near the man, and he had no way to transport an animal back to wherever he was coming from. Maybe the reason why the man was trying to rob her was because he was a terrible hunter and needed food. If that was the case, what else was the man missing? Then she noticed it.

Jennifer stood straighter and relaxed her defensive stance a bit. "You're robbing me?"

"Yes. Now drop your valuables, like gold or money. You're making this harder than it needs to be."

"Woozle, I think he is robbing me."

"Kid, I think he is robbing you. Want me to bite him?"

Unable to keep the smile from her face, "I'm carrying a mop. I'm in starter gear. And I have yet to find a quest or a job that pays money." With space between them, she felt the need to raise her voice.

"How much is the mop worth?" asked the man.

She thought about this for a moment and mumbled, "Okay, this man is trying to rob me." She let the mop hang in her hand and turned to Woozle. "So he must be a bad guy."

"I have heard of one guy stealing from the rich, giving to the poor, and only taking a finders fee." He was standing in his attack pose.

With a shout, she asked, "How much is your bow and arrow worth?"

"What?"

"Well, you asked how much my mop was worth. If you tell me how much your bow is worth, I think I can come up with an estimate if I have something to compare it to."

"You're being robbed, girl. Normally robberies don't have this much talking."

"It's my first time." She threw up a hand in exasperation. "That one arrow is probably worth more than a mop. And you're the first human I've seen so far, and it does feel nice to be talking with another person." She liked the fact the man called her a girl rather than a fragment. She was already tired of being called that. Jennifer was still not going to make this easy for him though. Woozle was motionless, but she knew the moment the fighting started he would be fighting along with her.

"Each rocket arrow is equal to 2 blues, and the bow is worth 1 red and counts as an exotic ranged weapon. Only a few in this nation can even wield one. Now how much is the mop worth?" The part of the man's face that was not covered in his mask turned red, which was a good sign.

She just had to keep this going. "How much is the minimum wage? Like this is just a normal mop, I wouldn't pay more than like two hours of work to get something like this, but it is sturdy. I hit a goblin with it once." She spoke with a raised voice instead of shouting, just the need to keep talking.

The masked man's arms were trembling under the strain of

holding the bow and the rocket arrow at the ready. "Just drop the mop and r—"

Jennifer targeted the man with a blast of Dark Pulse and darted to her right. Woozle darted to the left. As the dark attack flew towards him, he let the arrow fire. Once the arrow lept from the bow, it was propelled with the same roar she heard before. The arrow flew high and wide, the pulse of dark energy hit the masked man right in the face. He stepped back a pace and looked a bit dazed.

Jennifer turned uncaring to watch the arrow rocket up into the sky, leaving a small exhaust trail as it flew. "Was that a rocket arrow?" She tried to hide the amusement in her tone. She was no archer, at least she never remembered being one, but a rocket arrow was sounding like a fun weapon to get. Woozle matched her pace on the other side of the road as she strolled towards the man.

"Yes, and the next one will hit you, so give up."

Trying to keep a straight face, she looked at the man, glanced around, and focused back on the man.

"The next what?" Jennifer asked, trying not to sound smug.

"The next rocket arrow!" The masked man yelled.

Jennifer gave up on hiding the smile, and walked towards the man as he reached for his quiver. Then the man paused. She watched as he grabbed for something that was not there. Her smile broadened as she continued her approach.

His eyes grew wide, and he froze. Woozle was beside her as she walked up to be within arm's reach of the man. Stopped with Woozle by her side.

"If I asked you to. Would you bite this man's arm off? My little lynx shark." She over pronounced the last word.

"Clean off, with one chomp," he answered coldly.

"One arrow is all I will need." The bandit's voice was as shaky as he was.

"Oh, well. You seem to be missing one," she replied.

The masked man's skin went from an angry red to a fearful pale.

She made a show of licking her lips. "I'm a necromancer in need of a new skeleton."

When he fainted, Jennifer tried and failed to hold back a laugh. The man was a terrible highwayman, an atrocious shot, and probably a terrible hunter.

Jennifer smiled down at her defeated foe. This time, she did not have to hit anyone with a mop and had beaten him by using mostly words. When her amusement faded, questions clouded her mind. "So, Woozle, what should I do now?"

"Loot the body, tie him to a tree, and look for wanted or missing persons posters offering rewards in the next few days?"

She eyed her companion. Not only did that sound mean, but it also seemed like a lot of work. Besides, she did not have any rope on her.

In the end, Jennifer took the man's weapons off him and found a large hunting knife, and a bottle of water. She took the weapon and the bow, then she moved to a nearby rock to sit. She hesitated then went back for the man's water. After she finished the drink, she waited for the man to wake up.

To pass the time, she tried to combine her powers in various ways. At first, she tried to put the dark pulse inside a force field, but the pulse would either be too fast or the force field too slow. By the time one would finish casting, the other had already moved on. Woozle climbed back into Jennifer's hoody as she tried different timings while getting the same failed result.

The spider had gone off somewhere, in her menus his status was set to gathering. She guessed that the gathering was new to the spider, and she was excited to see what the little creature would bring back with him.

Jennifer was considering putting a force field on a potion when the man woke up.

Woozle poked his head over the edge of the hoodie and glared at the man.

Her anger at the man boiled over. Narrowing her eyes, she spoke even louder than before. "You were the first human person I've seen since getting here. I've found nice spiders, goblins that apologize, and a holographic dean. But the first two legged, non-green skinned person I see fires a rocket arrow at me in the middle of the road."

The man stayed silent while he slowly stood up. As Jennifer's voice rose, his eyes got wider.

"So, this is what we are going to do. You are going to walk in front of me, and we are going to go to town. Once we get there, I am going to find someone who will arrest you and let them punish you like the robber you are." Pausing to collect her thoughts, "And you are going to thank me for not turning you into a skeleton when I had the chance."

The man stammered, "Th-thank you for not turning me into a skeleton when you had the chance, ma'am."

"You got some pipes on you kid. I think that the leaves in the trees trembled when you raised your voice." Speaking only for Jennifer to hear.

"Now, start walking."

Obeying, he turned and started walking at her command.

She did not want to admit it, but her mini map had shifted, so she did not know which direction the town was in. If not for the man leading her, she would probably have gotten lost again. She hoped he was going in the right direction. Woozle kept watching the man from his position in Jennifer's hood over her shoulder.

Jennifer's spider appeared on her shoulder from a small trap door that disappeared in a puff of smoke after a heartbeat. He carried some mixed berries in a small piece of white tree bark. He held his gatherings out in front of him as he moved backward and forward. Taking this as an offering, she smiled at Rover, giving him lots of attention and pets as a thank you.

Opening up her menus, she found her inventory. Blueberries, raspberries, and even a strawberry as well as a piece of birch bark were now listed in her log. "Thank you, Rover." Smiling, she picked up the spider and gave him more pets. Rover leaned into the petting happily. She returned Rover to her shoulder and made sure she was keeping pace with the highwayman.

The man walked ten paces in front of her, staying silent the whole time. She had lost track of time, her spider was riding on her shoulder as Woozle relaxed in her hood. As they walked, the city and its trail began to appear. The town's wall was not impressive. Barely taller than her as parts of it had fallen down, revealing that it was made of thin wood planks. The town wall was just a badly maintained fence that could not keep a dog out, let alone a person. A guard station stood out like a scarecrow over an empty field. It was more of a shack with a rope across the path to block the way. The rope, about as thick as Jennifer's thumb, spread from the guard station to the fence. The space the rope occupied was about what Jennifer thought a wagon would be wide. Jennifer let the thoughts in her mind come out of her mouth, "This would not even slow down a bored goat, let alone a person."

Once they got closer to the gate, Jennifer realized there was no one in the shack. By her prisoner's actions, he had realized it, too. The masked man sprinted full tilt towards the town.

With a scowl, she powered up her dark pulse aiming for the man's back. She missed her mark and hit the man's left shoulder, causing him to fall off balance. He ended up stumbling at full speed face first into the shack. It turned out the man was tougher than the shack because it fell down around him. The scene ended with the man face down underneath a pile of scrap wood.

"That was the first person you have seen, and you used your dark attack on him twice." Woozle had leaped from his spot in her hood, ready to pounce, but the fight was over before he could join in the battle.

Jennifer held her lips tightly together, while her face was warm. "You are right, I need to find a way to do better."

She did not change her pace, and once she reached the man, his face was bleeding on the wood. Once she was beside the man, she cleared her throat. When there was no reaction, she decided a polite nudge to his side with her boot would be in order. The soft contact with her boot made him groan.

The noise of the shack collapsing must have alerted the town because two men approached Jennifer. She took in the sight of one man in a sports jacket and top hat, the other wearing black finished armor with a spear in one hand.

Woozle sat on his back legs between Jennifer's and the town. He started to clean his paw, but his eyes never left those coming to greet her.

Jennifer waved at the people approaching her while leaning on her mop. The two men exchanged looks with one another as they approached.

The man in the top hat spoke, addressing Jennifer. "Welcome to Hogback, parallel. My name is Jim Gigawatts, I am the mayor of this town." His words came slow and hesitant as the man with the spear stood right beside him.

Something about the way the spear man was moving gave the impression he was a warrior and not just playing dress up. Although, the spear may have helped with that assessment.

"This man tried to rob me on the way here. I want him arrested and charged," she announced in a loud, clear voice.

A groan escaped the spearman as the top hat man facepalmed. "I gave you an exotic weapon for hunting, and you tried to rob someone?" The man in the top hat said from behind his hand.

"But, Grandpa, I was low on arrows and th—" the highwayman was cut off by a glare from the man in the top hat.

"Your mom gave me your login key. If you don't want to play fair, you may as well not play."

Jennifer could easily see the familiar bond in their speech and decided it was best not to get involved. The man with the top hat had some power over the masked man, more than just being his grandfather. The words login key tickled her mind, these words appeared to be important, but she did not understand their meaning.

"You'll go and do some chores while you're in lockup. After the raid we will see."

The almost-thief hung his head as he walked in the direction his grandparent pointed.

The spearman turned to Jennifer, his face was expressionless. With the boredom of a well-rehearsed line he said, "Welcome to the town of Hogback. We are a good-aligned town. You must be neutral or above to enter. If you are traveling with a caravan, your alignment is waved, but you must remain with your caravan at all times. The entry fee to the town is two blues. Please enjoy your stay."

Jennifer thought quickly, not knowing what blues were. "Excuse me, but I only got here yesterday. What are these blues you're talking about?"

The man in the top hat perked up. His eyes brightened like a sales agent on the verge of a massive sale. She also noticed that she was a head taller than both the men in front of her.

"Careful, kid. I don't like the look in the mayor's eyes," Woozle whispered into her ear as he climbed back into her hoodie.

"As Mayor of this little border town. I take it you are a new parallel, and since you are new, don't worry about the entrance fee."

The spearman's eyes rolled as the mayor spoke.

"Since you are new to this part of the shell and you do not have housing yet, how about I give you a quest. Let's say you bring back fifty animal pelts, seventy wood, twenty metal, or eighty-five healing moss, and I give you a spot right next to the town square to build a house or business on? Just tell me what resource you want to start with. I will even mark the areas on your map where to gather the resources." The mayor spoke fast with a level of confidence she wished she had.

Her head moved backwards, taking in a sharp breath, her eyes darted over the words that appeared in her menus, "The healing herbs, I guess."

A prompt appeared in her vision. **You have accepted a quest from the mayor. Gather 85 healing herbs from the forest nearby. Reward: a place in the town to build a house or business and 150 experience points.**

"Oh, I have the quest now," escaped her mouth as she blinked. This was a lot for her to take in, and she was feeling rushed into something.

The spearman cleared his throat, with some level of harshness in his tone. "My name is Squad. I am captain of the town guard and bodyguard to the mayor. As a parallel, what do you seek to do here?"

The answer came immediately. "I'm a fragment. I'm here because I wish to enroll at Bishop's University and was looking for a place to stay in town while I start my quests." The answer came out more robotic than was natural. Looking at the log, she could see a skill called, **Answer Honestly**, had been used successfully on her.

She glared at Squad for using the skill on her, but all he did was laugh. In fact, he bent over laughing. She turned to look at the mayor in confusion. The mayor was facepalming again, and what little she could see of his face had turned red.

"I would have answered honestly without you using the skill on me," she said. She sounded hurt when asking, "Why are you laughing?"

"The mayor offered you a quest thinking you were a parallel not a fragment, and did that assuming the sale thing. He only gave you the options to accept the offer, while hiding the rejection or negotiation." Squad said between laughs. "If he had known you were a fragment, the quest would have had you gather ten times that for a lesser reward."

With raised eyebrows, she turned to a glare at the mayor. If she could shoot daggers out of her eyes, the mayor would be knife rack.

The mayor took a couple of steps back. "I promise to only give you better fragment quests from now, girl," the mayor said, raising his hand in front of himself defensively.

Her face warmed at this, equal parts anger and embarrassment. She did not like being called a fragment or girl.

Woozle's jets hummed with power as took up his attack pose next to Jennifer while letting out a warning hiss.

The mayor's head darted down to look at the lynx, having lost a bit of color in his face. "I absolutely swear. Only parallel quests for you, my dear."

She looked at Squad, whose knuckles were white holding the spear.

Nodding with a stiff jerk of her head, she said, "Good, I'm off to gather herbs." She left for a spot now marked on her map. Her face was still hot with frustration, and she wanted to hit something. Someone tried to rob her and his grandfather was on the edge of cheating her out of a deal. She mentally selected her dark attack, letting her anger fill the power. Releasing the anger, the breath she did not know she was holding, and the attack let loose. A tree on the side of the path fell over, as a notification came up.

Congratulations, you have leveled up to level 3. You may choose 6 power enhancements. You have unlocked the trait, Giant Intimidation. During conversations, you may actively intimidate. If looks could kill, yours would.

Jennifer turned back toward the town. Feeling flushed in the face, she decided to get some water and deal with her level up before heading out.

"I just leveled up. Is there a place in town where I can sit and get a drink while I look at my options?" Her tone showed her frustration.

The mayor, not letting any chance pass him by, said, "How about I show you around, girl, before you help the town by gathering much needed herbs." A forced cheeriness to his voice.

She took in a deep breath, closed her eyes, she let out a deep breath. Focused on slowing her heart rate down.

The mayor was still smiling, the smile looked odd to her, there was something off about it. There was a sparkle in his eyes she did not recognize.

"I would very much like to see the town, Mr. Mayor." She wanted to remain formal, she put an emphasis on the word mayor. She was going to need a place to live while getting into the school and taking classes.

CHAPTER 5

ONE MAN'S TOWN IS ANOTHER MAN'S KINGDOM

AS HE EXPLAINED THE lay of the land, the mayor acted like Hogback was the greatest town ever. "Oh yes, we have the town hall, three inns, four guard houses," the mayor put extra emphasis on the words guard houses, but continued normally after that, "two warehouses, a Museum of Natural History, an embassy for the Toarcian dominion, the micro foundry factory, and then a few houses for the townspeople. There are six farms set not far from the town wall. Most are for grain, one is for watermelons down by the bay, and the others are for meat. However, since they are outside the town they do not count as town buildings, but they are under the protection of the town, so they generate resources for the town."

She was unsure how to judge the town. All the houses were tiny with most being only one story high and constructed out of wood. The houses looked cold, dark, and damp. Most had no lights on the inside nor smoke coming from the chimneys. She tried to recall what houses looked like in her world and remembered colors on buildings, but none were distinct to her. Feeling a pang of emotion, at the loss of memory, in her chest, Jennifer decided she needed to add color to the town somehow.

Looking around, there are more roads than people. He talked about every house they passed by, when the house was built, by whom, and how much the house cost at the time it was constructed, and how much the empty houses cost to buy or rent now. Most houses stood empty. Jennifer ignored most of what the mayor said but kept taking in the town. Most of the houses were rectangles, but some were round, and a few looked like repurposed barns.

At the end of the tour, the mayor brought her to the center of the settlement. The town square was more of a rectangle, but she had the feeling that correcting the mayor on this would not go over well.

"Mr. Mayor, can you explain the meaning of what is on the flag?" Jennifer pointed up to the flag waving in the sky.

The smile reached the mayor's eyes, giving them a certain twinkle when he replied. "The red background notes that we are a Red Alliance town. The green vertical line on the left side shows we are a border town with the dinosaur lands, and we have a -" He seemed to be looking for the correct words or diplomatic phrasing. "We have a somewhat open border with the dinosaur land. They send their trading caravans, and we only hold them for twenty-four hours while we inspect them. Then they go to the larger cities, often taking goods from our town too."

The mayor's tone shifted from one of boastfulness as he no longer met her eyes while talking. His head tilted down to the right. Adding up the details of the changes in her mind, she presumed holding of the caravan seemed to be a point of contention for the mayor to point it out so much. "The blue outline of a bright violet lightning bolt is my mayoral symbol. The yellow line that crosses horizontally the length of the flag up to the green line indicates that we have a military unit stationed here. That unit fights the town's bi-weekly paper raid."

Jennifer was nodding along up to the part about the raid. The town center was just a grass space with a small grove of tall trees on either end on the long sides, and the flag standing tall in the approximate center. A stone walkway mimicked the yellow and green lines on the flag. Near the bottom left triangle of the walkway was a large fountain with a statue of a man holding a yard stick up like a sword while standing on top of a taxi. The taxi stood on its two back wheels. To Jennifer the fountain looked a bit silly, she did not understand how it had not fallen over. Judging on how maintained the statue and fountain were, it probably meant something to someone. A small stone wall enclosed the town center. It was around the height of Jennifer's knees and about two of her feet wide. This was the only area of town where she had seen many colorful, small plants growing on top of the wall, giving the whole space a garden feel. After noticing some benches positioned around the fountain, Jennifer walked toward them and motioned for the mayor to follow before asking her question. "What's a paper raid?" So much was new to her, and she wanted to learn more.

Woozle had been loping alongside the pair while the mayor lectured about his town. The lynx-shark had the zoomies. At first, just sniffing around, something caught his attention as he ran about. Jennifer noted that Woozle had started at about the size of a field mouse and was now the size of a small house cat. She smiled as she watched him run from place to place with his shark fins and fur coat shining in the sunlight. He looked happy just running around.

She realized the mayor had not spoken in some time, and he looked as if he was deep in thought. Wanting to give him the time he needed, Jennifer watched the fountain's water.

After a moment, the mayor spoke again. "You fragments seem so real and remind me of when my grandchildren were much smaller. You know you're a fragment, but do you know what that means?"

She tried not to glare. Feeling her answer would have a touch of anger either way, she let her frustration show. "I am who and what I am. And what I am is sick of being called a fragment. I feel whole."

The mayor turned, giving her a strange look as he spoke. "I feel whole too. I haven't left this world in over a decade. The next time I leave will probably be the last time too." Leaned back, lifting his head to look at the sky. "Well, to answer your question, a paper raid is a single monster that has been copied over and over. Like a picture photocopied many times." The mayor slipped back into lecture mode again. If the mayor were to ever become a professor at the university, Jennifer thought she would take his classes, but only if he stopped calling her a fragment.

"In my town's paper raid, it's always a monster that has been copied. Not a single person, or distinct entity. Always generic monster mobs, they are the easiest to fight and give the lowest of rewards. The monsters attack in waves, each wave becoming more difficult. The waves are timed, if the wave is beaten within the time limit, the next wave will appear normally a tier above the last wave of monsters. If the timer runs out, and the attackers have not been beaten, a boss will appear. The boss is either at the same power level of the last mob, or one above. They attack here once every two weeks and give decent experience points and loot but nothing fancy. Between the paper raids, caravans, and exports, we're a profitable town. That's how I'm able to stay here as a long-term parallel. It is now my play cycle, get game money, trade it for real money to pay for the game." The mayor looked down and added a half-hearted chuckle.

"What's a long term parallel?" She asked because it seemed to make the mayor sad for some reason.

The mayor let out a dry laugh. "My choices were to live in a retirement home or live in a game world where I can still be productive." Joy returned to the mayor's voice as he spoke. "This way I get to see my grandkids more often, and the pod I'm in makes sure I eat and take my meds. If the ads are to be believed, this has even added years to my life." The mayor looked up at Jennifer in spite of both of them sitting on the same bench. "So, girl, are you a giant sent to give the town a new quest line?"

Turning her head, Jennifer looked at the fountain and laughed.

The mayor raised his hands, palms facing out.

Jennifer turned back to him. "What makes you think I'm a giant . . ." Her voice trailed off as she looked down at the mayor and the realization of their size difference sunk in. "I am descended from giants," she recited her words from before. She asked slowly, "Am I that tall?"

The mayor replied, "I'm as tall as I've ever been. And I must be in the top one percent of all men in terms of size."

She smelled a lie. Men always added an inch or two. The mayor seemed to be no different, but he was a head shorter than her.

Before she could think of a response. Woozle came bounding up with something in his mouth. "Wook wha I caugh." Woozle's speech was muffled by the light brown thing between his teeth.

"Oh, your familiar seems to have caught a nice wild rabbicoon. Those are almost all pests around here," the mayor said.

Her mouth opened in gaped and she instantly went into her inventory menu. She brought out a healing potion as Woozle dropped a creature, which looked like a cross between a raccoon and a bunny, at her feet. She did not hesitate to give the creature the contents of the healing potion.

The small rabbicoon finished the contents of the healing potion and curled into Jennifer, getting as far from the lynx-shark as it could. She reached out to Woozle, petting his head. "You're a good hunter, but this one seems a little young to be catching." She looked down at the empty glass container in her other hand then over at the rabbicoon hiding in her robes before turning to the mayor. "Can you please fill this with water? My hands are full," Jennifer asked the mayor.

Not hearing an answer she looked back to the mayor, the mayor's eyes were wide open and staring at Jennifer. He took the glass container, strolled to the fountain, and filled it up. Jennifer ran one hand over the rabbicoon and the other over her lynx-shark, hoping to calm both by the time the mayor returned.

Focusing on her status bars in her menu, there was now a black bar on her stamina bar that would normally be gray after casting her healing potion power. When the mayor handed the glass container back, the black portion turned back to gray.

"Thank you, Mr. Mayor," remembering her manners. She took a large gulp of the water and offered the rest to Woozle. Woozle shook his head and bounded over to the fountain to drink from the source. As soon as the scary lynx-shark left, the buncoon took off towards the stone wall nearby, to an unseen rabbicoon hole or burrow.

"You can craft healing potions?" The words came hesitantly from the mayor.

Drawing her shoulders inwardly. "Alchemist is one of my classes. Healing potions was the first skill. The reason I took your quest to find eighty-five healing weeds was because it may help me craft more than the four I'm allowed now."

"Alchemist at the most basic level would be able to turn ten healing weeds into one basic health potion. But as a man worth his salt, I can tell that what you gave the rabbicoon was at least a rare healing potion." Astonishment resonated in the mayor's voice.

She tilted her head as an idea came to her mind. A smile crossed her mouth. "Do you want a healing potion?" She asked as innocently as possible and pulled a second healing potion out.

"Oh, yes," he answered without hesitation.

"How much?"

The mayor's eyes shot up from the healing potion. She could almost see his bartering mind at work. She moved the potion slowly from right to left and back again. Judging by the way the mayor's eyes followed the healing potion like a dog would follow a steak, Jennifer had the high ground in this exchange.

The mayor stated his opening offer. "Five oranges."

Thinking back to her exchange with the masked man, she remembered that she still had no idea what money was like here. "How much is a room at one of the inns?" Trying to find something to compare it to that she wanted.

The mayor promptly said, "Ten oranges for a night at the Dry Boat, twenty-five oranges for the Dancing Clock, and one yellow for a night with breakfast and dinner at the Chateau du Jim." The mayor's eyes narrowed at her as he spoke.

Making the connection to the mayor's name, she asked, "Do you own the Chateau du Jim?"

The mayor pursed his lips. "One night complimentary at my castle and ten oranges. That is giving you a place to stay while you complete the gathering of the healing weeds and start building your own place in town."

Jennifer saw how much the mayor's offer had jumped and

made a counteroffer. "Three nights at the chateau and twenty-five oranges."

The mayor eyed her with an appraising look. "Three nights and five oranges. And that's because I think having you in town is a good investment."

That sounded like a good deal. Jennifer smiled while she passed the healing potion to the mayor.

The mayor took the potion. "When you get to the Chateau, let them know you have room one-oh-three. Feel free to join the paper raid this week."

There was no feeling in the world like she felt now, having a weight she did not realize was there being lifted off her shoulders. She had slept on a couch in a school last night. She had no idea where she was going to be staying tonight. It may only be three nights, but in that time, she could gather the healing weeds she needed to get a parcel of land in town. Jennifer only had one question left for the mayor as he handed her an orange bill with the number five on one side and an owl on the other. "What's an orange compared to a yellow?"

The mayor's eyebrows shot up before he doubled over laughing.

When the mayor was able to calm down and sit beside Jennifer he explained, 1-99 are red and are basically change and only came in coins, 100-999 were oranges and came in 5-10-50-100 notes, 1000-9999 where yellows the same denominations as oranges but are small bars, and carried on as green, blue, indigo and violet. The gears of her mind were grinding, why not just use the decimal system and dollar? There was a place south of where she used to live that used a unit of measurement that had a strange ratio. Twelve to one, then three to one, followed my one thousand seven hundred and sixty to one. Someone had told her it was needlessly complicated, but too expensive to fix. This world's money was like that to her.

Jennifer thought about the comparison to her own world, which was a cent to a dollar. A hotel room on the cheap end would cost about one hundred a night. But comparing the cost of one thing was not enough to give her a sense of this world's money, so she searched her mind for something else. While there were medications on her world, she did not remember health potions being there. She needed to find apples and bread to give her a good idea how much this money was worth.

"This really is your first day here?" the mayor asked, the humorous smile stuck on his face.

Jennifer mock glared at the mayor.

A blue bird with a large X in place of his right eye which had a metal helm and a sheathed sword on a belt flew up to him. Jennifer thought of how cartoonish the bird looked.

The mayor lost the color in his cheeks. The bird beak was opening and closing, with the feather on its neck moving at regular intervals. There were no sounds or words Jennifer could hear, and judging by the way the mayor reached, the words were meant only for him. She guessed it was a system thing.

"They can't be coming here."

"Who can't be coming here?" She should have asked about the bird first because it vanished in a puff of smoke.

The mayor turned to Jennifer and talked very quickly as if his mind was running faster than his mouth. "We are going to need - Well that would need to be done. Who could do the catering? The baker man who lives by -? No, no. That burned down and the insurance paid out. Well the cattle, they must eat meat. Wait, no. His right hand man thing has only has those square teeth. They are dinosaurs; best not to make assumptions. So if not, who else? The king and queen and probably most of the royal court—" The mayor stopped all of a sudden. "There will be the royal guards and their mounts. OH! They're going to need a place to stay and what will they ride in . . .?" The mayor gave her a scrunched up side-eye look she did not like.

A notification came up in her menus.

You have been invited to join the town of Hogsback as a citizen. As a citizen, you will be granted rights and

protections under the town charter, including but not limited to, free entry and exit from the town, access to the water wells, and other such utilities. The town has a flat tax rate of twenty five thousand oranges a year for land tax. The only guarantee in this world is taxes. Death need not apply.

With a nod, she accepted the invite and immediately saw a new menu tab labeled Town Interface. Her access level to the town interface was set to basic, giving her access to a list of town quests, a list of needed supplies, and a weather report. New quests were being added every heartbeat like gathering hay, cleaning the stables, gathering foods, and cooking a dozen meals fit for royalty. The cooking quest was not up for long as someone quickly accepted it. Jennifer's eyes glazed over at all the quests. She stopped counting new quests after thirty.

From the mayor's mouth came a loud and clear command, "Temporary Mayor's Office." A large, hardwood, dark, L-shaped, fancy desk appeared next to the mayor. A line up of blue birds started forming on it. Where they landed was a miniature version of a landing strip that planes at airports would use. On the runway, in white block letters had the words, "Incoming messages." On the other end of the work surface was another air strip labeled, "Out Messages." The rest of the desk was spotless with multiple unused notepads arranged in a neat pile and pens standing inside an organizer. The town's flag was painted on the front of the writing station. The mayor took a deep breath. With a wave of his hand he said, "Fine office chair with back massager." The chair was made of redwood and black leather. The part of the chair that would meet Jim's back had moving bulges. The mayor took his seat.

The first one on his desk was a blue bird wearing a cheap looking pumpkin mask who descended from the sky. It was followed by more birds wearing an assortment of costumes. They lined up with their wings folded standing on their feet on the open spot in front of the mayor ready to take messages. The birds came in all shapes and sizes. She watched as the birds flew with grace and purpose after standing in line like soldiers awaiting orders.

A young man carrying a shiny new briefcase came running up to the mayor, huffing and puffing. "Sir, is there an emergency?"

Without ceremony, the mayor said, "We need to call a town meeting. Go door to door if you have to, but make sure everyone important is going to come. Post on the outer forums. Then gather the town guards. Make sure they're up to date and wearing the town colors. Make sure they will look the part. Then contact the red legion, get them to send some people."

The mayor kept listing off duties for the clerk.

Woozle was stretched out on the ground, and she bent down to scratch his ear. She checked her menus to see if there was any information on where her spider had gone off to as he was absent from her shoulder again. After clicking on her status menu, a Pets window appeared.

Rover: Status - Gathering healing moss.

Although the spider was at max health, his stamina would dip a bit and rapidly return to full.

Deciding to ignore the mayor as he spoke to the birds, she looked at her stamina. The normal grayed out part on her stamina bar showing she had crafted health potions accompanied by a black bar on the display. A countdown timer hovered above the black area, reading six days, twenty-three hours, fifty-seven minutes. Something clicked in her mind: giving or selling a potion without receiving the vial back resulted in a long recharge time.

The mayor sat at the large desk writing furiously on a piece of paper, then handed the note to the birds. With the mayor distracted, Jennifer had time to level up.

On this level, there were no new powers, only six enhancements to change her powers in some way. Most of her options were Use Less Stamina/Mana/Energy, Recharge Faster, Do More Damage, Take More Damage, Heal More, and Last Longer. She allocated three of her enhancements to her forcefield so that it recharged faster and lasted longer. It could take more damage. Jennifer's potions also took less stamina. Her last choice was used for her undead powers. Focusing, she found several options to enhance this ability. She could now summon two skeletons rather than one and both would have more health.

With that out of the way, she looked at the available town quests. The only one left was to clean the stables. With a sigh, she turned to the mayor, who looked very busy.

She thought about her quest to get into the university and what she needed from him to do that before walking over to the mayor. "I will take the clean the stable's quest, but I want a letter of reference as well as the standard reward." She emphasized the word standard.

With a wave of his hand, he said, "Yes. Yes." Then she got a quest update.

Clean the stables: moderate reward - 100 oranges, 10 city reputation, letter of recommendation from the mayor. 24 hours left for the quest.

She went over the quest a few times. It looked simple. When her eyes focused back on the mayor he was, with a raised eyebrow, pointing in an easterly direction. Jennifer blinked and realized he had anticipated her request for directions. With a bow of her head, she said, "Thank you," before going in that direction.

She quickly made her way over to the battalions. Thankfully, the building stood out and had a sign saying stables over the doors.

The animal holding building was three floors tall. The first floor was split down the middle with areas for horses, moose, giant cats, and standard size mounts on one side. The other side had booths for much larger mounts. Much, much larger ones. The booths were larger than some of the houses in town. A logo hung above the massive stalls that looked like the head of a three-horned beaked creature with a large shield-like appendage on its head.

The second floor was divided in half. One side had a landing area and the other had bird cages. The landing area had a long runway for landing and take-off; it seemed that most flying mounts needed some running room to take off and land. The bird cages were all much bigger than Jennifer.

The third floor was the smallest because it only covered the area over the enormous bird cages. This floor was where all of the mayor's blue birds were coming and going from. Even office cubicles for the bluebirds to work at. The workstations for the wings beasts where all the same, to spite her not seeing two birds that looked the same.

The messenger bird section was the only part of the stables that looked like it had been cleaned in the last week, or even the last year. The other floors were a total mess. The grime and debris was probably fossilized.

After returning to the ground floor, Jennifer stared in wide-eyed horror at how much muck there was. Woozle stood on his front legs while his hind legs were in a seated position. "Well, kid, I am happy to say I have no cleaning skills, so this one is on you." Woozle got up, walked in a circle, and laid down to sleep. He did not even try to hide the fact that he was happy that he was not going to be helping.

Thinking of ways that she could clean the stables fast, she asked, "Maybe there's a river I could divert to wash out the ground floor? I think a strong hero did that before."

"Nope, that would damage the structure of the building, and probably bring down a few of the other houses." Woozle replied.

Jennifer reviewed her options. Selecting one, she tried casting Mend on the building. If it did anything, she did not notice. As she looked over her powers, it hit her that one power she had was not yet used. Summon Undead. She did not like the idea, but there was no way she could do everything herself.

She did not mind using her dark attack powers or force fields because neither seemed evil. Summoning the undead to do her bidding felt wrong. The idea of bringing back someone from the dead for cheap manual labor just to clean the stables felt extra evil. The dead should stay dead. They had earned their rest, but she was out of options.

Taking in a deep breath, which she held for a long moment before nudging Summon Undead with her mind.

Nothing happened.

After letting out a long breath, she nudged the button again.

Nothing happened.

She started cognitively button mashing. Zip, zero, nada. Jennifer let out a huff of frustration.

"Woozle, why is my Summon Undead not working?" she asked, frustrated with still not fully understanding the system.

Tilting his head, he looked at her. "Do you have any skeletons in your closet?" The lynx-shark sounded far too amused at his own question.

"So, not only do I have to use my unholy powers to literally raise the dead. But I also have to first make it dead?" Her voice rose in exasperation.

"Well, you could just find one that's already dead," he replied, lowering his head and voice.

Sitting on the ground, she took a thinking position, chin on a fist, while she thought about the options. "People do eat all the time, and not everyone is vegan. So, there must be a hunter's guild somewhere out there that would bring something in for the fancy feast. Where would the hunter bring the animal? Do you think there is a butcher in town?"

"This is a good aligned town, I don't think they would keep someone like that here."

"No, I mean a shop that sells meat, poultry, pork and the like. Sometimes they take a whole beast and cut it down for parts."

Woozle shook his head. "The farmers do that here, then they send the meat to the town. A butcher here is kinda not a good person to other people."

She shut her eyes tightly. She knew of only one other place where she might find an animal skeleton she could get to quickly. "Do you think they have a pet cemetery in town?" She really hoped they did not.

"Hold up. I don't think we want to go down that path,"

Woozle said, letting the nervousness in his voice be heard.

"Alternatives?" Jennifer asked pointedly.

"Museum of Natural History?" The four words came out slowly, as if he was unsure of the answer.

A short rushed walk later, they stood in front of a large building marked Natural History.

They saw no ticket sellers, but saw the front door of the museum was unlocked. Jennifer tried knocking on the door first. When no one answered, she let herself in.

As her eyes adjusted to the inside of the museum, she saw a floor to ceiling mural, depicting what looked like a four-tusked, crystal, wooly mammoth with gem cut crystal eyes. After inspecting the mural from behind a cloth rope, she could tell that each hair on the mammoth was a crystal-like hair that gave off an iridescent look. She had to take a moment to collect herself after finding her mouth was dry from hanging open amazement at the mural.

Adding voice to her thoughts, "Isn't this beautiful, Woozle?" When he did not answer, she discovered that he was not beside her. Curious as to why, she went back out the front door to find the lynx-shark curled up in a sleepy spot. "Are you coming? This is no time for a nap."

He lifted his head and turned it to Jennifer. "No pets allowed. They have a ward up, so I can't enter."

She replied, "Oh," and stepped back inside the museum. She felt just as amazed the second time because of the wooly mammoth, but she could not delay any longer. She was on a time sensitive mission. Since she did not have a map, she only had two options, left or right. A gift store, with a closed sign on the door, was off to her right. She assumed the largest and most attractive creatures were by the store because those creatures would sell the most stuff. She chose to take the path on the right.

In the first room she entered, there were a lot of displays but nothing in them. The room had places to show off a lot of stuff but no stuff to show off. Disappointed, she walked into the next exhibit hall on the path.

A sign above the entrance way to the next exhibit read Fantastic Types of Parallels and Where to Find Them. This hall was completely empty as well with plenty of unused rooms here too. She could feel her hopes dying. If she was not able to summon any undead, she would need to do an impossible amount of work all by herself.

The next hall was labeled Once Caught a Fish This Big. She gazed up at a massive blue-colored manta ray. "Okay, that is a big fish," she admitted aloud. A lot of sea life in this room, both stuffed as well as an enormous aquarium filled with fishes of all colors and shapes. At least one fisherman out there made a lot of donations to the museum.

She could not see how anything in this room would be able to help.

Several exhibits had video monitors in front of them, so she walked over to a screen. Jennifer pressed the Press Here for Audio button above the screen.

The screen showed a buff man fighting a tentacle-faced, green sea monster. "This is Sam the Fish Hunter, fighting one of the terrors of the deep. Sam fought these terrors regularly, hunting down many of the exhibits you will find here today." The narrated video went on to describe some more of Sam's fishing adventures. Jennifer left the screen to look for something useful.

She found three stuffed turtles. Each turtle had an oversized under bite showing large, menacing fangs. All three were standing on their back legs, reminding her of a snapping turtle. Their fangs seemed to indicate that they were meat eaters. The first, which was the smallest, came up to Jennifer's knee. The second came up to her chin, and the third stood taller than Jennifer. The third was the strangest because of the two large cannons coming out of its back. She decided to move on but kept the turtles in mind as a possible option.

She breezed through many other exhibits. Another display had a turtle, but this one was a model. The label said World Turtle. It had thirteen shell large segments encircled by twenty-eight smaller segments, but each segment had painted lakes, rivers, and risen terrain. The three center large segments had gigantic mountains.

She smiled at the thought of how people used to believe that the world stood upon the back of four elephants who stood upon the back of a turtle. The sudden but fleeting memory of living on a turtle island had her frowning.

A small red flag on a shell segment that was closest to the turtle's back left leg distracted her from the memory. In tiny print on the flag, she read You Are Here. "No way. I'm on the back of a world turtle?" Jennifer glanced around but there was no one around to answer her question.

Not knowing what to make of this, she walked over to a large fish tank. In front of the tank blue-green lobster shells about the size of her arms. The claws on the lobsters were easily half the size of the whole creature. More of these lobsters were alive and fighting in the tank. Not only were they using their claws to snap at each other but they were shooting icicles. Each lobster moved elegantly in the water. If not for the two fighting, they would have resembled dancers.

The lobsters appeared as if they were trying to flip each other over. The tactic made sense since the armored section of the lobster looked more than strong enough to take what the other was dishing out. So, the underbelly must have been the weak spot. The lobsters were so intent on their fight that they caused ripples and underwater waves that smashed into one another. Jennifer looked away from the fight to examine the tank. It was easily the size of four backyard swimming pools.

She looked at her menus, bringing up her powers. This time, when she slammed the summon skeleton power, a few options came up. Blue ice lobsters were listed under the choice selection.

The blue and green lobsters that had been in front of the tank were now walking around on the ground. When Jennifer had summoned the undead lobster skeletons. More than half of her mana bar disappeared and a small prompt appeared on her menu.

Two Blue Ice Lobster Skeletons have been added to your inventory.

The blue creatures each got their own spots in her inventory. She made a silent promise to return the lobsters when she was done with them and practically ran out of the museum, heading back to the stables. The countdown timer said she had twenty-two hours and thirty minutes left to finish cleaning the stables. Woozle ran beside Jennifer the whole while.

Once she got back to the stables, she had formed a plan. At each end of the stables were large areas of gathering water that had faucets. She turned them as open as she could, attempting to flood the area as much as possible. While the water was running, she summoned her two lobsters.

As undead skeletons, they did not move much, but they were definitely animated. Jennifer pointed to the entryways at both ends of the stable. "I want you to create ice barriers at each end. Woozle, I want you to throw down dirt on the ice. If the ice melts, I don't want the water escaping out of the doorways." To his credit, Woozle showed no hesitation. The two skeletons took to their orders as well.

Once the barriers were up and the water from the taps overflowed from the basins, she spread the water around as much as possible with her mop. She cast Mend on the mop every once in a while, just in case. About a thumb's length of water flooded the ground, which had taken more time than Jennifer would have liked, but the water was not draining. She was thrilled her necromancer starting gear had waterproof boots. She knew her plan was working. Turning to the skeletons, if the water starts to drain, she would have the lobsters to ice up the drain. "I want each of you to find the biggest piles of muck and use your water claws and ice attacks to soften the packed sludge until it gets soupy enough to move. Get it all as soft as mud so we can move on to the next part." They started on the dinosaur side since it was the dinosaur people coming, and this was the most important side.

The lobsters were using water and ice attacks to move the liquid around. She kept a smile on her face as the lobster's water wave hit the large piles of slime. To Jennifer's amazement, the filth had a health bar, and after the first water attack, it quickly diminished.

When the muck pile's red health bar was down to zero, the gunk turned to mud and oozed toward the drain. Jennifer instructed, the skeletons used their ice to freeze the drain making sure this whole space would remain wet. She wanted the piles of yuck to be as liquid as possible before she let the flooded space drain. Jennifer was not a hero of legend so strong that she could move those buildings to form a river that diverts running water into the stable, however, she was able to at least make a pond. She noticed the skeletons were not at full health. Unsure why they were losing hit points, she cast her Force Field to help protect them.

"Woozle, I want you to use your hunting skills to track down any and all soap they have here." She was capitalizing on Woozle's want to hunt for soap, he ran off. He had not come near the grime and stayed outside, but by getting soap, he was helping.

Jennifer took her mop and concentrated on cleaning piles of the dark brown stuff. Each push of her mop moved the goo closer to her goal. All of the muck needed to be moved. She imagined she was a knight in combat. Each stroke of her mop was the stroke of a warrior fighting great evil. The water was getting deeper, but it was not enough to slow her or her two knights of the deep. Soap bubbles were forming.

After hours of work, there were no large piles of crud left, thanks mostly to the ice lobsters creating many water waves. They were brown with soapy bubbles.

She moved to the center of the stable and told the two lobsters to let the water drain out of the sewage spillway at the back of the nearest booth. Then she instructed each lobster to go to one end of the flooded area and make water waves to push the muddy water toward the gutter until the water flowed cleanly from tap to drain. She stayed near the drainage point to break up any large pieces with her mop, keeping the drain open and flowing.

It worked. After nearly eight hours, the dinosaur side of the stables was clean. Once all of the muck was defeated, she used her mop and the water wave attack to clean the walls of the stable.

She was exhausted. Her arms hurt from over exertion, her legs were barely keeping her up, and her eyes felt heavy, but she needed to keep going. Still, there was light in the sky, and this was a timed quest.

On the other side of the wall stood the area for standard mounts. She began flooding the regular, horse-sized stalls next. Knowing this would take some time, Jennifer found a bench to rest on. She took a seat and looked out on the small town. She could see both entryways into the town from here. The one that was falling down was the one she came through. The other entryway looked far larger, thicker, and well maintained. The wall was straight for a good distance.

Her mind kept returning to the red You Are Here flag on the back of the turtle. It was right next to where the segments of the turtle shell met. If that were true, the border should be between the segments that the town bordered on which was next to where the dinosaurs ruled.

She was lost in thought and must have nodded off because when someone poked Jennifer, it startled her awake. Instinct had her swinging her mop.

She realized it was the clerk that she saw the mayor order to go door to door earlier and she had struck him reflexively. Jennifer removed the mop from his face. "Sorry, I was asleep." Not wanting to explain the brown muck still clinging to the mop, she moved it behind her. If the mop was out of sight, it would not be on his mind, she hoped.

A trickle of blood drained from his nose. Jennifer handed him a healing potion. After a few minutes of apologizing and sending her lobsters to clean up the other side of the stable, she concentrated on the clerk.

"It's fine. This is the first time I've been hit with a mop, and the healing potion you gave me removed the damage. The mayor wanted me to check on all of the projects," the clerk said while staying outside of mop range.

Fighting back a yawn, Jennifer raised her hand to cover her mouth. "I should be able to get through the first floor tonight, take a nap, then start on the bird cages tomorrow."

"The mayor needs the whole stable to be clean." The clerk said, with an edge in his voice. "This is very important to the town."

She made eye contact with the clerk. "To me, tomorrow is just a Tuesday." She was tired, grumpy, and glaring at the clerk. "This is a side quest to me." Making eye contact was something she was unaccustomed to. It was not as far as taboo, just frowned upon.

Not only did she not care if breaking this unspoken rule was what made him visibly taken aback, or the glaring in general, but the clerk took a step back. His voice rose with every word. "You are a fragment. All quests you get are a gift."

Jennifer smirked at him. "My quests are, one, to become a student at Bishop's University; and two, take what I have learned to make the world a better place. When I say make the world a better place, I don't mean make a barn cleaner because someone was too lazy to clean it in the first place. I'm talking about making sure fragments, parallels, and all others will be treated the same and given the same opportunities." She took in a breath before continuing, "Or something, but I don't know. This is like my second day here, and people keep calling me 'just a fragment', and I am getting sick of that."

By the time she was finished, the clerk was looking down at his hands. "I remember going to the University of the Gilly and Lilly for law. I wanted to help the innocent to get the justice they deserved." The clerk's voice was low and his face was filled with sadness.

"Why are fragments treated worse than parallels?" asked Jennifer. She wanted to know, and changing the subject might make it easier on the both of them.

The clerk kept looking at his hands for a long moment before a can, which had a red moose with wings logo, appeared in his hand. The clerk handed it to Jennifer. She was thirsty, she was tired, and this seemed like a peace offering. She popped the top and took a sip. The drink was overly sweet but made her feel better and more awake.

"The drink cancels the tired debuff out for a bit," the clerk said before continuing with her head tilted, "Right! First days - Uhm, you seem, a debuff makes you weak. In the, humm, other world, people need sleep or they get weaker. The same thing happens here. You get weaker, you lose intelligence, and whatnot. The drink cancels those out, but only for a short time. Parallels respawn because they can never die; they just stop showing up." His confidence built as he continued speaking. "They can do more than anyone else and take the craziest of risks. Have a dragon stealing livestock? Send a parallel. They'll kill it just for fun. Need a castle built? They'll pull one out of their inventory. They're stronger, faster, and even smarter."

He frowned with sadness in his voice as he spoke. "I once saw a boy no older than eight years old. He had a flaming sword and the most glorious armor. He simply threw down a castle. Not a small castle either, but one of the really big castles that could keep out a million goblins without showing a crack. Why? Because it was better than setting up a camp for the night. He left it there in the morning. Just walked away from something that was worth more than I could make in a thousand years, as if it was nothing. He was, or if he is still in this world, better than I could ever be. That kid never came back. The town ended up selling the castle as materials." As the clerk spoke she turned away from him. The eye contact made her feel uncomfortable, but the clerk turned to Jennifer. "That's how this tiny town ended up being able to afford our museum. The mayor won some award or unlocked an achievement and wanted to show it off. For a while it was the only thing in the bloody place. Then we got that great fisherman to donate so much to the town, and the museum."

Panicked, Jennifer glanced at her two borrowed lobsters and back at the clerk. "I've seen the museum. It does seem kinda empty?" She spoke quickly as she recast the Force Field over the two undead workers and gave an awkward smile before taking another sip from the can of the red moose.

"The dinosaur lands are known for conquering each other. None of them have ever attacked another part of the shell, but we think they may be looking for targets. That's why the mayor is so concerned with their upcoming visit."

Mocking the situation, she stretched her words out like she was confused. "So, if the stables are not clean, it will show weakness, thus they will invade this small town?" She could not see the connection between the stables and an invasion.

"Exactly, if they see weakness, they will take advantage of that weakness. We are a small town. We can use every advantage we can get." The clerk replied without a hint of irony. "I am sorry. There are other projects in the works I need to check on." He left her to continue her fight against the mess.

Jennifer checked on her borrowed undead minions. Both lobsters were showing cracks in their carapaces. Just small hairline cracks here and there. Her heart was beating faster. She was going to be returning these almost meter long undead creatures back to the museum. Now that they had damage, someone will notice that they were borrowed without permission.

She looked over her character sheet for options, knowing she only had one. Jennifer tried to cast Mend. At first, the power did nothing. Then slowly, her mana bar went down a hair line. Her heart was beating too fast and nothing had happened. She felt a pang of sadness. She had already taken them, now she was going to return them damaged, someone was going to find out, and then she was going to end up in jail. She lifted one of the lobsters, petting its carapace by way of an apology.

CHAPTER 6

BREAK

THE WORLD HAS A way of challenging our perspectives. Is the glass half full or half empty. And how far can one go before they are no longer human?

Jennifer's mouth gaped open as wires descended from the palm of her hand that was petting the undead, blue ice lobster. The wires moved on their own, shooting small sparks that welded metal into the hairline fractures.

Multiple wires protruded from a small open port in her hand that she did not know she had. Her eyes were as wide as they could be when she said aloud, "Techno necromancer." The name made a lot more sense now. She heard the scream. It was coming from her own mouth.

Woozle shot toward her with rockets glowing, yearning for release, teeth bared, and ready to attack anything that endangered his human. She screamed until all the air in her lungs was used up, leaving her mouth open and frozen in silent dread. She looked back and forth between Woozle and the wires. The rockets on Woozle's back stopped glowing, and his head tilted as he stared at her hand. With air returning to her lungs, she needed to convey what was going on, but her mind raced, unable to get the words to form.

She watched in fascinated horror as the wires were intertwining, separating, then moving. The sparks at the end of the wires may as well have been feet. The movement of the cables were like a couples dance, each moving on their own but in sync with one another. Paired but separated. Moving from her hand, but not under the control of the hand. Things that were not alive, could not be alive. They swayed, whirled, and twirled by way of her command. Without her commands.

"I have a garage door in my hand, and there are living wires coming out of it." Jennifer nearly screamed that she could not look away. Something from her body was taking action for her, better than she could do, without her.

"Kid," he was speaking low with a gentle voice, "I have boosters coming out of my back."

The wires advanced on their task, skipping, prancing, and bobbing around, mending the lobster while Jennifer stared open-mouthed at her lynx-shark familiar. His words sunk in.

When she felt that the repair was done, the tiny tendrils of her receded back into her hand. The door closed. She put down the first lobster and automatically picked up the second.

"What should I do," bits of water formed on the edges of her eyes. The other lobster was beside her. It was motionless. The repaired lobster moved back to continue its task.

Silence that was too deep for her to think hung in the air. "Am I happy with my body?"

It was not a question and not a statement, just the mimicry of words her mind came up with.

"I need to repair the other lobster."

Emotions churned as the realization set in. She was no longer fully human. That someone had not only kidnapped her and dumped her into this world but turned her into something that was not whole. The wires coiled out from her palm when they had something to complete.

"No." The words flitted through her mind, but she was unsure if she had said them aloud or if she just moved her lips. "No." She did not know when she had finished repairing the second lobster or when the lobster left her lap, but it was gone now. "I refuse."

"What do you refuse?" Woozle asked, going from a laying on

the ground to sitting at attention with his signature head tilt.

She turned her head to her familiar. "I refuse this world. Not only am I a second-class citizen due to me being me, but I never ask to be here. I never asked to be taken away from my friends and family, and I never asked to be made into a . . ." needing to pause, she needed to find the words to express what she was feeling. She spat out the next word, "Machine. I never asked for any of this! I just had this thrust on me." Her voice grew cold, lacking emotion beyond the word machine.

"I did ask."

"I asked to be accepted into university. With learning I would transform into something more. By going to school, I would need to leave." Her palms clasped together, she needed to say this, "To leave my friends and my family."

"I was happy with what I was when I woke up, I may not like the job I am doing, but it is helping others in a way." She forced her eyes to close and open. Her head facing forward, to nothing.

"This was my choice, I'm now a second class . . . person. I was going to be a freshman in an amazing university, find my future love, get a job, and make my parents and grandparents proud. Now I'm here." She had remained calm and collected until the last sentence when her voice broke and turned shrill. "There's no going home, and all I have are the clothes on my back."

"You have me, a spider, and a mop, too." Woozle was looking down, unable to meet her eyes.

She faced her familiar. "I have an amazing rocket-powered lynx-shark." She reached out her hand, picked up Woozle, and rubbed her face against his. "And a trapdoor gathering spider, and a mop. But without that lynx, I would be even more lost." Her face softened. A smile grew on her face with affection for the lynx-shark as she spoke. "I need to keep going. I will not let this world stop me. I have the power to choose my own way, and I have my own wants and needs, but the world always feels like it's in my way. There is another copy out there somewhere who did choose her own classes, who will finish school, who will have her parents there with her at graduation. I am here now. I have a dream of going to school and graduating." Raising her hand to look at it, "I am who I am. I am what I am. I do not need to fully understand my body to accept it." She closed her hand in a fist. "I like who I am." She recognized she was talking her way through processing her circumstances.

"Woozle, can you tell me why there are welding wires coming out of my hand?"

"Do you remember when I said you were an incomplete fragment?" Her familiar asked.

"Yes, but I thought that meant I just forgot stuff like my fourth birthday or other little things?" She was not sure she wanted to know where this conversation was going.

"Memories are one thing, but the human body is complicated. Like, what does the human appendix, liver, or spleen even do?"

"Those organs filter toxins from the air, water, and food."

He continued as if she had not spoken, "Why does there need to be so many intestines or so many hairs on the head?"

She reflexively reached up and touched her hair. It was there and felt fine. "What's wrong with it? My hair feels like hair."

"Yes, but to save room, every fragment, and some parallels have some things…" He trailed off, and she assumed Woozle was trying to be diplomatic. "They have some things, not all things, but a few, for the most part. Some things are simplified. What is not transferred gets replaced with standard parts."

"I've had my liver swapped with an off-brand replacement?" Her eyes went wide, and her voice rose to eleven again.

"Well, no. It's on brand. Magic users all get the same magic-based replacements, tech-based get tech-based replacements, and pure bios get bio-printed replacements. So, everyone has the same stuff. You are magic-based and you get a magically made liver. I've heard some timelines have between eight to twelve different blood types. People with AB positive blood can use all the other blood types, but O negative types could only take O negative blood. But here, everyone has turtle-worlder blood. I think they did this as a time saver, or to save space maybe."

"So, because the system gave me future defense tech. I was forced to be tech-based. I now have wires and machines in me doing what my body did on its own before I was so rudely and improperly copied?" Her mood grew darker as she spoke.

"The simple answer is yes, and because you are tech-based, I am tech-based." Woozle wiggled the rocket tubes on his back.

"What would have happened if I said I was from the magical land of fairies and unicorns?"

"No idea, maybe I would have gotten wings and a unicorn horn? All of this is way above me. I am here to help the fragments. I have no idea how they copy people over."

"They really need to work on their copying skills," she said with anger and frustration seeped into her words. "And I don't care. What I want to do is make the world better. I was going to go to school before this happened, and I am going to go to school while I am here. I have a reason to keep going, so that's what I am going to do. This quest gives me land to build on, and on that land, I am going to build a house to live in. Maybe run a bar [RM4] [AP5] or something. With games and dancing.[SD6] "

She spent the next few hours using her anger to clean the other side of the stables. Her anger and frustration at the world drives her to clean better and faster. The two ice lobsters helped her clean the first and second floor of the stables. The third was clean enough, in her opinion, and most of the blue birds that carried messages were asleep with only a few stopping in now and again.

Jennifer felt rather than saw when her quest was complete because she sensed the rewards being added to her inventory, including the letter of recommendation. Curiosity had her viewing the letter of recommendation. "Dear person, Jennifer is good, and I recommend her. Signed, Jim The Mayor."

She laughed and moved towards the inn marked on her mini map.

The sky showed hints of blue in the sky as the sun was following its trail. The sun would soon be peeking over the horizon. The two ice lobster skeletons held their own spots in her inventory. She felt so exhausted that walking was like moving through mud.

By the time Jennifer reached the door of the inn, she was yawning with every step. In her menus, she could see a debuff icon under her status bar marked with a few zeds. As she was only a few meters away from the inn's door, Jennifer mentally clicked on the icon.

Exhausted: You should have gone to bed hours ago, movement speed has been reduced, and all skills/powers/abilities now take extra mana and stamina to take effect.

She dismissed the menu. The inn looked like a house. She knocked on the door.

"Come in." A female voice rang out.

Jennifer opened the door and walked in to find a smiling woman behind a counter. The innkeeper, although rather large and well past being called young, moved quickly from her spot to stand before Jennifer. The smile vanished after giving Jennifer the once over, and a frown cemented in place.

Jennifer said, "The mayor reserved a room for me."

"Have you been sleeping in the stables, girl? You smell like every horse on this shell ate bad tacos next to you. Get in the baths before going to your room." The innkeeper covered her nose with her hand using her free hand to wave her towards the baths. "Just leave everything to be washed in the bathroom. We can't have that smell here."

Jennifer pulled the neck of her robes and took a sniff. She had been cleaning the stables for hours.

"What room number?" Jennifer asked before heading for the baths.

"You're in room one oh three. Ladies' baths are on the west side. There will be bathrobes and towels waiting for you." She said, while making hand gestures at Jennifer to hurry.

Jennifer did as instructed and found the showers. She left her clothes in a basket near the door. She turned the knob to release water while controlling the pressure. The shower worked just the way she expected, with red runes on the right side of a knob and blue runes on the left. She tapped her hand on the red rune three times to get a good feeling for how warm the water would get before refining the heat to a more comfortable setting. She only tapped the blue rune once to cool the water down a tiny bit.

Walls stood on either side of the showering alcove for privacy in the public space. There was a lot of room on either side of her, so even if she had not been alone, she would not have felt cramped. She upped the pressure a few times and used the shampoo and soap supplied. She wondered who she needed to talk to in order to get them laundered.

She was tired, sore, and dirty, but at least she was fixing the dirty part in the shower. The hot water, the soap and shampoo, felt wonderful.

She left the shower alcove in a fluffy courtesy bathrobe only to find her dirty clothes had already been taken away. But, there was a hot tub filled with soap and water. She had no idea who had filled it, or even when, but Jennifer took it as an invitation. After getting into the hot tub, Jennifer realized she was not alone.

Her lynx-shark swam at the bottom of the hot tub. He rose to the surface of the water, with his dorsal fin being out of the water. Jennifer shrugged and entered the tub could have held at least a dozen more people Jennifer's size, with the middle going deeper than her height. She decided to just enjoy the soak, letting her eyes rest while her familiar enjoyed the swim.

At some point, she must have fallen asleep because woke up to find a cow entering the tub. The cow displaced even more water than Jennifer. The cow let out a "Mooo" of joy as she settled in across from Jennifer.

Jennifer blinked several times, wondering how the cow got into the bath. Her mind moved like the mud she had cleaned earlier. Unsure what to say yet feeling the need to say something. Jennifer spoke very fast, loud, and high-pitched "Hello. My name is Jennifer. It's my first time here. How are you?"

The lynx-shark's head popped out of the water. "My name is Woozle. I'm part shark, and I love the water." Instead of waiting for a response he submerged again.

The cow said, "Moo moo, momo, moo."

Jennifer glanced over at the cow. Trying not to stare, she noticed the black and white animal was wearing large, dark sunglasses. She wondered if this was the same cow she had spotted earlier in the field with the deer. "I'm sorry. What did you just say?"

One shimmering blur of vision later, the cow disappeared and was replaced by a blonde woman in sunglasses. The cheeriness of her voice was unmistakable as she said, "My name is Sarah No Val. I'm with Exports Du Universal. It's my first time here too." The lady had wrapped herself in towels, while Jennifer was in a wet robe, having entered the hot tub without removing it. Jennifer was unsure of the etiquette here, and she had been too tired to think when she spotted the tub.

"I'm doing some quests to get into Bishop's University and get some land in town. I don't have a job, but I would like to be a working student." Jennifer needed someone to talk to, and she felt comfortable with this woman, especially since it was just her and Woozle in the tub. "Can I ask why you are wearing sunglasses inside?" Jennifer asked the blonde woman.

"Oh my! I forgot I even had these on," Sarah said, not taking the sunglasses off. Jennifer felt like something was off, but the smile on the woman's face reached her eyes. "What do you think of this dinosaur king thing happening? I'm hoping to be able to reach a trade deal with the dinos."

Jennifer put her hand on her chin as she thought about the question. "I honestly don't know what's happening. I just cleaned the stables. I was there when the mayor got the news, and he was able to use his mayoring skills to get everyone moving. By the time I reacted, the only quest left was to clean the stables." She smiled sheepishly. "I don't think anyone else wanted to do it. As soon as I stepped into the inn, he sent me up here for a wash."

"Is it true the stables have three floors?"

"Oh yes. The first floor is split with one side for normal mounts, the other side for big mounts. It was more like two barns stapled together. The second floor has a landing strip and cages for the flying mounts, and the third floor seems to be the offices for those blue messenger birds."

Sarah snuggled down into a more comfortable position in the water before speaking. "I just got to town today. Would you be able to get me to the roof of the stables? It would help me get used to the area."

Jennifer waved at her and in a circular manner. "Sure, but later, I need to get some sleep in me first." Jennifer stood up. "Argh, what time is it?" Jennifer's menu showed the time as 0805. "How about we meet downstairs for lunch? After that we can go take a peak around together."

Sarah said, "Oh, let me buy you lunch. It's so nice to find a friendly face around here."

As Jennifer walked towards the door, she put on a dry bathrobe over her wet one, before letting the wet robe hit the floor. Woozle slipped out of the tub and followed her. To Jennifer's surprise, rather than having his fur soaking wet and leaving a trail of water, the lynx looked like he had come out of a light rain. A smirk grew on his face, Woozle said. "My shark half gives me underwater breathing and a high resistance to water, Meaning I can only get so wet even if I'm under water."[AP1]

Jennifer easily found her room. Hanging from the doorknob on a coat hanger was her freshly cleaned starter gear. She swore she was going to get more clothes soon. She opened the door, carried the clean clothes inside, and lay down on the single bed. a large window in the room, but the curtains had already been drawn. She closed her eyes and went to sleep.

CHAPTER 6

ON THE ROAD.

JENNIFER HEARD A HAUNTING distinct, loud, and low pitch whistle. It was coming from outside the room. The only context she could place on the sound was one of loneliness. The note played again. Jennifer's mind worked on where it was coming from. She slowly pushed herself to a seated position[RM3] . Woozle was curled up at the end of the bed and was asleep. On the third long pitched whale, she walked to the window. On the edge of town stood a blue train. It was in the shadows, with the noise coming from one of the three protrusions on the top of the machine. Squinting her eyes, she could make out the numbers 313 written in black. The word "Pretty," escaped her mouth as she went to rub the sleep from her eyes.

She opened her eyes again to an alarm going off. "Did I set that?" Looking out the window, she saw the train was gone and the alarm clock was in front of her with a display that read "WAKE UP." For some reason no matter how many times she tried to press the snooze button with her hands, it did not turn off. Flopping back into the bed with the alarm still going off, an icon of Woozle's face moved to cover the snooze button. It stopped. "Five more minutes," was all Woozle said.

The bed was the right blend of firm and soft. There was some resistance from the warm blankets holding her down. It was Rover poking her face and she knew it was time to get ready for the day.

She put on her starting gear. As soon as she was fully dressed, Rover appeared on her shoulder as if he had never left.

Your pet <Rover> has gathered 15 healing moss. Your pet cannot gather any more today.

The prompt told Jennifer what Rover had been up to. Letting her mind pass over her menu, she found a log stating the spider was able to gather five healing moss yesterday and ten today. She smiled at her spider and gave it a well-earned head scratch. "Good job, little guy."

The spider leaned into the positive affection. Deciding that was a good amount of praise, she turned to go. Jennifer picked up the lynx-shark, placed him in her hood, and left the room with her spider on her shoulder. On her way to meeting her new friend in the eating area, she reviewed her menus for the buffs and debuffs. A ten percent experience bonus from her nap with a two-hour timer. Jennifer searched for the tired debuff, but she could not find it, which she decided to take as a good sign.

She entered the common area. A lunch crowd gathered there. A total of three tables out of the dozen were being used. Jennifer felt a wave of loneliness wash over her. The world seemed so big and yet so empty. Everyone in the almost empty lunch rush seemed to be wearing the same large dark glasses. Jennifer assumed this to be a local fashion trend.

She noticed Sarah waving her hand. Jennifer smiled and waved back, not feeling as lonely as before.

As Jennifer sat down, the innkeeper showed up with a cooked egg and lettuce sandwich, with a side of what seemed to be deep fried scales that were about half the length of her pinkie finger, and just as thick. There were no utensils, but there were two napkins. Jennifer looked down at the plate in front of her. She was used to pointy metal sticks for when she ate, or at least small tridents like metal sticks people placed great emphasis on using with great ceremony.

Looking at the food in front of Sarah. She was eating some kind of fruit with a thin, green skin and what could be viewed as rubbery orange inside. The fruit had been sliced into eight wedges and came with a side of what could be long grass salad. Jennifer searched her memories looking for what to do, she was unsure if there should be words before a meal, or if she should just start eating, was she the guest in this case, or the host.

"Who ordered the food?" She did not mean to ask the question aloud.

"Oh I am not sure, I cannot remember the last time I even told anyone what I wanted to eat. How long have you been in the system again?" Sarah asked Jennifer.

Jennifer faced down as warmth spread across her cheeks. She held three fingers up.

"Oh, three years and you're already staying in the best inn in the city. I've been here for nine years. Since I have to travel around a lot, I've had to learn the little habits here and there. I'm sure I've made my own mistakes too. Only parallels order their own food. Most of the time the cooking staff are already preparing the meal. Most greeters, if not the server, have a skill to predict what someone is going to order."

Jennifer did not feel any better and quickly shook her head.

"Not what you wanted, or not three years?" Like a teacher searching the class for students with an answer, "Did you mean three months? That is even more impressive," Sarah said, with a bit of awe in her voice.

Jennifer moved her head to face Sarah's and whispered, "This is my third day here."

There was not a lot of noise in the dining area earlier. Now, it was quiet. She swiveled around, taking in the room. One of the other patrons was holding his sandwich up to his mouth, but his hands and face were frozen in shock. One of the customers had his large, dark sunglasses that weren't large enough to cover his bulging eyes and raised eyebrows. Once he noticed her noticing him, he resumed eating as if nothing had happened.

Sarah let out a long exhale before speaking. "How did you end up staying in this hotel?"

Jennifer simply pulled out a healing potion from her inventory to show her friend, and then picked up a deep-fried scale with her other hand. Leaving the potion in Sarah's grasp, Jennifer could not find her voice to explain the deal, so she decided to first focus on the meal in front of her. Jennifer put the deep-fried scale partly in her mouth and took a bite.

She was expecting to chew on something tough and leathery that had been battered, salted, and put into a deep fryer. Little resistance met her teeth as she bit on a firm but chewable morsel in her mouth. It was soft on the inside and crisp on the outside. Despite just coming out of the kitchen, it was not hot. "This tastes a bit like a french fry." She said, partly in shock. She took another bite.

She looked up before eating her second deep fried scale and saw Sarah still holding the healing potion. She realized everyone in the room was eying the potion. Taking a deep breath, she explained her situation. "The mayor traded three nights here for one potion. After selling the thing, I can only craft three healing potions rather than four for the next week. Do you think if I get multiple bottles that would change? Right now, I have another quest to gather healing moss. I think the mayor wants to sell the moss or to get me to craft more. But I don't want to give up any more bottles." It felt like everyone in the room was staring at her. Wherever she looked, they were staring at her.

"You're an alchemist?" Sarah asked in astonishment.

"Yup, I'm a techno-necromancer-alchemist." Wanting to add more she continued, "My familiar is a rocket-powered lynx-shark. I have a pet armored, gathering, trapdoor spider." She thought about what else she could share about herself. "I'm descended from giants, and my primary weapon is a mop. What's your class?"

Until she was given a question, Sarah's eyes never left the potion. She handed the vial back to Jennifer. Jennifer left it on the table in front of her plate. Sarah opened and closed her mouth several times, "Well I, umm. You see I -"

Jennifer picked up the sandwich and took a bite.

Sarah looked down and smoothed out her clothes with her hands. "I'm a Hunter-Gather. I'm only level five, but I'm hoping to get the deal maker prestige class. I took a trader sub-skill as well. That gives me a bonus in negotiations."

"My classes were more or less a random choice for me, I only really got to choose one." Jennifer admitted.

"I also did not get to choose my classes, their system gave me my primary and secondary powers. I do get to choose my prestige and other abilities."

Jennifer could not help asking, "Knowing what you know now, what would you have chosen?"

Sarah made eye contact with Jennifer, causing her to quickly look away. "I guess—" a disembodied hand protruded from a bright purple jacket with blue glowing lines where the seams should have been grabbed it. It was like heat waves came off of a large rock until the rest of the person appeared.

"Hey! That is not yours!" Sarah exclaimed.

Startled at the sudden appearance of a brightly colored person, Jennifer gave the man a once over as she quickly swallowed a mouthful of sandwich.

Like most people Jennifer had already met here, the guy was short, maybe reaching her chin. The bright blue hair that stuck up in all directions had a slight glow. Half of this persons' face could not be seen because of the bright purple fabric covering his nose and chin. Wrapped around his forehead above his violet eyes was a bandana with a metal bar on it. The metal bar featured a stylised pinecone. This guy wore a jacket despite being inside and the weather being warm. His jacket was zipped up and the same purple color as the mask the dude wore. His pants were black, but again on the seam lines was a blue glow. He wore a black glove on his right hand, and the knuckles of the glove had a hardened outline. The man's left hand was covered with an outline of a dragon on his gauntlet that had pointed and angled fingertips.

He held the potion up, inspecting it. Without turning to

acknowledge either Sarah or Jennifer, he said, "Scan," and a white sphere appeared. From the sphere, a blue light shot out, which produced a grid pattern surrounding the vial holding the potion. When the white sphere stopped analyzing the vial, the glowing one showed no sign of giving the potion back.

Jennifer slowly put down her sandwich, stood up, and reached out to take back the potion. Once her hand touched the vial, the man spoke without meeting her eyes. "How much." There was no questioning tone in his voice. It was more monotone akin to sounding like an old computer reading a line of text rather than a human.

Jennifer's cheeks burned, and she narrowed her eyes. He had not asked to see the potion, had not even acknowledged their presence, nor shown an ounce of courtesy. Jennifer glared at the newcomer but answered him in the same tone he had used on her. "No." Snatching the potion away from the neon garbed one, she put it back in her inventory. He turned his head to face Jennifer and looked her in the eyes.

Critical success. Giant's intimidation has caused fear for 10 seconds.

The notification popped in her menus. The man's eyes went from steely to wide-eyed. Fear only made her smile widen. She had not meant to trigger it, but happy it went off.

"Can't handle looking a girl in the eyes, ninja?" Sarah spoke in a mocking manner.

The ninja responded with "Listen, Cow—"

But Jennifer cut him off with a louder and more forceful tone, saying, "No." She slammed her hands into the table for emphasis.

The ninja fell silent.

Jennifer glared at the man, deciding what to do. "First, apologize to Sarah for being rude."

To his credit, the ninja turned his full body to Sarah and bowed at the waist. "I apologize for my earlier rudeness."

Before the ninja reverted from his bow, Jennifer continued to raise her voice. "Secondly, you are going to sit silently while my friend and I finish our meal together." As he moved to recover from his bow, she added more volume to her voice. "If you want to talk to me about my potions afterwards, you will show my friend the absolute respect she deserves. And no name calling."

Sarah had her eyes and mouth wide open.

Jennifer did not know if it was her knees or the table that was wobbling. She sat back down hard. The innkeeper had the same shocked appearance as Sarah. "Excuse me, innkeeper. Would it be possible to get some fruit or berry juice please?" The innkeeper nodded once, closed her mouth, and ran for the kitchen.

Jennifer took a breath to calm down and collect her thoughts. She had a lot of questions but did not want to pester her friend. "You said you wanted to be a deal maker. Is that one of those side power sets?" Jennifer was not particularly interested. She just wanted to get the conversation going again.

"Huh?" said Sarah, in shock. Once she recovered, she said, "Well, I'm level five. The area cap is level fifteen and the level max of this shell segment is level fifty. At level fifty, we unlock at least one prestige class. Deal Maker is one of the possible prestige classes. Although, I've been told it may be unlocked with a quest line."

"I'm still only level three." Jennifer reviewed her bars, and with a mental search command found her total experience. She was not near leveling up.

The two continued to speak and share what their goals and ambitions were. Jennifer wanted to go to school and make the world better, while Sarah wanted to climb the ranks within her company.

One of the servers took the empty plates off the table, leaving a tall glass of dark berry juice. Jennifer closed her eyes and took a deep breath. She held it for five heartbeats before opening her eyes and turning to the neon-colored ninja.

"Okay, Mr. Ninja, you were asking about my potions." She stayed polite, but Jennifer knew her smile did not reach her eyes.

"I would like one of the healing potions." The ninja spoke with no inflection or emotion.

Jennifer let her frustration speak for her. "Why?"

It took some time for the ninja to speak. As Jennifer waited, she counted the heartbeats it took for him to respond. She got up to twenty-two.

"I do not currently have any self-healing. This would allow me to adventure more and save more people."

"Do you currently need healing, Mr. Ninja?" Sarah asked.

"My name is Large Soup Bowl 14, I am currently at ninety-eight percent health."

Jennifer blinked. "That's technically a name . . . I guess." She gave the ninja a once over again. "Tell you what, Large Soup, I'm going to show my friend the view of the village from the top of the stables. After that, I have to visit the museum." She had no intention of explaining the lobsters and shifted in her seat at the thought. "Then I'm going to gather healing moss in the forest. If you would like to join me, and if we get enough healing moss, I should be able to craft you a healing potion. Maybe. It will be my first time trying . . . to do so." Trailing off, she shook her head and collected her thoughts.

"Agreed. I will follow you then complete the quest together."

Large Soup Bowl 14 has been added to your party.
Large Soup Bowl 14, level 5, has added you to his list of contacts.

The messages gave Jennifer an idea. She sent a mental command to invite Sarah to her party. She stood up, finished her juice, and gave a thumbs up signal to the innkeeper, making sure it was alright for her to leave. Her meal should be covered in the deal with the mayor for the room, but she wanted to make sure.

"Sarah No Val, the cost of the meal has been added to your room bill." The innkeeper smiled and waved her hand, signaling the group could depart.

A blue bird landed in front of Jennifer, depositing a note on the table. "Jim: On my way to stables, please meet me there."

The mayor was going to the stables as Jennifer led the group to the freezing and clean place. She had decided to leave Woozle behind and let him sleep in their room, and her spider sat on his preferred shoulder.

It was a short, quiet walk to the building. Jennifer took in the morning air and the peaceful town.

"So, when will you be done cleaning the stables?" The mayor asked.

Jennifer felt the urge to be snarky but resisted the temptation. "If you follow me, Mr. Mayor, you'll be able to make your own estimate for the time to completion." Jennifer kept the pleasantness in her voice as the mayor scowled. The mayor was under pressure and had time constraints. He signaled for the trio to continue.

"Hello, Mr Mayor, my name is Sarah No Val. I am with Exports De Universal. I was hoping to speak with you about some trade opportunities." Sarah's tone reminded Jennifer of a shark circling its prey in the open ocean.

The mayor stopped, causing the entire group to do the same. He stared into Sarah's eyes for a long moment before doing the same to Large Soup Bowl. Covering his face with his hand, he slowly dragged his hand down. "'The exports and ninjas go into retirement,' they said. 'It would be easy', they said. They never mentioned any of this in the orientation."

The mayor's cheeks flattened, the lines on his face accentuated his age. He raised his thumb and forefinger to rub his temples. He had the appearance of a man that was carrying the whole turtle on his back. Without notice, a smile returned to his face. His back stood straighter as he walked up to Jennifer. He put his arm around her waist, and walked towards the stables.

Jennifer was confused. She did not like him being so touchy and forward with her. She slapped the mayor, maybe a bit too hard.

Jennifer was larger than the mayor. Her hand alone was larger than his face. The left side of his head showed signs of swelling. The two other party members found interest in the fabulous architecture of one of the nearby buildings.

The color changed to the darker range of black and blue. Jennifer handed the mayor a healing potion. A moment later, the mayor handed back the empty vial as the color in his face returned to a refreshed state.

"I'm sorry. That was a bit presumptuous of me," the mayor said as both his cheeks went red. He was unable to meet Jennifer's eyes before returning to his normal voice. "However, did you know we've nearly tripled the town guard overnight without assistance from the League of the Double Red? They're the closest freehold city state. They have promised us an extra one thousand guards to protect the city from -" he paused, quickly glancing at Sarah and Large Soup Bowl. "They want to make sure that the visiting delegation goes well and no outside parties would interfere with the happenings of the town."

The lingering action hung in the air. Jennifer was really just confused by the sudden change of subject. Her cheeks turned red. She was also not willing to let his forward action be forgotten either. "I only gave you the potion because I hit you harder than I intended to. I'm not sorry for slapping you. I'm sorry for hitting you as hard as I did." She said as an honest apology in spite of her anger. She wanted to clear the air between the two.

The mayor was visibly taken aback but responded with, "I am sorry. I should not have done that with you or touch you in any way. I was—"

Jennifer cut the mayor off in a voice louder than she intended. "I accept your apology. You acknowledged your error and there is no excuse for you touching me without permission, but hopefully you will not make the same mistake again. I will make sure to use the right amount of force next time. " Her voice raised because if it happened again, she was going to hit harder.

Giant Intimidation has succeeded. The town of Hogback has been temporarily intimidated.

"Damn it. Was I being too loud?" Jennifer asked in a much

quieter voice. The mayor held his thumb and forefinger close together, signaling that Jennifer was in fact louder than she thought. "I am sorry for that, too."

The mayor's crooked smile and downcast eyes added to the sincerity of the apology. "If we keep apologizing, we'll be here all day. Let's move on with the business at hand."

The group moved towards the stables and Jennifer took a moment to take in her surroundings. She noticed a black and white cow chewing on some grass in the alleyway across the road. The thing that made Jennifer do a double take was the large black aviator sunglasses on the cow's head. The cow even gave Jennifer a nod, too. Curious about the cow, Jennifer raised her hand to point it out, but before she could say anything, Sarah interrupted.

"I can assure you my company does not want to interfere in any way with the glorious meeting between this town and the local dinosaur warlords. We feel that there is an opportunity to trade goods and services. People in the dinosaur lands use swords and bows, but not the wheel. We may be able to sell them carts, wagons, and maybe even the odd high-end sports car."

"I don't even have a car let alone a sports car," the mayor grumbled.

"I'm here for adventure, glory, and ninja honor," said Large Soup Bowl.

The mayor's head turned to face the ninja, whose hair changed from neon blue to neon purple for no discernible reason. "Let me guess. New to the game? Don't have a VR rig yet?"

"Correct."

"Don't worry, as a retired person, life is worth spending more time on the outside. No need to get a VR headset. Do try to use punctuation. It helps."

"Understood." The ninja made a heart outline with his hands in front of him accompanied with a large red heart appearing above his head.

"Good. I need to check out the stables." After a brief inspection, it surprised the mayor that the stables were already clean. He seemed like he was looking for a reason to chastise Jennifer by pointing out several very minor things but still gave out an experience bonus to Jennifer.

Taking the stairs and the group up to the roof, Jennifer showed them the view over the small town. Looking out from the top of the building, Jennifer saw two black and white cows wandering around town. The first cow was next to one of the larger houses, the second cow was near the museum.

"So, what does the town need?" Jennifer asked the mayor.

His Adam's apple bounced while he gazed down. "While this is a small town, it's fully self-reliant. Our principal export is specialized non-physical currency used outside the game. We use coffee seeds in-world for transactions." As he spoke, his shoulders moved back. He wished his chest puffed out.

"What needs to happen for the town to grow?" After finding out what the town needed, she might be able to find something to do. She wanted to help and getting direction from the mayor would be useful.

"I'm getting more fragments like you, parallels like Soup Bowl, and maybe even more cows." The mayor added a wink to the word cows.

She was trying to be as covert as possible, but the mayor had spilled the beans. She had no way to get more people to move to town. Though, she could look for farm animals. The town needed more. Jennifer added Find Farm Animals to her quest menu. She could not add any rewards, so it was more of a note.

"We've moved the paper raid to tomorrow. Are you three going to be taking part?" He said while facing Sarah and Soup Bowl.

Sarah was the first to respond. "Do you think it's a good idea to have a raid day when the king and queen are here?" Jennifer recognized the service industry smile that was on Sarah's face from a genuine one. "A lot could go wrong. Or is this all just a show of force to be used as a deterrent?"

"Yes, a good source for experience. I will join the paper raid," Soup Bowl said, as robotically as ever.

Jennifer nodded to herself. "I'll join as well. I'll be able to heal people and cast my force field to protect others."

The mayor nodded at this, while lifting the heels and rising up slightly. A smile crossed his face. "That makes three of you. Normally, a team has four members. Do you have anyone else in mind?"

Jennifer thought this was the mayor trying to be subtle and asking for an invite. She did not hesitate in asking, "Mr. Mayor, would you like to join our team for the paper raid?" The mayor's smile turned upside down, the inner corners of their eyebrows will be angled up. She spoke before the mayor could. "You have your own team, don't you?"

"I have a team with a few of the high-level town guards. It's better to present a united front in these things." His apology was unsaid.

Jennifer turned to the other members of the team, with one hand turned upward. With his arm out he said, "Ahh," like they had any idea.

Sarah shrugged. "I'm more or less a solo out here."

Soup Bowl stayed in place when a broken animated heart appeared above his head.

"While we gather moss, we will look for another member." Jennifer put her hands on her hips, and stood straighter.

The trio left for the museum so Jennifer could return the mostly intact blue ice lobsters.

Her heart started beating faster as she led her team to the museum. She needed to pat down her sweaty hands on her robe as they got closer to the large building.

There was no issue entering the building because no one manned the front desk. Soup Bowl would, at times, inspect the empty exhibit or empty display case and then he shared quests **Catch Poison-Breathing Parrot or Find Yellow Lady's Slippers.** Jennifer could not see the available quests that the ninja was seeing. She huffed at this. Again, she was being denied access to part of the world because of who she was. She did not mind that the ninja boy was able to see and choose the quests, but it irked her that she could not. She tried not to be jealous of the ninja but if asked, would admit to some envy over the fact the ninja's neon hair kept changing. That just seemed fun.

When the trio finally got to the sea exhibit, they heard an audible gasp from Sarah as they entered the space. A pair of wide, cartoonish eyes appeared above Large Soup Bowl's head. Jennifer kept walking around, trying to appear unfazed at the amazing exhibits around her. The group walked in front of the blue ice lobster [AP1] tank. Her heart raced as she focused on her breathing. She counted to three. She had just borrowed the lobsters for a quest. What was she afraid of? Nothing was wrong. She was going to have to wait until a distraction presented itself.

The group watched in awe as the living lobsters continued their errands and quests that only they knew. One stood on top of the highest hill in the aquarium with a crown and cape. The king lobster was at least as long as Soup Bowl was tall. They moved with grace that any ballerina would be envious of. The carapaces of all the lobsters [RM2] shone like ice melting in the spring sun.

Jennifer really needed a distraction.

"Hey, look, a distraction," Jennifer yelled, pointing in a random direction. With her companion's attention pulled, she put the two lobsters back where she found them. They were almost as good as new because she had repaired them herself.

"Sorry, what was the distraction again?" Sarah asked.

Jennifer was smiling, blinking rapidly, and looking away, trying to appear innocent. Her hands were behind her back, though she could tell her face was getting warm.

"Oh, it's gone now. But hey those lobsters sure are pretty. Look at these two on display here." Jennifer spoke quickly and without making eye contact.

A large question mark appeared above Soup Bowl's now neon-green hair. "Were those there before?" No inflection in the ninja's voice, but it was clearly a question.

"Well, of course they were here before, and they're here now. I think. Yes, time to go to the next exhibit." Her words ran into each other as she hurried toward the next exhibit. But the entranceway had an Exhibit Closed for Cultural Reasons sign barring her way. She hung her head knowing this was the end, case open and shut. Someone would find out what she did and throw her in jail. She had only been borrowing the lobsters. Plus, they helped the town.

Soup Bowl said, "Sure, why not? There's time for gathering moss, or maybe fighting some forest monsters."

His words gave Jennifer hope of being able to get out of the situation she had put herself in. She lifted her head and saw the ninja walking to the exit. She followed him without making eye contact with Sarah. Though, Jennifer felt as if the whole museum was now watching her.

CHAPTER 7

A WOLF IN WOLF'S SKIN

THE TRIO WAS HAPPILY walking in the woods to fulfill the quest. Or rather, Jennifer was happily gathering flowers, moss, roots, and greens while Sarah held a handgun at the ready. Large Soup Bowl was nowhere in sight. Jennifer was still getting used to the team interface. She could feel he was around and could also see him on the mini map.

"How can someone with glowing neon hair be so stealthy?" Jennifer asked while monitoring their direction on the map.

"Ninja skills," the tree replied. It sounded a lot like something Soup Bowl would say. Jennifer shrugged at this and went back to picking some nice yellow flowers that seemed to grow like weeds in this part of the forest.

"Incoming," Sarah yelled. She pointed her gun to the sky.

A very loud and drawn out "Kid!" was heard yelling back over the sound of rockets.

Jennifer put her hand to her face. She heard a few loud pops from Sarah's gun. That was followed by a laser beam which came out of her watch before Jennifer had a chance to stop her friend.

An impact that caused a wall of dust and a shockwave made the trio stumble. Woozle came out of the dust cloud, fangs bared, jets glowing, and dodging the bullets as if they were nothing but falling leaves. There was a ringing in Jennifer's ear as the ninja popped out of nowhere to deliver a strike with a glowing knife. Woozle dodged the attack, redirecting his mass with his rockets to deliver a powerful kick followed by a blast of hot exhaust that sent the ninja flying back.

"We're under attack. Get behind me. I'll protect you." Woozle sounded like a grizzled veteran of combat as he circled Jennifer forming a line in the ground around her.

Jennifer held her hand out and said, "Sarah, you remember Woozle from the hot tub, don't you? Large Soup Bowl 14, this is Woozle. He's my familiar, so none of you should be fighting." Her words came slowly, showing the others she was calm. The ringing in her ears stopped. She wanted to pick up her little protector and give him cuddles, but it did not seem like a good time to give him attention. She did not want to embarrass him in front of the team.

Woozle turned around to face Jennifer and sat on his hind legs with his head tilted. "What about the wolf?"

"Wha—" Her words were cut off as a large, powerful force came at her from behind, knocking her to the ground face first. She flailed around unable to get up with such a heavy weight on her back.

Unable to lift herself up, she shifted her weight to the right. Even before she finished raising, on a near instinct level, Jennifer started casting. The speed around her slowed as she took in the situation. It was indeed a wolf. The beast was attacking the ninja with its powerful jaws. Before the creature could chomp down on Soup Bowl's arm, she encased him in a force field bubble. Its fangs ground against the protective field.

Shots from Sarah's gun rang out, hitting the lupin but doing little to no damage. Switching tactics, she used the laser beam, leaving a black line across the wolf's fur. The animal turned to face Sarah, lowering his massive head and growling with such intensity and power. Jennifer's bones vibrated away. An alert came up in her menus.

Growl Debuff: Resistance Reduced

She heard a click in her mind that told her that her force field was ready to be used again. She cast a protective bubble on Sarah. The wolf dodged Sarah's ranged attacks while charging her. It's bestial fangs ripped into the force field. The animal was strong and fast. Sarah was the only one causing damage to the attacking beast. The force fields would not last long.

Large Soup Bowl charged in yelling, "Ninja Sneak Attack."

The ninja buried his blade deep into the fur covered side. This was the first time the wolf reacted to any damage. The beast's head turned to the knife in its side. Jennifer renewed her shield on Sarah as the attacker's head swiveled back[AP3] to face the ninja. With a growl deeper than before, the animal faced off with the ninja.

The Growl debuff stacking on the group lowered everyone's damage resistance.

The creature and ninja circled one another as the growl grew louder. Sarah reloaded her gun. Jennifer prepared her Dark Pulse attack. Ninja took the initiative, by throwing something on the ground. In a plume of smoke the ninja's outer lines faded into stealth. The tearing teeth met Large Soup Bowl before he was completely invisible. Thanks to the forcefield the ninja was knocked back, the protective field popping out of existence. Woozle landed on the wolf's back, biting down hard with his rows of shark teeth.

Rather than using her attack power, Jennifer used force field on Woozle.

The beast spit out a gob of blood onto the ground and shook off her familiar. The lynx-shark landed in front of Jennifer on all four legs and squared off with the threat. He was a protector between the beast many times his size and his person. As the hound moved the lynx-shark mirrored the other's movement while keeping himself between Jennifer and the beast.

With the force field cast on Woozle, Jennifer saw her mana bar was just over the halfway mark. She needed a plan. The wolf made a move to charge the much smaller familiar. As time slowed, Jennifer cast force field on herself. Sarah fired her gun which was followed by the ninja's sneak attack.

A plan, I need a plan. Just attacking wildly will not work.

Suddenly, she had a plan. Jennifer, with her mop in hand, charged in a rage at the creature. The animal charged at Jennifer in kind. She twisted her whole body, screaming incoherently as she swung her mop as hard as she could, and hit the beast's face.

An alert popped up. **Giant Intimidation successful.**

Jennifer did not have time to read the message, but she knew what it meant.

The animal was knocked to the ground and landed on its side. Time returned to normal speed. She had a plan, and the one thing she was missing appeared from a trapdoor on her shoulder.

The attacker stood up and took a half step back with a deep growl.

Jennifer hoped the spider would live up to one of his traits. "Rover, make a trapdoor in front of me big enough for that wolf." The spider vanished from her shoulder. "Soup, strike the line of shark bites. Sarah, aim for the head." Jennifer's words were emotionless.

The lupin let out a howl and charged at Jennifer. She glared, unflinching and unmoving. Her heart beat too fast to count. The beast charged her at a fantastic speed. Each step the beast took added speed. Jennifer did not raise her mop to defend herself or queue up her force field bubble. The beast was too close now. With each moment, the beast closed the distance.

Jennifer closed her eyes.

A smile crossed her face as she heard the crash. Opening her eyes, she saw the wolf was stuck and wrapped in a white net made of spider webbing. Jennifer raised the mop above her head. "Now!" She did not know whose attack landed first, or last, but after many strikes from the team. Jennifer whispered to the animal, "I'm sorry."

A laser shot from Sarah's watch finished off the beast.

Jennifer's mop had cracks running up and down the shaft. She inspected her teammates. In her team window she saw the others status bars. Sarah was uninjured, but ninja had taken some damage. He was still well above half health. One healing potion was left in her inventory. She also had not recast her healing potions either.

The group stood over the downed animal, as the creature changed from a terrifying beast into four **large cut steaks, two wolf hides, two wolf hearts,** and a **wolf skeleton.**

Soup Bowl was the first to move towards the dropped loot.

Jennifer's mind and body both moved at a much slower speed than before the fight but she was still fast enough to let out, "Wait." She breathed deeply and counted to ten. Her eyes combed the area. She easily found what she was looking for and took a few colorful flowers out of the ground. She created an improvised bouquet which she laid out before the beast's parts.

Jennifer knew she should say something but was unable to find the words. She opened and closed her mouth, searching for something appropriate to say. To her surprise, the ninja spoke. "We thank you for the offerings of your body, and we apologize for the way your body must be taken." The words did not feel correct, but the intention was there.

No one objected when Jennifer took the skeleton along with the fur. The other two members of the team took the rest of the loot. Woozle was limping, so Jennifer recast her three craft healing potions. Checking in her team's menu, Woozle had taken the most damage, so he received the first healing potion. Soup Bowl received the second.

Bringing out the healing potions resulted in more black and gray on Jennifer's stamina bar than she would have liked. She had not been expecting a fight and decided she did not enjoy it.

"I can hear a stream nearby. How about we go over there for the healing moss?" Sarah's voice distracted Jennifer from her thoughts, but she could still hear her blood rushing through her body and her heart pumped far too loud and fast for her to form a response. She nodded to her friend. Sarah took the lead with Jennifer and Soup Bowl following, and the group silently moved to the stream. Woozle returned to Jennifer's hood to take a rest.

No one spoke as they arrived at the flowing water. Jennifer entered the stream in her clothes, still feeling hot from the fight. The stream added green to her stamina bar, but there was still more gray than green. While in the water, Jennifer cast mend on her broken mop. She did not want to watch the wires do their repair dance, so she kept the mop under the water and her head above.

"Healing moss. Twenty pieces," Large Soup Bowl said as he moved to gather the moss. Out of the group, the only one that did not show signs of distress was the ninja.

Jennifer's eyes passed to Sarah and her friend's hands were still shaking from the fight. Woozle swam in the water catching fish. It was not until Sarah started to clean the fishes that she started to feel her heart relax.

In a low voice from her right side she heard Woozle ask, "Do you want me to catch more?"

Jennifer shook her head. Her familiar returned to her hoody and purred. The noise and vibration did settle her heart. "Thank you, Woozle." Her companion purred louder.

Small pops and crackling followed a welcoming woody aroma. Sarah started a fire in a circle of stone. The wood was arranged in a near up turned angle and Jennifer's memories sparked, telling her this was a teepee fire. Sarah was adding a handful of pine needles into the orange licks of fire. The smoke from burning pine needles added a distinct and pleasant aroma to the air. Ninja forced pieces of wood that were pointed on both ends into the ground. He then speared the fish on the free end of the pole. The smell of the natural burning wood, pine needles, and cooking fish created a spice in the air.

Jennifer lost track of time as she focused on her breathing to calm down. Closing her eyes, wishing to focus on what could still see her menus. The display of icons indicated the various conditions on herself and her teammates.

The conditions on Soup were rest, stealth, ninja reflexes, and ninja danger sense. Focusing her mind on the rest icon, the effect description stated that it added buffs to healing, mana recovery, and stamina recovery, but he was unable to move while under the trait's influence.

Jennifer opened her eyes. According to her menus, Soup Bowl was fully recovered. She watched his icon on her mini map, moving along the side of the river. Jennifer guessed he was probably searching for more healing moss or fish.

Her stamina was still low, and the smell of the cooking was the motivation she needed to leave the water. The fish she ate recovered most of her stamina.

Returning to her inventory, she had a way to go on the healing moss. Her eyes were drawn to her new wolf skeleton. Not knowing what to expect, she cast mend on the skeleton while keeping it in her inventory. She saw the skeleton's integrity go from sixty-five up to eighty percent.

Jennifer found her mind wondering. Her curiosity was piqued, and she did not want to hold back her question. "So, a golden gun and a laser watch are powers you get from being a hunter/gatherer?"

Sarah's hand went up to cover a laugh. "No, I get those from work—"

A howl rang out over the forest.

Jennifer's body went cold. A shiver went down her spine and she wrapped her arms around herself. "Rover, can you do that trap thing again?"

The spider shook its body, indicating a no.

Jennifer picked up her mop and pointed downstream toward the town. The stealth user of the group appeared next to the hunter gatherer. With a brief exchange, both Sarah and Soup Bowl nodded.

The group moved along the stream, making as little noise as possible. They kept their guard up as they moved. Jennifer repeatedly cast the force field bubble on each of the members of the group. The protective barrier would blink out after around a minute. This time needed to be different. It would go better and she wanted the group to be prepared.

Soup Bowl vanished in neon smoke as Jennifer saw a green-gray wolf just as large as before. The group was ready for this beast. Jennifer could feel herself smiling. It was not a smile of joy or happiness, it was a nervous reaction. She did not want to be smiling.

She was scared and she felt a pang of guilt at the thought of taking an animal's life. Even with this creature attacking them, she reminded herself that she needed to defend herself. She wished there was another way.

The animal with the gray-green fur circled the group. Jennifer knew from the markings this was the same beast. The wolf seemed to eye each member of the group. It occurred to her that this one was being more cautious, possibly choosing its targets before jumping into action.

Jennifer watched as the aggressor stalked around them. The last attack was a surprise. Now they were prepared, and she had a couple of fresh surprises in store for this lupin.

Jennifer counted aloud, down from three, to indicate when they should attack. Sarah nodded in her peripheral vision. While at the same time the beast's right ear twitched at two. When she got to one, she cast her dark pulse. Jennifer's chances of that attack hitting was low, so she used it as a distraction. The wolf jumped out of the way only to be hit by shots from Sarah's gun. But it moved in time for the laser to barely singe its fur. Large Soup Bowl yelled out he sneak attacked and reappeared. The wolf's teeth found the ninja's arm while his blade met only air.

The force field protected Soup Bowl at first, but the field went down as the beast shook its head, trying to tear the ninja's arm. When the field blinked out, the wolf's eyes brightened as he bit down hard.

Keeping her breathing steady, Jennifer knew her only option was to protect or to strike. "Summon Undead." As much as she wanted to protect, taking down the beast and passing out a healing potion after would be more effective. The words spoken battled against what she wanted. A wolf skeleton appeared. Its head raised to the sky and with the jaw making small movements. With no flesh, no blood, only bones, the world went cold at a soundless howl. The clean-boned skeleton charged its own kind. The wolf's eyes went wide as the animated undead thing came at him.

The skeleton took large bites out of the living wolf, but it took damage from the wolf as well. Sarah and Large Soup Bowl both attacked as quickly as possible, and Woozle jetted in to take a bite before jetting out again.

Jennifer cast Dark Pulse but focused her attention on the health of her teammates and the integrity of her skeleton. The skeleton lost integrity fast. When the skeleton dropped below a quarter of its hit points in the health bar, Jennifer dismissed the summoned skeleton back into her inventory and cast Repair. With every point of repair, she used a point of stamina.

The wolf pounced at Jennifer. In that moment, when her action should be, she froze. She was a deer in the eyes of a hungry predator. Before she could brace for the pain to come, a ninja stealth attack threw the wolf off course. She immediately handed the ninja a healing potion and cast a force field on him. She had used far more mana than last time and was under the bottom third of her mana bar now.

The gunshots and laser beams weren't enough. The wolf shook its head and body, letting out a soul chilling growl. The beast charged, catching its target.

Large Soup Bowl, to his credit, did not let out a sound of pain. The force field vanished with the wolf's bite, and Soup lost a third of his health. But he was not the intended target. The creature had the potion's container in its teeth. Letting the vial drop to the ground, the wolf broke the vial underfoot.

A second black section now hung on Jennifer's stamina bar along with a new weeklong timer counting down. She was now limited to two healing potions at a time. Jennifer was more prepared for this attack. She had a plan going in, but it was the beast who was winning.

Her health bar was full, Sarah's health bar was full, and the ninja still had more than half of his health bar. But the hunter gatherer's stamina was almost entirely grayed or blacked out, and her mana was less than one third of Soup Bowl's. The neon teammate had a bleed effect. She had to finish this fight now. The wolf charged at Jennifer, and she cast Summon Undead, costing Jennifer the last of her mana.

Their movements were oddly mirrored, as they both jumped at one another. The undead wolf met a living wolf in the air.

The skirmish did not end, and it wasn't like she could take a break. Jennifer held her mop defensively in front of her, hoping her mana would regenerate fast enough for her to cast a bubble around the skeleton.

The skeleton was back under one third before her mana regenerated enough for a force field. The team was not being idle and were using their attacks. If they were to defeat the animal, it was death by a thousand cuts. Each cut caused only slight amounts of damage, but the beast was going down. The hit cost a tick of health while the wolf's bite took larger chunks out of whoever found their way between its jaws.

This time, it was the ninja who scored the last hit.

Jennifer fell to her knees, let out a long breath, and looked over at her team. Sarah was on her back, breathing heavily while the Soup Bowl was posing with a large V over his head. He was the victor, but his health was still going down, with less than a tenth of health left. Jennifer tossed him a healing position. "I am going to need the vial back." She was too tired to be polite.

This time, the wolf left five steaks, one pelt, one heart, and one skeleton.

"Sarah, can you cook some of that meat? My stamina is way down after that fight." In spite of not taking a single hit, Jennifer was exhausted. The beating of her heart seemed too fast, and her hands shook uncontrollably. She didn't dare attempt to stand.

Jennifer let her zone out sitting on the ground, letting the world pass around her. She had no way of telling how much time had passed. What felt like a blink had been enough time for the wolf meat to be prepared. It was now hanging from a stick in front of her. She ate the meat as fast as she could, bringing her stamina up to around twenty percent. "I'm sorry, my stamina is at like one fifth. I'm going to need to eat more to be ready if we're attacked again."

Sarah and Soup Bowl appeared at one another wordlessly. The

ninja moved toward Jennifer and passed all of his food to her. Jennifer pressed her lips together, feeling wetness build around her eyes. "Thank you." After finishing the meal, she was able to have full stamina after refilling her health potions and casting Mend on the skeleton in her inventory. Her stamina was green and black. Leaving no gray, this was as much stamina as she could have.

After giving his part of the meal to Jennifer, the ninja was back to stealthing around the group. Sarah sat still eating a salad. Jennifer did not know where the salad had come from and thought it would be too impolite to ask. Instead, she moved to where the wolf had fallen and laid down a few flowers, mimicking the words Large Soup Bowl had said over the first wolf. "We thank you for the offerings of your body, and we apologize for the way your body was taken."

She took the skeleton into her inventory for the purpose of summoning undead but felt an odd resistance this time, as if she was opening a heavy door. The same amount of mana was used, and she could not explain the difference between the last time and this. Then the notification appeared.

You have summoned the skeleton of a defeated foe against his wishes, but an offering was made to summon this undead. These two actions balance each other out. Your alignment has remained unchanged. The best effect is sometimes no effect at all.

Understanding dawned on her about why it was harder to summon the second skeleton. The wolf was still out there. She cast force field on the group including her familiar, and a pet. Her mana had bottomed out with the multiple casting but recovered quickly. "The wolf's still out there."

Stirred to action, the group continued to gather healing moss and other items while hurrying their way up stream back to the village. Thanks to the group, Jennifer was well over halfway done with her gathering quest, including what her spider was able to gather before.

When another howl split the air, the group froze. The ninja had vanished. Both skeletons stood on guard as Woozle bolted up a tree. He was waiting to ambush the twice defeated wolf while Jennifer and Sarah scanned the landscape for any sign of the beast.

On a positive note, there was only one wolf to fight. On the downside, it was strong. The ninja was not getting stronger, but the group was running out of tricks to defeat the wolf. If this fight was the same as last time, Jennifer would only be able to repair one of the skeletons during the fight. She needed to be very careful. The last attack lowered the number of healing potions she could use at any one time and stretched her stamina nearly to the end.

The group was tense and waited a long time. Sarah spotted the animal first and simply pointed at the wolf. How could this creature continue to return after each encounter? Why was it not leaving them alone? The thought filled Jennifer's mind.

This wolf eyed Sarah, Jennifer, and the two skeletons. Its right ear twitched as it approached the group.

An idea popped into Jennifer's head, and she blurted, "I have a crazy idea, but if it goes wrong, everyone attack them." The chance of her plan working was slim, but something inside her told her it was better than just fighting again.

The list of things a parallel could do far outweighed what Jennifer was capable of as a team leader. Yet if her insane plan worked, it would stop the fight before it started and keep everyone alive.

Jennifer sent a group invite to the wolf that was gearing up to attack them.

The wolf stopped and sat back on its haunches like it had just been told to sit.

"No one attack," Jennifer hissed, the tension edging her voice. The wolf's head tilted as if in thought.

Kevin has joined your team.

"What the flying flocking flamingo?" The monotonous words

came from the trees which the team recognized as Large Soup Bowl's. The wolf turned his head to the noise and let out a bark. The wolf's bark was not one of aggression but more a mark of recognition. The new party member turned his massive head back to Jennifer.

Not dwelling on why such a fearsome beast was called Kevin, Jennifer put down her mop. She didn't want to startle the beast, so she slowly approached him.

"Kid -" Woozle cautioned her.

She did not know what to say or where this was going. "So far so good." She let her words hang in the air.

Jennifer got within arm's reach of the wolf. It was sitting on its haunches, eyeing her. She held out a hand for the wolf to sniff as she sucked in a deep breath, never taking her eyes away from the beast.

The wolf sniffed Jennifer's hand with deliberate and slow movements. Kevin huffed, stood up on all fours slowly. It circled Jennifer and sniffed her.

Once it was satisfied, the wolf gradually moved towards Sarah. The wolf's ears were pointed up, and the tail hung down as he sniffed her. "Are you sure this is a good idea?" Sarah's voice cracked with nervousness as the beast circled her.

"I have no idea." She was astonished that not only had Kevin accepted her invite but that this had not already broken into a third skirmish.

Sarah glared at Jennifer for a moment before watching the beast.

The wolf barked again, this time in the direction of where the ninja was hiding. Large Soup Bowl 14 appeared next to the beast. Startled, the wolf yelped and jumped away before growling at the ninja with its ears flat against his head. Regardless, the ninja reached out his hand for the wolf to sniff. At this action, the wolf's ears went back up, this time with a small tail wag.

Kevin circled the ninja, taking in his scent with deep breaths. This time it lasted longer than both Sarah's and Jennifer's sniff tests combined.

The force field bubbles had timed out on everyone. Jennifer knew she did not have time to recast them if this went wrong. Kevin could do some actual damage with his attacks. She pulled up his stats in the group's interface menu. Kevin was listed as a level eight Great Forest Wolf.

Apparently satisfied with the ninja, the wolf turned to move back toward Jennifer.

Woozle jumped down from the trees to stand between the wolf and Jennifer. Although, whether he did it to be counted as one of the group or to protect her, she had no idea.

Kevin paused but eventually moved to sniff the much smaller lynx-shark. They met nose to nose, sniffing one another. After a moment, the wolf made a very human gesture of nodding and moved to stand beside Jennifer. He pressed his body into Jennifer. Him leaning on her almost caused her to fall over. She steadied herself and pet the wolf.

"How can a wolf be a parallel?" Sarah asked no one in particular.

"I had no idea that was even an option," the ninja replied.

"Either way we have found our fourth party member," said Jennifer.

"First a half giant, then cows, then ninjas, and now wolves. What's next, dinosaurs?" Woozle grumbled.

"Oh, stop being grumpy. Even you must've realized things weren't going well." Jennifer reached down and gave Woozle a comforting scratch.

After showing the wolf a bit of the healing moss they were searching for, the group gathered everything they needed in half the time. Kevin was able to sniff out the moss far faster than the group could spot it. When the sun was a few fingers above the horizon, the group made their way back to town.

They had gathered more than was needed for Jennifer's quest, but she and Soup Bowl wanted to see if she could craft healing potions without activating her power.

The warm bright glow of the day had transformed into the

night, with the only light coming from the two moons by time everyone arrived at the gate house. Jennifer bent down to make eye contact with Kevin. She pointed with both hands to herself, then with both hands at the town. She then pointed at the wolf with both hands, then one hand towards the town and one away. Hoping the wolf would understand.

After a moment, the wolf nodded as a cartoonish shield appeared above his head. Jennifer took this as a question if it would be safe. She turned to face at Soup Bowl, and asked, "Can you do that shield thing? Was this just another thing fragments could not do?"

A shield appeared above the ninja's head. The wolf nodded and led the group to the guardhouse.

CHAPTER 8

A WOLF'S NEEDS

"YOU CANNOT BRING A wolf into town." The exasperated town guard repeated for the third time.

"Okay look, he has joined my party. He is part of my group. I think he should be allowed in." Jennifer was trying to keep her cool while dealing with the guard, but her frustration was mounting.

"Would you keep someone's pet dog out?" Sarah planted her hands on her hips, tapping her foot.

"If that was just a pet dog in this world, I would let it in. But in my world, we have leash laws to protect people from creatures like this." The guard raised his voice, attempting to speak down to Jennifer who was a head taller than him.

The raised voices caused Kevin to growl at the guard.

Jennifer put her thumb and forefinger against her temple, thinking as fast as she could.

The nameless guard shouted over the growling wolf. "See, this beast is far too aggressive. He cannot come into the city."

"Sarah, could you please?" Jennifer gestured at Kevin while trying to think. Sarah spoke quietly. Jennifer assumed Sarah was calming Kevin.

"Fine. What if I got him a leash and made sure he was being led by a parallel at all times?" Jennifer asked.

"Let me check his alignment. This is a good town. We do not

want a big bad wolf getting into town." The guard's lips twisted into a smug smile that Jennifer did not like. The guard took out the same square device that had shown her alignment before.

She nearly burst out laughing as the device asked, "Who's a good boy? Who's a good boy?" It pinged and announced, "You are." A note of shock passed over the guard's face as Kevin barked with happiness, waggled his tail, and ran in a circle.

The guard eyes moved over the group with skepticism at the other parallel in the group, Large Soup Bowl. "It will have to be a very short leash. At the first sign of trouble, the guards will be on him in an instant." The guard kept up his self-important air during his pronouncement. "You go straight to the foundry and get the leash made. If you don't go straight there, I will make sure you're never allowed in the city again no matter what the mayor says."

"I was looking forward to visiting the foundry anyways." Jennifer raised her voice above the guards but not loud enough to wake up the whole village this time.

Jennifer directed the wolf to the ground beside her. She made the gesture clear and hoped it did not come off as a command. Kevin walked to the spot Jennifer pointed to and sat. She pointed at the wolf then herself. She placed her hands close together but without touching. She hoped this would make it across the species language barrier.

The wolf took a long moment and nodded to Jennifer as she led the group towards the micro foundry.

After making the third wrong turn, Sarah took the lead, putting Jennifer in the middle. The wolf was on one side and a lynx-shark on the other. The neon ninja took up the rear. He had an exceptional glow at night with his colors constantly changing.

The wolf growled softly at Sarah but Jennifer looked down with a smile and spoke in a kind voice, "It really is for the best. I'd probably get us lost."

The wolf tilted his head as it kept walking beside Jennifer.

The micro foundry was an odd little building. The outside resembled a normal two-story house you would find anywhere in the town. The only exception was the dull orange light coming out of all the windows of the house. A robot sat on the porch.

The robot came up just shy of Jennifer's waist and had a ball shaped head with two square sets of white lights in the approximate location where a very young child would place the eyes. A long, horizontal bar flashed periodically where the mouth would be. The torso of the robot was clothed in blue coveralls. The body of the mechanical being was accompanied with more of a rectangular prism with rounded sides. Its arms resembled air duct tubing with strong, five-digit hands coming out of the end. The hands looked to be larger and stronger than Jennifer's. The robot had no legs but two large wheels on the side which was covered in a rubber tire. Just behind the first large set of wheels was a much smaller set that seemed more for balance than for maneuvering or adding speed.

"Welcome to Honest Grezzer Micro Foundry. What can I do for you?" The robot spoke with a long rectangular mouth lit up.

"Hello, I would like to get a leash and harness for my friend here." She gestured to the wolf.

The robot went straight to business. "Sure thing, ma'am. Coming right up. That will be twenty oranges."

Jennifer nodded. "Can you make the harness out of combat leather or some kind of armor?"

The bot turned its head away from Jennifer. The light in its eyes turned off and on again. Returning to face her, it repeated the process. "I cannot stretch any pattern too much, but I think I have got something that will do. Two hundred oranges at his level."

Jennifer eyed the robot up and down. Rust showed in several places along with severe scraps and a pockmarked shoulder. Taking a chance, Jennifer cast Mend and reached out to shake the robot's hand. When the robot took Jennifer's hand, he found he was being repaired.

After a long few moments, Jennifer let go and ended the Mend. The robot took a mirror out of his inventory and inspected himself. "I look one hundred years younger, and I am operating at two percent more efficiency."

Jennifer was shaky on her feet. The wolf whined beside her and licked her hand in concern.

"As long as I'm fed, I'd be able to cast Mend on you as long as I am in town." Her words came out slightly weak, but she showed what worth she had to the bot.

He nodded, "How much can you repair?"

"Depends on what I am using that power on. My guess would be up to eighty percent." Jennifer answered honestly. "And once a day until I reach your cap? As long as I've eaten, the repairs come out of my stamina."

The robot rolled back and forth for a moment, before presenting the offer. "Five oranges up front for the cost of the materials. You come by once a day until you repair me up to eighty percent. I understand life happens in the adventuring world. So you cannot miss over three days in a row. If you do, I will report a breach of contract to the Law Guild Second Division – Carl and Hamster."

She turned to Sarah who had remained quiet except for the slightest of nods. Jennifer handed over the five oranges from her inventory.

The ground beneath her feet rumbled as if an engine as big as a house had just turned on. In the house behind the robot, lights pulsed to the rhythm of machines. The front door of the house opened, revealing a conveyor belt that came down in front of Jennifer. It deposited a set of armor that would fit the wolf. Jennifer lifted the armor up to inspect it. On the back, seven bands of strong light metal parts overlapped one another. The suit even had shoulder armor with three of the plates. On the wolf's chest was a single triangle-shaped piece with rounded edges and a belt with pouches on the side.

The wolf made a questioning *awwroof* sound and turned to look at Jennifer.

She smiled at the wolf, pointed to the armor, and then at him.

Kevin let out several joyous barks before prancing toward the armor. Sitting on his haunches, he reached out with his paws. This wolf had five digits at the end of his paws and could equip the armor without aid. He did not put it on like she or Sarah would, but by touching and claiming the armor, he added it to his inventory. He then equipped it. The reason she knew this was because of the log in her menu telling her so.

The wolf's tail wagged hard and fast enough to work as a fan on a hot day. "What about the leash?" Jennifer asked.

"One moment. Do you want it to be just as strong as the armor?"

Jennifer smiled at the question. This was going to be easy. "No, I want it weak, flimsy, and just long enough to count as a leash."

The robot pulled some string out of his pocket and signaled for the wolf to come close. He tied the string in the shape of a bow and glued it in place. "Will that do?" The robot asked.

"Yeah, that'll do, and the leash will always be led by a parallel." Smiling, Jennifer waved at the robot and said, "See you tomorrow, Honest Grezzer." Jennifer took the leading position in the group to the inn. Sarah coughed and pointed in the correct direction.

Jennifer only got the team lost once before getting to the inn. She was first to walk into the inn and spotted the mayor sitting at one of the tables.

The placard embedded in the wood with his name and title was a dead giveaway that this was a mayor only table. He waved at her and went back to reading the paper in front of him. Things seemed normal at the inn. A mellow band played on the stage. There were more patrons here now than there were at lunch.

Quiet conversations were going on at a few of the tables. The only thing of note was a group of red-armored warriors sitting at a single table. Confident all was well, Jennifer looked back at her party, waving them forward. Everything was fine until the last member of the party entered the room. The room went silent as Kevin, the armored wolf, silently followed the team.

All eyes followed the wolf who did not seem to care about the scene he was causing. Although Kevin did have a prance to his step, despite not acknowledging the eyes that stared at him.

"That's a Great Forest Green Wolf. Is that now part of your team?" The mayor could have been yelling in the town square with how quiet the room became.

"Yup, his name is Kevin," Jennifer answered the mayor happily. Ready to turn in her quest, Jennifer put all eighty-five healing mosses on the table before the mayor. By the look of her experience bar, she would be able to level up.

"Isn't he one of the wolves that's been attacking travelers and livestock in the area for longer than I've been mayor?" The mayor's volume didn't change. She noted that the ninja vanished and Sarah found a seat far away from the pair.

"Yes. Well - probably. He nearly killed us twice and would've gotten us on the third time. Maybe. Definitely on the fourth time at least." Jennifer kept an upbeat and happy tone as she pet the wolf's head affectionately.

"First the judge's hellhound. Then the traveling musician. Now this." The mayor buried his face in his hands. "I send you out to get healing moss and you make friends with a wolf."

Jennifer reviewed her menus and found an add friend option, she sent out a friend invite to Kevin, Large Soup Bowl 14, Sarah No Val, Mayor Gigawatts, and Honest Grezzer. All of them accepted almost instantly.

"Again, yes, that's more or less how it happened. Now about this quest," Jennifer said, smiling.

The mayor groaned, accepted the friend request, and dragged his hands down his face just enough for his very tired eyes to look at her.

Jennifer kept the corner of her lips pointed up as she returned the mayor's gaze but only received a harrumph. To her surprise, the mayor gave a fifty percent experience bonus to Jennifer and her team for completing the quest. The experience points were pro-rated based on the time the team members had been with the quest and how much they had done during that time. Jennifer received the most, followed closely by Sarah, then Large Soup Bowl and finally Kevin. They all leveled up. "Thank you, Mr Mayor." Jennifer's response from the mayor was a dismissive wave of his hand.

Kevin followed Jennifer to the table where Sarah was sitting. As they weaved through the dining room, she almost had to rebuke the wolf. Not for anything major, just tell him to watch his wagging tail. Several of the inn's customers almost got hurt, barely avoiding the whipping fur stick. Kevin was a happy puppy.

Woozle was nowhere to be seen, so Jennifer assumed the lynx-shark had gone back to their room. She looked down at Kevin and guessed he too would be staying in their room. Jennifer's stomach growled. It had been another long day with very little sleep.

"It is time for rest. I am going to log off for the night." Large Soup Bowl faded out until he was no longer in this world.

"Do you know what you want to do with your level up?" Sarah asked Jennifer. Her eyes shifted from right to left, probably reading her menus.

She had twenty-four hours to choose her upgrades before they defaulted to random. Once was enough, and that just got her some poison resistance.

"Tomorrow morning I'll look at what my options are. With three power sets, I always feel a bit overwhelmed."

"I think this town has a social worker that can help you choose your level up," Sarah said while absently going over her options. Sarah whispered something that sounded like, "Token of Cowthulhu," but Jennifer wasn't sure if she had heard Sarah correctly.

"Token of what?" Jennifer asked.

"I unlocked an optional level up power. It seems to allow me to summon a -" Sarah paused and furrowed her brow. "Well, it is not clear what I would be able to summon, but it will be fun."

Her frown turned into a little smirk that reminded Jennifer of a kid who had just figured out how to get the cookies out of the cookie jar and did not want anyone to know.

Too tired to ask more questions, Jennifer concentrated on what to order. She had just narrowed it down to meat and filling when the innkeeper arrived at the table. The plates the inn keeper had with her made Jennifer's eyes go wide. A large green salad was placed in front of Sarah. This salad had lettuce, spinach, grass, baby tomatoes, yellow peppers, and strawberries. This salad was colorful and looked delicious. The innkeeper set down a plate of two bundles of wrapped bacon the size of tennis balls. The third plate was some kind of uncooked meat slices.

"Umm, who wanted the uncooked elk?" She asked looking around, her brow furrowed.

"How do you know what we want?" Jennifer blurted out rather than answering the Host.

"I use my 'always serve them what they want' ability. It's a passive power under the Innkeeper options," she answered, trying to find the intended guest for the meal. She wore a look of confusion on her face while holding the plate.

Kevin raised his head above the table, giving a polite little bark.

Her eyes went wide, and she shot an irritated glance at Jennifer. The innkeeper put down the plate on the ground in front of the wolf, who proceeded to wolf down the elk meat.

Jennifer used her cutlery to cut one of the bacon balls in half, revealing that the bacon was only the outer layer. From outside to inside, the layers were bacon, brown rice, ground spiced meat, cheese, more ground meat, green peppers, and onions, with a center of a boiled egg. The side salad that came with it was much smaller than Sarah's. This was easily the greatest meal Jennifer ever had, even if it was only the fourth or fifth meal she could remember eating. There was a look of satisfaction on all of Jennifer's teammates at the end of the meal, except for Kevin. The beast was looking up at her with big pleading eyes for whatever was on the necromancer's plate. When she showed him the plate he started to inspect the ground around the table.

Sarah went to her room, while Kevin followed Jennifer to hers. When Jennifer got comfortable enough to sleep, she realized she was going to need a bigger bed. Somehow Woozle took up more space on the bed than the two-hundred-pound wolf. Both the wolf and lynx-shark snored that night. "How could you two snore so much and so loudly?" She asked the sleeping creatures. Somehow, she was still able to pass out.

The next morning, Jennifer woke up with a lynx-shark sitting perched on her abdomen. He had grown again and was now larger than any house cat Jennifer had ever seen. The wolf sat in his battle armor at the end of the bed. Jennifer yawned, closing her eyes and stretching her arms and legs. Her feet were well over the end of the bed. She closed her eyes hoping for more sleep. The long note of the train pushed her to open her eyes. The lynx-shark and wolf were watching her. She noticed in a corner was a small spider web with Rover resting in a hammock-like structure. "Oh, I see the smallest of us gets a whole bed to themselves." She affectionately mocked the spider who wiggled its body in what she assumed was a morning greeting.

The wolf gave a wide yawn, showing off massive white fangs, before exiting the bed. The lynx-shark proceeded to produce the word, "yawn" with his double row of triangle teeth showing, but his eyes never closed. When he closed his mouth, she gave him head scratches. She smiled.

She needed to find a toothbrush and toothpaste. Pushing the thoughts of oral hygiene from her mind, she focused her thoughts on her status bars in her menus. Twenty percent of her stamina bar was still blacked out, but her other bars were full.

Still not fully awake, she reviewed her situation. She realized she had limited time left in the inn, but she had a plot of land in town with nothing on it.

She pulled up her menus to see her quests.

Get into Bishop's University: Letters of recommendation, mayor 1 of 1, parallel 0 of 1, and business owner 0 of 1.

[+ other quests, see story guide]

Gather grazing animals 0 of 5

Save the town 0 of 1. Save the nation 0 of 1. Save the world 0 of 1.

Her quest list was short, but she still had a way to go. She decided to give herself a new quest in the meantime.

Get a house 0 of 1.

After adding the quest, she looked down at the wolf in her room. She caught a stray thought listing off the parallels she knew. Kevin was a parallel and would be able to write the letter of recommendation. The only issue was that she had no idea how to mime, 'Can you please write me a letter of recommendation for my university?'

As Jennifer got out of the bed, Woozle and the spider followed. Rover opened a trapdoor and appeared on Jennifer's shoulder. "Are you coming?" Jennifer asked the wolf. The wolf placed a paw by his cheek, tilted his head, and closed his eyes, while unmoving from his new spot in a sunbeam on the floor. She believed that some things were universal and understood that he wanted to sleep more.

Jennifer went to the shower and bath for a quick soak, which allowed her to review her plan for the day. While soaking in the hot tub she set about planning her day.

1) Check out her plot of land

2) Find out how houses are built

3) Find quests to do

4) Go to Bishop's University and see about using their stuff to make a healing potion

5) Return in time for the paper raid

6) Repair Honest Grezzer

"Mend" She bolted upright looking for the source of the word. "Mend."

Jennifer not knowing the source of the word, she took in her surroundings. Aside from Woozle and Rover she was alone in the baths.

Again, her greedy, childlike voice said, "Mend."

Only when she noticed Rover waving at her, did she realize he had spoken. Her mind stalled at the double surprise of the spider's first words and the request to be mended. She eyed the little spider and thought it over. Mending a leg sounded good, but she had no idea if it was possible. "If this even worked, it might hurt a lot. I don't know the risks. Maybe we could talk to the other armored spider at Bishop's?" As much as she wanted to say yes, she had no idea how to go about regrowing Rover's leg. With what she understood about her powers, it could take a lot of stamina, and she already knew she was going to be spending stamina on repairing the micro foundry.

The spider's grandmother was huge, but Jennifer had no idea how old she was. Would Rover age like Woozle and grow with each adventure or encounter? He wasn't getting any bigger even with leveling up, but his back did shimmer with metal even though his carapace had not yet fully appeared. Did the fact that he only had seven limbs affect his growth?

"How about this, my little spider. I was planning on going to school today. How about we talk to your grandmother?"

"Goblin wolf, wolf to goblins," the little spider was able to say.

Confused at his meaning, Jennifer considered the idea of bringing the wolf to the goblins, and wondered why the spider would want them to meet each other. She took the suggestion as Kevin getting a pet goblin. "That may work? If there's time, we can do that." Jennifer responded. Rover's face was facing down and moving left and right. Jennifer was unsure if she was missing what the spider wanted or if she was just missing something. For all she knew, her spider was being mean and wanted her and Kevin to hunt the goblins.

"It must mean you want Kevin to get a pet goblin, right?" she asked.

Rover stopped moving. After a few heart beats, a trapdoor appeared next to him. As he left, his activity status changed to gathering.

She already had a long day ahead of her. Soon enough her pet spider would be able to speak more and say what he wanted. She sighed, put her head back, and let her shoulders dip below the water line. Waiting until the time felt right, Jennifer updated her mental to-do list. Before she went to Bishop's, she needed to go to see the town's social worker. With so much to do, she needed to prepare to meet the rest of her day. With no time to waste, she left the hot tub. Woozle had been swimming happily but left the hot tub alone too. As soon as she was set, so was Woozle.

Jennifer went back to the room to awaken Kevin. Before they left, the innkeeper handed a to-go box filled with food. He gave her a cheery smile. The inn was noisy and filled with people in sunglasses. She saw an empty seat in the dining hall. She wasn't sure if the box was prepared for her knowing she was going to travel or if it was prepared due to all the tables being occupied. It was a thoughtful gesture, so she thanked the innkeeper, and set out for the day.

The mini map in her menus indicated the spot where her land was. After following the map marker, she found herself in front of a small field. The land was adjacent to the town square next to one of the town's bars. She did not like being next to a bar, as it looked like a hole in the wall or a drinking room. On the other side of her plot of land was another vacant space listed as available. Jennifer had no experience in judging the land value. The space seemed like it was big enough to build a house, log cabin, or whatever she decided on here. Turning around, Jennifer studied the park with the statue of the man on the taxi. She could even see the town hall.

"This will be a good view. Now to figure out how to build a freakin house." The intense feeling of the weight of the world bearing down on her with each word, "Always more to do. Never enough time." She kicked the ground and smiled.

Jennifer marched over to the town hall, assuming that she could get advice on building a house and talk to a social worker. She walked through the doors with a spider on her shoulder, a lynx-shark, and a wolf by her side. The clerk behind the welcome desk went a shade whiter. She approached the desk and cleared her throat, buying time to think of what to say to this clerk.

Giant Intimidation Successful

The message appeared on her menus. Jennifer glared, causing the intimidation to be successful a second time.

Frustrated at her inability to control the trait, she tried to be as polite as possible. "Can you please tell me who I should talk to about getting a house built in town? Preferably a house that I don't have to slouch when going through doors?"

The clerk let out a fearful squeak, opened a drawer in his desk, and retrieved something. Jennifer was handed four business cards. She slowly moved her hand to take the cards, but the man's hands were shaking a lot, making it difficult to gently take them.

"Thank you." In her menus, she noticed Giant Intimidation had triggered again. Jennifer moved her hand to meet her face in a classic facepalm action. "Can you please point me to the level up social worker?" Jennifer asked from behind her hand.

The clerk pointed down the hall. "Third door on the right."

Remembering that her last thank you had triggered the intimidation, Jennifer nodded, before moving towards the social worker's office. Walking away Jennifer heard, "How rude," from the clerk with a volume he meant for all to hear. Without missing a step Jennifer lowered her voice so only Kevin and Woozle could hear, "Kevin, woof."

Kevin let out a large, loud bark then turned and looked at the clerk with a strange expression. She could not hide the smirk on her face as she glanced down at her wolf companion. Though, she could tell from the wolf's eye that he, too, was amused. "Let's hope he was wearing brown pants," Jennifer murmured before entering the social worker's office.

Moving down the white marble hall, she saw several brown wood doors on either side. Random plaques lined the walls. She did not read the portraits of people who were probably important at some point. To Jennifer's surprise, no one else was waiting in the waiting room. The walkways were white marble that had black chairs lining the walls. In the middle of the room sat an oval table covered in magazines. She walked up to a glass window with a desk behind it. A woman stood in white robes with red triangle cuffs. A small plaque on the desk read Town Social Worker. Jennifer was in shock for the moment and she nearly shouted, "The town social worker is a white mage? I could have been a social worker if I chose to be a white mage?" She could not keep the frustration out of her own voice. This was the job she wanted. She saw the option and had passed it over.

"I am a white mage, social worker, and plumber," the mage answered in a shocked tone. "You wanted to be a white mage?"

"I'm trying to get into Bishop's University of Magic and . . ." Jennifer paused trying to regroup her thoughts. "Bishop's University of Magic and Whatever to be a social worker."

"Why?"

"Why not?"

"Schools are not much use here when leveling up can give you more skills and powers."

"Leveling does seem odd, but before coming to this world, I had just been accepted into the school, and it's important to me to get a good education."

"Ahh, a new fragment. That explains things. Well, yes you can do university, but they tend just to teach you things, as opposed to leveling which gives you powers and abilities." The mage tapped the fingers on her right hand on the table rhythmically.

"Why not both?"

The robed woman blinked quickly at Jennifer's response.

"Well, that is one way of doing it I suppose. That just muddies the process, gives you ideas you do not need. Attending classes you do not need, taking tests you do not want to take, and how much of that will you really need when you are fighting a dragon or running a shop? Learning, questing, and leveling while attending university can happen. Look at it like this though, you will be splitting your time. It will take longer, and you will never be in the top five percent if you do both. So, why bother?" The white mage's eyes met Jennifer's, who quickly looked away. "But if that is what you want to do, you should do what you find fun. So, what can I do for you today -?" The white mage trailed off waiting for something from Jennifer.

"Oh, my name is Jennifer, and I just hit level three. I was told you would be able to help me with my leveling choices?"

"Okay, Jennifer, what are your power sets and add-ons?"

"Techno, Necromancer, Alchemist. I also have Mend, Speak With Turtle, Speak With Spider, Imperial Tea Tester, and umm, I keep triggering Giant Intimidation."

"Imperial Tea Tester? How did you get that?" The social worker leaned in closer to the glass, while she was sitting in her black office chair.

"I did the random option," Jennifer said with a shrug.

The mage moved her back in the chair. "Do you have any issues with your current powers?"

"I have a twenty percent stamina debuff for almost a week because I traded one potion, and the other potion vial was lost in combat. Is there a return vial option you can suggest?"

"The Dev, Oliver Thordescended gives his followers the option of three of his five powers. One of which is to have their thrown weapons return to them. He may be able to give enough wiggle room for what you want."

"What is a dev?"

The white mage made a 'shh' sound, and her eyes darted around. "Be careful, the Developers can be somewhat sensitive if you use the little d or the big D when people talk about them."

After checking her log, she did see that she used a lowercase D. "So, these Developers care about the size of their D's?"

The smirk twitched on the side of the social worker's mouth. "Yes, the size of their D's do matter to them. The Developers transform the thoughts and hopes of fragments and parallels from a concept to reality. They do this by altering the elements, creating something from nothing, and testing iterations of our reality to suit the needs of all. So, rub their egos a bit, and let them know you think they are big D's."

Jennifer felt awkward, wishing to change the subject back. "You were saying they could help with a recall weapon power?"

"You may also be able to convince some of the local trickster sprites to give you a granted power in exchange for a boon. However, dealing with trickster sprites is never an easy thing. The final option I can think of would be looking into one of the teleportation power sets. Some of those will have the ability to teleport the vials back to you. Since you're level three now, you'll be able to unlock your first travel power. Although, they don't get good until level fifteen, and most fragments -" the white mage placed a hand to her chest, "like myself, tend to only get to around level ten."

"Why only level ten?"

"Think of this like school. Sure you can get a master's degree, or whatever. The rent is cheap, food is cheap, and life is cheap. You can make a good living here with less than your high school, so why push yourself?"

"Why not push yourself, why settle when you can do more? Greatness does not come from looking up at the mountain, it comes from looking down from the mountain and knowing you will do more." A picture of an elderly man, holding a can to sprite who was sitting in a large soft armchair came to her mind. Those words were taken from that man.

The eyes of the white mage looked up, and her head shook. She sighed loudly. "You're one of those. I bet you always went for top marks in your class too. Happiness is subjective, when your needs are met there are only greeds. Anyways getting back to your powers, have you thought about who or what kind of trickster you may want to deal with?"

"Trickster spirits, like ravens and coyotes?" Stories that wanted to be told hovered on the tip of Jennifer's tongue, but her mind could not find the details. Her skin crawled. The hairs stood up on her neck. Something was not right. She was unable to see what puzzle pieces would form from the bits of memory. Her emotions warred between a sense of wonder and danger.

"Trickster sprites like imps, jinns, kitsune, or Devs like James Loki, Henry Lugh, or Kevin Alone-Home. Henry may be able to synchronize with your mend power."

Jennifer felt something in her memory that was just out of reach. Something that was important. "So where do I go to speak with the trickster spirits or Devs?"

"There is a non-denomination Dev interface request shrine on the second floor. There are signs to lead you to where you want to go. But I will mark it on your mini-map."

"I also have a plot of land in town. Any suggestions on how to go about building a house?"

"There are a few builders in town who you can commission. If you want to make the house by yourself, there's the generic Whale Builder Quest powerset options for crafting and well mining. It's a pretty basic power, but it's good."

Something about the name did not sit well with Jennifer. She was not going to take that option.

"Okay, that does help. I think I am going to go to the Dev shrine, thank you."

"You're welcome. Just one question. You have two pets: a weird looking cat and a wolf?"

"Oh, this is Woozle. He is a miniature giant, flying, rocket-powered lynx-shark. He's my familiar. The wolf is named Kevin, and he's a parallel not a pet and he's a friend. The spider on my shoulder is named Rover. He's my pet. Thanks again, I should really get going."

Jennifer left the office of the white mage and proceeded to the Dev shrine. Following the signs, Jennifer ended up visiting the city hall library, the Department of Sanitation, and the Department of Ghost Busting while moving towards the shrine. She really needed to put more points into navigation.

CHAPTER 9

HOW BIG CAN IT REALLY BE?

SHE WAS WANDERING around city hall looking for the Dev shrine
after completely losing track of the signs that guided her way when
she came across an old man sitting on a bench. He had the
appearance of someone over one hundred years old, and that would
be an underestimation of his age. His dark skin resembled tree bark
with deep crevasses. Looking at him, she felt the touch of nature,
wood, and leaves. It was as if she was standing under a tall tree,
protected from the sun. Something strange and powerful washed over
her, but not on her skin. There was something inside of her she could
not name. He was a being of some other nature. A small nameless
touch inside of her told her that he was just pretending to be a man.
His mouth was a knife slit, and he was wearing an animal hide jacket
with light yellow coloring, and many matching long cords. He had
a classic cane made of dark red wood and wore blue jeans. The man's
hair was short, messy, and black as if the only thing that time had
left untouched was the color of his hair.

Jennifer almost passed him, but his jacket caught her eye.
Without thinking, she blurted out, "Is that a deer hide jacket?"

The old man lifted his head with unopened eyes to face
Jennifer. "It is a deer skin jacket."

"It is a very nice jacket." Jennifer spoke honestly.

A younger voice came from down the hall. "It's old school. I
prefer a new suit."

There was something off. She could not place what it was.

The new speaker was a man who had the head of an orca. Her skin was touched with a cold breeze. Her mind took in the killer whale, questioning if he was the boy on the cover of the book she'd read in the library. He wore a cream white suit with black pinstripes and black pockets. The orca-man's limbs were human. At the end of his arms were hands that had at least one gold or silver ring on each finger. He wore expensive looking watches. The one on his left arm was gold, and the one on the right was silver. The orca-man wore no shirt, displaying the physique of a professional bodybuilder. In spite of not wearing a shirt, he wore a black vest and a matching tie. The tie covered where the orca flesh met the human flesh. His mouth had a smile that revealed sharpened, pillared teeth spaced far apart. The black and white colors were sleek and streamlined. The large dorsal fin reminded Jennifer of a punk hair style.

The orca-man did a spin, like a catwalk model having reached the end of the runway, and ended with a flourish. His left arm was across his chest and his right arm was straight. It was off somehow. About a hand width away she could feel embers brushing up against her, followed by pin pricks of ice. She was unable to explain the feeling. Looking at the large black and white head of the creature, she knew the only reason she could feel such things was due to the proximity of being far more powerful than her. He bowed deeply and looked at Jennifer straight on. He smiled and said, "I'm new, so I have no name for the Devs to take. And may I say what a pleasure it is to meet a descendant of the giants. They were always my favorite." He took Jennifer's hand and gave it a kiss.

Something was off. Something that was causing an itch in her mind that she could not scratch. She took a seat on the empty section of the bench, not taking her eyes off of the killer whale man.

The old man spoke. "I am so old that the Devs have forgotten my name, so they cannot take it. I would not take what this one offers." He made no movements but was clearly referring to the orca-man.

"Hello, my name is Just Jennifer. And umm, I was searching

for the Devs shrine or trickster sprites to talk about my leveling options." The apprehension gripped her when speaking to the two. She realized that she was sitting beside the old man, but did not remember sitting down. The orca-man before her seemed to be one of the two candidates she was seeking. The old man's mouth produced a carved smile, and impossibly, the orca-man's smile had broadened.

Although disturbed by the pair, she had to keep referring to them in her mind as an old man and an orca-man. For some reason she was having trouble distinguishing the two. She continued with the introductions. "And this is Kevin. He's a parallel I met yesterday." She looked down and realized she was alone.

Both the orca-man and the old man spoke as one. "We know."

Only the orca-man continued, motioning to the old man. "And that one speaks too much. I have chosen to ignore him. So, my lady, what is a good girl like you doing talking to someone like me?" He didn't let Jennifer answer the question. "Well, I could offer you some things to make some real changes, powers that can help you burn down those barriers you want to tear down."

Jennifer was taken aback. A trickster spirit was offering a deal. Every hair on her body stood on end. In that moment, she knew two things, her heartbeat was hard and loud, and there was no other noise in the hallway. Gone were the normal background sounds of the building. Everyone else had disappeared. A small winged insect was motionless, mid flap near the wall. A quick look around informed her that Kevin, Rover, and even Woozle were absent from the scene. All of the alarms in her mind were going off. She was forgetting things. Jennifer turned her gaze to the eyes of the old man and the orca-man, studying them. The orca still wore a wide smile, but his eyes were now closed. As for the old man, his eyes remained closed, but the smallest curls of a smile played at the edge of his mouth.

Something just was not right. Thoughts kept tugging at her mind. Looking around, she realized there were two people in front of her. One was an orca sitting where a man's head should be and an old man. They were speaking to her. She needed to pay attention.

"I do want to make the world a better place, and some things could be changed for the better." Though confident in her belief, she let the words come slowly, as her beating heart told her she should not be racing into this situation.

Her palms were warm and sweating. There was something just a bit off. She needed to focus on details like how one was an orca-man and the other old man, or for some reason, she would forget they were there.

"Do not be so vague. You are leaving so much room in your words. The turtle we are on could fly between them." The old man's words were deep and meaningful.

Words, Jennifer needed to use her words. Maybe saying something would knock the orca-man off-balance and buy herself time to think. "Why are you dressed so well? Do you have a party to go to?"

"If you cannot be good, you may as well look good. To be the one to make the changes you want, good is not going to get you there." His words dripped like honey. "Change always requires someone to get hurt."

"I do want to be good, but I do not want to hurt others." Something clicked in her mind as if she found a puzzle piece she did not know she was missing. Neither of the two before her had names, so the Devs could not find them. "I was copied to get here. How did you two come to be here?" Her brows knit together as she asked the question, attempting to buy time.

The old man answered first. "A friend was returning a favor, and I came from a turtle island to this turtle world. Turtle island was dead."

The orca harrumphed at the old man. "Where I came from, the world was running headlong into the unmovable object and was most certainly not an unstoppable force. So, I took the first train I saw." He seemed proud of his actions.

"You both came from timelines that were ending. One with the help of a friend and the other by train?" she asked, simplifying what she was being told but unsure what to make of the train.

"I came here by way of my own power." An edge of warning creeped into the orca's voice.

"One came by way of their own power and the other with the help of a friend." Jennifer clarified out loud.

"Yes, and -?" The orca-man rolled a hand in a circular motion trying to get Jennifer to continue.

Her heart slowed, giving her body's energy to her mind as she tried to process what the orca-man hinted at. She knew he was trying to lead her somewhere but she did not know from where or to where.

It was her turn to speak but with what, a conclusion? Jennifer had no conclusions, but like any child, she had more questions. "How can timelines end? The universe I came from was supposed to be infinite, and with every choice we make, we make a new timeline. So, infinite timelines, with infinite choices, in infinite space -" She let her voice trail off while she processed what she knew.

The world slowed down for a moment. Both the old man and the orca stopped moving.

The old man chuckled as he said, "Infinitely finite."

"You can lead a horse to a power station, but you can't make them an engineer," the orca said dispassionately, then glared at the old man.

This was confusing. She needed to focus, but the thought of the two before her seemed to drift away from her mind unless she focused on the two before her.

The orca was visibly frustrated, his arms crossed in front of him. "How do I explain to an ant who I want to make into a giant when they are in the multiverse?" After a moment, the orca threw up his hands. "How do I explain to someone who thinks they are big that they are in fact tiny, when someone, someone," he used both hands to point at himself, "wants to take that tiny person and make them truly big?" then pointed at Jennifer.

The old man took on the tone of a lecturer. "The friend that brought me here explained it like this. Imagine a bracelet that is thin and curved. It's wrapped around your wrist, but the two edges on the bottom of the bracelet never touch. Those two edges that were closest together were both the ones and the zeroes, the alphas and the omegas, both the beginning and the end."

"Which one is the beginning and the end?" Jennifer questioned.

Without missing a beat, the old man continued, "Both the beginnings and the ends. The two edges are the closest together in reality, but the furthest apart on the bracelet. The ends would go from zeros or ones, to twos, to fours, to billions very quickly."

"I can feel an edge of the bracelet but not a second edge, but I can feel the curve. It may feel straight, and linear. Just like with space and time, it is not." The orca-man said soberly before letting the old man continue.

Jennifer closed her eyes so she could picture a bracelet in her mind. The moment her eyes were shut, her mind screamed a warning, shooting her eyes back open. She needed to concentrate on something.

"With numbers, we can have an infinite number of numbers. We have prime numbers, which are whole numbers that can only be divisible by itself and the number one. Prime numbers must also be infinite. But they can never be so infinite that there are a greater number of prime numbers than non-prime numbers. So, there are different sizes of infinite."

The orca interjected, louder than the old man, "There are also pairs of prime numbers like one and three, eleven and thirteen, ninety-one and ninety-three, these numbers become farther and farther apart, but must also go on forever even if they are rarer. With timelines, there are forces at play that limit the infinite. He and I both know this."

"So, timelines are like prime numbers or pairs of prime numbers, but they have a value of infinite that is a lesser infinite than something else." Jennifer's words were a reflection of her stumbling to understand the concept.

"The bracelet is wider in the middle. Either side of the middle is getting smaller because timelines get cut off," the orca-man said with a hand chop to punctuate his words.

The old man added to his lecture, "Or the timelines get merged. That is why some people remember things like the great freedom fighter of a faraway land who was killed in the past decade, when he is really alive."

"Or they remember different names for a family of bears in a children's book." As he spoke, the orca's tone conveyed an eye roll, though he had not opened his eyes yet.

"The Dev that made this world did so smartly, powerfully, and controlled." Sorrow laced the old man's voice, but Jennifer did not know why.

"And the Dev had the drive to complete the project that we now live, work, and play on. Forever taking his cut." The orca may as well have been painted green with envy from the way he spoke.

She could not think of anything but the orca-man and the old man. It was the only way she kept them in her memory. Even blinking caused her to forget who she was speaking to. Once she saw them, she recognized them, and something in her mind told her it would be important to remember this encounter.

Age marked his tone as elderly man spoke. "My friend suggested there were two basic ways to create a new timeline. Along each string of atoms can be thought of as a single timeline. This line is straight, until it is not. One string is added next to or on top of the first line, creating a mass. That bit of creation of something that is straight at every point, becomes a curved mass. This is from where we are on the bracelet. The first way to create a new timeline was to create a choice in the universe so great that the universe is forced to. It is not as simple as choosing to go right rather than left. History for all that it is, is uncaring of small things. There must be something that affects the change so much that there is no choice but for the universe itself to split, so it can see what difference that choice truly makes. The second way—the more common way—is for a timeline to create a simulation of a timeline, a simulation so great that it too could create a simulation." The old man spoke with the clarity of understanding but in a way that made Jennifer feel like she was still missing something, or a lot of somethings.

Jennifer focused on the orca-man's words, making sure to keep the old man in her view the whole time. "So, rather than turtles standing on turtles, it's now simulations of simulations, and mad men pointing at the horizon saying the earth is flat or saying that the moon is a hologram because they have never tried to see what is over the horizon. We are who and what we are. It doesn't really matter why."

He smoothed out his suit as he continued his lecture. "The Dev made a simulation but was somehow able to move the simulation out of the line of simulations. This simulation interacts with other timelines in a way that appears to be a game to most of those timelines. So, this simulation is affecting and is affected by so many timelines that it's now its own timeline. If one of the timelines it's affecting ends, this one will continue. This timeline cannot end unless all other timelines they interact with end."

Without opening his eyes, the orca man turned to face Jennifer directly. His mouth was already wide and he made a smile that sent a shiver down her back. "So, the Dev made this world his lifeboat to the end of time. I intend to make this boat my own and ride it to the end. You can add your paddle to mine and help steer the boat."

Jennifer's head was spinning, trying to make sense of what these two were saying, but she was starting to see what the orca was offering.

Her mind was confused. They were playing a game at a level beyond her. She was here for help with her level. "So, I'm looking for a power that will return the vials of my potions, or a building power that will let me make things like a house."

The orca-man's words swam from his mouth like music from a master musician. "Oh, I can do that easily my dear. That is only two powers out of the five I can give. And with my powers undefined and you being the first to follow me, you would have a great say in how my powers grow. Do you want the vials returned to you by fin or feather?"

"In exchange for?" Jennifer was leaning in, waiting for the catch.

"This world, like any other, is run on favors. A favor here and a favor there. All in the name of good, of course. Me offering you a power is just me affecting the world I now find myself in, much like yourself." The orca's words sounded like honey to Jennifer's ears, inviting with sweetness but also an invitation to bees. Bees are known to sting.

"The bullet train to the infernal levels is made of gold smelted from good intentions." The old man quoted a proverb to her, reinforcing the sense of danger.

"If you are willing to talk to the devil, you have already made the deal. You are just haggling over price." Jennifer quoted back a proverb at the old man, causing him to open his eyes and turn to her. "And better the devil you know," she said.

This offer was not something that happens often. She wanted to make a choice. Her mind wandered back to the deal with the mayor. He too gave her an offer leaving out a choice that she could say no.

"There are other options." Her words were not firm, but she let the statement hang in the air.

She knew her choices were accepting an offer from the orca-man in his fine suit or asking the old man if he would grant the power. There was no doubt in her mind the old man in his traveling leathers would be able to grant such powers. Why would he be here when he came from another place just like the orca? The difference is how he got here. Both nameless, both radiating power she could not explain. She did not know what either of the two beings would be asking in exchange. It came down to accepting an offer, asking for an offer, or walking away. The fact that her own mind would not keep either of the beings in her memory while only accepting the most superficial information about them, she wanted to ask one question before making her decision.

She moved her mouth, but it was dry.

Before her words could escape, both the beings spoke in unison.

"Names carry power and are not things to be shared so lightly."

The old man continued, "We have but a short time, and you know your choices. Ask the goblins for their names. Now make your choice."

Her lips curled in a scared smile. Nodding, she made her choice. It was the best choice she could make. Powers undefined were powers that could make change. Change to make the world a better place. She wanted the power. She needed the power. Confidence grew in her. She straightened her back, she knew her choice, and she made it.

CHAPTER 10

BACK TO SCHOOL

JENNIFER LIFTED HER HAND to cover her eyes from the sudden brightness. Her eyes adjusted quickly to the light as she turned a corner. Her heartbeat was pounding hard and fast. Woozle walked slightly ahead of her with Kevin in front of him. She brought up her menu. Rover was listed as gathering healing moss. On her power tray, a new one had appeared.

Anadromous: Activation on an item, Cost: A minor amount of mana will return the item to caster. Tiny cooldown time. Like salmon, what goes away must come back.

She stopped in her tracks and reread the power description. She could not remember when or where she got the power, but in her heart, she knew this was important. Her mind drifted to the facts. Orca eat salmon, but the salmon returning home was told in old legends.

Something bumped into her leg, bringing her out of her thoughts. Looking down, both of her companions were giving her a tilted head look. "So, I have a power that can return used potion vials."

Woozle scoffed. "Bah, we missed the show. Normally, the Devs like to make a show of these things. They must be behind in tickets or something. I bet it was Dea Tacita Cass, they do not want to be seen but could be around every corner. I guess we have one less thing to do kid, what's next?"

Jennifer jogged beside Woozle on the route back to Bishop's University. When she leveled she had three new powers to add to her growing collection. The first was taken up with her new return item power. It was just simpler for her to think of the power in terms of what it did rather than what it was called. The first power she selected came from her alchemy tree, craft stamina potion. The last power she had at this level was to upgrade her navigation trait. She could start thinking about her future travel power. There was always a pressure to decide now, for things that will affect her future.

Closing her eyes, she pictured the way she used to travel. She was always the passenger of something moving. There were times she was on trains, buses, or cars. Pulling up her options for cars, she found the option was grayed out. Checking taxis she said that option was **BANNED**. In red letters, even. She liked the idea of using a train for travel, but decided against it. The travel powers were for her and Woozle. She saw the options for Superspeed, Teleportation, and flight. She liked the idea of flight, but unsure how that would work.

Mentally flipping through the flight options, she saw jet packs, wings, and even planes. None of those suited her, she wanted something she would be able to get from point A to point B. A plane was just not an everyday mode of transit for her. If only there was a car version of an airship.

The search for a suitable power did come up with something. Her eyes shot open.

Personal airship. At this level the only option was **Flight Navigation, a passive** skill that would also synergize with her navigation trait. Her ability to not get lost would improve by fifty percent. Looking at the powers in this tree, at level fourteen there was a power called **Falling with style - Falling is the easy part, the ground not so much.** It was not until level twenty eight she would be able to fly an airship.

She wanted something like a canoe with a hot air balloon above it.

She tested her new abilities. The power added a fish head, tail, and fins to whatever item she wanted to return to her.

The craft stamina potion came with a couple of downsides. Drinking one stamina potion recovered half the cost of making it. So, having one on hand would greatly aid her in times of need but could not be created in the moment she needed one. The second downside was that she was only able to carry two stamina potions at a time in her inventory. If she had access to all of the slots it would bring her total potion count up to a total of six.

The return item power had a low mana usage, but the longer the distance the higher the mana use. The items looked pretty on the return trip and always landed neatly in Jennifer's hand.

The navigation skill was always on. Although, it did not consume any mana or stamina. Having it constantly running did lower her stamina recharge speed, but unless she was tracking that bar, she would not notice.

She smiled and felt good about her choice. With the paper raid coming up, she knew the return item power would come in handy.

Jennifer jogged back to the university at a pace that did not consume much stamina long term. She was trying to make up for lost time. Running faster would cause her stamina to drop to a point she needed a longer break. The pace she was at allowed a constant speed. Kevin hopped alongside her with his tongue hanging out, making him seem happy. The wolf could probably run much faster. Four legs seemed like they would just be faster, but she needed to conserve her stamina.

Woozle stayed neck and neck with Kevin while not using his jets and showing no sign of running out of stamina.

Jennifer's spider was nowhere to be seen, but he had a teleport power with his trapdoor ability and could return if she needed him. Or when he wanted to come back.

The group reached the school rather quickly. Opening her mini map, she was able to quickly navigate to the dean's office.

She opened the door to the office. "Hi!" she yelled. She turned in the mayor's letter of recommendation to the dean hologram who read aloud, "Dear person, Jennifer is good, and I recommend her. Signed the mayor." The dean was clearly not impressed, giving Jennifer an eyebrow raised glare. But the letter of recommendation was a letter of recommendation.

Jennifer looked back at the dean and smiled.

"And the next letter?"

"Oh, I am working on that." She looked down.

"You could have waited until you had all three."

She left the office, without another word. Closing the door behind her, she promised the next time she would have all three.

Jennifer spoke to her empty shoulder, "Okay, my little spider. Can you get your grandmother to come out?"

A trapdoor appeared on her shoulder, and Rover scurried out. The arachnid jumped to the ground and ran off only to disappear behind a grandfather clock. Jennifer sat on a nearby bench to wait.

The dean came out of his office. She could not tell where the light of the hologram was coming from. The transparent blue man walked towards her and gave her a questioning eyebrow. Weighing her options, she decided to ask, "Do you have other appointments?"

The head of the school quickly looked down and brought up a holographic calendar. It was empty and blinked off. Lifting his head back to Jennifer. He asked, "So, why take classes, when you can have power and skills added with quests?"

"I want to learn. I want to learn how to make the world a better place. Power may help me make the world a better place, but knowledge will keep me from making the same mistakes others have made."

"So, you can blow up the beehive, but you want to learn to move the beehive?" the dean asked.

She blinked slowly at the university's top person, not fully understanding the reference.

"This school was put here as a point of access for fragments. And as a possible school for parallels to attend when in-person classes from their own world weren't possible or when it made more sense to attend virtually." The dean seemed saddened at the lack of the need of the school. "This school has been so ill used. There is a goblin colony here now. The last time it was used was during one of our connected Earth's regularly scheduled plagues. Even though I miss having full classrooms, hoping for another plague just seems wrong."

She wanted to point out how the dean did not have an immune system. Changing course, she asked, "Why not teach the goblins?"

The dean burst out laughing.

"Why not teach the illiterate, unwashed, cannibal, green skins." He laughed and said, "I don't think they even know not to soil the land they live on."

She eyed the dean. She was going to see the goblins for herself before accepting the judgment. Since she did not remember if goblins were real in her world, and having only ever met three, she did not know if what he said was true or not.

"When the school was running, I gave out quests to kill mammoths. The goblin's main food source. Every dead mammoth equals ten goblins gone," the dean said with a chuckle.

Jennifer got up, went back into the dean's office, and unplugged him. "That's better." She looked at her companions through the door, who were both napping in the hallway near the bench she had been sitting on. Looking around the dean's office for something to do, she read the names of the books on the shelves.

She eventually found a book with an interesting title, pulled it off the shelf, and went back to the bench to read it. The book was called, "Classical Guide to Sociology." On the cover was an old man in traveling leathers sitting by a river. After opening the book, Jennifer discovered that this world also had phone books.

The book had a good title and a good cover, but it was just window dressing for an office. "Never trust the cover of the book."

"Those are good words. My grandson said you wished to speak to me?" The giant armored trapdoor spider said from on the ceiling.

Jennifer squeaked in surprise. "How could something so big be so stealthy?"

Kevin was up in an instant, jumping between Jennifer and the giant spider, barking.

Kevin's heart was in the right place at least. Woozle had only swiveled his head to look at the source of the noise. She reached out her hand to pet and soothe the great beast.

"Kevin, this is my pet spider's grandmother. She's not a threat." She made sure her voice was calm but loud. Kevin went from loud barking to low growling.

"Kevin, this is a friend. Friend." She put emphasis on the second friend. Kevin stopped growling, but he did not relax his stance.

Jennifer took this as a sign to continue her conversation with the older spider. "So, your grandson asked me to cast mend on him. I don't know if that will hurt or help him."

"Speaking human already. What a smart boy he is." The grandmother spoke with affection.

"He is. He laid a trap that helped our adventuring group greatly." Jennifer turned to see Woozle, who only raised his head to yawn then went back to his nap.

"Hmm, mend. What are your classes again?" The monstrous arachnoid asked.

"Techno-Necromancer-Alchemist. I have the navigation, mend, and can return items." She counted off on her fingers.

"And you are at least partly organic?" A note in the spider's voice that told Jennifer the eight-legger was trying to be polite.

She hesitated, for several heart beats. A few days ago, she would have said she was fully organic. Looking at her hands, she remembered how there were wires that moved under their own power. "I'm not sure."

The giant armored spider paused for a moment, then bobbed her body in an approximate nod. "May I bite your hand?"

Her head jerked up in surprise, "Wait, what?"

That, in turn, caused Kevin to growl again.

Jennifer knelt down beside Kevin, soothing the beast once more when Jennifer gave him pets. He took a deep sniff but continued to watch the giant armored spider. After a few pets, Kevin seemed less nervous but never let down his guard.

"Why do you want to bite me?" She had run through the question in her mind a few times, not finding an obvious reason.

The giant spider answered in a caring tone that only grandmother could. "To see the color of your blood, dear."

Woozle added his voice to the conversation from under the bench. "So, if it's red, she's human with bits of the system. If it is black or green, she is not?"

Jennifer wanted answers, so she held out her hand to the giant armored spider that could easily take her arm off. She was unable to meet the spider's eyes with her own. The legs of the spider alone were menacing. Smaller spider legs had small hairs. On a giant version, there were more spikes. If this one stepped on her accidentally, it would be like having a car drive over her foot.

Jennifer looked at her pet spider as a way to both distract and to remind herself of the missing spider leg. Spiders should have eight not seven. Jennifer felt her brows coming together, standing straighter with her hand reaching out firmly towards the mandibles of the spider. She never saw the pointy bit coming but felt a pinch on her hand. Looking back, she saw a red line of blood dripping down onto the ground.

Jennifer kept herself from screaming. The larger spider was fast and powerful. That, coupled with the sight of her own blood, made her heart pound. She looked at her log and status bars.

You have been bitten by a Giant Armour Spider for 5 piercing damage.

She saw her total health bar had barely budged. It was only a little blood.

Turning her attention to Rover, he bit the end of one of his legs. Jennifer's eyes widened in surprise at the blue droplets of blood. Kevin gave a low growl, but Woozle sauntered over to sniff the spider's blood.

The red and blue blood pooled and combined on the tile floor creating little rings of purple. The blood samples were not acting as water and oil. Jennifer glanced up at the old giant armored spider.

"So, is it working?" Jennifer's voice cracked as she spoke.

After a few moments, the giant armored spider's body seemed to move in a mock nodding motion. "As an armored spider, I believe your mending should work. If your combination of mend and healing potion gives my grandson here a new leg, that leg will grow with him and be part of him. His body should accept the leg and should be able to heal the new leg as if it was his original."

Woozle spoke before Jennifer could. "I am hearing a lot of 'should' when you speak. What happens if the kid casts mend and it goes wrong?"

"I have other grandchildren, but you will not be able to have another one as a pet." The giant armored spider's words cut Jennifer's heart. She knew a warning when she heard one. She did not want to make an enemy of the spider and wanted to help.

"My little spider, are you sure you want to try this?" Jennifer asked, with a sinking feeling.

The little spider moved its body up and down in a nodding motion. Jennifer turned to the older spider. "What are the chances this goes wrong?"

The giant spider seemed to think on the question before answering slowly. "One in five is the worst case I would say, but I would give you a one in three chance because you have at least quested together."

Jennifer turned to the softly growling Kevin. She wondered what he was thinking. Kevin had been logged in from his world for a long while now without logging out. In that time, Kevin had realized they were at least able to team up with others, but they could not communicate beyond basic movements and interpretations. Jennifer reached out to scratch the beast's chest and focused on what she needed to do next.

Jennifer picked up her little spider and put him on the dean's desk. She steeled herself for the next part. Her stamina and mana were as high as they were going to be. She opened a stamina potion and health potion. Preparing for the operation, she moved her hand over the patient spider and uttered the word, "Mend."

The wires of her hands began their dance.

Little welding sparks traveled over the spider, cutting, and burning while only being a means to repair.

She watched her party interface. Rover's health was going down, and a metal bar icon which turned gray then blinked white. She assumed the blinking indicated that the effect had not taken yet.

Seeing the health of the spider dip below the one third mark, she opened a health potion with her free hand and placed it before the subject. "Drink it slowly." She could hear the panic in her voice.

Kevin barked a panicked warning but thankfully did not attack anyone.

The grandmother spider was so still she might as well have been a statue.

The healing potion was working or at least keeping the spider's health from going any lower. But Jennifer's stamina was almost out, and her mana was below half. She reached for her stamina potions but dared not move the hand that was performing technomancy. She reached for a stamina potion but could not open it with one hand. Her free hand was numb, and she could not grip it well enough to get the top off.

Jennifer's eyes went wide in fear. She needed the stamina potion quickly before she crashed. "Woozle, I need you to open the stamina potion!" As soon as Jennifer yelled, Kevin howled a long deep howl.

"How? I don't have thumbs." Woozle yelled back, attempting to be heard over the howl. It only made Kevin howl even louder.

The giant spider moved.

Kevin stood between Jennifer and the spider, barking, and howling.

Jennifer fell to one knee. She knew if she stopped, it would be the end of her pet spider.

Kevin turned. In less time than it took Jennifer to blink, the spider moved, but Kevin moved faster. Darkness surrounded Kevin, causing the spider to miss its intended target. Kevin appeared next to the spider, flanking as he bit into one of the spider's legs with glowing blue fangs.

Jennifer's stamina was less than one tenth, and a warning appeared on her menus. Mana was being consumed to replace the stamina, but her mana was going to crash very quickly. Woozle was beside Jennifer pawing at the stamina potions on her belt. The noise of the room became very loud. Jennifer's body weakened, her energy draining even faster than before. Her mana is being used up very quickly. "Kevin, please," escaped Jennifer's lips.

Jennifer knew only two options, keep the mend spell up and her spider would live, or to stop and Jennifer would live.

She kept the mend going.

Jennifer looked down at Woozle. "Sorry, this was a short run after all."

"To the infernal levels with that." Woozle stopped pawing at the potions and charged into the melee between Kevin and the spider.

Woozle bit Kevin's tail, holding him in place. Kevin could have easily dislodged Woozle, but he did not, stopping the melee.

Woozle had his jaws firmly on Kevin's tail and was trying to drag him toward Jennifer. The wolf looks back, his eyes meet Jennifer's. Kevin rushed to her side and licked Jennifer's face.

Her mana had crashed. Her stamina was at one percent with her health now melted away. Jennifer could no longer speak or move. She had resigned herself to mending the spider for the rest of her very short life or walking away with an eight-legged spider as a pet.

Cool glass touched her lips. When Jennifer opened her eyes, Kevin held a potion in his paw up against her mouth. She drank it down and thought it was the best thing she had ever tasted.

Her stamina ran out again after fewer heart beats then she would have liked. With her health slowly melting away, Kevin pawed her a health potion. Jennifer looked down at her hands, watching the wires continue to mend Rover. She was all in, and while the stamina potions had added to her, they were just a temporary stop. The health potions were a stop gap at most.

Jennifer watched as her stamina was at one percent again, with her health ever closer to zero with each heartbeat. She did not feel terror. She felt pain as the wires used her body, her health, as they continued their dance and did not know if this was going to end in destruction or creation.

She screamed as the wires receded back into her hands. They had finished, and she was alive. Jennifer peered down at her pet spider.

Rover did not move.

Kevin pressed his massive nose up to the spider and took in a big sniff.

The spider remained still.

Jennifer looked at her party interface. Rover's name was no longer listed.

Woozle stepped up and nudged Rover with his nose.

Her eyes watered. She had taken all of her available potions, ninety-nine percent of her stamina, one hundred percent of her mana, and ninety-six percent of her health.

But the spider was unmoving.

The dean lit back up, giving everyone a slight shock of electricity.

A glowing purple dot appeared on the back of the spider.

The spider was unmoving but glowed.

The dot became a glowing line.

Yet the spider was still unmoving.

She had been holding her breath. It was all for naught. She collapsed on the floor, breathing heavily and trying to hold back her tears.

A plate carrying a few sandwiches descended on a large spider leg. On top of the multiple snacks stood a small, eight-legged spider with glowing purple straight lines adorning his carapace. A metal leg waved at Jennifer.

The spider was moving.

Jennifer reached out to touch the spider. Rover picked up a sandwich intercepting her hand. She was going to pet him if not for the food. A smile and a tear found their way to Jennifer's face. She picked up the nourishment and ate all of the food on the plate as she watched the spider get used to the new appendage.

First, Rover walked forward and backward then left to right and right to left. The spider did a roll and what looked like an attack with his now needle-like leg. When the spider reached his adult size, he would be deadly.

Both Jennifer and the much larger spider let out an audible, "Awww." Rover climbed up Jennifer's arm and settled into his normal shoulder seat.

Unlocked Blood Ritual trait: You can now add blood to a ritual to enhance any ritual. Blood, it is in you to share.

Jennifer murmured, "That can't be good."

"What cannot be good?" the grandmother spider asked.

Jennifer looked down, not wanting to meet the spider's many eyes and kicked at some imaginary dirt. She spoke quietly, "I unlocked a blood ritual trait. But I'm a good person not . . ." Jennifer trailed off. "I'm not evil."

The giant armored spider moved its body up and down like someone's head would move when laughing uncontrollably. "My alignment is near the end of the evil side, and I bake cookies for new students and travelers alike. Alignments do not make you who you are. It is just a system thing. They like putting things in neat little boxes."

That made her feel better, "But the town I live in is good-aligned, so I have to at least stay on the better side of neutral."

The giant armored spider went to inspect her grandson and check out his upgrades. Kevin licked the bite marks on his tail, Woozle curled up on the dean's couch, and the dean glared at everyone. "What the infernal level was all that? I nearly had you die on my floor, and not even one of you acknowledged me. And stop unplugging me. It is hard getting the plug back in!"

Jennifer unplugged the dean again. She did not know who had plugged him back in, but she did not want to deal with him.

Although Jennifer was very low on health, mana, and stamina, she had things that needed doing. Courtesy of grandmother spider's sandwiches, her stamina was over half recovered. Her health and mana were also on the rise, but they were taking their time going back up.

She turned to look at her upgraded spider. "If you are well enough, can you gather some food?"

The group saw a trap door appear next to him, and he disappeared quickly into it. The spider was not gone long, reappearing with some kind of meat on a stick.

Jennifer took the stick from her spider but stared at it in wonder, unsure where the stuff was gathered from. Being too low on stamina to think about it much, she ate. Before she was done with the first, her spider had gathered a second. She gratefully ate the food because the paper raid was coming up in town, so she would need to have her health and stamina potions restocked. She had other items left on her to do list.

Jennifer stood up and prepared to get lost again. She smiled at Kevin and said, "Let's go goblin hunting." Woozle was already beside her, and a glowing spider sat on her shoulder prepared for the rest of the day.

CHAPTER 11

IT WAS ALL IN THE HAT

STEP ONE OF JENNIFER'S plan was to find the goblins. So far that plan has not worked well. A chance encounter led to meeting the goblins before, so she did not know how she was going to find them again. She had no tracking skills and no idea how to mime, "Find goblins," to Kevin. So, she got lost and hoped for another encounter.

At one point, Jennifer exited an empty food kiosk onto a grassy square with old red brick campus buildings on all sides. Turning around, the kiosk had disappeared. She shrugged; this was all part of her getting lost plan. Although the grass around her was green, it had not been well maintained. A strange looking cow in sunglasses was filling up on the overgrown grass. The black and white cow had long shaggy fur, a mane, and beard under its chin and a long tail with a tuft of hair at the end. He had a big head with short black horns and a hump on its shoulders. Compared to the other cows, this one was a high capacity assault cow. The creature let out a long moo while looking at her.

Jennifer did not have much time to keep looking around if she wanted to make it back to town on time. She went up to the cow. "Hello. Um, do you know where I can find the goblins?" She felt she had been lacking intelligence when she left the dean's office. She should have asked the older spider for directions.

The cow looked at Jennifer through the thick, dark aviator style sunglasses. Jennifer had no idea if the cow was a fragment, parallel, or functionary. She swore she would treat everyone the same and was going to wait and see if the cow reacted. Kevin was laying on the ground beside her. She realized that she might be lucky, and the wolf had not tried to turn the cow into a meal.

The cow gave out a long deep, "Moo," turned, and walked away.

Jennifer glanced at Kevin who had his head and ears perked up. Looking at Woozle, Jennifer shrugged and asked, "Do you have a better direction?"

Woozle simply shook his lynx head 'no'.

The group followed the strange black cow. A Beefalo ID tag appeared over the cow. Jennifer was unsure if the word was a description or the name of the cow, but she turned off her navigation skill and followed.

The cow walked through the archway, turned a corner, and went through a door. When the group suddenly came out of a tent door in the middle of a goblin camp, Beefalo was nowhere to be seen.

Jennifer did a double take in spite of the fact that she knew the map had been moving around her rather than her moving around the map.

The encampment went silent as the goblins stopped what they were doing and stared open-mouthed at Jennifer's party. A lot of the goblins were doing what she expected to see in any town. The only difference was that rather than buildings there were tents. Two green tents had a logo on the top of a mermaid in a white circle. Chairs were set up outside where goblins were drinking beverages. Jennifer made a mental note to visit those tents when she had a chance, because the drinks looked tasty.

After a few moments of Jennifer taking in the view of the goblin tent town, she realized that the goblins were still staring at her party. She had the plan to get here, but had no idea what she would do when arrived. With a nervous smile, she raised one hand in front of her and wiggled her fingers. "Hello."

As soon as the word left her mouth, the goblins went into full panic mode, running in all directions while yelling in their guttural tongue. The goblins that were carrying supplies simply dropped them, leaving them where they fell, and dashed away. The beverage drinking goblins also left their drinks behind.

She looked down at Woozle and Kevin had taken prepared stances, eyes and ears looking forward ready to launch at any moment. She was happy neither went charging after the goblins, so she reached down and pet them. The goblins sprinting every which way reminded her of children playing tag in a school yard. Jennifer frowned slightly as she could not remember ever being in a schoolyard before becoming a fragment.

Once the area in front of Jennifer was deserted, she called out, "Hello, umm, anyone out there?"

From behind one of the larger tents, two rows of four armored goblins came out. The goblins wore purple tunics and bronze body armor with matching bronze caps and carried spears. A drumming goblin followed the armored goblins.

Jennifer blinked at the attack force. She remembered only a few days ago when she met goblins for the first time. She thought they were just strange looking green-skinned children with long pointed ears. She looked over the goblins with their weapons in hand coming toward her and smiled. The world was not as strange to her now as it had been only a short while before.

She recognized the second goblin on the right as one of the first goblins she ever met and talked to. Thinking quickly on what to do, Jennifer pointed at herself and said her name.

The goblin's eyes opened in surprised recognition. The goblins legs gave out from under him, causing the soldier in the back to walk straight into him before falling over. When one fell, the others followed like dominos. They were definitely not an elite goblin attack force. The tall goblin she recognized scrambled to his feet, looked at the lead goblin, and started the march again. The other fallen goblins had far more trouble standing up.

The lead goblin held in hand up with a fist, Jennifer guessed this was a signal to stop the goblins.

Jennifer put one hand on her face, while using the other to point behind the lead goblin that stood at the pile of green skinned warriors on the ground. While her palm was still covering her eyes, she noticed the spider was twitching. She guessed he was nervous about meeting the goblins. Rover was using one of his natural legs to rub his new metal one. Taking her hand down, she looked at the goblins.

A cloud of dust surrounded the tangled goblins as they fought amongst themselves with fists flying at one another. The lead goblin yelled at the others only to have another goblin throw a punch at him. The goblin she recognized smartly moved away from the brawl. He was sidestepping his way towards her party.

Kevin edged forward to meet the goblin, but Jennifer decided to greet the goblin first. There was no sense in risking a misunderstanding. Woozle was right beside Jennifer the whole time, staying silent while the known goblin approached the group.

She did not know what to do next

The hesitation was all the goblin needed, but she wanted to act first. The smaller one reached out a hand in front of him and made a petting motion. "Soary," he said with a toothy grin.

After blinking a few times, Woozle was unable to keep in his giggles. Her smile had gone from a smile of greeting to one that was barely holding in a laughter.

Towering over the goblin, she knelt down and hoped that by going to one knee she looked less threatening. She pointed at herself and spoke her name then introduced Woozle and Kevin. She picked up the spider from her shoulder. Rover was excitedly moving around, but she frowned slightly. Rover was vibrating like a car's engine before a race. "Don't worry Rover. They will not hurt you. Even if this does go wrong I will protect you." Looking at the goblin, hoping he would understand, she said, "This is Rover. Do you remember Rover?"

The goblin pointed at himself and said, "Goblin." He petted the spider. "Soary."

Jennifer tilted her head and looked at Woozle. "Goblins have names, right?"

Woozle looked back up to reply. "I've only been assigned to human players. I knew a familiar who was assigned to a train once. Turns out trains have names. But goblins -" he trailed off for a moment. "I think the only named goblins I've ever met were big bosses, like dungeon or raid bosses."

Kevin had circled the goblin and was sniffing him intensely.

There was an itch in her mind that kept repeating itself. *Do goblins have names?*

The question was persistent in her mind. It was important, but she could not remember why.

The goblin did the same to the wolf, sniffing him all over.

Thinking fast for other ways to communicate, she pointed at herself and said, "Human," and pointed at the goblin and said, "Goblin."

Pausing in his sniffing of Kevin, the goblin nodded vigorously at Jennifer.

Speaking to herself, Jennifer mumbled aloud, "Ideas can either be good or bad. Sometimes you will not know which is which until you act upon them." A Cheshire smile made its way onto Jennifer's face as an idea grew in her mind.

She needed to show the goblins what she wanted. Rather than wondering if this was a bad idea or not, she picked up the goblin, turned to Kevin, and said, "Up." Kevin was on all fours with his head leaning to one side looking at Jennifer. Before either the goblin or Kevin could protest, she put the goblin on Kevin's back. "Ride."

To the goblin's credit, he reached right for the welded ring on Kevin's armor, which was in the same place a riding horn would be and did not pull on Kevin's fur. She pointed at the goblin, "Rider." She made sure to say the word loudly, clearly, and with a firmness in her voice.

The goblin looked down at the wolf's head, which was almost as large as the goblin, then back at Jennifer. Kevin's eyes were wide staring at the goblin on his back. The goblin hopped off the wolf's back, shook his head, and waved at Jennifer to follow.

She had been worried that the wolf or goblin would freak out, but them rejecting the idea so plainly had not occurred to her. She wished the wolf and the goblin would have been an instant pair, but her leaf-colored friend led her around the still fighting goblins and the pile of dust they kicked up.

Kevin and Woozle followed the goblin, leaving Jennifer in the back of the line with Rover on her shoulder. The spider was no longer moving or vibrating. Jennifer assumed he was just as shocked as she was when they followed the goblin. She hurried to keep up, not wanting to get separated.

The group followed the goblin who led them through the camp. Jennifer could see as they walked by, many goblin heads peered around corners and through tent flaps. She could not tell if the goblins had recovered from their initial panic or not. She was not attacking them and was even being escorted through the encampment by one of their own. She hoped it was a good sign.

The goblin led the group up to a tent. While not the tallest or biggest, it was on the larger side. It had more of a round, barn-shaped top. Three exposed rings of black poles were used to form the shape of the tent. The rings were held in place by a series of connection points. The tent had an archway with an extended opening, where a goblin sat in a rocking chair beside an open case holding a violin.

The goblin had a striking appearance. His gray mohawk and well-groomed, thick, gray beard would have been enough to stand out since most goblins in the camp had black hair, if any at all. He also wore a black leather jacket that sported metal spikes. The elderly goblin did not stop rocking in his chair, the goblin's eyes narrowed as the group approached.

Her goblin friend stopped a few paces before the gray-haired goblin and spoke loudly. She assumed the younger goblin spoke clearly and loudly due to the older goblin's age.

She looked around as more and more goblins came out from their hiding places to see what was happening. Jennifer made a waving gesture, her palm out adding more wiggling fingers than moving her full hand. A few of the goblins even waved back.

Wanting to make sure her friend was not aggravated, she looked at Kevin. She could tell he was interested in the goings on. He was sitting on his haunches, ears, and face focused on the gray-haired goblin.

Jennifer had no idea what the goblins were saying. She would not be able to make many of the sounds they made. They moved their mouths, but their language was so different and seemed to involve a lot of spit as they spoke.

The gray goblin did not raise his voice as he spoke to the goblin that led them here. The aged goblin looked down and shook his head often.

It occurred to Jennifer that her goblin friend may have been speaking loudly to draw the attention of the other goblins because more were showing up with each passing exchange of words.

The older goblin looked around the group then inspected Kevin. He shook his head once more.

As a crowd formed around Jennifer's party. A goblin pulling a street food wagon also showed up. Jennifer waved beckoning at the food merchant who smiled and threw food her way. Paper wrapped bread smelled delicious. Biting into it she found sautéed meat inside the crispy bread.

Either the fact she was still recovering from mending the spider, that she was starving, or the bun was just that tasty. She decided to get more later.

Without warning, another small goblin with short, chopped black hair ran past Kevin yelling, with anger in her eyes aimed at the gray hair goblin. As more goblins shouted at him, the gray-haired goblin glared at the crowd. The goblin spoke a word in the guttural tongue of his people, and the crowd instantly went quiet. It stood up and reached for the violin. As the old goblin did this, Jennifer looked around at the crowd searching for the possible meaning of this. Gasps and quiet muttering came from the crowd of goblins.

The goblin touched the violin case then looked at Kevin. The goblin said another word Jennifer could not understand but understood the meaning as Kevin stood and walked up to him. Not knowing what to do Jennifer watched as the goblin had said come, or a similar command, and Kevin understood it.

Taking a musician's grip on the violin, the gray-haired goblin's skin faded, revealing his skull but leaving the beard and mohawk. No skin, no muscles, just bone and hair. Grains of sand swirled around the bone goblin and began to flow across him, covering his skin. Where his eyes should have been sat two purple-blue cut gems. As the goblin began to play his beard went from well-groomed to moving wildly under its own power.

Jennifer looked down at her hand being reminded of the wires inside. Those too could move under their own power.

The goblin that led the group here moments ago went from standing proud between Kevin and the sand goblin to cowering behind the wolf. The Great Green Forest Wolf stepped towards the sand-covered goblin, head held high, ears facing forward. He let out a short loud bark, then he took another step forward.

As Kevin moved closer to the sandstorm, that was once just an old goblin, his fur transformed from greenish gray to snow white, the color of snow that forms on a cloudless day in the coldest of winter.

A shiver at the memory of the cold went through Jennifer as she looked at Kevin. His paws and muzzle turned black, as if they had been in the cold for far too long. Where the goblin was heat and sand, Kevin was cold and snowy.

The goblin stopped playing and used his bow to point at a thick old tree. Kevin turned to face the tree and made it as if to bark. But no bark came out. Instead, the howl of the blizzard wind and the snow and ice of a winter burst forth. A short blast of the frigid north hit the tree and cut it cleaner than any axe could.

The sandstorm goblin held the violin in his left hand, as the right hand moved slowly with the bow. The mellow tune coming from the violin became a single note, as both transformed beings returned to normal. Jennifer could see that Kevin was tired and panting from the short transformation. According to the team's menu, Kevin was out of stamina and mana.

The gray-haired goblin looked at Kevin and nodded. He shouted something at the crowd. Half the village seemed to form a line, most came running from behind the tent.

Jennifer moved up to check on her wolf party member. Although his stamina and mana were both recovering, he looked a bit wobbly on his feet. Jennifer checked his paws first, as the gray-haired goblin walked up and down the line of goblins. She found no damage on her friend and scratched him behind the ears before he lay down.

Jennifer thought briefly about crafting potions for Kevin, but her stamina was low, and her mana was only slowly recovering. She was in no shape to be crafting.

She had not realized it, but the goblin leader had walked up and was now standing beside her. Kevin stood up and eyes narrowed at the gray-haired goblin. He took a step between Jennifer and the encroaching green one. He put a hand in front of him with the palm out. Kevin did not move anymore but remained on guard.

Jennifer had no idea why the goblin was looking at her with such intense eyes. The gaze caused her to wrap their arms around themselves and sway slightly where they were standing. He pointed at Jennifer's hand which she very reluctantly moved towards him. The goblin took her hand in his and traced the lines of her palm.

Kevin let out a warning growl.

She was unsure why the older goblin was fixated on her hand or why Kevin was so nervous about it. Both behaviors added to her apprehension. She did not want to be transformed if that was why he was interacting with her.

The goblin paid Kevin no mind, but the line of green people behind him began to thin. When the goblin let go of Jennifer's hand, she sighed with relief and Kevin stopped growling. The gray-haired one put his index finger up to the point of his thumb and made a motion towards his face.

She assumed the goblin was asking if she was hungry, so she smiled and nodded, rubbing her stomach in a circular motion. Jennifer had either answered that she was hungry or pregnant. Either way, the goblin turned and yelled something. The line quickly scattered only to be replaced moments later with goblins bringing her food. One way or another, Jennifer was not going to be hungry.

The first goblins to return brought simple things like fruits and vegetables. She ate the food as it came in. The next wave brought sandwiches, followed by cooked meals. Most brought Jennifer food, then got back into line. She was only able to finish the food from the first five goblins, Jennifer's stamina was as full as it could get. Her health and mana were also full. She decided to store the food that would not go bad in her inventory and just nibble the rest. Sitting cross-legged, she watched the scene before her.

The gray-haired goblin brought other goblins up to Kevin. He would smell the goblin, circle the goblin, and either shake his head or nod.

Jennifer had no idea what factors played into Kevin's decisions. Those who received a nod, moved into another queue. While those who got the shake either left or sat near Jennifer and waited.

As the second line continued to fill, the elder goblin had a quiver filled with arrows delivered to him.

Jennifer imagined they were for some kind of archery contest. She pictured a goblin riding on the back of a wolf shooting arrows.

The gray-haired goblin led the second line of goblins to a tree near the one that had fallen to the blizzard breath. He took an arrow out of the quiver, put the arrowhead against his throat, and leaned toward the tree, resting the butt of the arrow against the bark. Dropping his hand, he saw the only thing holding the arrow in place was the weight of his neck.

Time slowed. Jennifer's voice caught in her throat as she instinctively crafted a potion and started to rush to his aid of a goblin who just stepped into an arrow. She was trying to make sense of why a goblin would do this to himself when his neck would be cut.

But the shaft of the arrow snapped before she got to her feet. When the goblin turned, only a small cut on his neck remained. It was like a cut someone would get while shaving. He held the two parts of the broken arrow, one in each hand. The goblin talked to the crowd then motioned one of the selected goblins forward to do the same.

Relieved, Jennifer went back to her position on the ground. She knew what was going to happen but remained just as tense. Something could easily go wrong. The body of the arrow might not break, or the tip of the arrowhead could be extra sharp, or the arrow could break entirely and the sharp wood could slice into them.

It only took three goblins breaking the body of the arrow before one did go wrong. Jennifer rushed over and poured the healing potion directly on the goblin.

The words of the old goblin came out slow. Even in another language, the meaning was clear. She was not to interfere. The next goblin to make an error with the arrow, would not be receiving a healing position.

That was not something Jennifer could do. She glared at the smaller green one before her, twisting her lip into a snarl.

Giant intimidation has failed.

She swore she would help the next goblin. Kevin clamped onto her robes with his teeth and pulled Jennifer back. When she returned to her spot, the ceremony continued.

Thankful for the excess of food she had, she was able to regain her lost stamina from casting Craft Healing Potion. She could even refill her two stamina and healing potions for when things went wrong. Not if, when.

The line thinned quickly because many goblins left after the first goblin failed the test. But there were no more punctured throats. After the last goblin broke the final arrow, the gray-haired goblin spoke in a loud voice to the successful goblins. The crowd watched. When the gray-haired goblin finished speaking, all of the goblins moved around the encampment with purpose. Some went to gather firewood while others laid out stones. The villagers made a long and narrow firepit about the width of Jennifer's leg and about eight of her paces long.

She figured they were going to make an enormous fire then have the goblins walk over the coals. She vaguely remembered doing something like this at some point but could not pin down the memory. Then Jennifer had an idea. She took one of the sticks meant for the fire and then she used Dark Pulse on the tip. The stick did not catch fire. After several attempts, she finally got it to light. It was the same yellow orange flame as normal. She was hoping for a dark fire similar to the attack, but all she did was use a lot of mana.

The gray-haired goblin came up beside her. This time Kevin did not make any attempt to intercept him. The goblin looked at Jennifer's lit stick and smiled. Jennifer handed it over, and the elder goblin called to the others, speaking in a loud voice while holding forth the burning stick. After a few moments of speaking to the other goblins, the gray-hair goblin turned to Jennifer and made a gesture with his free hand. With his arm and palm out, the goblin made a pew-pew noise she recognized.

A smile broke out on her face, and she understood what the goblin wanted.

The fire ignited with the first blast, burning brightly, and quickly. While the wood was burning, the gray-haired goblin once more took up his violin and, with soothing musical notes, transformed. While in his sandstorm form, ground moved, almost danced over the fire. Initially, the fire glowed brighter, but as the sand fell, the fire went out, leaving only steam and red coals.

Leaving his sandstorm form, the old goblin took off his shoes and socks and walked barefoot across the coals. He moved deliberately, each step showing confidence in his stride. He stepped in one of the glowing red spots as if it was nothing. When he was done, Jennifer rushed over to give him a healing potion. He smiled through his beard and gently pushed the healing potion away.

Jennifer had mixed emotions about this. She wanted to help and heal people. On the other hand, it was the goblin's choice, and this was probably something cultural for them. Plus, she respected that by refusing her help, the older goblin showed that he was not a do-as-I-say-not-as-I-do elder.

When coming here, Jennifer had assumed that Kevin would find a goblin in a cowboy hat, and that goblin would become his rider. Kevin would have a partner and be stronger. And that would be that.

So far, Kevin had to accept the rider, then [AP1] they had to have the bravery to almost impale their throat on an arrow followed by literally walking over fire. Jennifer felt herself shaking, she lit the fire they would be walking on. They would be hurt, and she would not be allowed to heal them. She sat down cross-legged and tried not to ball her fist in anger. Kevin came up beside her, nudged her with his head, and lay down with his head in Jennifer's lap. Jennifer smiled at Kevin and pet him behind the ear.

The gray-haired goblin yelled at the remaining prospects who stared at the field of coals, one by one the goblins attempted the crossing. Most did not make it to the halfway point. Out of the many who tried, only three goblins made it all the way.

Kevin inspected the three remaining goblins.

Jennifer could not tell much about the goblins other than one was female and the other two were male. Or rather she assumed the one was female because of the chest band she wore. She had trouble telling most of them apart. Since the game system copied people, she figured it must be the same with goblins. The goblins were not exactly the same, but many closely resembled another.

Jennifer looked up in the sky. The sun was much lower than she was expecting. This had taken more time than she thought. She got up, dusted herself off, and called to Kevin, pointing at the sun, hoping he understood there was a time issue.

Kevin made a circle around the goblins before choosing the one she assumed was the female. Jennifer turned to Woozle who watched the whole process in silent interest. They stood to go but stopped when the gray-haired goblin held a bag up for Jennifer.

He passed her the bag, and when she looked inside, she saw something that made her smile and her eyes well up. Inside were two items, a purple Bishop's University hoodie, the word Bishop's was printed in black on the purple top against a gold backing. The second item was a pair black sweatpants with the word Bishop's printed in purple with a golden backdrop down the right leg. She put the new clothes into her inventory.

Jennifer immediately hugged the goblin in thanks. The goblin patted her on the back as the two embraced. When the hug was over, he spoke to another pair of goblins, then hurried to Kevin who then gave a low bark.

Jennifer looked over her menus for the party interface and did not see the new female goblin as part of their group. She tried to send the goblin a party invite but received a notification that the recipient of the party invite was invalid.

"The goblin counts as Kevin's pet," Woozle answered before she could ask. "If you look at the party menu and focus on Kevin's name, you should be able to expand for more information and see the goblin as a pet."

Jennifer did as she was instructed and looked for the goblin's name but only found him listed as 'Goblin'. She was able to see the goblin's health, stamina, and mana bars. As a precaution, she cast her force field spell on Kevin and his goblin partner, and it succeeded without issue.

"I guess all goblins are just called goblins. Unless they're a goblin boss." She shrugged and looked at Woozle.

She thanked and said her goodbyes to the gray-haired goblin and the goblin from the attack force. She turned on her navigation skill and headed back to town.

CHAPTER 12

PAPER RAID

JENNIFER JOGGED TOWARDS TOWN. She picked up the pace yet never let her stamina drop too low. She slowed periodically to allow it to build back up.

While she was setting the pace of the jog, Kevin easily kept up, but the goblin rider had trouble staying on his back.

She stopped to take a break and eat some of the food in her storage because she needed to keep her stamina topped off. She also wanted to change into the Bishop's sweat shirt and pants but did not like the idea of getting undressed and redressed in the open. When she entered her menus, she figured out that with a few mental commands, that the change could be done instantaneously. She changed clothes.

Bishop's Hoodie and pants - set bonus plus 15% experience.

Kevin removed his armor, too. When the team began running again, the goblin was able to hold on much easier but was covered in sweat. Jennifer saw how much effort the little goblin was putting in just riding. She hoped when the goblin leveled up, it would be able to choose a skill or power that made it easier to ride.

After two more quick breaks, the group was able to make it back to the town just before sunset. When Jennifer got to the guard house, the gate had been left open with no one inside. She was impressed that it had been remade and upgraded with a metal gate and a stone guard house. A sign on the outside of the guard house read, "Raid night. Enter at your own risk. Evil players will be rejected from the town." She shrugged and entered the town.

Even after participating in the blood ritual, she was not considered evil. Woozle had no issues. Her spider used a trap door to go from in front of the guard house to Jennifer's shoulder rather than wait. Kevin and his new pet goblin also had no issues entering the gate. The town had changed a lot as barriers were set up and the windows boarded up. It was a strange sight, but the town was getting ready for a raid, so it made sense for them to be prepared.

Jennifer looked at her friends list in her menus to find Sarah No Val and Large Soup Bowl. She sent them group invites. Both of them accepted quickly. Jennifer followed her mini map markers, which showed the two were in an open field.

Sarah wore a new black and white suit and she looked ready for action. The ninja had on the same clothes he always wore. As Kevin put his armor back on, his goblin looked around confused.

Jennifer was either going to have to learn goblin or that goblin was going to have to learn common. The same went for Kevin. Jennifer knew taking the mining skill would be helpful but being able to speak to others would be nice.

Dozens of other teams gathered and waited for the raid. Her heart was racing. A smile edged onto her face. This was going to be her first raid and something was going to happen. Which was something she really should have asked before.

"Hey listen!" A red robed, gray bearded man said while tugging on his companion's green tunic.

"Hey, listen?" The one in the green asked. The one in the red pointed at Jennifer.

"Hey, listen!" The one in the robe repeated with a laugh.

"Hey listen, you really should get rid of the familiar. They're just annoying. They are only helpful to noobs." The one in green said. Jennifer had no context to interpret the two repeating the words 'hey listen', or the word 'noob' but she felt offended.

"I am useful?" The words were quiet. Woozle was looking down at the ground. His ears dropped to the side. "I am useful."

Jennifer picked up her familiar and put it in her hoodie. "Yes, you are."

"No, he is not. All he will do is repeat things and point out the obvious. Water is wet and you should not walk into walls. Bah, get rid of him so we do not have to hear it speak." The gray bearded one spoke.

"He is my friend." Jennifer glared at him.

Giant Intimidation Successful

She ignored the two men and turned back to her group.

"So, what's a paper raid?" Jennifer asked her party.

Sarah's facepalm was so aggressive she almost slapped herself. Large Soup Bowl had a huge question mark above his head. But Kevin and his goblin just looked around at the other groups. Jennifer was happy at least they did not think her question was bad.

"Request more information on raid," Large Soup Bowl asked with no emotion in his voice.

Sarah blinked rapidly in Soup Bowl's direction, in what Jennifer assumed was surprise. "This is the town's paper raid. It's called that because it's a single enemy that will be copied many times. Like creating photocopies of the same thing. The enemy type is going to be a basic AI, so no copies of any person."

"There are faction scores with each of us belonging to a different one. My part of the faction score is going to the company. Jennifer, as you're part of the town, your faction score goes to the town. I have a vague idea where Soup Bowl's or Kevin's are going to go -" Sarah trailed off thinking about something but waved her hand before continuing on, "Then there's a team score. We're team Jennifer because she counts as our team leader, and she hasn't changed the name. There are individual scores, also."

"So, my name will be on the scoreboard with how many of the copies I'm able to defeat?" Jennifer asked, knowing with her power set that she was not going to be doing much damage in this raid.

Sarah smiled at Jennifer's question. "The point total is calculated on what participants do. Healing does a lot of good and scores a lot of points."

"Normally, this town starts off at a gray level. They get to green about one in ten times. But with the dinosaur team and all the other teams the mayor was able to bring in, I wouldn't be surprised if we get to blue or maybe even yellow." Sarah rambled without explaining everything.

But before Jennifer found a place to ask, Woozle interrupted and took the tone of a lecturer. "When you see the names of others, there is normally a color or black. Black means they're too low to get experience from. Grey is the lowest you can get experience from. White means equal level, so white can fade to black, or fade to red, and rise through the colors. Orange, yellow, green, blue, ending in purple. There are rumors that there are silver and even gold, but I've never found proof of those."

Jennifer cast bubbles around her party, including pets, and waited for the raid to start. She did not have to wait long. The mayor made a speech from on top of a bench in the field. She was not paying attention to what he was saying. She was rubbing her palms together in excitement for her first raid. She caught bits and pieces, something about showing the dinosaurs a good time, prosperity for the town, and the micro foundry being repaired. For all the speech was worth to Jennifer, the mayor could have been saying, "Blah, blah, blah."

The sun was down, but the red smeared sky had not embraced the night yet. Loud, clear words came from all around, "Paper raid starting in ten, nine, eight…"

She pulled her focus to what her team would need as her pulse raced. She recast her Force Fields on the group while keeping her only weapon, the mop, ready.

Descending from a cloudless sky, came large rectangular gray pieces of paper. Once the papers touched the ground, they became large beavers twice the size of goblins.

Jennifer let out a loud audible, "Aww."

Only a handful of heartbeats later, the rodents charged the line of the town's defenders. The sharp, barred teeth of the beavers made them far less cute and more threatening.

Casting her Force Field onto the other defenders so they would not receive tearing bites while maintaining a watch on her mana, Jennifer focused on her team. She only gave out protection to others when her abilities and status bars allowed her to do so.

While she stood behind the front line, the furry attackers broke through and charged at Jennifer. She was not sure why she had waited, but she activated the dark power, "Summon Undead." One of the undead skeletal wolves instantly took on bodyguard roles. Any beaver that got too close would be intercepted by her soulless minions' fangs.

Sarah No Val was using the same attack pattern she used when Kevin had attacked them: two shots with her gun followed by a laser blast from her watch. Each attack took down an invader.

Large Soup Bowl did his ninja vanish and attacked with a high degree of frequency. He would attack, throw three knives, and then vanish. While this pattern was longer, it only took down two beavers.

Kevin would do the hit and run like the ninja, but he would vary his attacks. Sometimes he would do an ambush attack that cloaked Kevin and his goblin in shadows, then he would jump out with glowing blue fangs. The illuminated teeth of the wolf would rip hard into the beaver that he crunched down on. Other times, he would body check or attack with his paws and use the Growl Debuff, which also worked as a taunt.

While Kevin's goblin was new, she was the most ineffective member of their group. She did not have an effective power or ability to fight with. She was the only member of the party that could not take down a beaver on her own.

Jennifer's Dark Pulse did not have the stopping power that her teammates' had, but the silent predators on her side made up for it. The priority for Jennifer was maintaining the Force Fields on her teammates and shielding the front liners when she could. As the defenders pushed forward, she was thankful that she had not needed to use any of her potions.

She decided to play it safe and de-summoned the skeleton wolves, tagging them for repairs. To her shock, just tagging them triggered her mend skill, removing what minor damage they had received. The difference between her stamina usage when she repaired them inside versus outside of her inventory was negligible.

The papers fell and the beavers came. At this level of the raid, they were no threat. It was repetitive, attack, attack, attack, or casting Force Fields whenever her mana refilled. It was all going well. Almost no one was injured, so Jennifer felt no pressure to pass her healing potions out.

The sky blended colors from red to orange.

Jennifer realized that the town had moved past the easy raid because the rodents were now wearing dark gray padded vests. The attacking beasts now had a layer of protection on.

Kevin bit down on a padded vest. He was no longer able to defeat the attackers in one bite. The larger armored beavers were attacking faster but were not enough to be a threat. She knew she was the team's support system, and focused on her role in the battle. The Force Fields were coming down more often, which put a slow drain on Jennifer's mana so it never fully recharged.

Kevin had his shadows, which made him harder to hit. Large Soup Bowl had his ninja vanish, which briefly made him impossible to target. Jennifer had a skeleton bodyguard. Sarah only had her tailored suit and Jennifer's Force Fields. In terms of protection, the one from the company was dressed for success in the boardroom not the battlefield. Eventually, Jennifer could no longer cast the Force Fields on anyone besides her team, but none of the other groups seemed worse for wear.

The beavers were tougher and hitting harder. Jennifer did not feel any sense of fear. She focused on helping her friends with her powers and abilities.

She was casting a new protective bubble when a car honked and an engine revved. At the noise, the battle stopped as everyone looked for the vehicle. It turned out to be a large, black car with the word Taxi written in silver on the front hood. Several more taxis followed the first.

Jennifer stared in wonder.

The taxis were not stopping as they raced out onto the field. With their high beams on and gaining speed, the vehicles raced right for the raiding party.

CHAPTER 13

GOTTA KEEP MOVING

EVER FEEL LIKE A deer in headlights? A whole raid group was feeling like that.

Jennifer was willing herself to move faster and get out of the way, but she was so much slower than the taxis. She kept thinking, *faster, faster!* only to realize she was also yelling it to the other defenders.

The taxis sped closer with every heartbeat. They were too close and too fast for her. Feet became inches, and she saw the fear on her face in the reflection of a windshield.

The taxi executed an impossible swerve, hitting a beaver, then another, and another. Her eyes went from wide-eyed shock to wide-eyed realization. The vehicles were attacking the rodents as hit and runs.

The orange sky melted away into green, her mind barely registering when the sky was yellow. The taxis were escalating the raid quickly and forcing the defenders farther apart from one another.

It could have been mere seconds since the taxis joined the defense, but those distracted moments could have cost some defenders their lives. Realizing she had not moved in some time, Jennifer shook her head and checked on her own party using her menus. Not only were they still alive, their status bars showed they were safe and doing well.

Woozle stood beside Jennifer, and her spider sat on her shoulder, but she did not see any of her other teammates around. She brought up her mini map. Sarah was the closest, so Jennifer rushed towards her. Woozle jogged along beside her as they ran around the mayhem. She let Woozle and her skeleton wolf attack anything hostile around her.

Jennifer met up with Sarah as the sky showed the threat level go from green to blue. The scenery would have been picturesque if not for the carnage. The noise of the battle and the cars was too great for anyone to communicate verbally. Jennifer pointed at Sarah, and put a thumb up. After a blast from her laser watch, Sarah returned the gesture.

The new wave of beavers had heavy armor, thick helmets, and looked like they spent most of their time in the gym. Plus, they either had a thick black stick with a ball on the end or a futuristic handgun. The blasters came with lots of silver add-on parts. It shot a blue beam of something that did damage and slowed people down.

She quickly cast Force Field on Sarah and checked her health. So far, Sarah had taken less than ten percent damage. Her healing potion would do more than Sarah needed, so she should save the potion until later. Sarah made eye contact with Jennifer while she attacked. Between the taxis, beavers, defenders, and other random noises, it was too loud to talk. Jennifer waved at Sarah to follow, moving towards the next closest companion, Large Soup Bowl.

Large Soup Bowl was harder to track because his ninja vanish made him invisible on the mini map. But Jennifer knew roughly where he was, and since his health was only down a sliver, she wasn't worried. She and Sarah defended themselves as they ran. The attackers were no longer going down easy.

With a sickening crunch, a beaver's long black weapon hit Sarah in the left arm, stopping their small party and blocking their path. With too many of the rodents around them, the pair was unable to run from their attackers. After two of Jennifer's Dark Pulse attacks and Sarah's two gunshots and a laser blast, they only left small dents on the beast's armor. The jaws of a great wolf and her familiar appeared, teeth first on the sides of the beaver's neck. It struggled, trying to dislodge them. Afraid to use her range attacks, Jennifer used the only option remaining. Her mop.

Whacking her opponent in the face was the distraction Sarah needed to unloaded her pistol at close range into the unarmored sections of the attacker. Not staying to watch the animal fall, the group rushed to find Large Soup Bowl.

Stopping in her tracks as the sound of a deep howl came from another direction, her bones chilled from the howl. It was a howl of sadness, a long drawn-out sadness. The icon on her mini map showed her that the ninja was heading to the sound of the howl.

Jennifer recast Force Field on Sarah. Around the group was a lull in the battle. Jennifer sucked in a deep breath. She had no idea if this would work, but she felt what she was about to do was a good move. Letting out a howl of her own, she channeled her fears and anger into it. She poured all her strength into her lungs to make the howl as loud as possible.

Kevin stood beside her before she finished the howl, adding his voice to the call. Other groups headed toward her as well. The beavers and taxis were dealing with each other while other groups found members, forming a new line of defenders. Jennifer smiled and felt proud at how effective her first howl was.

Jennifer used the tip of her mop to draw a circle in the ground. She then drew a larger circle. In equal spacing around the outer circle, she drew smaller circles then arrows pointing counter-clockwise from one circle to another. She put a larger J in the inner circle, and an approximation of a healing potion on the side closer to Jennifer. On the opposite side she put on a scary face with large rodent teeth. She hoped everyone would understand this, as she made eye contact with her teammates. Her group took their places and prepared for the beavers to charge.

She looked around her and saw that other teams seemed disorganized while grouping together, just holding their weapons waiting for the beavers. Jennifer saw one of the taxis explode before hearing the booming noise. For a moment, all she heard was the ringing in her ears as she looked in confusion. She did not have much time before the fighting resumed.

Looking around but not sure who she was looking for, she searched for someone who would be able to organize the defenders quickly. Jennifer pointed at someone that she hoped would fit the role nicely.

The mayor had a dumb look on his face as he pointed at himself.

Jennifer smiled broadly and beckoned the mayor over, flinching as another taxi exploded. As the mayor came closer forward, Jennifer made eye contact with another member from another team and beckoned him over.

As the two were moving towards her, she got back to drawing out her plan in the dirt at her feet. Jennifer drew a line in the dirt. On one side, was where the big teeth and scary face was. On the other side of the line was her already drawn plan. Jennifer drew two more circles, one for each line of defenders on either side of her team.

As expected, the mayor and his team got to Jennifer first. When he arrived, Jennifer pointed at herself then at the middle circle. She pointed at the mayor then at the circle on the right. A look of understanding crossed the mayor's face before giving her a questioning look.

After the second group came up, Jennifer repeated the process. The other person she had summoned was a large teddy bear with a black beard, red cape, and a permanently stitched on jovial expression. The bear seemed to be the leader of the second group. At the very least, she would be able to call others over, give them a plan while preparing for another round of combat.

The stuffed bear took his group to the left, and the mayor took his group to the right. After the mayor waved his team into position, he moved behind Jennifer. Strangely, the mayor's desk appeared between them. She did not know what the mayor was going to do, but she turned so the beavers were in front of her. The mayor and his desk were behind her. A good leader was an excellent communicator, and she hoped that in the fog of war, he would still be able to get the word to the remaining defenders.

Jennifer took in a deep breath and closed her eyes. Even with her eyes closed, she could see her menus. Thanks to the taxis, her team had recovered their health and stamina. Her stamina was partly grayed out, but her other status bars were full. The summoned wolf skeleton's health was down to slightly below half while her de-summoned skeleton was back up as full as she could make it. She switched out the wolf skeletons and started the repairs.

When Jennifer opened her eyes, the sky was blue, with the last taxi speeding towards Jennifer. Looking to her right and left she saw other teams setting up to re-engage the beavers. With more teams taking up their positions, time slowed. With the last taxi heading her way, her mind worked faster. Jennifer had no idea what the intention of the taxi was but trusted it would not attack any of the defenders. Risking a look, she glanced over to see what the mayor was doing. He was at his desk, writing messages and handing them to those strange blue birds.

Jennifer turned as the taxi swerved to a stop. A tall dark-skinned man stepped out of the vehicle with a dark blue fedora in one hand and the neck of an electric guitar in his other. He smiled warmly, put on his hat, and walked by Jennifer.

The beavers were too close for her to focus on him. Jennifer cast Force Field on the two teammates in front of her, Kevin and Large Soup Bowl, just as the beavers hit the line of defenders.

The battle was on them now. The line held but barely, and the Force Fields were going down faster then she could cast. After Kevin's shield went down, he ran behind Jennifer. Sarah took his place and finished off the rodent.

The beavers were now wearing shiny, thick body armor with dark-visored helmets that covered their heads completely. Half of them were attacking with glowing, blue, long swords that shot bolts of crackling lightning when they made contact. Those that attacked at range were either wearing wizard hats, casting flying wooden stakes that flew at high speed, or wielded large shoulder mounted cannons shooting blue bolts.

Jennifer cast Force Field on Kevin when she heard the electric guitar play behind her. It was loud, clean, complex, and rich in sound. She did not recognize the tune, but it had a good beat. She saw two new icons showing two buffs in her menu, **Perfect Timing**, and **Eclectic Rock Blues**. The buffs affected her entire team. She did not have time to check what the buffs did, but she was able to cast Force Field faster, both in how fast she could cast and between castings.

Each time a teammate's Force Field went down, they would retreat behind Jennifer until she could recast it. With the use of the protective bubbles, her teammates only took a few points of damage. At any given moment, two of her teammates were in front of her with one behind. Even with the musically induced decrease in casting time, Jennifer never had time to cast the protective bubble on herself, Woozle, Jennifer's skeleton, or Kevin's goblin. All three were acting as Jennifer's bodyguards and attacked any of the raiders who got close to her. Jennifer's mana was slowly going down because she was casting faster than it could recover. Since her summoning and repairing the skeletons was draining her stamina too, she needed to be careful.

The music played and the battle continued. If it was a movie, it would have been awesome. Jennifer was terrified. Beavers were screaming as they attacked. She could barely keep up with her Force Fields, and her teammates were taking damage. They were winning every fight but were on track to lose the battle. The attacking rodents were unending, and defenders were going down slowly.

Her teammates were getting hurt. Sarah was the first one to lose enough health for Jennifer to hand her one of the two healing potions she had in stock. As soon as the potion was drunk, the vial swam through the air, returning to Jennifer. As soon as the vial was back, she recast a healing potion, which dropped her stamina below the halfway mark. Weighing the odds, she downed a stamina potion. The green contents of the container recovered her stamina, but it would just add fuel to her tank for a short time.

Jennifer was in a good position with stamina and health, at the moment, but her near constant casting of Force Fields had her mana below the one third mark. She had no way to recover it. If this kept up, she would be useless. The only thing that kept her going was her refusal to give up.

Two loud chimes rang out over the battlefield, and a cheer rose up from a lot of the defenders.

The sky was blue. The beavers did not change, but more papers fell from the sky. The music kept Jennifer in a rhythm of casting, handing out healing potions as needed, or eating something rather than taking her last stamina potion.

Before she knew it, a few things happened. First, Jennifer ran out of mana. With her mana recovery, she would only be able to keep up a single force field about half the time. Since Sarah did not have any dodge abilities and had taken the most damage, Jennifer decided to focus on her.

The second thing to happen was the defense line fell. She only found out at a later time, the other defenders not only moved back but many fell in battle. On her mini map, she saw the other defenders as blue dots and the attacking beavers were red dots. The green dots were her team. With the battle escalating, blue and red dots were blinking out while her team was still at full.

Finally, she got a new notification. Full. Jennifer could no longer eat to recover stamina, and she was in no position to recover stamina safely. She smiled. Right now they were going to lose and she had no intention of giving up or abandoning her team, no matter the cost. She was not going down without making them pay in fur for every inch they took in their onslaught. She had already faced a scenario like it today, and she would not let this new threat stop her either.

The man with the guitar belted out a song. "Got to keep moving, got to keep moving. There's a hell hound on the trail." The words sounded a bit off, but Jennifer felt a new buff. **Got to keep moving**. Jennifer's mana and stamina changed from draining to recovering, but it was not enough.

A green dot went down, but she refused to give in. Kevin's pet was no longer throwing stones. Somehow, the little goblin had gotten a hold of one of the blue energy spouting blasters. She smiled as she kept pulling the trigger, missing more than she hit, but every little bit helped.

Jennifer continued to triage her team. Her teammates were below half in terms of health, while she was at full health having not been injured by an attack. Large Soup Bowl had less than half his health bar, but his mana never moved. His stamina remained over seventy-five percent. With his ability to ninja vanish, he was by far the hardest to hit.

Kevin had the most verified attacks, along with his goblin. This made him the highest damage dealer, but he paid the price for it. He took most of the potions but his health was only around one third, and his mana and stamina were below half. His armor looked like it was going to need repairs.

Sarah had no dodges but seemed to be able to take attacks the best. For some reason, Sarah was attacked the most. Sometimes when the rodents were attacking others, Sarah shot them and they would charge her, leaving themselves open for whoever they were attacking before. She had a little over ten percent health. Her mana was around three fourths, and her stamina was about the same.

The blues player's chorus of "Gotta Keep Moving" was Jennifer's mantra. Not stopping and not pausing, she kept on going. She was huffing and puffing in spite of having done the least damage. The summoned wolf skeleton was around twenty-five per cent, so Jennifer switched them out. She wanted to start repairs, but that was not a good idea, and she knew it. The battle had become a blur. Her movements on repeat. Casting force field, using a healing potion, return the vial, and stand on the circle. The only attacks Jennifer had made were with her mop when a beaver got past her minion protectors because she could not spare the mana for her dark attacks. Her arms felt like jelly. Each action she took was weaker than the last.

The beaver's battle line was thin, but so was the defender's. Jennifer could not tell who was falling faster at this point. Thankfully, no more papers fell from the sky. The revitalisation from the song was helping, but not much. She could cast one more craft healing potion before tapping out, becoming a liability rather than an asset. She just needed to keep moving, keep going, and not to stop.

At the start of the battle, Jennifer estimated that there were around two hundred defenders. She estimated that there were around fifty left. She was still standing and defending. Sarah, Ninja, Kevin, his goblin, and a wolf skeleton remained.

The beavers suddenly stopped attacking and reverted from rodents back into paper. The papers turned to ash.

Jennifer dropped to the ground in exhaustion, breathing heavily.

The battle's anthem stopped playing. The blues man packed up his guitar, got back into the taxi, and left without even a goodbye wave.

She cast her final craft healing potion, as she called to Sarah.

Sarah rushed up to Jennifer. "No time for rest. Now it's time for the hard part."

Jennifer felt her breath catch, but she was too tired to display her reaction. "That was the easy part?"

Three chimes rang out over the battlefield followed by the words,

Raid Boss Incoming.

Jennifer's heart sank. That sounded bad.

She looked on as the ash gathered, turning into the last piece of paper falling from the sky. This one was far bigger than all the previous papers. It was larger than Jennifer.

The mayor and his team were on her right, while a new team that she had not seen before stood on her left. They seemed to be some kind of lizard folk. Slightly shorter than Jennifer, the lizard in front had dark gray skin, which was more like a hide with folds, giving it an armor-plated appearance. He had a large, thick looking shell on his back with spikes coming out of the sides. Powerful arms, as thick as Jennifer's thighs, flexed and swung a war hammer with a mini jet engine on one side. The lizard man also had a tail with a bulge on the end.

The second more attractive dinosaur wore clothes that accented her features but gave her no protection from the battle. She had an exotic curved bow but no arrows.

A colorful bird-like creature that stood on two legs was the third member of their party. It had a flat snout, short forelimbs with oversized hand-like talons, and a large sickle-shaped claw on each foot. Its feathers were royal purple, and he had a matching pointed wizard's hat and a staff that was illuminated with gold on one end. He also had a long cap that came down over his shoulder, being held in place with a golden rope. Under the snout of this hung a fake beard that looked taped on the sides, leaving a gap under the mouth.

The last member of the team was a head taller than Jennifer, wearing thick, black body armor that looked like it came off one of the beavers. Black metal armor encased his legs and arms. This one seemed to be the tank of the group, who was able to take the most damage and be on the front line. He had three horns and a large shield-like crest growing out of his head along with a beak-like mouth. This triceratops lizard man was armed with a thick white shield of unknown material and a sword that Jennifer would have trouble carrying with both hands. He was also taking practice swings.

Jennifer focused on her breathing, trying to remain calm when she turned her attention back to the falling piece of paper that would be the raid boss. Time slowed again as she watched the page fall. Having no idea what to expect, fear creeped into her heart. It was too much. She was exhausted and could not keep the self-doubt from racing through her mind.

The longer the paper took to fall, the faster her heartbeat.

When the page finally landed, a dozen strange birds burst out of the ground. They were large webbed foot creatures covered in light brown feathers, where each row of feathers was marked by a white line. Their necks were black, long and elegant, ending in a snake's head. Many of the birds hissed a warning.

Jennifer whispered to herself, "Cobra-chickens." She had never seen anything like these birds before. Some forgotten memory told her these avians were to be feared.

From inside the birds' circle, a metal creature clawed its way out of the ground as if it came from the underworld itself.

As the final boss popped out from the hole, relief washed over Jennifer. Behind a clear protective layer on the head was a beaver with an eye patch. The raid boss seemed to be just another beaver. A beaver that was wearing exoskeleton power armor and a greatsword with leaves that spun around it. But still. She had been worried that something even more monstrous than the cobra-chickens was going to come out of that circle.

Kevin was the first to charge, taking out one of the cobra-chickens with his glowing blue fangs before attacking the exoskeleton. The beaver swung its sword to meet Kevin straight on. The leaves that spun around the sword cut like razors before the sword sliced into him. The blade passed through the great forest wolf's body as if he was nothing but air.

Kevin was gone, the system removing the remains. Kevin's goblin also vanished. The battlefield went silent.

Jennifer stared dumbfounded at where Kevin had been. He was tough, so going down like that stunned her. She now realized that the bigger threat had to be the beaver, but she still felt more terror looking at the cobra-chickens.

The mayor's voice got Jennifer moving again. "Tanks up front. Damage dealers attack at range. Focus on the add-ons first. Melees be careful!"

Jennifer was confused at the word use of tanks. She looked around. A few potential candidates stood among the defenders that fit the description. One was a female humanoid in a uniform, sporting high heels and a backpack. Her feet never touched the ground. She floated in the air with two ship hulls each having naval cannons protruding from her backpack on both sides. She was a mix between a girl and a ship, and yet there were no actual tanks. The defenders could have really used one.

Jennifer had no idea what an add-on was, and she was no damage dealer. The triceratops lizard man rushed into melee range, ignoring the cobra-chickens, and flashed red and blue lights on the top of his shield. A siren sounded from the shield drawing all eyes to him. The head of the exoskeleton turned to face the triceratops. It was clear he wanted the boss's attention, and he was getting it. Jennifer cast her Force Field on him.

The raid boss's leaf sword came down in an arc of destruction but was blocked by the triceratops's shield. Jennifer's bubble popped like a balloon before the blade even reached it. The mayor appeared on top of the exoskeleton in a blinding flash of light, bringing a violet colored arc of electrical strikes down onto the boss.

Sarah shot at the cobra-chickens, as did most of the remaining town protectors.

The wizard hat wearing lizard man group cast a high-speed, small meteor at the beaver's exoskeleton.

An elf with dark skin rushed past Jennifer. The elf's skin was not just dark but wooden like, having the appearance of having grown out of wood found in dark forests. Her pointed ears overlapped with her short black hair. She wore a red pullover with a logo of a black handprint on a black dress. The elf laughed with a disturbing hint of insanity, and shouted, "Pop quiz."

Her power was aimed at the cobra-chickens, who were suddenly sitting at a desk and hunching over with trembling muscles.

"Nightmare quiz. Power of the substitute teacher. Recess is canceled. I am calling your parents."

The words alone made Jennifer's spine shiver with fear even though the powers did not affect her, but she wished to avoid substitute teachers like this wooden elf in the future.

Mentally shaking herself, she did not feel useful to the events happening around her. She felt the need to do something, Jennifer recast Force Field on the triceratops, but she knew that was little to no use. The cobra-chickens had all been taken out, leaving the defenders to focus on the boss who was attacking the triceratops.

Whenever the beaver sword met anyone other than the Triceratops, it would end that defender's time on the battlefield.

Jennifer did not want to think about where the defender went or who they would be leaving behind. She was saving others by being on this battlefield, but it hurt even letting her mind wander in that direction. She just needed to keep moving like the musician's song. She was low on stamina and mana. Her summoned skeleton was down to less than twenty-five percent health, Woozle was nowhere to be seen, her spider was still on her shoulder, Kevin was gone, Large Soup Bowl was attacking and vanishing as fast as he could, and Sarah shot her gun and laser as fast as she could.

With the barnyard serpents out of the way, the final one falling to the unannounced tests, the remaining teams attacked the beaver's exoskeleton, but it did not show any signs of slowing down.

The triceratops's shield cracked with a metallic noise that rang out over the battlefield. They were losing again. The defenders outnumbered the raid boss forty to one. But their forty had been fifty not long ago, while the beaver showed no signs of being defeated.

Jennifer stepped back then took a second step. Being out of the danger zone, she closed her eyes and took a deep breath. She needed a moment to think. Giving up was not an option to her.

Opening her eyes, she looked for a weakness. The beaver's primary attack was with its sword. However, Jennifer noticed a weaker and much slower punch came from the other arm. Both attacks were telegraphed, easy to see when it was coming and where it was aiming. She watched the raid boss make another attack and realized that the upper body of the exoskeleton must be on a swivel. If Jennifer could somehow stop the mechanism from swiveling, the exoskeleton would not be able to attack.

The mayor was still on top of the power armor, riding the beaver like a rodeo cowboy , continuing to bring down the lightning on the external covering of the raid boss.

Jennifer examined where the waist would be on the exoskeleton, but she saw no way to get in and stop the attacks from that point. Looking for another weak point, she noticed the punching arm was the counterbalance. If she caught that punch, they would be able to stop the attack, but then what? Even if the beaver's arm was stuck, what else could she do?

The right side of her mouth curled into a smile. "When in doubt, go for the knees!" Jennifer was now the woman with a plan.

"Get ready to web someone," Jennifer said to her spider as she started to run up to the triceratops lizard man. He was by far the most likely one to fill the role of the rock, while everyone else was going to be the hard place.

The shield of the triceratops was broken in two, but The lizard man was now taking the attacks on the remaining part of his shield. She rushed up next to him and yelled her question between the swings of the sword. "How strong are you?"

He shouted, "I am the strongest!"

He was either an egomaniac or their best shot. "Drop your shield and catch the next punch." She instructed the prime defender while miming what she wanted done.

The triceratops gave her an are-you-crazy look.

She was not going to let any doubt play on her face. "You got a better idea?"

The triceratops deflected the sword blow, threw down his shield, and caught the arm of the boss.

"Rover, web them together!"

As he did, the triceratops eyes went wide in panicked confusion followed by the dawning of recognition. The lizardman and the beaver were now in a contest of strength, neither able to move but both struggling. The mechanical augmented monstrosity only took steps when it was not attacking. There was only a binary option, move or attack. Both of these options used many of the some components, much like how people only need to bind the wrists or a person to stop their arms. Now the beaver was trying to step back as the triceratops was trying to hold it in place.

The defenders were all attacking wherever they could. Most of the attacks landed on the armor where it was thickest.

Walking with purpose and far more confidence than she felt, she moved over to the beaver. Jennifer made eye contact with the mayor as he was raining down lighting using his own body as a conduit. Her actions made him stop attacking and watch her.

Now or never. This was going to work, or they were going to lose. Jennifer only had one weapon, a mop. She was going to have to use her weapon in an expert manner for this to work. She stood right in front of the exoskeleton and could see the milky black eyes of the beaver. There was fear in those eyes. This was working.

Jennifer rested the tip of her mop against the inner elbow of the raid boss's exoskeleton outstretched punching arm. Where a hinge was locked in place until the last moment of the attacks were delivered. Jennifer looked up at the mayor and nodded. After she got out of the way, everyone on the battlefield attacked that spot. Jennifer rushed back to the triceratops and waited for the next part.

Seconds is all it took before bits of armor fell off from the battle damage. The lizard man, wielding the jet hammer, broke off the exoskeleton's arm.

The triceratops lizard man still held the exoskeleton in place on the still attached arm. As she hid behind the lizard man, Jennifer pointed at the left knee gear using the tip of the mop again. The survivors took the prompt and attacked the knee joint. Again, the lizard man and his rocket hammer struck the last blow, and the leg broke off at the knee joint.

The exoskeleton could not make any attacks while missing its primary attack weapon having its punching arm held in place and now missing one leg. Jennifer dashed out from behind the triceratops lizard man and pointed at the shoulder joint that connected to the remaining arm with her mop.

Again, the remaining defenders knew what to do, they laid on all they could with arrows, lighting bolts, and throwing axes. After a short pause, the melee defenders lined up for a turn, each using their most powerful attack. This gave the range users time to reload or recover mana.

"Ninja attack." Sounded out as the arm broke off the mechanical body.

Something moved inside the exoskeleton.

She took in a deep breath, holding it in anticipation.

The wreckage broke off in small parts, and rained down from the beaver's body as he left the protection of his machine armor.

A chorus of battle music played from the same place that had signaled the stages of the raid, and the sky went a few shades darker.

The beaver wore the familiar padded, black body armor and carried a cannon, which looked like it belonged on a pirate ship.

The music sounded as if it was sung by a choir in an ancient language, a route tongue language, with easily pronounced words. Most of the words ended in an "us" sound.

She glared and marched up to the beaver. "Surender now!" The words came out as angry as she was, loud and hot. She held her mop ready. Time slowed as the other defenders readied themselves, many looking exhausted. Jennifer assumed others were hoping the raid would be over after defeating the exoskeleton. Jennifer held her breath, trying to steady herself on her feet, waiting for the beaver to either comply or attack.

After more heart beats than she could count on her fingers and toes, she let out her breath. "Umm, hello?" she said, trying to prompt the beaver into deciding. She looked around at the other defenders, but they were also frozen. She had no idea what was going on. When time slowed a moment ago, she had been fighting for her life, so she assumed it was from adrenaline. But not only did time slow down, it had stopped.

"Did you ask one of the greatest threats to the turtle to surrender?" asked a voice that dripped with disbelief.

Jennifer looked around to see where the voice was coming from but could not place it. She answered with far less confidence than she felt, "Yes."

"That is very much not something that happens when beavers come down for real raids. It is more boom boom, bang bang." The cultured voice sounded like someone educated trying to talk to a child.

"This has happened before, but never with beavers," another female voice said.

But again, Jennifer could not see who was speaking or from where.

A third deeper voice with more authority said, "This was just a paper raid. According to the system notes, surrender is possible."

The first cultured voice said, "Yes, but from the players, not the paper copy. We have no data on what is needed to be done for him to surrender. He always fought while the other grabbed whatever wasn't nailed down."

"Umm, hello, my name is Jennifer. Could you come out please?" She had no idea what was going on or who was talking, but this world did make someone crazy.

"She wasn't stopped?" the female voice asked.

"She was the one asking for surrender, and she's barely more than a paper copy herself," said the cultured voice.

"I sped her time sync up with us. The Dev is too busy for this, so it's up to us to decide. Besides, I wanted to hear her opinion," the deep voice said.

"Umm, which Dev are we talking about?" Jennifer had some idea on who the Developers were, but maybe getting a name of one could help her.

"The Dev." Three voices said in unison.

A short man in a red lab coat appeared before Jennifer. The little man had the letters GM embossed on the coat. He had the same beard as the little man that had handed Jennifer the red egg that became Woozle, but his hair and build were different. Recognition filled her mind as the man appeared. A woman and another man, both in lab coats, appeared before her. The woman was poking the beaver with a stick, and the other man looked disinterested.

Jennifer was nervous and the silence made her more uncomfortable. "What does GM stand for?" she asked before she could stop herself.

The woman answered first, "Game Master."

The second man with the cultured voice said, "General Manager."

The one with the deep voice answered, "Ghost in the machine. There is some debate as you can see. Now, before you ask any more silly questions, what were you going to do if the beaver surrendered to you?"

She looked around, unsure what to say. Her eyes fell upon the mayor, still frozen and looking like he was about to shoot lightning out of his hands. With a shrug, she said, "I would make him work for the town and repair any damages, or task him with improving the town?"

Jennifer glanced at her teammates seeking advice in their frozen forms. Her forehead wrinkles thinking about what she should say. Tilting her head from side to side, weighing choices.

"Bah, she has no idea. She is no general, king, or even mayor. If we let the surrender happen, it's just a wasted path," the woman argued.

"Hostages," the cultured man said. "They come for the hostages."

The words sent a chill down Jennifer's spine. She did not want to be a hostage taker, and she glared at the man who made the suggestion.

The one with the deep voice smiled. "As a gnome, a keeper to the system I declare. Your Giant Intimidation racial ability has activated on the beaver, and he has surrendered to you. Good luck." With a finger wave the trio disappeared, time resumed, and the music stopped.

"Victory goes to the defenders," said a powerful voice that seemed to come from all around.

The defenders cheered as the beaver dropped his cannon to the ground and looked down.

Jennifer searched frantically for her teammates, glancing at her team interface to check for their names. She froze. Kevin's name was still grayed out, as was Woozles. She made sure one of the skeletons was in her inventory, but the one that was out had been destroyed. She had lost track of it in the battle.

She needed to find Woozle. Her eyes darted quickly from person to person on the battlefield. Seeing how few of the defenders were left. They were cheering and looking like this was all fun and games, but so many were missing. Her heart raced to the point that it hurt. She could not focus on her breathing. Her heart was beating so hard she could hear it. Her hands were clasped together so tightly they were white. She had no idea what to do next. She needed guidance and someone to talk to. She needed her first friend from this world. What was she going to do? When Jennifer saw the mayor, her eyes watered.

***

Intermission 1: Kevin

Kevin breathed out as he exited his game pod. The village won the raid. His team even came in fifth overall in terms of points. He had no idea how the points were totalled, but since this was a beta version of the new game, and no one else was playing it yet, coming in fifth to non-player characters seemed like a let-down to him.

He had not expected the game to be so good when he got the envelope from Turtle World Games. He had never heard of them before. Apparently, they were a new gaming company with full virtual reality gear to connect players to the game. Everything felt so real. The company delivered the game, and the virtual reality pod free of charge and even encouraged him to stream as he played. After being in the pod for days, he could see why they wanted him to stream. The game was amazing. When connected everything felt so real. The touch of grass under his feet, the taste of the grass under his feet. There was a physical, tangible, real sensation so really it was easy to forget he was just playing along.

When he played, he was no longer just a corgi with an office job and a small team working under him. The game was a chance for him to be a warrior of old, righting wrongs, and doing good.

The first monsters he had come across were strange humans, and he did what he would do in any game, fight the monsters. Somehow, they had sent him a team invite, which started him on a new adventure.

The elders told stories of an ancient civilization of humans that kept the Canine race as pets or trained the dogs to do the tasks humans did. It was all hog wash. The Humans extinction was just the most recent extinction event. They, like so many other animals, just disappeared. He thought about how this was 1998, there just was not time for those kinds of stories. The Eiffel Tower was made by pre-writing Canine civilisations, not some ancient humans.

But in this game, sometimes the humans seemed to communicate as if they were Canines, anthropomorphising the humans so well they were almost Canine. Kevin had no idea why the developers of the game would take this route in their story. Ancient human theory was a fad long past its prime.

Something stuck in Kevin's mind though. When the human guard said he was a good boy, his streaming numbers went up quickly. He had over a million viewers now. His office even offered to keep his salary if he advertised their company logo on the corner of his stream. People, including his bosses, wanted to see more of the game. He knew that he was going to get better deals from others to have their logos on him, but he was loyal. His work pack could always use the boost. Plus, Monica was due for a promotion. If she took over his team, they would be in good hands.

Kevin may have erred, resulting in his character dying in the raid, but he wanted to go back to his game pack. Plus, he had a new outfit already picked out for his pet goblin.

***

Intermission 2: Working with the Dev

The Great Ajax was the primary gnome, he was attached as assistant to the Dev. He reminded himself of this every day, having held the position for several million millennia now. When someone says the days start to run together, they give no idea how true that is when you are near immortal and working in the same position for so long that apocalypses seem to run together. But something was changing, and he could not put his finger on where it was coming from.

The lunar beavers had maintained their peace treaty for a few hundred years now. When the beavers arrived, they raided for resources. The Developer wanted this, although Ajax never understood why. The beaver timeline was coming to an end, and they had somehow brought over their whole world, which was something the gnomes had not seen before. Something new was something interesting.

There had never been any beaver players before. For a time, their presence brought war, raids, and many changes to the turtle world. Players and the beavers grew tired of the wars, and a peace treaty was signed. Very little trade had been done, and the refuge planet filled with beavers became the second moon to the turtle.

The first moon, the larger of the two moons, was in fact just a giant beehive. It was here before he had been given the position of the Primary Gnome. Ajax knew nothing of the hive moon, but it interacted the least. The tool and computer making insects never seemed interested in playing games, so seeing bees appearing never seemed right. They pollinated and farmed multiple forests of plants. The trees are just as much as the flowers. They did not interact with the system but allowed themselves to be tracked. Their names were random letters and numbers.

Ajax looked at his monitor, searching for what was causing all the small issues. He believed, something akin to the beavers and bees, there was someone new on the turtle's back. Whoever or whatever this whole was, they were able to take on a new and unknown role in this world. The gnomes could only see the effects from the whole's actions, and until they were tagged, they were unknown elements.

Coupled with more sightings of the one that called himself Taxi-Man, so he was still active. But that one did not seem like he would be able to make such changes Ajax was seeing.

The Dev spoke. "Ajax, some kind of shark on the infernal levels is making changes."

Ajax looked over at the Dev, who normally took the form of a spiral galaxy. But today, the Dev stood in a form he had never seen before. The Developer had marble white skin with the arms and chest of a man but the lower body of a quadruped hooved animal. This form reminded Ajax of the centaur, but the proportions were off. The back legs were lower than the front, with a back sloping down at nearly a forty-five-degree angle. It had large and powerful legs; they were just in a strange placement. The Dev still had no head or face but took the dark outline of space, with unending blackness spotted with stars and galaxies. The sky in the game had to be maintained to look earth-like. Seeing the Dev like this reminded Ajax of the note on one of the monitories. The sky must be alike so hope remains alive. In this space no stars here, just a shifting color palette of orange and reds. A contrast to what the Dev showed.

Ajax's voice cracked, dry from disuse. "We are seeing more holes making their way here. Normally, we only see one every hundred years, now we are seeing one every month!" They rarely needed to speak, and had the compunction to move a few things around to keep everything going. "Do you know why they are all coming here?"

"This would be your first reset. This is normal. Rats will attempt to board lifeboats on a sinking ship just as people do."

Ajax nodded and turned back to the data. Something was coming. A shark was in the infernal levels. All he could do was sit and watch.

The Dev laughed deeply. "Release the Commodore."

Ajax looked up at the Dev, too tired to move any of the muscles on his face. He did not know why they would release something so dangerous into the game. But he obeyed then turned back to the data.

An idea occurred to Ajax. Maybe it was not a shark. Maybe it was a whale, a killer whale that was affecting the infernal levels.

***

Intermission 3: Warlord of the Dinosaurs

Hellion's man was in a mood.

"We came in sixth!" David raged at his team. "We were supposed to take this town as an outside settlement. What were you all doing out there, looking at the daisies?"

They had all fought, and the paper raid had escalated farther than they thought it would. They were all long-term players in this game. At times this game was just as hard as real life. With each passing day, this world felt like more of a job.

She reminded herself why she was here.

When Hellion was diagnosed with cancer, her choices were to live for six more months in the real world or spend decades streaming and playing the game. The game sounded a lot more fun than the chemotherapy.

She had been tapped to play the role of wife to the emperor, who was to be the dinosaur warlord of the thirteenth shell in an expanded and concurrent game. She went along with it and had chosen the form of a Parasaurolophus. Sure, it gave her a weird forehead. Old science fiction shows gave aliens strange new foreheads all the time. She was able to wear whatever she wanted, the dress she wore faltered her body to the point everyone turned their heads as she walked past. Just the way she wanted, she craved that attention, from all.

David, who she had never met before, had taken the form of an Ankylosaur, the armored dinosaur. With his set up, the more he was attacked, the more damage he could do. He was always fighting on a knife's edge, augmented by the rocket hammer. The hammer needed to be repaired and refueled after every engagement.

Greg, the one playing the tank of the group, was the team member that got the most points, having tanked the raid boss. After the raid, he went from level thirty-seven to level thirty-nine. It was becoming more and more rare for any of the inner circle to gain levels.

The group had been playing together as long-term members of the game for around two years. None of them had hit the max level, but level thirty-eight was a milestone because it gave access to the strongest power in the primary power set. As a tank of his class, he very well may be the first one to get it. The dinosaur races were considered new in the game. They had fewer players, and with no one having reached max level yet, there was always more to find.

David was a good leader, and he played the part well, but all he cared about was winning every battle. For the most part, they did win every battle, but the man had no idea how to lead an army.

Sometimes he reminded Hellion of one of her favorite quotes, "My logisticians are a humorless lot . . . they know if my campaign fails, they are the first ones I will slay." David may be able to fight well, but armies only move when they are fed. Hellion had been arguing for peace and trade in the last few months. Their supply lines had gotten long and thin. But David was still pushing to conquer this trading town and add it to his domain.

At this point, their group controlled two hundred forty-two cities with populations between ten thousand to one hundred thousand. Most of the land was devoted to farming and military production. Not much trading to be had on the last shell segment with the expanding conquering army. Army building and near endless battles were good for business, but only for local business. How can you sell something to the town next door, when you know, they are going to attack you sooner than later. Withholding the trade may delay the attack. Many players came at the call of coin and experience. Not many stayed. Their little empire was made up of NPCs. Other warlords did the same, and most of the time, whoever had the most troops with the best equipment.

"They weren't looking at the daisies, dear. They were fighting, but the resources needed to take and hold that town were greater than we anticipated." Hellion let an edge seep into her voice. "Not to mention that we would be starting another border war. A war on two fronts is a fool's war, and we have wars on five fronts now."

"Four. Allstone fell three days ago." David replied with frustration continuing to show.

"Our sponsors like it when we win, but how long until the

betting houses see how things are going and start betting against us?" The wizard lizard said.

The room went silent. Everyone knew what he meant. Even here, coins were what turned the world. They needed their streams. Being sponsored was how they afforded to stay in as long-term players, never logging out but adding time to their lives with nutrients and monitoring. Their minds were active here, but their bodies were as broken down as old cars after a weekend at the derby.

Hellion's grandkids logged in every Wednesday to see her. But she would do anything to be able to see her family in real life. At some point they could, individually or as a group, be asked to take a loss. No one in the group was really in the position to say no to a bribe. Her family came first, the youngest grandchild was entering university soon. An expensive one at that. A bride that paid for the school would be enough. Leaving the game was a final curtain call, the bribes would allow an encore, just at another venue.

"The name at the top of the leader board was redacted. I have no idea what to even make of that. They were third in terms of damage overall, and I'm a damage dealer." David would not let the scoreboard go.

Hellion replied, "The mayor is at max level fifty, and has prestige classes and levels, possibly a decade of play time on us. Not to mention items, power ups, and whatever else he has up his sleeve as mayor. It would take at least a legion just to take him out, if not more. The lightning rod power alone deals massive damage, and he was able to add superior holy damage." She was trying to state how hard it would be to take this town.

The group remained silent for a long moment.

"The low-level necromancer that led a mixed NPC player team could be more dangerous than the mayor." The triceratops spoke quietly. "She reorganized the defenders, and then picked the weak points on the raid boss. I only ever saw one skeleton out at a time. If we send troops to take her down, everyone we send could end up being a weapon in her tool belt."

"Fine. Two legions for each of them, plus an extra for the rest of the town. We import food for around seven legions. They haven't been min maxing their farms, so it would be worth at least twelve legions. We're going to be hitting a plateau soon. The super nations are going to start to look at us, finding ways to use us or abuse us. The higher the numbers on our side, the better."

David had a point, but the risk benefit analysis did not make sense to Hellion yet. "We can't go to war with any of the super nations unless we have trading partners. If we have a sudden shortage, we will need a way to trade to get those goods." This was an old argument, but she tried to delay the inevitable. Hellion knew in her heart, they would be going to war on this town soon.

***

Intermission 4: The Commodore

The commodore looked out over what was once a living town. Buildings burned, bodies littered the ground, and blood splashed walls. It was beautiful. Each of his strikes cut down at least one person, building or even creature. Nothing could stand in his way. Like a master painter, each stroke and each movement was intentional. When more than one fell from each slash of his claws or swipe of his tail, well, those were just happy little accidents. He looked down at one of the town guards still alive under his foot. The commodore picked up the man, who was—to his credit—still squirming.

He had petitioned for so long to be able to play as a dinosaur. Everyone wanted to build. He wanted to tear down what they had built. The world could always use a bit of a shaking up.

"What is your name," the commodore asked the guard.

"Nash McCrae Emmett Lambton Kaleb the twenty-seventh," the guard said.

"Run. Run and tell everyone you meet Commadorous Sixtyfourous is here."

It was all just a game. He was going to do what he wanted, nothing mattered.

It was all just a game.

CHAPTER 14

BACK TO TOWN

JENNIFER RAN FULL SPEED towards the town hall. The mayor had said if Woozle was anywhere, that is where he would be. Her eyes watered, her heart pounded, and her lungs burned. The paper raid field was within the city border of Hogbacks. Her emotions drove her on, it was not a skill, power or ability that added to her speed.

A crowd of people stood in front of the city hall. Jennifer did not look at any of the people as she ran. They could have been waiting for other survivors, or just spectators. As soon as she entered the building, she veered toward the receptionist. The dark-skinned woman with dragonfly-like wings was speaking to another winged person. In her distress, Jennifer rushed over and blurted out, "Woozle, a miniature giant flying lynx-shark, where is he?"

Jennifer knew she was interrupting whoever the receptionist was talking to and that she would have been yelling if not for the need to catch her breath, but her worry over Woozle made her forget her manners.

The receptionist, to her credit, looked at Jennifer calmly. "Down the stairs to the left, second meeting room."

Jennifer rushed down the stairs and found the room she wanted. Someone had laid single person beds out in orderly rows. People in gray robes with red crosses on write robes moved from patient to patient. She froze, her eyes taking in the room. Everyone in this room was also on the battlefield earlier. Dozens of teams began the battle, but only around twenty people survived. All of the defeated were in this room rather than lying where they had fallen in battle. The system must have moved them.

A loud bark tore her mind away from her taking in the scene before her, and she immediately turned to see Kevin sitting next to Woozle's cot. Her feet automatically propelled her toward Kevin before she could process what she was seeing. When understanding hit, she had already wrapped her arms around the greenish gray wolf and let her tears flow freely.

"Where is Woozle?"

Kevin raised one of his front legs and returned the hug, resting his large head on her shoulder as she cried.

"Kid?"

Woozle's voice was normally gruff, deep, and always reminded Jennifer of a grumpy old man. Now his voice was weaker and did not have its normal lust for life, which made her pause her crying to look down at the prone body on the cot.

Woozle lay in his monorail position, belly flat against the cot with paws spread out. The shark fin on his back that normally stood straight up dropped to the side as his unfocused eyes glazed over. Woozle opened his mouth in an attempt to yawn and started to stretch out but stopped suddenly, wincing.

She desperately wanted to pick him up, pain etched his movements. She needed to hold something, and Kevin was real, and alive. "I am so sorry. The battle . . ." she trailed off as the tears came back. "Kevin was killed, I couldn't find you, and-and . . ." She let the tears pour out onto the wolf's fur.

Eventually, she steadied herself, wiping away her tears and getting her water works under control. Edging away from Kevin enough to look the Wolf's in the eyes, she almost lost it again. She saw him get killed. But for some reason, she had forgotten he would be coming back. At the moment, she did not care what the rules of this world were. She was happy Kevin was back.

Woozle was another story. She had the option to dismiss her familiar, but what about losing him in battle? She had no idea.

Composed, she gazed around the room. "If I'd died, I would have just been transported here?"

She did not direct the question at anyone, but a young boy answered. "The only ones that wouldn't have been transported here would be functionaries. They would have fled before fighting though." He wore gray robes but spoke with more experience than his age should have allowed. "Was this your first raid, miss?"

"Am I that obvious?" She focused on the floor and kept her voice low.

Kevin moved his head and snout to nudge Woozle gently as the young boy in the healer uniform talked. "This goblin was quite insistent that I come and check here. Hmm, I don't recognize this patient's species."

Jennifer turned to look at Woozle. He had remained unmoved in a monorail pose, but his eyes were closed. Something was missing, something about her familiar that was normally there but was now absent.

She whispered, "His tail. His tail is missing." His beautiful snow white and light gray patched fur-covered shark's tail was now only a small nib of a tail. The tail of a lynx.

Looking around the room, she did not see anyone else missing arms or legs. She did not understand why only her friend, her familiar, had lost a part of himself.

"Miss, can you check if you have a new quest?" the robed boy asked.

Her head tilted to one side before she opened her menus. There was a new quest marked with a red exclamation mark.

Why is the lynx-shark's tail missing? Your familiar had its tail stolen. Find out who stole it and get it back! Personal story line, multi-tiered rewards based on tier progression.

One of Unknown. Find your familiar's tail or dismiss your familiar.

At first, she did not understand the message. When comprehension hit, her eyes narrowed, she felt her anger rise. There was no keeping that emotion out of her voice. "Someone stole his tail." It was not a question. It was confirmation on what fuels her anger.

"Kid, I don't need a tail. I'm still a good familiar. I won't give up. Please." His voice remained weak, laced with more than a hint of fear infused in his voice.

Jennifer looked down in confusion. There was nothing to be fearful of. The room was filled with warriors. Anything that could cause fear would be stopped before it reached the door.

The kid in one the gray robes said, "It would be best just to dismiss him. Starting familiars are never useful in the end." He shook his head and left.

Jennifer glared at the back of the boy's head as he walked away to check on others recovering from battle. How could he even suggest that? They were not strangers passing each other in the night. They were not weak-willed simpletons willing to give up when things got hard. Woozle was the first person she met in the new world and was ready to defend her at any moment. He may be hurt now, but he will get better, won't he? Letting her anger pour into her words, she said, "As long as you want to stay, I'm never going to dismiss you. I'm never going to run around and leave you. I'm never going to say goodbye."

Woozle groaned. "Yeah, I can't remember that song either. But for now, put me in the hood, and let's go see the scoreboard."

Jennifer picked up Woozle in her arms. Checked on Rover, who was sitting on her shoulder. She nodded at Kevin, and made her way out of the emergency infirmary. After five steps, she put Woozle back down.

The problem was he was too big to travel that way. As she leveled up, he had gone from the size of a field mouse to a normal sized lynx or large dog, both of which were too large to fit in her hood. She looked around for an alternative, but nothing was built for carrying a creature like him. She turned the blanket under Woozle into a sling to carry her friend.

Leaving the room, Jennifer walked past a large board listing the names of the top teams along with their rewards. The top team and top three individuals had their names blacked out.

Her team was fourth, just behind the mayor's team. While her team was low on damage, they had received high points for organizing, healing, and buffing. Each member had won half a green, and as team leader, Jennifer controlled the division of winnings. Without a second thought, she decided to split the money evenly. Looking through her menu, she found where and how to split the reward. Remembering how the mayor explained this world's money, she recalled that half of a green was five hundred yellows, so each party member would receive one hundred twenty-five yellows.

She was still somewhat confused about money in this world, but if reds were pocket change and oranges were dollars, then yellows were thousands. However, that conversion was not perfect because inns for a night cost less than a meal, and that did not seem right. Either way, it felt like she was carrying more money than she ever had before.

The scoreboard also displayed a loot selection area. Again, Jennifer scored high. She assumed that was because she had not been transported back to the hospital, so she had automatically received the options of a generic drop that she would be able to use or sell, or receive a drop that would be tied to one of her power sets.

Jennifer was already feeling rich with the cash prize, so she chose to go with the random drop that would be tied to one of her classes.

Congratulations: You have received the item - brewing station- . This station will allow you to craft potions far better using ten percent less ingredients with a thirty percent chance of critical successes or failure.

The word brewing station was in purple lettering, but Jennifer had no idea what this meant. Would she be able to craft more potions, better potions, or both?

The scoreboard's total loot inventory had a list of items that players could bid on. The bidding process was relatively easy. She could tag any items she wanted, and if no one else bid on them she would receive them. If multiple people tagged a specific item, they would have to roll to see who received that particular item. The person higher up on the scoreboard was more likely to win. But the more items a winner bids on, the more likely they are to lose more items than they win. The balance was either bidding on a few items that she needed or bidding on all the items she wanted.

Kevin had tagged a few items: a beaver armor set, some boots, a sailor costume, some beaver blasters, and a couple of rings. Sarah tagged a beaver skin top hat, a beaver pistol, and a beaver watch. Large Soup Bowl, on the other hand, had tagged a lot of items. There were so many items tags, her eyes just blurred over the options.

She again felt lost. For the most part, it was mostly beaver droppings. Nothing she felt really suited her. That was until she saw the Beaver School uniform. The educational outfit is a five-piece set with shoes, pants with buckle, purple dress shirt, gray sweater vest, and a black tie. Their purple was not quite the same as Bishop's, but in Jennifer's excited eyes, it was close enough. Not wanting to waste her bonuses, she tagged each item of the school uniform.

Jennifer looked through the rest of the drops and ended up putting her name on two more items that caught her fancy. One was a ring that boosted her mana pool, and the other was a compass that would boost her navigation skill. Piles of coins as well because there were a lot of piles of money. Normally, only one or two people tagged that loot, but the larger piles of coins had more tags. She guessed that more tags meant less chance of winning, and that was why people spread out their tags a bit more when it was just money.

The snoring coming from her sling was loud enough to split the noise of the crowd in front of the scoreboard. Kevin was roaming around the park sniffing people. Her armor spider was on her shoulder. Jennifer found a bench to sit on. She was trying not to cry. The battle was scary. She saw people kill or be killed. The strangest thing for her was that they did not stay dead.

She remembered the mayor telling her that parallels would almost always come back. Apparently, at least in the paper raids, she would come back too. But the difference between knowing and experiencing was staggering. Jennifer put her face in her hands, the battle still fresh in her mind. She had let Kevin down. She had let Woolze down. She had let so many people down. They had fallen when she could have healed them. She had let Woozle down so much that he was scared of being discarded. She constantly reminded herself that the beavers were not really alive. They were just copies. But she was just a copy too.

Her hands were covered in wetness, but she could not stop the tears. She just wanted to go to school, learn, and make the world a better place. But less than an hour ago, she was fighting armored space beavers. She did not know what she had expected the battle to be like. It could have been anything, but it was not just good guys fighting bad guys. The explosions, the magic being cast, and so many parallels and fragments hurting and being hurt It was all too much.

She was sobbing uncontrollably, her mind went to her current situation. She felt worse that she had no idea where she was going to be sleeping tonight. This world was what it was, and it hurt.

Her hands moved because Kevin nosed them aside. A big, wet wolf tongue licked her face. She went from crying uncontrollably to uncontrolled giggling. The wolf was the best thing in the world at that moment. When she was able to get a hold of herself, Kevin's goblin burst out laughing as she took in what the goblin was wearing.

The poor thing was wearing a blue and white sailor suit and was not looking happy about it. The goblin's face was set in a frown, her ears were not as perky as before, her shoulders drooped. Jennifer moved off her seat onto her knees and pulled the goblin into a hug as she laughed. The goblin flailed around for a moment, but after a few heartbeats, the goblin returned the hug.

When the two separated from the hug, Jennifer was no longer sad. She wiped her eyes clean. The goblin was still frowning, but she was no longer dropping her shoulders, and her ears were pointed up again. That was a good sign, so she turned to hug Kevin as well. He scoffed a bit, but he too returned the hug.

All her negative thoughts were shoved to the back of her mind. She was here. She was with friends. A wolf that was trying to kill her only two days ago was now the best emotional support wolf in the world for her.

"Oh, there's a goblin here, dude. Free XP."

The words caused Jennifer's heart to freeze. Kevin growled at the intruders as she turned towards the player who spoke.

Giant Intimidation: successful - Area of affect – line of site.

"This goblin is my friend." Jennifer spoke in a loud voice, adding as much command and warning as she could. The notifications for Giant Intimidation all came back as successful or critically successful. The difference was how long the intimidation lasted. A smile crossed her face as she scanned the frozen crowd.

"Kevin, speak."

He barked at the command, which caused the people to run in fear.

Turning to the goblin, and sarcastically, she said, "I'm sure they all just remembered the oven they left on."

The goblin smiled at Jennifer, and she smiled back.

"Normally, girl, I would not want you to do that, but they need to know not to mess with my town." The mayor's words were slurred, and he was not walking in a straight line. "So, are you two coming to the after party? You should come so we can"—he slurred his words— "rub our win in their face." He walked towards her, and the smell of liquor hit Jennifer well before he came close to their little group.

She had no idea there was an after party, and the idea of the party caused her lip to curl down in a scowl.

Giant Intimidation failed

"Why in the infernal levels would I want to go to the after party?" Her words were pointed and cold.

"Well, there goes my buzz." The mayor gave Jennifer a look. She was unsure if it was due to the content of his blood or something else, but she could not discern the meaning of the look. "What did you think you did today?" The mayor's words lost any hint of a slur.

The question caught Jennifer off guard. In her mind the mayor was right along with her the entire battle. She raised her hands to her head and massaged her brow. With her voice more under control but still loud, she said, "I fought in a pointless battle where a lot of people got hurt."

"No girl, you just saved the town." The smile on the mayor's face made his eyes twinkle.

Jennifer took a step back.

CHAPTER 15

EXPLAIN THAT ONE AGAIN

BEFORE JENNIFER REALIZED IT, she was back in the Chateau De Jim, trying to get the mayor to explain to her how she saved the town.

"My girl, this is like leading a horse to water and the horse expecting you to hand feed him too." Stiffness revibrated in the mayor's movement and words. He was still smiling, eyes however were glazing over.

"The warlords of the next shell over are playing some kind of empire expanding game. They mostly have functionaries doing the fighting with a few parallels. They feel strong, and probably are stronger. One on one, maybe. Since they are used to fighting the functionaries like the ones that were in the paper raid. They did well, and you did better."

"All I did was give out a few healing potions and cast my force field. Oh, and raised undead a few times. The only reason I scored high was because I survived. Others beat the beaver."

"Yes, all you did was play a support, almost no one does that here. You also took the beaver prisoner when it was about to transform into a new form. When bosses transform, they become more dangerous, they get some new power up or ability. Sometimes their hair changes color and becomes ten times stronger due to some prophecy. I could have revealed my loud trump card or let the beaver kick our behind so hard that the town might have lost some profitability."

"So it was good I asked for it to surrender. It stopped the fighting." She did not know why she felt the need to defend her actions. They were the right actions.

"As someone who buffs like, your force field, and heals, you got a lot of points. Then you rallied us and came up with a freaking on-the-fly plan to beat the boss. And with the web trap from your pet, we were able to win. Girl, without you, we would've failed. You did the right thing."

"Without me, the raid may not have escalated so far. And what was the deal with the taxis or the blues playing man with a hellhound?" The frustration of the world was getting to her, and she had to vent. "All Alice had to deal with was a mad hatter and a rabbit that was late. I have monsters, goblins, an electrical mayor, and a wolf named Kevin. And I somehow saved the town?" She checked her menu. The Save the Town quest marker was still not completed, so the system did not think she had saved the town yet either.

"Yes, girl, you saved the town. And now the town is drinking until the ship be sinking!" The mayor sang out his reply, and the other patrons at the bar joined in.

Jennifer massaged her temples. It was all madness. Before she could come to grips with her own thoughts, the dinosaurs walked in.

All was silent.

The air crackled with tension as the dinosaur leader scanned the room for his quarry.

When he laid eyes on Jennifer, she smiled warmly back and gave a friendly wave. Reading the expression of the dinosaur was not easy, but the death glare she received was a glare to behold. Grinning, she mimicked the glare.

Fusing Dinosaur Intimidation glare and Giant Intimidation failed. Giant Intimidation on dinosaur warlord was successful. Due to frequent uses you can now assign points into intimidation as a passive power.

Jennifer had forgotten to check if she had leveled up after the battle. With a mental flick she checked her stats.

Congratulations: You are now level 10.

Despite her misgivings on the paper raid, it gave her a lot of powers and enhancements to choose from. Glancing over her choices, she got a little overwhelmed. She decided to wait until Woozle felt better and would be able to give her advice. The power options were nice, but what she really wanted was to be able to craft more healing potions, so she wanted a lot of her enhancements geared toward that.

A fist slammed into the table in front of Jennifer, pulling her attention away from her menus. The offending dinosaur slurred his words as he raised his voice. His rancid breath could have felled a moose with or without the alcohol. "I was talking to you, fragment. What's your price?"

She looked the dinosaur man up and down, making the movement apparent to everyone watching. She did not like the way he asked the question, how he referred to her, the tone in the man's voice, or how he looked at her. The line, when they go low, you go high. Play on the friend of her mind. She decided on what position to take in this argument. "I find you lacking lizard man." No emotion entered her voice as she talked. She felt her words may have come from someone straight out of a renaissance story plus, the wording would aggravate the warlord enough for him to leave her alone..

The dark leathery brown of his face turned red before he made an offer. "One purple per battle."

At his words, the female dinosaur, with the strange horse-like mouth and long tubular horn coming out of the back of her head, snapped her mouth shut. Her head shifted back, leaving the rest of her body still. The dress she wore was red, and sparkly.

Keeping her poker face, not knowing what she was asking for, "One purple per battle sounds nice on paper, but how often will I even be in battles?" Jennifer raised a hand to signal the barkeep that she would like another drink. "And you are paying for my drinks tonight." She was having half blueberry lemonade, half ice black tea, that cost five oranges. She did not order the first one, the innkeeper brought the first one out and my mayor paid for it. She really liked them, but they were overpriced. If they did not pay for the drink this was going to be her last one for the night.

She watched the gears grind in the dinosaur warlord's head.

As his mouth slowly opened, the female dinosaur butted into the conversation with a rush of words. "One green per victory with four yellows a month guaranteed no matter what. We will include dental and one full cosmetic change per year. You will get a two-year contract with options to renew with a twenty percent bonus and three minor cosmetic visits per month."

The whole situation just annoyed Jennifer, and she did not want to deal with these lizard people. She was happy to be in this town. It was close to school. She was trying to get them to stop making offers. She wanted to let them down easy, show them why she was saying no, without saying no. "I have land here in town—"

"We will buy that land, and give you double the space." The warlord interrupted. "You can choose any land, even in our capital."

Her blood boiled. While she tried to be diplomatic, these people were trying to bribe her to work for them. She wanted to help others, but these lizard people were warlords. She wanted to go to school and better herself then find her place in the world and add her name to the side of good. These dinosaurs, literal dinosaurs, wanted nothing but war.

"No," was her only reply. The whole room fell silent. A maid placed Jennifer's drink on the table, then quickly moved away. Jennifer watched the warlord's face turn even redder.

The colorful feathered lizard man in the wizard hat spoke next. "You said land, not a house. If money you do not seek, what interest would peak?"

Jennifer guessed the wizard cast a spell so she was compelled to answer. She could not see it in her log, but she did not want to share the information. Trying to hold back the words, as the spell took effect. "I'm on a quest to reopen Bishop's University of Magic, but I have no house and no place to stay tonight." Her eyes narrowed as she glared at the lizard wizard. In a voice filled with a venom she did not know she had, she said, "Because of that, I will never work for you."

"A house on a hill, that will fulfill. Next near a school, that will not be cruel, for you to anew." The feathers on this lizard man shimmered, changing colors as he spoke.

The vibrant display drew her in, making it seem like it was the most attractive thing in the world. As a calming breeze swept over her, she could not look away from the dazzling wizard lizard. But something within her screamed defiance.

"I am going to smash my mug on your head, rip your throat out with my bare hands, roast your hide, and eat what is left. I will use each of your wonderful feathers to decorate my future bedroom. Then I will use your bones as my summoned skeletons. Did you notice the plural? Because I know I will be able to do that over and over again because you come back each time. I will keep doing this until you can no longer come back." Her words formed from the compulsion spell; those words were something she would never say aloud. She also had the feeling that she licked her lips as she spoke but glared at the feathered lizard wizard, who interestingly enough, lost all of his colors except for his belly. Those feathers turned yellow.

The words that came out of Jennifer were not her own. They came from somewhere, almost as if she was possessed for a moment.

You have resisted further hypnosis. You cannot be hypnotized for another 24 hours.

Jennifer took in a deep calming breath. Waved the mayor over. When he arrived, she passed him a sling with Woozle sleeping in. "And please hold my drink." She stood up, she towered over the three dinosaurs before her. The only one taller than her was the triceratops lizard man, but he was not with them for some reason.

Jennifer stepped up onto a chair then onto the table. Her hair brushed against the ceiling now towering over the warlords. Jennifer raised her voice, and she began a verbal bombardment

Achievement unlocked: - Removed from diplomatic event - Ever get thrown out of a bar, after publicly insulting visiting nobility to their face? We recommend not doing that. Again.

CHAPTER 16

WHERE TO GO FROM HERE?

"I THINK AFTER I threw my drink in the face of that ankylosaurus was when the guards came for me." She rubbed the sleep from her face. "But maybe my comments about that lizard's hammer were what made him the maddest." Jennifer's hand was on the side of the micro-foundry with the mending power active.

The robot avatar of the building moved his head up and down.

Jennifer assumed that the movement showed that the foundry was listening to her.

"So then what happened." Lights lit up where a mouth would be on the face of its round head.

"Well you know how it goes, you find a weak spot and you exploit it, just verbally. It is when they go down crying that you know you have your own." She took a swig of her stamina potion so her mending could continue. "Anyway, can you craft a house?"

"I can craft a doghouse. Guild rules bar me from fabricating more than cosmetic changes to a house. You would need a functioning door to your house before I can craft a house." The machine bowed its head.

Watching her stamina, she waited until it was just under half before toggling off her mending skill. She walked to the front of the building "That's too bad because the inns are full. After a raid people like having a place to rest their heads."

"I believe there is an old tradition of people sleeping in empty train cars. I am told Train is rather nice."

"From hero to zero before I even get a parade. Can you point me in the direction of the train? Also can you make a sleeping bag and cot for me? The first thing I'll do tomorrow is find someone to build me a house." A yawn escaped her lips, and she raised her hand to cover her mouth. She glanced up at the sky. The inky blackness contrasted with the silver moon hiding behind a smaller yellow moon. She paid for the sleeping gear, starting off towards the train with Woozle in a sling on her back. "It's so different, and yet this place is feeling a lot like home."

***

Jennifer went looking for the train. She had seen the machine a few times, the whistle she heard far more often.

There were no tracks leading to the train, the black cylinder stood out in the night. Three box cars were attached to the engine, in the second segment in bright blue letters, "you are safe here" painted on both the outside and inside of the metal structure. The inside was larger than the room she slept in before. Without a bed, she had to put her head in one corner and lay with her feet on the diagonal opposite corner. The sleeping bag was also too small and ended up being a throw blanket. Woozle slept in a free corner with the blanket sling as a nest.

***

"Jim who?" Jennifer asked about the banging noise on the side of the train.

"Me. The mayor, Jim Gigawatts. Dude with a big hat. The guy who runs the town you are sleeping in. That Jim. The man who has a train running late because you are sleeping in him. That Jim." His voice sounded pleasant and upbeat but with hints of something Jennifer could not quite catch.

Jennifer rubbed the sleep from her eyes and yawned while looking around. She remained fully clothed under the too small sleeping bag. Her feet were too cold last night, so she had put her socks and shoes back on. She gave a half-hearted shrug. "Give me a sec. I'll be out." Her head brushed the of a low hanging back in the train. Jennifer pet the car wall, "Thank you train, I had a good sleep."

Leaving the box car, she left the door open and stood between it and the mayor. Kevin stood next to him. The look on the wolf's face and the tilt of his head made her think how silly it must look for her to sleep in a train. Woozle was still curled up in the blanket, sleeping. She did not know where Rover made a web to sleep in.

"So, the town is now at war," the mayor said, while eyeing Jennifer.

She lifted a hand to cover a yawn and stretch before saying, "I'll go make a recruitment poster."

The laughter that burst out of the mayor had her looking down at him in surprise.

"Jennifer, you had those dinosaur warlords running a code brown out of town. You yelled at a group of high-level, elite warlords as if they were kids with their hands in the cookie jar." The mayor was trying to control his laughter, while speaking, "There's no way they are ever going to be threatening this town with you here."

"So no war posters then?" Her head tilted, as she tried to recall every detail of the night before. She remembered the feathered one hypnotizing her. Or was it a trance of some kind? Her sleep-soaked mind was not fully up to speed.

"The infernal levels have no rage like a woman who has been scorned."

The mayor's saying didn't sound quite right, but she let it go so that she could piece together the night before. She remembered being angry.

"As soon as the log out glitch is over, I'm going to have my grandson find out if anyone has a recording of it."

"Log out glitch?"

The mayor waved a dismissive hand. "You don't have to worry about it. It's something us parallels have to deal with from time to time. Now come, we have a mountain of food waiting at the inn. We can have breakfast while you tell me what you need to get the school open again." The mayor left the field with a wide smile on his face.

Confusion and sleep addled her brain. Looking around, her eyes came to rest on Woozle. He opened his eyes, stretched out his legs in front of himself, and yawned with his tongue curled up.

"Are you ready for the day?" She did not bother concealing the concern in her voice.

"Kid, I lost my tail, not my will." When he moved to stand, he stumbled and fell over. Before Jennifer could reach him, he stood up and took a few practice steps. She watched as he tested each movement. The floor of the car was flat, making it better to practice here rather than outside. From the look of things, he was getting better after each step. Jennifer pushed her lips together and rubbed the palms of her left hand on her sweatpants. She had no idea how much of his balance had been lost when he had lost his tail. She also knew that when she leveled up again, he would get bigger.

As Woozle took practice laps around the encampment, Jennifer brought up her inventory menu. She had won everything she had bid on. Rather than needing to undress then redress, she was able to change her outfit from her menus. As simple as mentally dragging the clothes out of her inventory, and imaging the clothes appear on her. The clothes she was wearing automatically went into her inventory. She liked the new uniform but it did not have a hood that Woozle could ride in. Something she would miss. She was still planning on getting a robe to go over the uniform. With having leveled so many times last night, she was going to have to pick her new powers soon. With every level he got bigger, she was unsure how long that would last. Thinking it over, she decided that she would visit the micro foundry and see if the robot could do alterations to the uniform.

She politely told Jim that she would meet him and Kevin at the inn, as Woozle became more sure-footed. She also reviewed her quests.

Enroll in Bishops university, 1 of 3 complete.
Gather farm animals for the town, 0 of 10 complete.

Repair the micro foundry, health 67 of 80 complete.
Story line: find your familiar's tail, 1 of unknown complete.
Build house, 0 of 1 complete.
Explore Bishop's University: 72 of 100
Save the world: 0 of 1 complete.
Save the Nation: 0 of 1 complete.
Save the world: 0 of 1 complete.

So much to do. While the side quests she was doing were helpful, they were slowing her down. She needed to find a business owner to get a second letter of recommendation, and she had no idea what kind of side quest they would require in exchange for the letter. Jim owned the inn, but he already wrote the first letter. The micro foundry was a business but, when pressured when she was repairing him, was only a maybe after repairs were done it would write a letter. He said he would need to talk to his guild, and they have their own sentient resource people he would need to ask first. She felt that would lead to more side quests at this point. After spending a night in the train car, to spite how safe she felt in there, she was more motivated to get her house built. On her way to level ten, she had received three enhancements at level six. Thinking this over, the powers she found the most useful was Mend so she added a reduction in stamina requirements, faster repairs, and the ability to repair more.

For her level seven, she had received a new power, Drain Life, in her Necromancer power tree.

Drain Life: Diminish the health of one target, moderate mana, moderate cool down. Part of the health you drain will be transferred into team members and allies who are within line of sight. The closer the target, the greater the effect. What were they doing with their life force anyways?

It was a combat spell. While she had not liked combat, if she was caught in one, she would be able to heal others better this way, so she took the spell.

Her level eight choices were another three power enhancements. Since she used her last enhancements on just one power, she felt it was better to spread them out this time. Currently, she only had one skeleton left in her inventory, but it was useful. Her choices were to make them hit hard, be hit harder, have more health, hit more often, have an extra skeleton, with her final option was to take less mana to summon the skeleton.

During the battle, she had set her summoned skeletons to act as bodyguards, a force field that made them tougher, making them better for that job. The reduce mana use when summoning, option also did not seem as much of a boon because she did not use much mana. The same resource pool as her future defense tech shields, she needed to summon summon skeletons far less often. She was about to pass up that option completely, but instinct told her to look it over again. In the raid, she had not used her dark attack much so that she could continue to resummon.

She decided to add a reduction of mana use for both her Drain Life and Summon Undead skeletons. The final power enhancement went into reducing the mana needed to cast the protective buff.

At level nine, she had the option to add another power. With no new powers available for her three main trees, Jennifer looked at her side powers.

At level five, she had the option to select the power Craft. The craft power came from the same generic power tree set from which she received her Mend skill. After selecting the power, Jennifer felt an itch in the back of her mind, followed by a massive headache as information was added into her brain. The splitting headache lasted for only a few moments. "I can now craft pottery. I guess that's useful," she said, speaking more to distract from the headache than anything else. "I hear those are in demand over in Otherule. They have a hero who hates them, while villagers love to hide things in them."

"Good to know, I am just going over my level up process. If

you don't mind waiting?" It was more that she was using this time for him to get used to his new body, rather than her waiting on him.

Looking over her character sheet, she had only two levels left to sort through, the fifth and the tenth levels. Every fifth level had an asterisk next to new power. Focusing her mind on the symbol, instructions on how to change or modify a power appeared.

Level 5* You will be given a token from the system to change one of your already existing powers. You will be given 3 options for each of your main power trees. The options will be chosen at random, and from those options you will be able to choose what best works for you. Once the token is given freely from the system, you cannot trade it to another, but it can be used whenever you want.

The same was true for level ten, but there was also an additional power to be used in a minor power set.

Jennifer took in a deep breath, used one of the two tokens, and looked through all of the upgrades and options available.

Necromancy

Dark Pulse turned into Flaming Darkness, [+ description] low mana use, can be toggled on and off. This is the flame thrower option.

Summon Undead turned to using the Best Parts, you can pick the best bones from multiple sources [+ cost and toggle/recovery]. This is the "we have the magic, we can rebuild them, we can make them better" option.

Drain Life turned to Drain Sewer. You can now drain any sewer [+ cost and toggle/recovery]. This is the never call a plumber option.

Summon Undead: Due to your crafting powers, alchemy, and blood ritual, an additional option has been unlocked. You may now modify your minions using additional materials onto your undead. This option will require additional stamina, and additional stamina will be required to repair the materials. This is the "I'm Canadian. Bub." option.

Future Defence Tech

Force Field Weapons: Rather than casting a Force Field, you can now cast weapons made out of force fields [+ cost & toggle/recovery]. This is the "why defend when you can attack" option.

Force Field Shield: Rather than being inside of a force field, a floating shield will protect the one you cast on [+cost and toggle/recovery]. The shield will last longer and protect more but will cost much more. This is the "shield over bubble" option.

Force Field: Rather than a transparent blue, your force field will be rainbow colored. This is the "rainbows make everything better" option.

Alchemy

Healing Potions: Changed to acid, [+ cost & toggle/recovery] Why heal when you can melt?

Mana Potions: Rejuvenation potions give minor healing, minor stamina, minor mana recovery, and a stimulant bonus. This is the "get back up" potion option.

Healing potions turned to bonus health. This potion does not heal but will increase the health pool of the target by 20% for

15 minutes. Once the time runs out the health pool will return to normal. If a person has a pool of 100 health, after drinking this potion they will have a pool of 120, if they take 15 damage at the end of the timer they will have 100 health, if they take 25 damage, they will have a pool of 95. If a person who drinks this potion and they are at 5 points of remaining health of a pool of 100, they will have a pool of 25 points.

Her jaw fell open. Each of the choices were good options, but there was only one worth taking.

"Kid, I can feel your excitement. What are you going to go with?"

Her lips curled into a smile, as she imagined what she could do with the option. "Woozle, I'm going to have the most bedazzled skeletons. Where can I get some shinies?" Her words came out loud and fast.

"You have the option to have metal skeletons with armor and weapons literally welded on, but you want to put shiny stones on them."

She let out a long, happy hissing, "Yes." Mentally slamming down on the "Canadian" option.

Jennifer decided the next thing she had to do was review what was on her plot of land. She looked down at Woozle as he was prancing around. He was at the height of her stomach.

"Oh boy my how you have grown." She said mockingly.

He wiggled his ears, and gave a shark smile.

***

"Yup, this is land alright." The words came out dryly as if that was not what she was expecting. It was just a square of land next to one of the inns. The grass was tall, blue, and unkempt. Jennifer and Woozle explored the area looking for anything interesting.

It turned out that the land did not even have rabbit holes. But there was a blueberry bush and another bush that had large pink flowers on it. Jennifer's alchemy powers told her that the blueberries were tasty and the pink flowers could be used to make tea, which sent Jennifer's mind into overdrive. She had not seen tea yet in this new world. There were a lot of inns and bars but no tea.

She turned to Woozle to ask about the tea, but the sight of his missing tail faded her smile. She chose to enter the raid, and she lost track of him. Her familiar's missing tail was her fault. She only had one main quest, to get into Bishop's University. The sad thing was, she felt all the side quests pulling her in all directions, including helping her familiar. If she was going to help him, she would have to do some side quests that would lead to other side quests.

She nodded as she made a mental list. First, they needed a place to stay. The land she owned had the potential to help her finish her quest to get into Bishops, to have a roof over her head, and to have an after-school job. The next thing she needed was to build a house.

"Woozle, do you know how to build a house?" she asked, not really expecting anything other than his usual snarky answer.

"I know where we can find one." He put his nose to the air and sniffed.

Jennifer with her metal spider on her shoulder followed Woozle, who followed some unseen trail. While Woozle was on the hunt, Kevin wandered up to Jennifer with his goblin on his back. He leaned his head into Jennifer's lead with large eyes asking for something. She knew what her wolf friend wanted, and she scratched him behind the ears. She patted the goblin on the head in greeting making sure she was not left out.

She and the group followed Woozle all the way, to three buildings down from her land. The group walked through the door to one of the inns in town, Jennifer was hit by the smell of stale alcohol. This inn was dark, gloomy, and looked like a fight would break out at any second.

"Are you looking for a quest or offering a quest?" said a voice from beside Jennifer.

The voice startled her. Kevin gave a warning growl.

Collecting herself and putting a hand on Kevin, she replied, "I'm looking for someone who should be here already."

Taking a quick glance around, she took in the blacked-out

windows that blocked the sunlight before she focused on the speaker. He looked like a bronzed statue with twin smokestacks arching over his shoulders toward her. He wore a green apron. At first, she thought he was wearing a helmet, but then she saw the metal skin move as he spoke.

"Speak the name of the one you seek, and I shall show you to them." The voice was deep and carried a metal note in its tone.

She turned her head to Woozle while keeping an eye on the metal man. "Do you have a name?"

"Carpenter level twenty-two. Has the Warhammer Knight secondary class. Big in the shoulders with blond hair." Woozle returned to sniffing the air.

"Follow," the bronze metal man simply said. Jennifer shrugged and followed the man, who led them to an empty table. "Stay here. If he wishes to speak with you, he will be here soon." He then pulled two large mugs out of holders where human biceps would normally be.

As he put the mugs on the table and eyed the group, Jennifer realized she should give him a drink order. "Umm, I'll have some berry juice and water, please?"

The bronze man hovered his pointer finger over the first mug. Red liquid poured out of his finger, filling the mug. He moved onto the second mug and, this time, water came out. "The price of the drink will be included on your table. The price of the table will be ten to fifteen percent of the transaction. This includes goods and services. A cost meter can be viewed in your menus as the deals are made. Thank you for your patronage." The metal man left as soon as he finished speaking.

Jennifer looked at her companions. Kevin's fur made him look bigger. Woozle found a spot he liked on the table and laid down. This was not the kind of place Jennifer liked to be in. It seemed like a cross between a bar shown in old westerns and the kind where health inspectors left with fatter wallets. The juice was good though.

The group did not wait long before the blond guy showed up at their table along with a donkey that had a squid on its head. "So, what services can Hammer and Squid provide for you today?" The blonde spoke in a fake, upbeat customer service voice.

Woozle raised his head and looked at the two. "How many points have you put into the carpenter class?"

The blond poked his elbow into the donkey. "See, I told you taking that class would get me places."

Jennifer closed her eyes, parted her mouth slightly, moving her lips to make a "what" sound silently, before opening her eyes, when she noticed the donkey had six legs and was wearing a pink collar.

She was still staring at the donkey with the squid on its head when the blond went into the sales pitch. "I can build you anything from a chair to a sailing ship or—"

"Can you build a house?" The question that came from Woozle cut off the sales pitch and got them to the point.

The blond man again nudged the donkey, and the squid rolled its eyes as a projected image appeared on the table. The projection was blue with white lines.

"Is that a blueprint for a house?" Jennifer asked in astonishment. Looking back up to the squid, she noticed a wizard's staff in one of the squid's arms. The staff, with its large pearl on the end, was glowing blue.

The blond replied, "Yes, this is the basic house design. One floor, two bedrooms, large living space connected to the kitchen area, as well as a bathroom, and laundry room. If you invite us to be a member of your party, we can see what bonuses you have that can add to this."

Jennifer sent the mental command to add party members.

"Tenchno-Necromancer-Alchemist and a Great Forest Wolf. Odd matching. A few pets. Humm. As a necromancer, your bonus seems to be able to switch basic stones and bone stones. And as a tech base, you can have a seventy percent reduction in power needs. None of the other classes add to the building, but the forest will double the bonus from gathering wood."

Jennifer blinked. She had forgotten Kevin had been with her when she added the quest, but she was the only one to turn in the quest. She did not mean to share the quest with him, but of course, Kevin was always welcome at her place, but the house was just for her. She turned to Kevin, not knowing how to mime any of this. But Kevin was not paying attention to her anyway. He had his head tilted, looking at the blueprint projection.

"Umm, the house is just for me, but maybe we can add a doghouse later?"

"Of course, of course. So do you want us to go with this design or do you have something in mind?"

Jennifer looked into the blond's eyes as a smile crossed her face and her eyes narrowed.

Giant Intimidation partly successful. Target's current actions have been interrupted.

Jennifer asked, "Do you have a pen I could use?"

Once the hammer wielder was in her party, she could interact with the blueprint, just not well. Her lines were not straight, the curves were not uniform, and the corners were not at ninety degrees. The aerial view of the building looked like the letter U reaching with the bottom of the u facing the back of the property. Outside, between the ends of the U would be a garden.

Jennifer explained that the arm on the right was the entry hallway. Her house needed an inner and outer door so people could only come in one at a time. The entryway opened out into the living area. To the visitor's left would be the exit hallway, having the same inner and outer door as the entry and allowing only one person out at a time.

The living area, with floor to ceiling glass windows, looked out onto the garden and the town square. Behind the living area was the kitchen. Beside the kitchen, was storage and stairs going up and down. Upstairs would be the living area with a bed and bath. The bathroom needed to be extra-large in order to have a bathtub large enough for a half giant. The large basement would be unfinished, but she decided that laundry machines would be going down there along with her alchemy. She also wanted to have wall mounted sconce lights on the sides. After being in the dark inn she wanted the place to have lights.

With Kevin at the party, he added a room for himself.

Looking at the wolf. She wanted a place, but after not having a place, she decided she wanted a home with an open door. So, her friends, allies, or people she met would also have a safe place to stay. She decided to label the room as a guest bedroom and added two more rooms to the second floor. Closing her eyes, she took a deep breath. She would need to work out how much rent would be if people needed to stay a while. She felt conflicted. Kevin had been with her the most out of any of her party members, but what happened if he decided to leave? What if she decided to leave? She wanted to be close to her friends, but would they want to be close to her?

Kevin changed the name of the guest room to Kevin's Room. Was he asking to stay with her, or was he demanding to stay with her? She looked over at the fanged beast. He would need a place to stay. By adding his name, he wanted to stay with her at the least. She had a plan, but what if she needed to stay in the dorms during the week and could only come back on the weekends?

As she was considering the situation, the wall between Kevin's room and Jennifer's was removed. The room was labeled Kevin and His Human.

She did not mean to do it, but she growled.

The great wolf did a quick lip lick, and the room's name changed to Jennifer and Kevin.

She added the wall back in. She still did not know what was going to happen, but in the end, Kevin wanted to stay, and she wanted him to stay too.

At first, the blond man looked confused but said he would add bathrooms on the first and second floors.

Jennifer looked over the plan for her house and smiled. It was going to be a wonderful home for her and allowed her to have an open door policy if her friends wanted a place to stay. It would serve her purposes.

"So how much will it be?" Jennifer dreaded asking the question. The economics of this world made no sense to her, but she had earned a lot of money from the paper raid. She just hoped it would be enough.

"Seven hundred wood, five hundred stone, or one hundred fifty wood and one thousand five hundred stone. We will also need eighty metals, fifteen glass, five coral, and fifteen clay. It will have standard energy and water hook up from the city. City rules are standard for the building so fifteen yellows, and two thousand five hundred yellows added for the work and making sense of this. But we're only staying in town for the next three days, mostly doing repair quests and local quests before moving on. The fragments coming in have a lot of repairs that need done, and it's good XP for us."

Blinking to reign in her running thoughts, the first being that the cost was a lot less than she was expecting. Even after adding on the ten percent the table was going to get from the deal, the plan sounded too easy to be true. Then she remembered she would need to get the materials in less than three days.

What were her priorities?

Her mind flashed with barely connected thoughts. In order to help Woozle, she was going to need more skeletons in her inventory. She did not like her necromancer abilities, but the set was powerful. Remembering when they killed Kevin, she laid flowers and thanked the wolf for the first of the fur, meat and bones. She was hungry, she would need to get food soon. She believed the wolf to be a beast and not a person. It was not like she could just walk up to the grave and speak to the dead.

There was so much more to do, and it was tiring. With a dry mouth, she reached for her drink. As she picked up the cup, she paused. What was stopping her from going to a grave and speaking to the spirits? There was no harm in asking a question. A no was a no;[AP1] a yes was a yes. And if they made her do a quest, at least it would be better than digging up the bones.

"How do I speak with the dead?" she asked absentmindedly.

The donkey spoke in a well-mannered voice, with clear

pronunciation and near musical tone. "Historically, mediums have used coins—normally silver—to help communicate with the dead. Each flip of the coin is assigned an answer with more coins leading to a higher accuracy in communication. Birds, like crows and ravens, have also been known to send messages from the living to the dead."

"I've seen crows," said Jennifer. "They're blue here and already doing the messenger thing." She mimicked the movement of flipping a coin. "But for coins, I don't know. I wouldn't trust a coin flip."

"Psychopomps like angels, willow whips, owls . . . Hmm. I hadn't thought about this, but a lot of winged creatures seem to work well for speaking with the dead. The game normally operates on near functionality of our myths and legends. If this was the real world, how would you attempt to speak with the dead? Maybe put in a request with a mod?" He was well spoken, and considering that he was a donkey with a squid on his head, his mannerisms were even more impressive.

"Umm," she said, as her mind kept turning. Multiple worlds here. Coupling that with the fact that she was missing much of her memories from her old life, his statement only confused her more. Nothing in her mind to speak with the dead, beyond becoming dead, and that was out of the question. She had too much to do. Put simply, she was too busy to die.

"Are there graves here?" She had not thought about it, but there had to be a place where the dead go. Not to mention leaving loot behind. There had to be more to it.

Again, the donkey spoke. "There's Hogan's Field, an enemy mob called the Grave Digger's Union, and lots of gravestones." The hesitation in the donkey's voice could not be missed as he added, "We've not been given a quest line to go there yet, but there are some interesting rumors about the area."

"Can you give me the location? Do you want to come with me and Kevin?" Jennifer could feel the excitement in her voice. She thought if they were unionized, there had to be someone to speak to.

The blond man, the donkey, and the squid all exchanged looks before turning to Jennifer and saying in unison, "No."

"Well, what about the location?"

The squid and donkey's moved in an approximation of a shrug, and a squid icon appeared on Jennifer's mini map. The location was well south of the town.

Jennifer was unsure if their party was two or three people, so she simply thanked them as a group.

Once outside, she waved at one of the many blue birds flying around. One alighted on a nearby branch. Jennifer spoke clearly to the bird as she had seen others do. "Message from Just Jennifer to Sarah No Val and Large Soup Bowl Fourteen. Going to speak to a union. Want to come?" With that, a small blue bird flew off.

The group took some time to gather. Mostly because Soup Bowl needed to finish his homework before joining the group. Jennifer did not have many memories of doing homework but remembered that it took a lot of time. As soon as he arrived, they all headed down the road.

"Where we go? Why we go? What loot?" Soup Bowl's words sounded more robotic than usual.

Jennifer looked back at Kevin who walked behind the group. Sarah led the way, but Woozle walked beside Jennifer with Soup Bowl on her other side. Rover kept to Jennifer's shoulder, and Kevin's goblin, in her sailor costume, rode Kevin's back.

"Umm, we're going to a field to speak to a grave digger's union. I want to learn to speak with the undead. As for the loot, I'm hoping we'll find something." She was unsure how looting would work. To her knowledge, none of them had any archaeology traits or a graver robbing skills. Besides, there were probably union rules about that kind of thing. Curiosity had her reviewing the loot they had received from defeating Kevin, the paper raid, and the plant gathering.

Lost in thought, she almost plowed into Sarah when she stopped abruptly in front of the group.

Soup Bowl asked without inflection, "Side quest?"

"We're going to see the grave digger's union so you can learn to speak with the dead?" Sarah asked without turning around.

Jennifer looked down, letting out a weak, "Yes." When she looked up again, Sarah's clothes had changed from casual wear to her business suit.

"Grave diggers bad?" The inflection of Soup Bowl's words caught Jennifer by surprise.

"How bad can a union really be?" she asked, honestly unsure why Sarah was gearing up just to talk to some unionized people.

Sarah raised her voice and turned toward the group with eyes wide. "We don't even know the class of union members. There have been rumors that they are bards, fire wizards, spirits trapped in masks, a legendary ghost, and necromancers."

Jennifer felt her spine straightened. "What's wrong with necromancers?"

"They're evil. They defile the dead. They're . . ." Sarah's words trailed off. As she looked up into Jennifer's eyes, Jennifer could not hold her gaze for more than a heartbeat. "Oh my Cthulhu. You want to learn from them."

"I want to learn from them so that what I do isn't evil. My alignment didn't change when I summoned Kevin's bones, but I don't want to fight and kill someone just to use their bones. I don't want to defile the dead." Jennifer looked at her shoes, not wanting to meet anyone's eyes. "I want to find a way to get permission from the dead to use what they've left behind. I don't even know if Kevin is okay with me using his bones, and I lost one of his skeletons in the paper raid."

Soup Bowl came up and hugged Jennifer.

It was the most robotic hug she had ever had, but a smile crossed her face. She returned the embrace.

"Summon Kevin," his words were clumsy, but she understood the intent.

Leaving the embrace, Jennifer rubbed what she was going to call dust out of her eyes and summoned the skeleton.

Soup Bowl walked up to Kevin then emojis appeared above Soup Bowl's head. The first was a set of oversized cartoon eyes, followed by a finger pointing at Kevin. As Kevin's head tilted in what she assumed was a questioning look. She realized her head was also tilted.

Woozle answered the unspoken question as he too watched the exchange. "They're communicating through emojis, because they don't speak each other's languages."

Above Kevin's head, a question mark appeared.

Soup Bowl nodded twice. A large red heart appeared followed by a broken heart. Soup Bowl pointed at the skeleton before pointing a finger at Kevin. The next emoji was a cartoon man shrugging.

Kevin went up to the skeleton and sniffed. The skeleton did not react as the wolf it came from circled it. Kevin stopped in front of the skeleton, barked, gave a play bow, where his front legs stretched out and his head dropped below the skeleton's head. He held the position as his head tilted from right to left. When his head stopped moving, he barked again.

The skeleton may as well have been a statue. With no reason to move, so the skeleton did not move. At least that was what Jennifer thought until she saw a small movement in the tail bones of the skeleton. Jennifer gasped and her heart skipped a beat.

The skeleton wolf's head slowly tilted to one side. As it tilted, the tail wagged more. Without warning the skeleton did a play bow, resulting in the pair playing dog tag with one other. Jennifer smiled. She did not know if the skeleton was gaining personality or if it was just mimicking the movements, but they seemed to be having fun.

Kevin came up to Jennifer, pressing his full weight against her body with his head looking up at her. While her skeleton chose to sit in front of her. As she gave Kevin scratches, she asked the group, "Does that mean he's okay with me using the skeleton?"

No one met her eyes.

"Kid, you are talking apples. He's talking wolf . . ." Woozle's voice trailed off.

Soup Bowl was the one to give an explanation. "Wolves are pack animals. Kevin playing with the skeleton means acceptance. There is no way to tell if he understands this is his skeleton or not, but he is not intimidated or frightened by it. He accepts you into pack. This is good sign and skeleton plays now too."

That was the most Soup Bowl had ever spoken. Sarah was squinting with her left and raised half pointing at the well spoken ninja.

The feeling of happiness in her was enough for now. Not wanting to be left out of the fun, Woozle chased the skeleton when it and Kevin renewed their playing. Jennifer took in a deep breath, counted to three, and turned back in the direction of the grave diggers before she let the breath out.

Kevin's goblin walked beside Jennifer as the group moved towards their destination. Kevin, Woozle, and the skeleton continued to play as they walked. Daylight seemed to fade with every step the group took. Jennifer noticed the sun was hanging around the mid-afternoon area of the sky where it was supposed to be, so the sun was just less bright here.

"Is it just me or is it getting darker?" she asked the group.

An emoji of a nodding man appeared above Soup Bowl's head.

Sarah said, "I thought it was just my imagination, but we've believed for a long time that the sky is a lie. Rumour has it, we're headed to a place of darkness where the sun doesn't even go." A visible shiver ran through her body.

But all kept moving towards their destination.

The group came up to a line across the dirt road and stopped. On their side of the line, the road was a light brown, but on the other side of the line, the road was dark flat stone. Jennifer looked around. Unlike the trees around town, which were much taller than Jennifer, on their side of the line, the trees were no more than double her height. But at least there were trees. On the other side of the line stood no living trees. They had fallen over and petrified long ago.

The path they had taken was far from flat, but it did not compare to the road ahead. It was hard to tell what was in the distance, it was almost ink black against ink black. The two moons were overhead, but it was as if someone had thrown a shade over the sky.

Kevin let out a low growl and changed into his full armor. He continued to growl as he crossed the line with his sailor suited goblin on his back. The goblin looked grim, with one hand on a saddle horn and the other on her glowing sci-fi gun.

Soup Bowl crossed the line next in his full glowing neon ninja gear. Once over the line, he vanished. Jennifer wished she could vanish like that.

"Kid, if you want to turn back, no one will think less of you. Plus, if there's any danger." He put an ellipsis on the word danger and showed his teeth off in a wicked grin.

Hesitating for ten heart beats. Jennifer quickly crossed the line before she lost her nerve. The sudden temperature change from warm day to a cold night took her breath away. As for her spider, Rover summoned a trap door on her shoulder and dropped into it, disappearing. Woozle shivered as he crossed.

Looking back, the only member of the group that had not passed over was Sarah. Her skin lost most of the color so much so that even her patchy dark spots looked pale. She stared at the line then at the group and back again.

Jennifer began to reassure her. "If you—"

Sarah cut Jennifer off. "No, we go as a group." Taking a deep breath, she crossed the road.

Sarah activated a power that Jennifer had not seen before. Dark shadows flowed up from the ground in a counterclockwise motion around Sarah, forming an outline of a shield that was a meter in diameter. With a rigid spine, she marched to the front of the group.

Jennifer checked her menu, wanting to make sure her skeleton, who was walking behind her, was set on bodyguard duty. She noticed a buff on her skeleton.

Due to steps taken on an unmarked quest line, as long as this skeleton is out, there is a fragment controlling the summoned creature. Sometimes it is a ghost in the closet, machine, and sometimes in its own bones.

She could not tell what the buff did or how it worked. Kevin was alive, so how could his ghost be in the bones? Was that why it was playing and acting more lifelike earlier? She shook her head. She did not have the time to dwell on such things.

Sarah was the only one in the group that knew anything about the area, and she was scared, so Jennifer needed to stay focused. Although Sarah could take a large hit, she did the least amount of damage except for Jennifer.

Jennifer smiled. She had a plan, but her plan did not involve fighting. The group followed in a line, with Sarah in the front, Kevin following closely behind and to the left, and Jennifer in the back. Soup Bowl used his ninja vanish power to move around. Woozle stood next to Jennifer, standing in an alert posture With the path coming to a fork in the road, the group remained silent. All eyes turned to her. Breaking convention, Jennifer simply pointed up the hill rather than at either path.

Sarah nodded first and led the way up the hill.

While the hill was steep, it was not a long or hard to climb. When they got to the top, the view showed the same hills and valleys repeated for a great distance in front of them. Jennifer squinted, looking for light sources or smoke. She saw neither. She scratched her chin as she thought about what to do. When she glanced at Sarah, her lip curled up in a smile. In her mind, If she could not go to the grave diggers, she would bring them to her.

With a shrug, Jennifer turned, looked straight at Sarah, and asked, "So, how's the weather?"

Sarah looked back with a blank expression followed by a series of quick blinks.

"We have not had rain for a while." Sarah looked confused but played along.

Jennifer scanned the ground at the bottom of the hill as she spoke. "This will be my first winter here. What will it be like? Does it get cold and wet, or cold with snow?"

She continued to ask questions at random to keep the

conversation going, but there remained no movement. Nothing was coming.

Sarah looked at Jennifer with her head tilted. "I guess no matter what you do, you can't make talking about weather exciting?"

The group waited in silence for what could have been an hour, Jennifer had not asked a question in a while. "Have you ever seen a lightning storm, just in the clouds, and no rain on the ground? It's beautiful. You can lay on your back looking up at the sky and watch. There's just a flash. No thunder, no rain. Just sparks so big you can see them from miles around, with lighting that never hits the ground." While she felt the passion in her voice, the plan was not working, nothing in the dark was coming for them.

Not willing to give up, another idea began to form.

While looking at the ground, Jennifer wondered what lay beneath her feet. She realized she had a skill that might tell her.

"Summon Undead." The power activated. In her menu, a tide of options flooded her vision. There were too many to count. The shock and horror of standing on a burial mound had Jennifer's heart racing.

"Run," she shouted and bolted down the hill. The voices of her companions called out behind her, but she could not make out the words. "Run, just run," she shouted again.

Woozle ran beside her along with the skeleton. Kevin and Sarah kept up without showing much effort.

"Why we running?" Soup Bowl's voice rang out in his robotic voice.

"It's not . . . a hill . . ." Jennifer said between gasps as she ran. "Burial mound."

The group sprinted down the mound and made it back to the road. They did not stop until they were a fair distance from the burial mound.

The group slowed as they neared the lit torch that stood in the middle of the road on the dark side of the road. Staying alert for threats, Jennifer again activated Summon Undead. Fewer options were available here but still more than she could count.

She was a necromancer. As long as her mana and stamina held out, she could summon undead for years here. She swallowed hard as the sudden realization hit her. The moment the group had crossed into this land, it was a trap for all who were not necromancers.

"If it comes down to it, don't fight, just run. You don't stand a chance." Jennifer tried to keep her voice steady while she lifted the mop in front of her and took a defensive stance. She had come here hoping to talk, and she was at least going to do that.

Walking closer to the flaming torch in the road, she felt the urge to speak. Finding no reason not to, she said, "My name is Jennifer. I come from Hogback. And I am a necromancer."

"My name is Count Vald Fam. I come from the land of the dead. I am a necromancer." The voice sounded like a voice from a bad vampire movie. It was not lost on Jennifer that he had mimicked her introduction.

"I am here to learn." A cold sweat came over her as her eyes darted around looking for the source of the voice.

"I am here to keep people out," said Vald Fam.

"Why?"

The eerie voice in the darkness said, "What did you come here to learn? You can already summon the dead."

"I want to learn to speak with the undead."

Silence returned except the crackle of the fire.

Jennifer kept her breathing calm, and even as her heartbeat hammered in her ears, she looked around.

"That is an interesting power to seek."

"There is a fine line between grave robbing and archaeology. Between light and dark. Between good and bad. I want to ask the ghost if I can use its bones, not just leave an offering and hope." Jennifer did not let her guard down as she spoke.

"Good, bad. Most consider themselves good no matter what the system says. The bones are just what people leave behind." Amusement lilted in his voice with an upturned note here and there as he spoke.

"Good is asking for permission. Bad is asking for forgiveness when you have the chance to ask for permission."

The ground before the group trembled. She remembered an underground pipe bursting once, causing a sinkhole. The noise was not too dissimilar, so she backed away.

Two horse skeletons dragged themselves out of the earth by claws protruding from their hooves, pulling a black and red carriage behind them. The carriage door opened and the voice of Vald Fam came from the inside. "Get in and let us speak."

Jennifer turned to look at her group. Sarah trembled, and Kevin's fur stood on end making him appear even larger. Woozle stared unblinking at the count, ready to attack at a moment's notice. The team's ninja was hiding in the darkness.

Trap or not, Jennifer felt herself moving towards the carriage, those actions not fully in her own control. Sarah's words made Jennifer stop. "What are your terms?"

No reply came from the carriage. Jennifer continued to keep her breathing steady, and after a few breaths, she repeated Sarah's question. "What are your terms?"

"What do you want them to be?" The levity had left his voice.

Jennifer had no idea what she wanted her terms to be. Risking a glance back, she asked Sarah, "What do I want the terms to be?"

Sarah moved up beside Jennifer. With a reassuring smile, she took over the negotiations and spoke as a businesswoman. "Hello, I am Sarah No Val, from the Exports De Universal corporation. I wish to speak on behalf of myself, this group, and Jennifer. Do you all accept."

"Does this cow speak for you?" Pleasure returned to his voice.

Jennifer's cheeks grew hot and raised a finger, but Sarah stopped her. Sarah's reassuring smile and nod was all Jennifer needed to calm her irritation, so she simply said, "Yes."

"A wise man once said, may you live in interesting times, as he continued to live a boring life. Let this be so. I accept you as speaker for your group." The merriment accompanied with his accent colored every word. "What are your terms?" There was no questioning inflection in his words. She guessed that the tone he used was either at the novelty of the situation or trying to give them a false sense of security before closing a trap.

"No one is to be harmed during our discussion. Once discussions are completed, both parties may leave unharmed. Our party will be allowed safe transport out of the land of the dead. Nothing that would harm any member of our party shall happen through action or inaction during or after discussions."

"I will do no harm to anyone in your party through action or inaction unless in self-defense."

Jennifer nudged Sarah. "Not everyone in our party understands the rules."

"Not all members of this party have the ability to communicate verbally with one another and actions can be easily misinterpreted. Do you have a way of correcting this?"

An unearthly howl sounded in the distance, sending chills down Jennifer's spine. The howl lasted much longer than one of Kevin's.

When Jennifer realized that she had been holding her breath and clenching her jaw, she forced her muscles to relax.

A man covered in light gray fur, wearing shiny blue pants and red suspenders, appeared. While his shape was human, his head was that of a wolf. On the wolf's head was a knitted hat with dangling knitted extensions on the side.

"Are you a werewolf?" The words came out of Jennifer's mouth before she could stop them.

"How's it going, eh? Me and some beavers were setting up a meet to compete for some meat that you eat."

His accent reminded Jennifer of some northerners.

"Meet meat? Or meat meet?" Sarah asked.

"Yah no, it's a meat meet, down by the meet up, where you compete to get the meat."

Kevin let out a cross between a whine and a woof that spoke of pure confusion.

"No, well, yah, but it's not always easy going down this path. I was a man, then I drank from the same water a wolf both stepped in and drank from. Most towns take out their torches and pitchforks when I dry to get a drink at an inn. The buffs are nice."

Jennifer turned from the werewolf to Kevin, whose ears were standing upright, while his head nodded when the lycanthrope spoke.

"Can you ask him if he is okay with me summoning his skeleton?" asked Jennifer, interrupting their conversation.

"Well, don't you know it, he kinda likes it. You won it in combat and even gave an offering. He didn't know you back then. He thought it was a sign of respect."

"Damn, Liam, we're playing roles here, and that's not the right accent." The man from the carriage yelled out, losing his bad accent. "We're playing the roles of the undead. There should be a certain . . ." the carriage man paused, obviously trying to think of the word. "A certain accent for the part."

"Oh no, sorry, Tim. Most of the time it's just all the smacking. I forgot we's supposed to do the accents when talking. So why are we talking?"

"The necromancer wants to use one of her free traits to learn to speak with the undead."

"Oh, does she now? That sounds like a good thing." The werewolf nodded approvingly as he spoke.

"Yes, well, we are evil, eh. We need to think of some side quests for her."

Jennifer groaned at the words 'side quests' coming from the one in the carriage and let out a yell, "Why is there always a side quest? Skeletons are everywhere. Nothing but death around here, and you want more side quests. Life should be more than side quests."

The one in the carriage stepped out as he spoke. "All life is a series of side quests and taxes. Want to go to the store for eggs and milk? Not only is that a side quest but you have to do a side quest first." The man wore a red sports jacket, with patched pants, and a dark gray vest and tie over a black shirt.

Jennifer thought the man in the carriage should have worn very old yet high end nobility clothes. An odd thought passed through my mind. How long from her time would it take before this was high end nobility clothes?

"Kid, are you sure this is a good idea?" asked Woozle.

Jennifer shook her head. "No, this is not a good idea. Side quests were the first thing I understood from this world. And it doesn't look like we are fighting."

While Jennifer grumbled, Sarah took control of the negotiations. "Okay, what is your side quest? Since there is nothing out here, I am betting on a fetch or gathering quest." It seemed like Sarah was trying to add authority to her voice by deepening it and adding some projection to it. "And when we're done with the fetch quest, I would like to add your grave digger's union to the list of our trading partners at Exports Du Universal." Sarah put her hands on her hips, striking a power pose.

Jennifer did not begrudge the action, her friend was a good deal maker.

The werewolf and vampire were giving each other confused looks. The vampire spoke up first. "Who the infernal level is the grave digger union?"

"Umm, they are the big bads of the area," Jennifer answered with a shrug.

Sarah added, "They've been running this area since the Devs only know."

"Never heard of them. Were they big back in the day?" The Werewolf played with his suspenders as he spoke.

"No idea, but that's who we were expecting," said Sarah

"Well, they're not here now. Shall we?" The vampire motioned to the carriage.

With some reluctance, everyone piled in. Amazingly, they all fit comfortably into the black carriage, and it carried them farther into the land of the dead.

"So, why were you acting so spooky and stuff earlier when you're really, umm," Jennifer's hand was pointing up while she searched for more polite words, "Northerners?" Hoping that was a polite term.

"Oh, and what role do you play?" the werewolf asked.

Jennifer scowled in irritation. Making sure not to direct the gaze at anyone. This world was just a game to some, but it was her life. She never thought about her role in it. "I'm a necromancer?" She felt more than just a little annoyed at the question.

Sarah's voice held more than a hint of pride as she said, "I am a lead trade advisor for Exports Du Universal and the tank of a mixed group."

"Ninja level seven surge damage stealth," said Soup Bowl in his robot speech.

The werewolf bared his teeth at the group.

Jennifer tightened her grip on her mop before realizing the werewolf was smiling.

The lycanthrope said, "This world tried to dumb down the roles so everyone can easily succeed, eh. What do you do for the world, boys and girls?" As he spoke, a red and white can appeared in his hand and he took a sip.

Their country accent was giving Jennifer a headache. She wished they would go back to being creepy, evil creatures of the night. At least that way, they were easier to understand.

"I'm trying to be a student." Jennifer searched for something better to say, before remembering something important. "Hey, Soup, can you write me a letter of recommendation so I can get into Bishop's University?"

A thumbs up appeared as an emoji above Soup Bowl's head.

"In this world, stereotypical roles are easier to get, keep, and understand," said the vampire. "We were creepy because that's the role we have as members of this society whether or not this world is real, a simulation, or unreal. Since we're dealing with you as equals, we can take our masks off and be more ourselves." The vampire spoke in a lecturer's tone.

If he was one of her professors, she would happily attend his class.

"When I received the status effect of vampire, I decided to also play the role of an undead count. The role of a vampire is expected to be dark and creepy. So, that's how I acted, especially when dealing with adventurers and parallels. It's a little different with you lot because you're not emo kids coming and asking us how to be vampires because vampires are cool."

"This is a lot of words, So, where are we going, and can we set up a trade deal?' Sarah asked bluntly.

Jennifer was interested in this societal role play, but she too was interested in completing her current task.

"How would you go about speaking with the dead?" the werewolf asked.

"Go to the land of the dead, talk with some vampires, maybe some werewolves, and just throwing this out there, learn to speak with the dead by speaking with them?"

The vampire and werewolf looked at each other before looking everywhere but at her.

"You have no idea how to teach or learn speak with dead, do you?" Sarah asked

"And now we are in a carriage, with no idea where we are going," Jennifer added.

Kevin growled.

"Time to fight," added Soup Bowl.

"Wait, we have an idea," the vampire nearly shouted. "We're going to a mana spring. If there was a way to speak with the dead or your ancestors or whatnot, it would be there. We're willing to help." The vampire looked over to his werewolf companion. "Besides, if we fought, you'd be at a severe disadvantage considering we're both way higher levels than you."

Jennifer put up a hand for the team to wait. Thinking aloud, she asked, "How was I to speak to my ancestors?" She tried to reach something in her mind that was just out of reach.

If ideas were clouds, the sky would have gone from clear to dark thunder clouds blocking the sun so completely it may as well have been night. When lighting crashed, Jennifer had a plan.

"I'm going to need stones, animal skins, water, wood, and fire," said Jennifer.

The carriage stopped as the bewildered werewolf asked, "Are you telling us what to do?"

Jennifer glared at the werewolf.

Giant intimidation failed. You cannot trigger this ability again for 60 seconds.

Her reply was simple and straightforward. "Yes, please."

The werewolf and the vampire looked at each other. She could not tell which one of them folded as they shrugged simultaneously. If there was going to be a fight, it was now or never. She liked her odds.

Turning back to the group, the vampire answered first. "Okay." The carriage started moving again.

"We'll get there soon, yah," said the werewolf.

"So, how about we start talking about those trade opportunities? What is it the land of the dead needs and wants? I will tell you how we can get those things for you." No question in Sarah's voice, was clear the land of the dead was not ready for a sharp saleswoman.

The carriage slowed as it neared their destination, the land of the dead was going to be exporting bone bricks, museum pieces, and travel permits to high class vacationers who wanted a calm, out-of-the-way place to go. In return, the land of the dead was going to be receiving some herbs, non-adventuring guests, a sports complex to house a new sports team, and some other stuff that Jennifer had less than zero interest in.

In truth, Jennifer had stopped listening to their trade negotiations and was thinking about her plan. Her mind was still lit up trying to find the missing pieces for what she wanted to do when the carriage stopped.

She stepped out of the carriage into a densely wooded area with a small lake. The light from the sky was still dimmed, this was clearly still the land of the dead. The trees had no leaves, they were trunks, and branches so close together it would be hard to navigate. A stream trickled out of the still water near the group. The pond should have been on dozens of postcards with the pale blue glow coming off the water. In the middle of the pond, sat a small island supporting a single tree with glowing leaves.

Jennifer explored the area with all of her senses, trying to find a good spot to start. The water called to her, not in song or in movement, but in a way that spoke to her being. Any plan she had was lost as she gazed across the still water.

"What is this place?" asked Sarah, her words soaked in bewilderment.

"Tis a mana spring. At the end, many adventures come to see it before their end. We see many strange things come and go from here. Those who stay . . ." the werewolf trailed off. On the grounds there stood no huts, tents, or signs of people staying in the area.

"What should I do?" asked Jennifer.

"That's up to you. We'll be back tomorrow," said the werewolf before turning away. "Kevin, there are some fetch quests you can help us with. The ninja can tag along too." Without ceremony, the parallels in the group followed the werewolf and vampire back into the black coach.

Jennifer looked over the remaining group at Kevin's goblin, Sarah, and Woozle.

"Kid, I'm not going to - to be able to follow you into that. I'm too system-em." The lynx-shark stuttered as he spoke, unable to meet Jennifer's eyes.

With a nod she said, "Well, that means we have someone to watch our stuff while we swim." She could have placed the whole group's items into her inventory, but she did not want her familiar to feel bad about not joining them.

The group prepared for the swim, leaving their gear in neat piles on the shore. Jennifer was the first to enter. When her skin touched the cold liquid, she lost connection to her menus. A shiver went through her body. This came with both a loss of something familiar to her as well as the warmth of wholeness as she entered the deeper water.

The goblin swam next to Jennifer, as she was only halfway submerged. When she looked behind her, Sarah had not yet entered the water. Jennifer waved at her to enter the lake. Sarah backed away from the edge of mana infused water. Thinking back, Jennifer had seen Sarah had enjoyed the hot tub, so her hesitation could not have been a fear of water. Sarah had entered the water willingly. Then it dawned on her why her friend was now scared. "You are going to lose access to the system and the illusion. Stop worrying and come as you are. The water is fine."

"You knew? Then why are you always mad when people call me a, a . . ." Sarah was unable to say the word herself.

"You present yourself as a strong woman, so to me that's what you are." Jennifer spoke while at the same time focused on treading water, she was expelling more energy then she was expecting staying above the water line.

The goblin made a strange noise and started splashing in the water. The small green one was looking directly at Jennifer making distressing sounds. She did not show any distress from swimming, and was using her hand to point at Sarah. Jennifer smiled at the goblin, and nodded, but after a few heartbeats, the rider stopped splashing. She moved her head back and forth from Jennifer to Sarah several times, shrugged and continued her swim to the island.

Time became meaningless as Jennifer reached the deep water and swam. Her body became heavy, then light, followed by heavy again. The sounds of the running water and her fellows breathing and splashing. No sounds of birds or beasts could be heard. The lack of other noises resonated in a way that created an atmosphere of silences dialed up to eleven.

As she swam, Jennifer looked down but was unable to see far due to the glow. A shadow, a dark spot that moved under the group as they swam to the island. The goblin was the first to set foot on the shore, turning to sit while the others made their way.

Jennifer was next, and she wiggled her toes as blades of grass played beneath her feet. She let the glowing moisture fall from her form. As the droplets fell to the grass, the plants instantly grew at least a fingernail length.

Sarah moved slowly, dog-paddling from shore to shore, always keeping her head above the water. Of course, she kept the sunglasses on. When she reached the shore, she shook the water off of, sending out a fine spray which watered the sprouting grass.

As if by some unspoken agreement, the group faced the other side of the lake and remained silent. Sarah was the first to look away, but Jennifer was not yet ready for the next step of this journey. The shadow that had followed the group from under the water grew darker as it broke the top of the calm pool. The head was not unlike a barracuda attached to a long, slimy neck with dark outlines of scales. In spite of creating a great shadow beneath the waves, the creature was translucent, casting the same blue light as the water it came from. Its eyes were large and spoke of an ancientness that Jennifer could not describe. A light chattering noise came from the creature's mouth.

When the creature dived back into the depths, Jennifer turned towards the tree. The bark on the tree was such a deep color of brown she thought it was black from the shoreline. As she got closer, she could see not only the true color but the deep and jagged lines of the bark. When she touched the bark with her hand, the spot melted revealing hollow innards. The bark continued to dissolve away, creating a portal large enough for Jennifer to step through. Closing her eyes, she took a deep breath and stepped into the unknown.

The grass was green, the birds sang, and a tan colored deer looked up from chewing on some grass. She knew without looking that a large house sat behind her, but no entrance, exit, path, or road broke the treeline near the house. A large bear came up and sat next to her.

At this point, the strangeness of sitting there felt normal. The deer was just a deer, the grass was green, the sun was real. The bear handed Jennifer a cigarette. A completely normal thing for a bear to do. She was not a smoker, so she gently pushed the cigarette away but smiled at the bear's thoughtfulness.

She took a deep breath. The place smelled like home. When the bear got up, so did she. After waving goodbye to the house, she followed the bear into the woods.

No words were spoken between them when they reached the river. The bear simply stared into the water for a long time. With a quick swipe of its claws, the bear pulled a fish from the water. The bear motioned Jennifer over to the fishing spot. She dutifully took the spot and looked into the water.

Her arm moved on reflex, and before she knew it, a fish appeared in her hands. She was not hungry and had no use for the fish. Eyeing the bear, she knew it was not hungry either. She put the fish back in the water.

The water was clear, the sun was high, and Jennifer saw her reflection. She did not recognize the reflection at first. She could not remember ever seeing her reflection. There was just a sense of how she looked on the back of the turtle. This was the first time she had seen herself. Her small eyes, dark skin, and long black hair were in the reflection. Small marks were there as well. One scar just under her left eye less than the width of her Pinky finger nail, the other under the lip around the same size. This was the face she had seen before on the back of the turtle.

She nodded and went back to sit by the bear. She felt the bear looking at her and frowned as she watched him light a cigarette. The bear gave a questioning look but took a puff before putting out the smoke.

She could feel that the bear was wondering why she was there. Without words, she conveyed her story to the bear. The bear nodded and, with one paw, hit the ground.

A small cardinal flew on red wings to land on Jennifer's outreached finger and looked into her eyes. The bird tried to teach Jennifer something, before flying off, scared away by a large blue jay.

There was no malice in the blue jay and it just wanted to know what was happening. The bird gave Jennifer a seed before it too flew off.

The sun lowered in the sky, and it grew dark, the moon rising to take its place. Jennifer had learned something, and the bear headed back to the cabin. When Jennifer tried to follow, the bear turned, picked her up, and carried her into the river.

"No need to rush, stubborn bear. So much to do."

CHAPTER 17

I WAS BUSY FISHING

JENNIFER STOOD ON THE shore opposite of the tree and could not help yelling at the vampire. "What do you mean it's been two days?"

"You were in there for two days. What was taking you so long?" The vampire snapped back in amusement.

"It only felt like . . ." she trailed off. Was it minutes? Was it hours? Time was strange at times.

"Well, it worked," the werewolf eagerly replied. "You got the trait, right? Speak With Dead. We're just waiting on that greenling."

Jennifer checked her menus. It had been two days, and the trait Speak With Dead was now on her character sheet in purple writing. Everything else was in black writing.

"Yes, I got the trait. This world makes no sense," she said in a huff. "Now I have less than a day to get the supplies I need to build a house."

"Yah, no," said the vampire. "Since you shared your quest, the rest of the group did that while you were stuck in that tree. We were not able to save the town, nation, or world. Or get a business owner to sign off on a reference letter."

"Yah, Kevin even went to the pup's starting location to find out. Best he could do is find a division supervisor to speak to. Everything these days is getting corporate," the werewolf said.

"So, where is my group then?" She brought up her mini map in her menus and saw the names beside the dots showing where they were.

Large Soup Bowl was just three question marks, Kevin was closer to the center of the shell, Sarah was heading back to their location, Woozle was close by, but Rover was off gathering healing moss.

"Woozle," Jennifer yelled, trying to get the attention of her familiar. The sound of a rocket engine powering up came from her right, before going fully powered up.

The lynx-shark, who was now the size of a small horse, rocketed into Jennifer's chest, knocking Jennifer to the ground. The lynx shark was getting bigger, and now hunting rabbits. The lynx dropped the rabbit it had been clutching in its jaws and rubbed his head and face over Jennifer as much as he could. She held her familiar up to look at him before holding him close for scratches and pets. He was big, but she was a half giant.

"So, you've taken up rabbit hunting?" she asked her familiar.

"Yah, that kitty has been rabbit hunting and keeping us fed. Those are tasty little guys." The werewolf licked his lips.

Woozle spoke with a mixture of pride and grumpiness in his voice. "I'm looking for clues. A rabbit stole my tail. So, I've been looking into rabbits. They're everywhere now and the only animals within a day's travel."

The rabbit was quickly skinned by the werewolf, cleaned, and put over a fire.

When Sarah arrived, she was followed by a caravan filled with goods. People in sunglasses pulled large carts or had oversized backpacks. "So where do you want me to set up shop?" Sarah asked the group.

The vampire raised his hands, interacting with his menus, and a blue bird with a black cape landed on his shoulder. Sarah and the vampire spoke with each other for some time as Jennifer ate.

Her stamina had not gone down more than five per cent in the last two days. Doing nothing for two days did not use much stamina.

Jennifer received a curious notification

Congratulations, Goblin target not found. You have been given. Target Not Found. Error.

The group was silent as the small, green-skinned female left the edge of the water. She had on a black t-shirt with white writing "I went on a deeply spiritual journey and all I got was this shirt and a log." She carried a log as thick as Jennifer's arm and as long as her leg. The goblin carried it as if it weighed no more than a piece of paper. After depositing the wood at Jennifer's feet, she waved her finger between the log and Jennifer and spoke in her guttural language. But the goblin looked just as confused as the rest of the group.

Jennifer made a mental note to learn to speak goblin. She picked up the log and put it into her inventory. The log was labeled Ghost Wood in the same glowing blue as the lake. Thinking about it, it was the same blue as the dean too.

"Okay, we need to get to the goblins, then back to town—" She stopped when she spotted something she had not seen in her menus before. A new, shiny purple button labeled Speak With Undead. Jennifer closed her eyes, took a deep breath, and counted to three. When she opened her eyes, she exhaled and pressed the new button. The mana bar did not budge when speaking with undead toggled.

Jennifer moved her focus to Summon Undead, and a list of nearby skeleton options came up. Some of the skeletons were highlighted with purple. With a smile, she selected a purple highlighted skeleton. Jennifer turned Speak With Undead off and on again attempting to trigger the trait.

"Umm, hello, who is this?" The voice sounded as if it was coming in over a staticky radio.

"Hello, my name is Jennifer. I am wondering if I could have your bones?"

"You woke me for a bone-ing?" A note of disbelief echoed in the disembodied voice.

"Yes, please." She did not care if her enthusiasm showed.

"Okay, do what you want. Just don't wake me up again." With that, the line went dead.

That could have gone better, but she did have a shiny, new skeleton. Well, a dirty, old skeleton that was standing in front of her with rags on. She put the bones in her inventory and set her mending to work on it.

She could have three skeletons active at one time, so she was going to need to think of names for each one. This one, she decided to call Andera. She had one set of Kevin's bones left and naming them would make it easier to have six skeletons in her closet. Each set of bones only took up one slot in her inventory. She was unsure how many she could put into a stack and still keep their names.

Most of her contacts with the dead went the same way as the first, with comments like, "Just get on with it," and, "I have better things to do with my afterlife than care about those old things," and, "I was in the middle of plotting out my book then you go and interrupt me." But when It asked, "Are you offering me a job?" that threw Jennifer off.

Blinking at the question, Jennifer took another bite of her rabbit lunch, then a drink of cold river water. Her words came out long and slow. "What kind of job did you have, before, errr, staying dead?"

"I was a pre-law student at the Gilly and Lilly University. I was also a bartender on the campus. Before that I worked at several fast-food places. Oh, and I had a paper route when I was a kid." The deceased's voice was filled with eagerness.

"Okay, so if I hired you, what would you want?" Jennifer had no idea what she could offer this dead person in exchange for work.

Jumping on her words, the ghost replied, "Ten percent of all experience points, and one out of ten pieces of gear."

"Do skeletons even use gear or experience?"

"No idea, but I do."

Jennifer waved at Sarah to get her attention.

With both a curious and confused expression, she walked over, and Jennifer repeated the spirit's demands.

Jennifer could see her friend's brows furrow above her sunglasses.

"That does seem a little high, and what happens if the ghost wants to quit, or you want to fire the ghost?" Sarah asked.

She relayed the question to the ghost, who replied, "I get to keep the experience and gear, and you keep the bones?" After relaying the terms to Sarah, Jennifer gave a half-hearted nod.

She used Summon Undead on her new skeleton worker, which appeared with the name Henery Woker highlighted in blue. Jennifer shrugged at the name and put the bones in her inventory.

When her stamina fell below seventy-five percent, Jennifer turned off her Mend power.

"Okay, I have more than enough skeletons in my inventory now, so I need to get back to town to get the repairs done on the micro foundry. Do you have anything to do here, or are you coming back to town too?" Jennifer asked her friend.

"I'm going to need to oversee an expansion office here, but that will only take a day or two. The road is safe if you and the goblin want to make the run."

With a smile, she went over to the small goblin and summoned the Kevin skeleton. The goblin blinked and her eyes widened as she gazed at the skeleton. She turned to Jennifer and pointed at herself.

When Jennifer nodded, the goblin got on the back of a skeleton but instantly dismounted. The green girl went over to the pile of rabbit furs and quickly made a riding blanket. When she threw the blanket over the skeleton, the skeleton's nose turned red and nodded at Jennifer.

Jennifer took this as a sign to get going and gave her goodbyes to the vampire and werewolf, who were giving pets and affection to Woozle before they departed.

Setting off at a jog, Jennifer noticed they were running faster, and she felt lighter on her feet. At this rate, she would be able to make it back to town faster than they had arrived in the shadow land.

In the distance, the town's walls looked like they were crawling with ants. Once they got closer, she realized people were working on the wall.

The old guard shack had been replaced with a large structure. A small window was set in the square building and a thick garage door gate stood to the side.

The group slowed to a walk as they came up to the new entrance.

"Well, Woozle, it looks like the mayor upgraded the wall." Jennifer was stating the obvious, but she wanted someone to confirm what she saw.

Woozle did not disappoint. "Yes, the question is why?"

A shiver went down her back. She looked at the goblin on the back of undead Kevin. The goblin who shrugged and urged her skeleton mount towards the gate that was now much less inviting.

Once they were at the gate, the guard said "Papers, please."

"Umm, what papers?" Jennifer tipped her head back and inspected the new construction. Days ago, it was barely a fence. Now it was a proper town wall.

"Argh, what business do you have in the town of Hogback?" The voice came from a small speaker under a one-way glass window.

"I want to see my new house, and I need to repair the micro foundry," she said while counting on her fingers. "Then I need to find a business owner to sign off on me going to Bishop's University. Oh, and I will need to gather herbs."

"Okay, you can enter, but the goblin and the shark thing cannot enter."

"Excuse me? This Miniature Giant, Rocket-Powered Lynx-Shark is my familiar, and that goblin is something to my party member's. And we all took part in the last paper raid."

After a few long, tense heart beats, he said, "Fine, but the goblin cannot come in, they are not on the approved list."

Her face grew warm in anger as she glared at the glass.

Giant Intimidation blocked

"Who is in charge of the approval list?" Her voice dripped with menace.

Giant Intimidation successful

The trait, Giant Imitation, has evolved into Giant Imitation II. Who said size does not matter.

"The only one that can change the approved list is the mayor." The voice from the speaker held a note of fear.

"Get the mayor." Each word came out hot.

"I can't just get the ma—"

"Get. The. Mayor." She kept the same tone.

"I will let you in, and you can talk to the mayor yourself." A buzz came over the speaker as the garage door opened.

Although she mumbled, "Thank you," Jennifer could not help glaring at the gate and its hidden guard as she walked away.

The trio first went to the micro foundry and fulfilled her promised quest. The effort of turning on her mend power reduced her stamina below ten percent. With her anger cooled to a low simmer, she made her way to the mayor's hotel, Chateau du Jim.

As she passed by the town square, Jennifer's jaw dropped. A tent city, more orderly than the goblin encampment, had popped up in the park. The tents were set up like rows of tiny houses. The top of the tents were below her shoulders. Jennifer looked down at Kevin's goblin and pointed at her then the tents. In front of the line of tents someone had left a sign. "I hear the beating of war drums, the cost of bread and freedom are on the rise."

The little goblin moved her head left and right, a clear no.

Turning to Woozle, the lynx-shark answered before she could ask the question. "I don't know. I've never seen something like this. From the setup, it looks like a camp of functionaries. This isn't a good sign."

With a shake of her head, Jennifer moved on slower than before. She stopped in front of the door to the hotel, closed her eyes, and took a deep breath. Exhaling, she opened the door.

The mayor sat at his table in a corner. The room was full but much quieter, as if the joy in the room had been tied up in the back. Her companions followed Jennifer to the mayor's table. He did not look up as the chairs were pulled out.

The blank look on his face told Jennifer he was in his menus. She politely cleared her throat with no effect. Before her annoyance triggered Giant Intimidation, she asked, "Woozle, how much damage does a shark bite do to a mayor?"

"I don't know. Let's find out, kid." Jennifer smiled in anticipation.

The mayor shot up out of his seat, using words a sailor might use after stubbing his toe and finding his bottle empty.

Woozle was curled up at Jennifer's feet as the mayor looked around for the source of his pain. Both the necromancer and her familiar looked on in curious innocence. The goblin giggled as she peered over the edge of the table.

"Did you see what bit me?" the mayor asked in frustration.

"We only just got here, but we were hoping to speak with you." Jennifer tried to sound as innocent as possible while batting her eyelashes at the mayor. "I had a bit of an issue getting into the town today, and I've not even seen my new house. It was so worrisome, I had to come straight to you."

"Oh, fallen to the dark side, have you? Necromancy will do that. I'll add an exemption for you." As the mayor spoke, he waved his hand in a circular motion.

"What? No. Inferno levels. I have a way of summoning undead without gaining evil points. I meant the goblin." She dropped the innocence act at the assumption of being evil.

"Not evil yet. So, what was the issue?" The mayor looked her up and down.

"The guard wasn't going to allow the goblin in or Woozle" With her frustration rising, Jennifer wondered how long it would take for her Giant Intimidation to kick in.

"How did you sweet talk the guardsmen into letting you in?"

Jennifer focused on the ceiling until she calmed down. "Yeah, sweet talking is something I can do." She tried to control her tone, knowing she should get back to the point. "I think Kevin's goblin should be allowed in. All goblins really."

The mayor did not respond but had the blank stare of someone looking at their menus. "Very scary giant lady with a clean skeleton was let in the main gate at three-oh-one. Nothing to report." The mayor's left eyebrow raised, and made eye contact with Jennifer. "I wonder who that would be."

"So, Woozle and Kevin's goblin will be allowed in along with Kevin." She focused on a spot on the table.

"A goblin guest will be allowed in with approved adventurers or townsfolk."

A barmaid Jennifer did not recognize left drinks on the table

"So, what's happening with the tent city? And the town wall?"

"War." With that single word, the mayor was the center of everyone's attention. "In the last two days, we've had more functionaries fleeing the war shell. They mention a T. rex. It's a little cliche, but the T.rex has been fighting hard. The warlord you met during the raid is the biggest concern."

"I did not like them trying to buy me off, but why them?"

"They're getting desperate and have lost a few towns. This town is a strong defense territory. If I were them, I'd make a temporary bridge a day's ride away from the town, with my remaining forces, take this town, and rebuild my forces." A grim determination filled the mayor's voice.

"Why not just go the normal way?"

A three-dimensional map appeared over the table, and the answer became obvious. A bridge crossed from one hexagon shell segment to another. She did not want to be stuck on the bridge with an army at her back when she would not be able to turn around. "One wants to be trapped on the bridge. The main bridge leads into town, where you have a gate." Her words came out flatly.

"The reason why this town is here is because of that bridge. It was here before the town was founded. If they crossed here, we would be able to see them. This is a small trading town. Bigger, thicker, tougher walls is what I have the town focused on building" A note hung in the mayor's voice that she could not identify.

The mayor needed a pick-me-up, but she would need to be subtle. Perhaps, even convince him it was his idea.

"Well, since you wanted to make sure I got home safe, you said you were going to show me to my new home?"

"Wait, what?"

From his reaction, she felt she nailed it. "My house should have been built by now, but it's so scary out there with all the unfamiliar faces. What if I get lost again?" She did her best to look innocent. "Oh, and I am going to borrow this table and chairs. And this water." She did not give him a chance to protest. She reached her hand out in front of her, trying to be ladylike. "Your hand, sir?"

The mayor automatically reached out and stood up. Before he could say anything, the table and chairs disappeared into Jennifer's inventory.

She half dragged him to her new house and let herself in. The light outside was growing dark, but the lights inside illuminated the flower garden on the other side of the glass.

"I see why you needed to borrow the table and chairs. There's nothing in here yet." A frown creased the mayor's face as he looked around. "Well, it's very nice. I like how you can see the flowers outside, but I really must be going."

After Jennifer placed the table and chairs in front of the window, she turned to the mayor with a glare.

Giant Intimidation II successful

He took a seat. "I guess I can stay a little while."

"Good, this won't take long." She pulled a water jug from her inventory and made her way to the kitchen. When she noticed the goblin was following her, Jennifer pointed at one of the other chairs with a smile.

Jennifer looked around the kitchen at the layout she had

picked, including a space for her alchemy station. After taking the station out of her inventory, it fit in the space nicely. She walked outside to one of the bushes and some moss on a rock, gathering the ingredients for her plan. Jennifer bustled around lighting fires under beakers, adding the water, and starting the brewing process. Jennifer activated Does This Taste Like Poison, Craft Healing Potions, and hoped the Alchemy part of her powers would help keep everything up as she continued to mix and heat.

She really hoped her plan would pay off. She came out of the kitchen with what had been clean, cold water and was now a green, warm liquid. She put it in front of the mayor. A devilish grin lit her face.

"I don't know about this." The mayor did not meet Jennifer's eyes.

Her smile widened and her eyes narrowed as she said two words, "Drink it."

The mayor looked at the drink in front of him. His Adam's apple bobbed up and down as the mayor took a sip. A bead of sweat ran down the side of his face.

"Tea. You made tea." The look on his face was priceless as his eyes slid in horizontal lines, indicating that he was reading his menus. "It's a healing tea that gives a buff."

"Thank you. I made it myself." She could not help but let pride fill her voice.

"So, you dragged me away from my duties. While the town I am leading is on the verge of an invasion, that could happen any day. Just so I could try tea?"

"Yes, do you like it?"

"Yes, it was very good." He took another sip of the drink.

Woozle's head came up from behind the table. "Kid, you can make tea?"

"Yup, it is basically hot leaf juice and some skills"

"And Jim, former adventurer, and current mayor of the town of Hogsback. Would you pay for this tea?"

"Oh ya, if I could get it from a store. I would definitely pick a can of this up, especially if I was going into a fight." The mayor answered with enthusiasm.

Woozle turned his head from the mayor to Jennifer, and back again. He rolled his eyes and coughed. Both Jennifer and Jim looked at him. "Okay so Jim, yes or no would you buy this drink?"

"Yes"

"Jennifer, you can make this drink?"

"Yes?"

"And all three of us are in a room with a table and chairs?"

"Yes." They both answered. Jennifer did not know where Woozle was going with these questions.

One of Woozle's paws went up to his face. "Would this space make for, oh I do not know, a good tea shop?"

Jennifer's face went slack, her eyes slowly moved from Woozle to Jim. She stared at the mayor. Her mind spun at the question. "How much do you," she trailed off and stiffened her back, deciding to inspect her nails. "How much do you pay for the tea in a tea shop?"

Jim gave Jennifer a blank look. He sighed, looked down at the ground, then up at the ceiling. "If you find the cost of the ingredients, double that price and it would be a fair price. The tea gives a medium health regeneration, and a tiny boost to stamina. It will be a great benefit for combat. In fact, the town would be willing to put in an order. If you bottle it, we can get it equipped to the guards."

"Wha, double? Are you sure? There are literally three ingredients: moss, leaves, and water." Her eyes moved from the cup to the mayor.

"Then triple it. It is business, you have a good product, you will have a good customer base among adventures, and are in a good location. I believe you will do well. And this did get me out of my own head space, if you got more chairs and tables, maybe add something to the atmosphere."

"Cat café," the thought so loud in her head she said it aloud.

Woolze's head looked down. "I do not think tea made of cats would be good."

The mayor's head tilted at Woozle.

"No, a cat café is a shop that serves tea, and has cats who are up for adoption roaming around the space."

The room was silent for several long heart beats.

"What if you adopted familiars?" Jim asked slowly. "Most of the time, people dismiss their familiars because they are not suited to the role of the people they are attached to. Here they may be able to find one they like, and will keep rather than sending them back into the system".

Jennifer looked at both entrances, "One was meant for guests, and the other for everyday use, but yes. Yes, that could work."

"I think I can get you the business license for a familiar café." The mayor stood up. "Thank you for this, it did get me out of my mood. Time, tide, and war waits for no one."

After Jennifer and the mayor said their goodbyes, she decided to explore her new house. It was empty, but it was what she wanted. It was a win for Jennifer. Making her way upstairs, she found the first alteration to the blueprints.

Doors marked with Large Soup Bowl 14, Kevin the wolf, Just Jennifer, and Sarah No Val. She made sure there would be room for her in her blueprints. Kevin was the only one who pushed for his own room at the design phase. He was also the only one there. Smiling, she shook her head at the thought of roommates. She was not going to be alone in this house with just Woozle, her spider, and a bunch of skeletons. Well, Kevin was already staying here. She had not meant to share it this way, but because they helped with the quest, how could she not? If they did not want to stay here, she would still have room for people to come and have a place to stay. Something she did not get when coming to this world. Besides, something comforting about not living alone. Opening the door to her room, she realized that she was going to need to get some furniture.

After rushing over the micro foundry, she ordered a bed, a small table, a chair, a desk, and a wardrobe. Disappointment rose in Jennifer when she found out those items would not be available until tomorrow at the earliest. Thankfully, she had an adventurer's sleeping mat from her night in the train car. Thanked the robot, and trudged home.

She was tired, more emotionally than physically. It had been a long two days and Jennifer wanted to sleep in. Finding her room again, she unrolled the mats and made herself comfortable. The goblin took up a spot on Jennifer's lower midsection and curled up. Woozle was too big to curl up on Jennifer, so he took up her left side. Rover teleported from the trapped door on Jennifer's shoulder to a corner where he made a web nest in a corner. She took Kevin's skeleton, who took a spot at the end of the mats at Jennifer's feet. She was unsure if she should take out the blue skeleton or not. She decided he could wait till later.

With her eyelids getting heavy, she looked out the window at the honey-colored moon in the sky. She thought, "This place is feeling a lot like home," before she drifted off to sleep.

She woke up once to let the living Kevin in, and again to let Kevin in though she couldn't remember letting him out.

When she awoke for the final time, the light was high in the sky. Judging from the brightness, it was midday. Jennifer let out a yawn and gave a stretch. Woozle was lying beside, and he too yawned. She was in her own home and in no danger. There were no giant spiders. The mayor was not knocking on her door. It was a very nice way to wake up. Woozle purred, sending a comforting rumble. Jennifer closed her eyes to savor the relaxing sensations.

She felt The goblin rested on her left side. Undead Kevin was on her feet, living Kevin lay his full body on her right, and other Kevin was keeping her head warm with his fur. It was nice. Just her, Kevin, Kevin, Woozle, and a goblin resting together like a pile of puppies.

Her eyes popped open. There were too many Kevins and only one with fur. Carefully, she looked over Woozle's fuzzy form and could just make out the top of undead Kevin on her feet. Living Kevin was on his side to her right, and the goblin on her left too. Her brain was not firing on all cylinders yet, but she realized whatever was sleeping above her head was not a Kevin. Whoever or whatever it was felt furry and warm. Jennifer turned over, pushing Woozle unceremoniously on the floor, and gave another yawn.

Her movements caused the others to wake. Twisting around she saw a long sleek head and neck attached to a strong muscular body. The frame of this new creature was similar to Kevin's, holding the shape of a canine, but it was taller, thinner, and had more tightly packed muscles than Kevin.

The coloring was also off, with pitch black fur and warm red embers glow that created a soft pond of red light around the new Kevin. Her eyes went wide as she recognized the species. "I have a Doberman from the infernal levels sleeping at my head. Sure, why not. You're now new Kevin." With those words, Jennifer decided to go back to sleep. She would deal with finding its owner later.

When the Doberman pawed at the door to be let out, Jennifer decided that this was as good a time as any to start her day. She needed to head to one of the inns for breakfast to recover her stamina. It was far closer to ten percent than she cared for.

When she pulled herself to her feet, the Kevins also woke up and started barking. Only the living Kevin could actually bark, but the skeleton was making the same motions. The living one's ears were pulled down and back.

Jennifer put her hand over the snout of the living Kevin in order to make the barking stop. "Some guard dog you are," she said, and moved to let the Doberman out.

"Umm, kid, did you get a new familiar for the tea house when I wasn't looking?" Woozle asked while he eyed the Doberman.

Its red embers were getting brighter.

"No idea. He was here when I woke up. Personally, I think this one was less scary than the spider. No offense, Rover." Jennifer opened her bedroom door and followed the new creature down the stairs and out the front door. Both living and undead Kevin followed behind Jennifer.

But instead of heading to the inn, she trailed the Doberman to the back entrance of the town hall. She had not planned on going there, but curiosity kept her on its tail.

The beast scratched at the back door, so Jennifer opened the door. Kevin entered next, never letting his eyes leave the body of the Doberman, while his goblin looked like she was sleeping in her saddle. Woozle proceeded next.

After being behind the hound as he walked down a few halls, a voice caused her heart to beat faster. She sprinted towards the voice coming from a courtroom, loud and clear.

Entering the room with the group behind her, she saw a woman sitting in the judge's seat. Her eyes went wide and let out one word. "Mom?"

The Doberman headed straight to the judge, jumping over a few benches and a barricade.

"Cruirse, I told you no jumping in the courtroom," said a uniformed minotaur. He caught the hound in mid-air as if the hound was just a puppy and glanced at the judge. "Well, ma'am, I found Cruirse,"

The minotaur looked at Jennifer and turned back to the judge. "Jennifer, you didn't tell me you had a kid."

Both the judge and Jennifer replied in unison. "I don't."

Jennifer's heart sank as they both spoke as one again, "Just a copy."

Jennifer grasped at the air near a chair, needing to sit down, while her mind repeated, "Just a copy."

As her hand made contact with a chair, a familiar voice said, "Clearly you all got something going on. So, let's just say innocent, and we can all—"

Jennifer's rage steadied her as she turned to the defendant, not caring how loud she was. "You tried to rob me, and you're claiming innocence."

Judge Jennifer on the bench raised her voice. "You tried to rob me?"

The rocket bowman quickly yelled, "Not guilty on a technicality?"

"Bailiff, please export the combat log," the judge ordered.

The minotaur made his way over the bowman.

"Guilty, with a mandatory quest that will benefit the victim?" The words rushed out of the bowman.

"I need herbs for my shop and a lot of them," the younger Jennifer said.

"Three thousand units of herbs to be gathered before any other quests can be accepted or completed." The older Jennifer hammered her gavel. "And you, my office."

"Can my party come?" Jennifer asked, not wanting to be alone with herself. She had never seen what her eye roll looked like but was now clear on the effect. She motioned to her party to follow.

Inside the office was a simple desk, two seats, a small black couch, and a work surface . Every wall that was not a window or door was covered with rows of books from floor to ceiling.

Jennifer followed the older version of herself and realized she was much taller than the other woman. Her grandmother had also been shorter than her. Contemplating this, she wondered if she would shrink in her old age.

The older, smaller Jennifer asked, "Let's get the big question out of the way. Why are you so tall?"

"Umm, half giant? You?"

"I took the descended from Atlantis option, which gave me a magic bonus."

"Ahh, and the judge part?"

"I just graduated from El Queen Jackson University and day-care for the rich kids. When I got here, I had just earned my law license. Took a while but I unlocked the prestige class of judges. I've been working here as a judge since then."

"I'm still in my first week. I'm opening a tea shop, so I count as a business owner, so I can write myself a letter of recommendation for Bishop's."

"Sociology?"

"Yeah, did you do that?"

"I did. But Dad wanted more, and I already had a minor in law by the end of the second year. So, I switched into pre-law, then transferred."

"Was Dad happy with that?"

"When is Dad ever happy? But he did have a smile on his face when he dropped in for graduation,"

"So, copies."

"So, copies. Just from different points."

Both Jennifers looked down. It was all getting a bit difficult for the younger Jennifer. "Do I call you older Jennifer?"

"Judge will do fine."

"Have you ever met another Jennifer?"

"Yes, but she's a pirate with red dyed hair. We met up in a pub. She started a bar brawl. Decided it was best not to follow in her footsteps. She arrived after watching some movies about pirates and orientation week. You?"

"You are the first. I am Necromancer, Alchemist, Future Defence Tech, the last one is mostly force fields." She cast one on Woozle for effect.

"Lawyer, Law Office Worker, District Judge, Infernal abbreviator and infernal contract law." The judge paused. "Don't ask me why but both infernals are one power set."

"I'm guessing that's where the 'H-E-double hockey stick' hound came from?" A knowing smirk crossed the adolescent's face. "Did you like those sets?"

The judge looked to her left, "Oh, yes. I found them very rewarding. So, necromancer?"

"Glitched, I didn't have much time to pick, and I didn't really understand what was happening." The necromancer looked down, still unable to look herself in the face.

"So, you're evil?"

"No, I just unlocked Speak With Dead, so I can get permission for stuff. So, no evil."

"Ahh, that makes sense. So, you're still going to University?"

"Yup, I'm going there after this. The dean will have to accept me."

"Let me know how—"

The two continued to ask each other questions for some time.

Jennifer was able to emotionally connect with the older version of herself. Jennifer's chest ached with a question she needed to ask but was afraid to hear the answer.

"Are there versions of our family? And how do you deal with just being a copy?" the younger one refused to meet the judge's eyes.

"I've never found Mom or Dad, but there's at least one version of our brother out there," the judge said, looking up with a finger on her lip.

"We have a brother?" Jennifer did not remember having a brother. Her brows came together while she searched her memory. "I guess my brother was one of the memories that didn't get copied over." The sorrow in her soul sung out in her words.

"One thing I have learned from this place, with all the parts being taken from other timelines, time periods, and having such poor timing is. Just because we are the same person, from different points, does not mean we have the same background. I have a brother. You may not have a bother."

"I feel." The newcomer to the world tried to put words to her emotions. "I feel like I miss a brother I never had now. And I will now always be comparing myself to you."

"Father said that I was just one of the many university's graduates. He said the doctor with the lowest passing grade is still called a doctor. I looked him straight in the eye and told him it was my feet that took me to class. My brother told me, no matter where I stand, my willpower took me places. Not my name. Not who I knew. My own actions. As a judge, I say you should only judge yourself by what you can do, and what you do. Be the main character of your own story."

The judge's words were cutting into Jennifer, " So I should take my own path."

"I'm a judge. You're a necromancer. We may look the same, but we go under our own sails. I went to university for the education not to impress anyone. I was copied into this word just at a different point in our lives."

"I think I can see why one of us turned pirate." Jennifer

wondered what a pirate's life might be like. She thought about how she would one day be getting a ship of her own, even if it was just a personal airship.

"Be who you are. Be true to yourself. Never let yourself or others believe you are nothing but a copy. You are your own person."

The words lightened Jennifer's heart. "I'll be my own person. There is too much to do to let being a copy slow me down anyways."

"Dad would be proud, no matter if he says otherwise. If you need someone to talk to, I will be here for you. But please do not show up at the courthouse looking for a legal loophole for a deal you made with an undead sea captain."

She was new to this world, and she was happy she found herself here on the back of the turtle.

***

Renewed, Jennifer set out with her group to Bishop's University. As they walked, she checked her inventory. A letter of reference from Large Soup Bowl. The reference letter simply said, "I, Large Soup Bowl 14, recommend Just Jennifer for school." Straight to the point with no room for argument.

Jennifer was receiving a speed buff from Kevin, making the trip shorter. Woozle, Kevin, and Kevin's goblin flanked Jennifer as she stood in front of the dean of Bishops University.

In the blue light of the hologram, the dean inspected the three letters on the table in front of Jennifer. Her heart beat faster with each passing moment. Everything she had done led up to this moment. She was going to get accepted to Bishop's.

"I accept the letters; They will be placed under review," said the dean.

"Review?" The word struck so heavily in Jennifer's mind, that it escaped her lips.

"Yes, your file is now under review." The dean quickly added, "And if you unplug the projectors again, you will be rejected."

She had never felt the urge to burn down a building more than this moment. "How long will this review take?" Her tone must have dripped with anger because Kevin growled and Woozle hissed.

"Between tomorrow and the death of your universe." The dean's words could have been used to smoke a dead deer with his smugness.

Jennifer swore to herself that if she got rejected, this building would be lit on fire with the dean still on. Thinking of the look on the dean's face as the office burned around him, she smiled.

"Thank you for accepting my letters of recommendation," forcing herself to smile, "and considering my application to this university."

They left the dean's office and the building. In spite of being in a bit of a huff, her group was greeted by a goblin. Kevin's goblin jumped off the wolf's back into the arms of the strange goblin, and with cheerful sounds, they greeted each other.

Jennifer turned and looked at Kevin, who looked back at her. Kevin gave a shrug and moved his head indicating the direction of the goblins. Jennifer shrugged back, and the team followed the goblins back to their encampment.

An elderly goblin in an ornate black robe and large pointed hat stood on the path. To Jennifer's surprise the old goblin barked at Kevin who barked back.

"Okay, next side quest. Learn speak with Kevin." She meant to say it quietly, but she was not quiet enough.

"You should learn not to interrupt other people's conversation first." The old goblin spoke with a peculiar accent but clear diction.

"What the muffin? You speak my language?" Jennifer put a hand to her open mouth.

"Yes, I do like muffins."

"Hello, my name is Jennifer?" she said, as the group walked into the goblin encampment.

"Greetings, human, my name is Goblin." In spite of the deep lines on its face and slow movement, the old goblin spoke with a young man's voice.

Her curiosity got the better of her, and she asked, "Are you using a trait to speak with me?"

"No. Talisman speaks for Goblin. Talisman speaks human to Goblin."

"So, why set up the encampment outside of school?" She was trying to make small talk despite the translating skills not being perfect.

"Goblin wanted education, so Goblin came to school. School closed. Goblin try to turn school into a dungeon to raise more goblins. Camping on campus until goblins allowed in residence with classes. Goblin wished for degree in education with young goblin." The more the goblin spoke, the more Jennifer empathized with the goblin, and the more her ears hurt.

Large Soup Bowl was easier to understand, and he did not come with the accent. Looking to the wolf, Kevin's tail was wagging hard, so Jennifer continued with the small talk as the group made their way to a campfire. "Do all goblins want to go to Bishop's University?"

"Yes. Goblin of Bishop's University."

The group sat, and a deep-fried bird leg was brought to the group. Picking up the food in her fingers, Jennifer took a bite and found the chicken very good. It also caused her stamina stats to jump up.

"I completed the entrance quest, but my application file is under review," she said between bites.

Kevin was also enjoying the chicken.

Woozle walked over to the goblin by a large pot with a dead rabbit in his shark mouth.

"You understand quest to get into school?" The Goblin's mouth hung open.

Being distracted by the goblin cleaning the rabbit, she casually said, "Yes. Do you want a letter of reference?"

"Goblin not know what letter of reference is. What is letter of reference?"

Rather than try and explain what a letter of reference was, she took one out of her inventory and handed it over. The look of shock on the goblin's face was worth it.

The green person looked at the page. He yelled something in their language. A pile of paper, and a few pens were quickly deposited in front of Jennifer.

Jennifer took the first sheet of paper and wrote, "I, Just Jennifer, recommend the holder of this paper for Bishop's University."

Handing the paper to the elderly goblin, she said, "One complete. Goblin needs two more." A pang of guilt settled in her chest, as she thought of a way to explain. Goblins were left out of the cities, the dean disliked goblins, and the world just did not like them. Even if they got the letters, there was no guarantee they would be let in. "I'm a shopkeeper. You need a letter from the mayor and a parallel. Two more letters from two different people."

"How get?"

For such a simple question, Jennifer had no answers. The people in the village only saw goblins as monsters.

"Side quests?" She had no solutions to what seemed like an impossible question. "Are goblins fragments?"

"Goblins are goblins."

Her thoughts recalled an old saying. Well, not all questions give answers.

"I will find the ones who wrote letters for me and see if they can do the same for you." She sighed. That was going to be a hard side quest. She watched as a new notification appeared in her menus.

Get the goblins into Bishop's University– impossible

Jennifer did not want to believe it was impossible. "This one won't be easy, but worst case, all of my classmates will be little green people. At least they're not the red planet eat-whatever-moves variety."

Kevin growled, and Jennifer was on her feet with a mop in hand searching for the source of the danger.

Kevin's fur stood on end as he stood between a white chicken with a silver tiara and a goblin in a dirty apron holding a butcher's knife.

Jennifer let down her guard, walked over, and picked up the chicken. "This one is Kevin's now. No hurting," she announced to the group of goblins.

Kevin tugged on Jennifer's school uniform with his teeth.

She let him pull her away from the goblins and gave a polite wave goodbye.

Woozle comes bounding up with a fried rabbit in his mouth. The movement was more of a prance, showing off the meal.

"You're going to let me have a bite of that, right?"

Woozle gave Jennifer a dirty look and powered up his rockets. With a gust of hot air, Woozle blasted off faster than either Jennifer or Kevin could chase him.

"I guess that's a no." The rabbit looked and smelled delicious. Jennifer could not help pouting. "I always share with him."

The group made it to town with Jennifer carrying the white chicken the whole time. When they arrived at the house, there was a line in front of her café. Her unopened café.

"Excuse me," she said, squeezing her way through the crowd. "Shop owner coming through. We'll be open as soon as I make the tea."

Once inside, Jennifer used Summon Undead on the blue skeleton. She called it that because, unlike the others, there remained a strange blue haze of the spirit surrounded it. "Okay Blue, start seating. There's only one thing on the menu."

Again, she used her power to summon two common skeletons. "The two of you, start gathering water."

Jennifer started brewing tea before realizing there was only one glass in the house, and it was dirty. Having only one borrowed table with two chairs in the café was not going to get her very far either. Making her excuses, she bolted over to the micro foundry only to find out that her order was not finished. It turned out that the mayor had set priority production on tents for the fragment refugees fleeing the dinosaur warlords. Their numbers were increasing, and they were coming into town with nothing but the clothes on their back. At least they got tents.

"Why go to the foundry when you can get what you need from Exports du Universal," Sarah said from behind her. Her friend stood confidently in a new suit with a golden name tag pinned on her chest. The very image of a manager that could handle everything. "We are not open for regular business, but do you want to be the first customer for my shiny, new branch?"

"Sarah, I'm so glad to see you. Can you? Really?" She did not bother to keep the panic out of her voice. Sarah's timely arrival had Jennifer wanting to pick up the woman and hug her. "My hero. Glasses, pitchers, tables, chairs, café stuff, soon. Can you rush the order and be there in an hour?"

Sarah struck a classic superhero pose with her hands on her waist. "Of course."

"Wonderful," squealed Jennifer, who hugged Sarah. "I need to make tea!"

The movers arrived at the café within minutes of Jennifer getting back. The blue skeleton took charge and did a good job directing the movers to where everything should go. His help allowed Jennifer to focus on her job as the two other skeletons brought in buckets of fresh clean water. She did not know where the buckets were coming from and was too busy to ask as she emptied the water into filling stations on the alchemist set.

She used her powers, traits, herbs, and knowledge at her alchemy station crafting teas. Some teas came out green, others yellow, and one rare purple. Even with using all the same ingredients, the system added randomness to something that should not have been randomized.

She continued to work until her stamina fell below the halfway mark. Taking a look outside the kitchen, she saw Kevin and his goblin greeting each of the guests. The wolf would sniff them, wagging his tail, and the guest would smile, giving him head scratches. A few people tried to pet the goblin, but she moved away from the outreached hand and clung to Kevin's furry rump.

Woozle, on the other hand, jumped from tabletop to tabletop. How he managed to do this and not knock anything over was a mystery. Considering his now pony size, this was even more impressive. He head butted or rubbed his face on any willing guest and purred so loudly that Jennifer could hear him from the kitchen door. The rockets periodically revving only added more rumbling to the purring.

One patron got a little too close to the engines and singed their beard. The thought of something or someone getting sucked into Woozle's intake valves had Jennifer wondering how many warning signs she would have to put up. But would anyone read them?

The chicken had roosted in a corner. People kept feeding her grains that they pulled out of their inventory.

"I've started a pet café. How did I start a pet café?" Jennifer took a quick glance at her menus, wondering where Rover was.

Rover Status: Gathering

Jennifer focused her mind and intentions.

"Rover, please return."

A trap door appeared on Jennifer's right shoulder, and out popped her pet spider. Unsure how Rover would react, she turned on to Speak With Spider. "So, I started a pet café. Do you want to go out there and get pets?"

The spider did not move for several heartbeats, and Jennifer feared she had somehow offended him. Suddenly, his neon legs lit up with green stripes that continued up his body. With a jumping loop, the spider leapt to the floor soundlessly and scurried into the dining area.

Rover climbed the nearest table and started dancing. Jennifer stared in astonishment. The only thing she had seen Rover do so far was gather berries and web something in combat. With his moves, he would easily win every dance completion in the area.

Jennifer tried some of her green tea. Not only did it taste wonderful but by the time the cup was empty, her stamina was full. She went back to work, until the light in the sky went dark.

When she closed, she was tired but happy. Blue set the ordinary skeletons to cleaning while he made sure everything was in order for the next day, freeing Jennifer to crawl into bed.

She slept deeply, but woke up to a rooster's call coming from outside. The white chicken pecked at the bedroom door to be let out. Still groggy but wanting to keep her white chicken safe, she followed it, yawning the entire way. Even sleepy eyed, Jennifer could tell the racket came from atop the roof, and the chicken wanted out of the house. Stepping outside, Jennifer looked up at a black rooster on the roof. But it was not an ordinary rooster with his white domino mask and red satin lined black cape. He had a red rose in his beak.

With the quick flick of a wing, three roses shot towards Jennifer. On instinct, she cast a force field, which deflected two of the roses and brought the third to a standstill in front of Jennifer. "I never knew throwing roses could be deadly."

The white hen's feathers puffed up as she strutted and clucked loudly at the rooster. Unfortunately for the rooster, when the caped chicken landed with grace in front of the white chicken, she received him with a wing to the side of the head.

Even Jennifer winced at the hit and heated scolding.

Jennifer picked up the white chicken and headed inside. With the now dejected caped rooster following.

Woolze and Kevin left for a morning hunt, planning to bring back rabbits, while Jennifer prepared for the day. On the teashop's second day, she gave out fetch quests for ingredients and a deep fryer.

On the third day, Jennifer sold fry bread with rabbit in the center.

Everyone fell into a routine for the next few days. The morning consisted of gathering and fetch quests while the afternoon was for making tea and frying bread for her guests.

The number of chickens grew to four, including a large golden chicken with an axe tied to its back, and a chicken with red on top and black on the bottom. The red and black chicken wore a pirate hat as well as a cutlass.

Each night, Jennifer would put them in a chicken coup she had made just for them, but they would disappear by morning. Since they would always reappear by the time the restaurant opened, Jennifer did not worry too much about what they got up to.

Jennifer did not know where they went or why, but they always came home safe. They even grew used to Kevin coming up to them and sniffing them when the café opened.

When Jennifer pulled herself away from her alchemy station to inspect the café, she gazed at the shelves filled with rows of sealed jugs. Each of the containers held 4 healing potions. They were all labeled Jennifer's Healing Tea. Cups and saucers were set up, ready to receive either hot tea or tea with ice cubes and cooled.

The guest space had every seat filled, and a line of guests queued up outside waiting for their chance to come in. Her blue skeleton wore a matching blue suit and escorted guests to their table. Each guest would receive a filled cup of their choice of hot or cold. As well as an unopened package of cookies.

Jennifer had made a deal with Sarah, and by extension her company, to buy the snacks. Jennifer bought the snacks at a discount, but after resale, they would cost the same as if the customer bought them anywhere else. The café would make a profit, the corporation would receive a profit, and the guest would pay the same. If a guest did not eat the cookies, they were not charged for them. The downside of using skeletons as wait staff was that they could not communicate with the guests. So, most guests did not know that they had the option to not eat and not be charged for the cookies. But then, who could resist cookies?

One of her other skeletons cleaned the tables, set the napkins, and washed the dishes. No one seemed to mind skeletons that walked around with all of their bones showing, and Jennifer wanted to show off her upgrade power.

Jennifer gave the busboy skeleton a coating of white metal that helped as it increased the durability, nearly doubling its hit points. But the true purpose was to make it easier to paint. Jennifer was no artist, but over the past few weeks she had found paint and enjoyed slashing paint on the bones. Not enough bones for her to have a proper canvas. The solution? An upgrade to starting metal armor. The skeleton became a walking piece of street art with additional glow in the dark paint. Her knight skeleton did not have metal gauntlets, but rather rubber yellow gloves for washing dishes. On his shoulder sat a yellow duck. She had no idea where the duck came from, but made it a point to start upgrading that pile of bones to look more like a pirate.

Jennifer placed a glowing skull on the chest piece of the glowing blue skeleton, along with rings of glued-on gems that a guest had used to pay for the higher-grade teas to take with them.

The familiar café had come a long way since she had opened it. Days became weeks, but every day she woke up wondering if this was going to be the day she would receive the letter of acceptance. On bad nights, she would fear a letter of rejection. Things were going well, other than the looming war. The influx of functionaries seeking refuge never waned, the chickens disappeared each night, but the café showed a profit.

Jennifer was lost in thought, gazing around the crowded café, when Blue poked her in the arm. Not hard, just enough to get her attention. "Speak With Undead." She did not need to say the power, she just liked to. "What's up, Blue?"

"Master, I have a guest who wishes to speak with you." The ghost of the skeleton spoke in a funny accent that should have stayed in the old monster stories.

Jennifer waved her hand for him to lead the way. "Why do you insist on sounding like Bela Lugosi? No one else can hear you."

The skeleton straightened as it walked and lost the accent. "Bela Lugosi is still undead. Well, I like it. It adds to the charm of this place."

"I'd like it better if you did the Son of Dracula or one of those circus vampires if you really want to play the part."

"I'll think about it. Anyway, the customer in question keeps pointing at the healing potions and a chest at his feet. I believe he wants to make a trade."

Happening more and more. An adventure would come in, offering a trade, anything from gems to money to supplies, and a few familiars. Jennifer was back up to having four of her own healing potions in her inventory, but no matter how much she tried, the healing teas were never as good as the ones her powers made. She would offer the teas she made, most would accept the lesser quality. She was being offered so many trades she was no longer accepting money.

Mechanical words left the shirtless, oiled up, loin cloth wearing man. "Trade for healing potion."

Focusing on the man, Jennifer was able to see the parallel's name, Barbarian the Barbarian of Barbarian 5. She shook her head. "Trade declined." She was used to this.

Normally, customers gave up after the first no, but this man would not take no for an answer. "Counteroffer, pet plus five sapphires high quality." He spoke with the same flat voice and speech pattern as the ninja on her team. Around a dozen of her regular customers talked the same way.

Looking over the barbarian and the treasure chest, Jennifer did not see the creature that the barbarian could have been referring to. She wondered if it was stuck inside the chest. "What pet?"

The chest looked like the typical trunk with a half barrel top, metal binding, and a big lock. Battle marks scared the chest as if someone had tried to smash it open rather than pick the lock. The middle of the lid of the chest went from rigid to sagging. The line along the bottom of the lid made a sad face. "Me."

Jennifer's eyes widened in confusion followed by anger. "You want to trade your familiar for a potion?"

"Yes, mimic good for trap. Enemies attack him rather than me?"

This barbarian was the same as her teammate Large Soup Bowl, both were what the mayor called Console people. The way they spoke was so wooden. She could never see their reactions.

Jennifer refused to let the familiar leave with someone who would let him be attacked. She raised one finger and pointed at the barbarian, but before she could say her peace, a horn blew in the distance. Everyone in the café stopped what they were doing, some mid-sip, and turned to look out the window. This was the single that the siege would start.

The entire town knew what the horns meant. It was the same sound used when the warlords showed up the last time. One upside to having a café in the middle of a town of adventures was safety. Whoever attacked would have to get through a wall, the parallels that find defending hogs back from monsters, and make it to the center to threaten the familiar café.

Every person in the café pulled out weapons, including the chickens. Where Jennifer expected grim expressions, she saw smiles. Some people were grinning like maniacs. The muscles on her face contracted into a nervous smile.

Jennifer turned to the barbarian. "Accepted. When potion is used, the vial will return." She slapped the potion into his hand, and told the mimic, "Find a safe place to rest. Sorry I can't show you around right now. But when this is dealt with, I will." Woozle rubbed his head and face on the mimic. "Don't worry buddy, you're in a safe place now."

The mimic's attempt to hold back its emotions, as the barbarian left followed by everyone who carried a weapon.

Jennifer was the last to leave. She stopped to give the chest a hug, reassuring the new addition to her home. Her teammates waited for her outside. Even the chickens were tapping their feet with impatience.

"Woozle, are you ready for this?" Jennifer clutched her mop so tightly her knuckles were white.

"I believe so."

"Are we ready for this?"

Woozle turned his head to look at Jennifer. "As long as you let me, I will always be by your side."

His words cause Jennifer to ease her grip on her cleaning tool. She took a deep breath.

The mayor had spoken about how the dinosaur warlord would

attack from a random point on the wall, so she was surprised to hear the rallying call coming from the gate to the bridge. The pass was wide enough to have wagons pass each other. Jennifer could not see the end of the bridge while standing at the entrance, and she could not see the bottom of the gap it crossed. Clouds and fog obscured the bottom. If there was a bottom.

CHAPTER 18

WAR

JENNIFER SHOOK SO BADLY she could barely hold her mop. She led her group to take up a position near the back of the line on one side. The group arranged themselves in a diamond formation with Sarah in front, Kevin on the right, Soup Bowl on the left, and Jennifer in the back. The pets were scattered close by with the exception of the chickens, who had formed their own diamond shape.

Jennifer kept trying to take deep breaths, but panic kept breaking through her calm. If the fight did not begin soon, she feared she would run in the other direction. Looking around, her reaction was not unusual. There was a divide in their army. It took several short heartbeats to understand why. Parallels were excited; fragments were afraid. There was no raid alert. The fragments that were choosing to fight knew that if they fell, they might never get back up. The parallels would return no matter what.

The mayor stood front and center. Jennifer's gaze shifted between him and the farthest point of the bridge. The warlord himself led the invading group over the bridge. She selected the warlord as a target, but the only thing that was stopping her from firing her dark blast was that he was out of range.

Oddly enough, the warlord walked down the bridge holding a banner instead of running. One slow step at a time, he held his banner high as he approached. But by the way he moved, it looked like he did not want to be there. Before, he would walk around with his head held high, looking down on everyone around him. Now, his shoulders sloped and his eyes looked down.

Every member of the warlord's army wore white arm or leg bands. Some even had bands around their heads. When the invaders got closer, Jennifer realized Red stains on the white bands. Staring at the banner was not a mark of intimidation. The mental shock hit hard, and she dropped both her jaw and her mop. The banner was a sign of desperation and a mark of surrender. A white flag.

Some people groaned with disappointment, while others signed with relief, but everyone rushed forward to help.

The warlords leading the army were taken to the town hall, and Jennifer's group turned into healers. When she had time, She made tea and healing potions. Jennifer considered returning to her café to get more of the drinks. The shelves in her café's kitchen were stocked with healing teas, but those were weaker. Her potions healed most fragments by half, but her teas helped by giving a regeneration buff. Anyone who drank would have health points recover at a faster rate than normal.

For parallels, the results were far more random. Her personal potions healed them completely or did almost nothing. Someone told her that the healing potions would heal five hundred points of health, while her teas healed about half but over half a minute. Her potions would always do the same, but not everyone had the same health pool. The higher the level, the larger the pool.

Warriors who were left behind with the lowest health pool were the ones Jennifer's team did triage on. When a bluebird landed on Jennifer's shoulder with a message for her to meet the mayor at city hall, she was worried what else could happen. Something important enough to summon her would suggest someone was hurt.

The sky turned silver as she left her team, who continued tending to the remaining wounded lined up in rows on the ground. One glance up at the sky cleared her hazy mind. A dark and ominous count-down clock hung in the sky. What was going to happen in forty-eight hours?

No greeting came from the mayor's lips as she entered city hall.

In a flat tone, he said, "The warlord and his armies were beaten by a single raid boss."

The female dinosaur added, "Whatever was attacking us did not trigger the normal options. When you take a town or city, there is an option to convert or raise. To take it or burn it to the ground."

The warlord's voice was low and full with emotions as he gripped his rocket hammer. "I always choose to convert and add the conquered city to my territory. That thing just beat my armies and left the cities to burn, not taking the raising option. He left the resources, the non-combatants, but no way to use the stockpiles. The fragments didn't have the script. They just fled."

"Why did you call me?" Jennifer felt like the odd one out in a room full of fighters.

"You came up with the plan to beat the last raid boss on the fly. We need someone to come up with a plan." The mayor's face looked grim. "And we need a plan in less than forty-eight hours."

"Have you tried not fighting?" It was the option she wanted most. "You know a battle not fought cannot be lost?" She shrugged.

They were not amused.

The head warlord roared, "I told you asking fragments for help was useless."

"We are going to need a bigger army." The triceratops ignored his leader's outburst.

Jennifer stared at the ground. The thought of putting anyone in danger turned her stomach, but she had given her word. "I can get you an army," she murmured.

"How?" asked the mayor without hesitation.

Jennifer shuffled her feet. "Letters of recommendation from the mayor, a business owner, and a parallel."

"Well, we have a mayor and a group of parallels." The warlord beamed and rubbed his hands together.

In spite of herself, Jennifer looked him in the eye with a smile, then looked down. "With the timer, that means this is a raid. Will fragments respawn?" The last word hurt coming out of her throat.

The others looked at one another then at the mayor.

The female dinosaur asked the mayor, "You've been playing the longest. Have you ever done a silver raid?"

"Why do you think he's been here the longest? I just got the ten-year badge," the dinosaur in the wizard hat asked.

"I stopped counting," said the mayor. "But no, I've never been in a silver raid. I'm playing the role of a mayor, not an adventurer."

By the huff in the mayor's voice, Jennifer every fiber within her being told her, the mayor was lying, but decided not to press. "So, do we know if fragments respawn?" She asked the question again, the final word came smoothly from her. While she still did not know the process, after going into the tree it was easier to understand such words.. She needed the answer.

The mayor spoke slowly and deliberately. "The strongest raids I've been in have had raid-specific rules, 'fragments respawn' was a case-by-case basis. Judging by the fragments that came here after the last battles, I would assume they will respawn."

"From the number of cities that fell and how many are left, I am assuming fragments will not," said the warlord, glaring at the mayor.

"So, a chance, at best." Jennifer looked down, trying to think of a way to keep her promise without endangering the goblins. "Okay, a chance is a chance. It will be up to them if they join. Mr. Mayor, you'll need to come with me to make the offer."

"I'm needed here to prepare the defense. There's no way I can go." The mayor raised his voice as he stood. He was clearly looking for support from the others as he looked around. The knuckles of his hands went white while leaving the table.

Jennifer raised a finger pointing at the ceiling and narrowed her eyes. "The mayor needs to be the one to make the offer."

"Look, there are things I'm going to be needed for here." The mayor crossed his arms and scowled.

The leader of the dinosaurs looked at the mayor in confusion. "Like what? We're the warlords here. We can set up the defense."

"And we can organize the lines of parallels and set up fallback points," the female dinosaur added while eyeing the mayor.

"But we need more bodies to fill the line," said the triceratops.

"I can cast fireball." The wizard lizard's comment made it clear that he was not the brains of the team.

The mayor rubbed his forehead. "I'll set up a town buff for the raid, then follow Jennifer to this"—he paused for a moment before adding—"army."

Seeing the opportunity, Jennifer added, "I'm also going to need more metal and healing moss."

The mayor rolled his eyes. "I'll spend more town points on fetch quests as well."

An hour later, the mayor met Jennifer at the town's gate on the road that led to Bishop's University. The mayor wore an oilskin hooded cape, a belt with a lot of pouches, his normal bone bead chest piece, and a walking stick.

"Where is your top hat, and coat? You have gear for just traveling?" Jennifer tilted her head slightly. So far, she only had her school uniform and starting gear.

"I have one hundred twenty-seven sets of gear for nearly any occasion."

"And you only ever wear one outfit in town?"

"When you have the perfect outfit, why bother."

Jennifer's lips tightened, and her eyes narrowed on the mayor. "Where do you even store it all?"

The mayor smiled and handed Jennifer a pouch for her belt. She took the pouch. After adding it to her belt, her menus posted an alert that her storage space had increased. Checking her inventory, she had gone from twenty slots to thirty. An additional four stacks of fifty steel ingots. She never paid much attention to her inventory, preferring to keep it as clean and empty as possible. Her mop and a few odds and ends were the only constants.

The mayor kept up beside her as they walked to the university. Not wanting to endure the trek in silence, Jennifer said, "So, this will be your first silver raid."

"Yes. The highest I've ever done was against a living, moving castle made out of flaming squids. It was more of a puzzle raid than a combat raid, but the reward was unlocking a prestige class. Of course, I took the mayor class." A slight smile crept across the mayor's face.

"So, Jim the Electric Mayor?" Jennifer felt it was a good question.

The mayor chuckled. "Electric, Invulnerable Mayor."

The mayor trailed off, Jennifer added "And?"

The mayor gave her a side-long look. "Cheese maker."

Jennifer stopped in her tracks. "Cheese maker?" Her jaw hung open before adding, "That means you have four main power trees, right?"

The mayor waved his hand, urging her to keep moving. "Well, three and a half. When I level up, I get the leveling options as if I have three power trees."

"I thought parallels only got two power trees and then optional power sets?" She took a few large steps to close the gap between them as they walked.

"We start with two, then we can unlock others. It's difficult, but it's doable."

"How did you unlock Cheese maker?"

"By making a lot of cheese. The things you do when you're young and want to impress a girl."

"You became a cheese maker to impress a girl? Did it work?" Jennifer could not imagine being impressed by that.

"That's how I met Belle. And now I'm a grandparent, so I would count that as a win." The mayor looked up with a dreamy expression on his face.

The two continued their small talk as they walked to the university.

When the two reached the main gates, the mayor asked, "So, an army of students. I vaguely remember something about people who enlisted getting the chance to get an education too. Yes, I think I could work with this. So, where are these students? In the dorms?"

"They have an encampment on one of the quads. I'm hoping this time I get to have some of that deep-fried rabbit." She licked her lips just thinking about it.

When they turned the last corner before the encampment, the mayor yelled, "Look out! There are goblins," and turned on his buffs.

"Yup." Jennifer walked past the mayor, waving cheerfully at a few of the goblins she recognized.

"Your army is an army of goblins?" The mayor looked aghast. "You want me to give a bunch of goblins letters of reference to get into the university? In exchange for fighting?"

"Only if they agree to it."

"This was a waste of time." Anger ripped through the mayor's voice. "They're less than people, only good for dulling weapons."

Jennifer's hand shot out so fast, neither could stop it. The mayor stumbled backward as a handprint outlined on the side of his face. "Are you a beggar or a chooser?" She raised her voice. "They have the same feelings as you or I. They have their own wants and needs. They want to get into the university just as much as I do. The world can only be made better with education for all."

"The world can be made better by exterminating all goblins. No man would willingly fight next to one, and we cannot beat the green off their skin," said the mayor coldly.

She felt her face growing hot. "Do you want allies or enemies? How many times have you fought goblins, but they're still here?"

"No matter how many rat traps there are, there will always be rats." The mayor was practically spitting his words out.

Woozle appeared next to Jennifer. Where he had come from, she did not know, but his engines revved in aggravation.

"With education, they will add their own knowledge to ours and everyone will learn more." She glanced in her menus and prepared to queue up her skeletons for a fight.

The train whistled in the distance and the two glared at one another. It felt like a warning somehow.

The mayor's face went red. With a twitch of his hand, he moved towards Jennifer. But before he took a full step, a pie slammed into his face stopping him in his tracks.

The pie stayed in place for a few heartbeats before it fell to the ground in a whipped cream mess. When he blinked, Jennifer bent over in uncontrolled laughing.

Between laughs, the elderly goblin Jennifer had previously met walked over to the mayor. Reaching up, and standing on his toes, a swipe of his finger, he wiped off the cream. "Banana cream pie, best aggression stopper."

A goblin speaking English caused the mayor to blink faster. "You speak our language?"

"Yes. How many languages do you speak?" While highly accented, the intelligence in the goblin's voice was unmistakable.

"I don't want you in my town's army," the mayor blurted.

"It's okay. We will watch your town burn. The commodore will crush you." The goblin shrugged and half grinned.

The mayor's eyes narrowed. "How do you know about the raid?"

The goblin's smile widened, but he did not answer.

The mayor looked sideways at the goblin and chewed his lip. "What do you think our chances are?"

"Without Goblin, bad. With Goblin, not as bad."

"That good, eh?" The mayor sighed and looked down. "How much to join?"

The goblins' eyes narrowed. "School."

"No." The word shot out of the mayor.

The goblin's smile returned. "No goblin."

Jennifer looked down at her familiar and mouthed the word, "Rabbit." Woozle nodded and bounded off. Jennifer returned her attention to the mayor and the goblin, trying to judge the chances that the pair would come to blows. The mayor wiped away the remaining mess on his face, as the two continued to speak to each other. She did not have the experience to know if these two were arguing or negotiating, but with nothing to add to the conversation. She slowly edged away. Her aim was to help the goblins start packing up. They would either need to leave town, or find a new place where they would not be bothered. She wondered if they might like swamp land. If the town did fall, she would like to move into their camp.

Sometime later, with a plate of deep-fried rabbit in her lap. She watched the goblins take down their tents, as Jennifer happily ate the rabbit. Woozle was on at least his fourth. Half an hour later, the entire camp was packed up and the goblins were off to Hogback. Not all goblins followed the trail to town. groups of four to six left in other directions. The ones that left either refused to meet Jennifer's eyes or glared at her with such vigor it made her giant intimidation look weak.

The only remaining creature in the quad was the beefalo with sunglasses. Jennifer walked slowly over to the creature and hugged its side. "We'll be back." A noise like an accented happy moo came out of the cow hybrid.

She contemplated staying and waiting for the battle to be complete before returning to the town. Thinking of the battle made her skin go cold. She was not a fighter, she wanted to be a student. The places her mind went when thinking about the upcoming battle were places she did not want her mind going. She forced the thoughts out of her mind, squeezed her eyelids as tight as she could, and took in a deep breath.

A few things happened over the course of just a small handful of heartbeats. The mayor and the goblin shook hands. The goblin town started towards Hogsback. Finally, Jennifer received enough experience to leave up. Joining the walk back to town, Jennifer looked at her leveling options. She received three power options with simple choices. She took Summon Large Undead, raising the limit of her crafted potions from four to eight, and a power called Boom Shield.

Summon Large Undead: You are now able to summon one large skeleton. This power does stack with other skeletons. When in doubt, go big or go home.

Looking over the stats, she could have her normal three skeletons or one large skeleton. Jennifer sighed. She needed to go back to the land of the dead and find something large she could summon.

Boom Shield: When the force field is removed by force, the shield will cause knock back damage around the one that was protected by the shield. You take this down, you go down.

With her final power option, she chose Crafter, which was the next power after **Mending** in the generic power tree she took so long ago.

All the powers she selected were powers unlocked at level eleven, and she felt this was a clean simple level up. She did not have to weigh her options, coupled with the simple choices, she was happy. Looking at Woozle, he was the size of a mini pony before, but now a regular size one. She missed having a small ball of purring fluff riding in her hood. She wondered if she got a backpack, would he willingly ride in it.

She walked silently next to the mayor on the way back to town. Bisow was trailing behind. The sunglasses made him stand out.

With every step she took, her legs felt weaker. She was sweating more, and needed to calm her breathing as the green army moved. She focused on not panicking as they approached the wall.

Jim waved his hand and the gate opened. Goblins walked through head held high. Apprehension turned to surprise and curiosity at the line of people winding around the town square. At the end of the line stood three robed people standing before a sword in a stone. The next person in line walked up to the sword in the stone, gripping the hilt of the sword. Even from a distance, Jennifer could see the bunching muscles on the person's arms ripple as he pulled the sword from the stone.

"What is your name, chosen one?" asked one of the robed people loud enough for the cheering crowd to hear.

"Umm, Hamill Gastly," said the man holding the sword.

"As was prophesied, Hamill Gastly is the chosen one who pulled the sword from the stone. Next!"

The next person in line was clearly a wizard, wearing a blue pointed hat, matching robes, and a long white beard. This time, a staff appeared in the stone.

Jennifer turned with head tilted toward the mayor who seemed to find something interesting off in the distance.

"Have you heard of the king under the mountain?" the mayor asked sheepishly.

"I've heard of the chosen one. It's been done." She paused to look at the long line of people. "It's been done a lot."

"Yeah, well, as mayor I got to choose the name of the buff. Everyone wants to be the chosen one. Everyone wants to be the hero in their own story, right?"

"You have people lining up to be the chosen one in the battle to save the town. That's not a bad idea." She wanted to chastise the mayor, but a good idea was a good idea.

Goblins joined the line of people waiting to be one of the many chosen ones. While no one interacted with the goblins, no one started any trouble with them either. People were, however, crossing the street and keeping their distance.

"Okay, let's see how they're setting up the defense." The mayor waved for Jennifer to follow.

She was underwhelmed by her first time in the mayor's office. A desk, the town flag, a window, and a picture of a woman in a green military uniform standing in front of an old school military ambulance. The map on the mayor's desk had little potions at small barricades with marginal sized arrows scattered all over its surface. Points to stand and fight, fallback points, and healing points. There was a legend at the bottom of the map to decode the colors and simples making interpretation easy to understand.

The people around the map were silent, moving icons around. The looks on their faces were deep in thought.

The setup confused Jennifer. "Why not just carry a healing potion and drink it as needed rather than having healing stations like water stations on a marathon?"

The triceratops answered her question. "Have you ever tried to drink something while fighting? It's a good way to get stabbed more."

Jennifer squinted at the triceratops, who was the only one in the room she had to look up at. "I use a diamond formation. The person needing healing gets behind me for a potion."

"Me getting behind anyone just puts a target on the one in front of me."

"So, you want your hands free for fighting." Jennifer's mind raced as she talked, trying to think of ways to deliver a hands free healing potion.

"Do you have a helmet I can see for a quick sec?" The smile on her face was somewhere between this-is-a-bad-idea and this-is-the-greatest-idea-ever.

The triceratops man took a custom black and gold helmet out of his inventory and handed it to Jennifer.

Just by looking at the helmet, she knew it was made by a master, it had a purple label on the inside saying as such. "Be right back." She left the room and used her crafting skill to make simple, two potion holders on the one on each side of the helmet with a tube.

Once finished, she walked back into the mayor's office. The mayor, the old goblin, who arrived when she was crafting, the leader of the dinosaurs, and his lovely dinosaur planner were all arguing about the placement of barricades. Jennifer felt the triceratops's eyes following her as she walked up to him, hiding the helmet behind her. She was really trying to hide her smile.

"So, I made you a thing," she said.

"What did you do?" he asked as his eyes narrowed.

She took the helmet out from behind her.

"Where I came from, this is called a drinking hat." She was proud of her little creation. She put two of her potions in the waiting receptacles. "Hands free, and ready for use when you need it."

The mayor was face palming, the elder goblin was staring open mouthed, and the dinosaur leader looked confused.

"Goblin want to know how many metal hats you have. How many potions you have?" He was the first to speak,

But before Jennifer could answer him, the dinosaur warlord spoke. "She can carry a max of four. Normally, she only has access to three due to trades."

Jennifer looked at the warlord with a side eye. "How did you know that?"

The warlord's smile widened. "Some people know who to ask the right questions to." His tone mocked Jennifer, as she processed what he had said.

With tension building in the room, Jim attempted an obvious de-escalation. "The corporation is good, but sometimes they sell information too. The cows are always watching."

Stunned at these revelations, the only thing Jennifer could say was, "Oh." She did not know how to process that. She trusted Sarah, but how many of the people wearing sunglasses were watching her? How much did they know? The gears of her mind spun faster with each heartbeat. What does the corporation do? Do they have a headquarters? Do they accept Sociology students as interns for summer break? Is it all one corporation, or just a few working together? What would their lunchroom look like, would it be just a large salad bar?

"Jennifer, are you not paying attention? The goblins will be here soon. Can your party go out and hunt with the goblins? The town is going to need a food supply."

The mayor's voice shocked Jennifer back to the task at hand. She checked her menus. Sarah was in town, Kevin was in the town square, and Soup Bowl's name was grayed out, meaning he was in another world. She sent a blue bird to all of them so they would meet in front of her café.

"Well, Woozle will enjoy going for a hunt, but we're missing a member of the party." The words were in the air for a moment. She looked at the goblin. When she sent an invite to him, she received an error message.

Invalid target.

"Will you join my party, Goblin?" While she would not be able to see him or his status in her menu, she could have him around.

The old goblin nodded once before answering. "Goblins come to town. Set up camp. Prepare for fight. Goblin go with giant. Get big food." He added a smile and rubbed his stomach.

Jennifer left the meeting with her green friend, leaving the rest of the strategy meeting to the mayor and the warlord.

It was not long before they were outside the city, following behind the goblin. Jennifer had no idea what the goblin was watching out for, but he looked like he knew what he was doing.

Woozle was beside the elderly goblin, periodically pausing to sniff the ground. She knew him well enough to know he was not finding anything.

Kevin was at the back of the group. Once or twice he had given Jennifer a polite bark when she had turned the wrong way. Even with the two navigations on, she still sometimes got lost. She did not know why, but it was happening less and less often. She would give him scratches behind the ear when he helped her stay on the right path.

Sarah was in front of Jennifer but behind the goblin. She was in the suit she wore for combat.

Jennifer's mind wandered back to the warlord knowing about her potion limit. Her heart was beating faster than it should. Jennifer needed to know but could not bring herself to ask. Would asking betray Sarah's trust? How could it not? Others in sunglasses that may have known.

"Did you tell Export du Universal about my powers?" She had not meant to say it aloud, the words coming out unintentionally. Sarah turned around, then all eyes turned to Jennifer.

Sarah straightened her back. Jennifer could not see if Sarah's eyes were darting around the group or not behind her dark sunglasses, but her head movement suggested it. Jennifer looked into the large dark sunglasses of her friend, waiting for the answer.

"No, I did not." Sarah was looking straight at Jennifer when she spoke, but something was off about her friend. Her body language told Jennifer there was more to it.

"But?"

Sarah could not meet Jennifer's eyes and was looking down. "We do not sell information on people we team with or people we have deals with. The main export for the company is information. One of us did sell that information."

"Goblin think. Company not bad. Company in system. Goblin make deal to not sell where Goblin is." The goblin moved to Sarah's side. He patted her side. "Goblin speak with non-goblin thanks to company." The goblin pulled out a plain circular copper amulet from under his shirt.

Sarah was unable to meet anyone's eyes. "I was the one that made that deal. We hope to help the goblins in spite of them not being in the system. If they could communicate better, they would be accepted."

Something itched in Jennifer's mind. She thought back to the night when she was cleaning the stables. She wanted to reject the system. She was going to go to school to help fix another system. Sociology was the study of society, by following this field she wound to answer, what binds people together, why people work together, how to enable people to work to better all rather than themselves? The system in this world was what bound people. All people playing by rules, set forth by the Dev. As she was system touch, the same system that let her look into her menus. Her attention was drawn to her anadromous power, the one that allowed her recall items. It was in the system, but she knew it was not from the system. Jennifer had an image of an old man in her head. Something itched in her mind, how do people live here, but live outside the rules?

The words pop into her head, she mimicked the old man's words. "Why do goblins not have names?" The words came slowly because she was unsure why that question was so important to her. "Is it because if you had names, the system would be able to track you?" The information was there, but something was not connecting for her.

"Goblin reject system. Dev came after Goblin. Goblin refuse

Dev. Dev told all to hunt Goblin." Notes of sadness rang in his voice.

"You reject the system, so you're treated badly? Did you do anything wrong?" Jennifer could not see how rejecting the system would cause them to be hunted.

Sarah's voice wavered as she spoke. "The corporation thinks the Dev needs to maintain control. We don't know why. When coming here, those in the corporation receive a choice. Accept the system or ." Her voice broke, unable to speak the alternative.

"Those who reject the system are punished by the system." Those simple words should not have gone together so easily, but they did. Her menus were always on hand. Even wishing that she could reject them too, there was no way to go back. In her own world, she had a menu in her pocket that was always able to bring her information just like now. That hand held menu connected her with the world by text or voice, played music, and allowed her to look up information faster than learning it herself.

"Goblin sees goblin mark. Hunt this way."

Jennifer could not meet anyone's eyes. It hurt her to be touched in memoirs. Such conveniences allowed so much control. With the connection of that device, she was submitting to having something that could track her every movement. Here, by interacting with the system, they could track her every moment. It would be much harder here to disconnect.

"Goblin who protect my heart is ahead." He pointed down the wide path the group was walking on.

Moments later, another elderly goblin embraced their group's goblin. The two spoke in their language.

Jennifer moved up beside Sarah. "I'm," Jennifer cut Sarah off before she could continue. "I know trust is a hard thing." Sarah wrapped Jennifer in her arms in a bear hug. Sarah was one of Jennifer's first friends here, but she never noticed the height difference between them.

"Are you taller than me?" Jennifer asked before breaking the hug.

"Well, yes, but only by a few fingers." Sarah's head tilted to one side. "Did you never notice? I was a bit surprised you never asked if I was a half giant like you."

Jennifer looked Sarah up and down. "I mean, yes, I should've thought of that."

A loud warning bark came from Kevin. his goblin moved from a bored posture in the saddle to holding her weapon pointing up and her other hand on a saddle horn.

The elderly goblin that was guiding the group shushed Kevin. "Goblin who test Goblin is ahead. They found food."

Leading the group around a bending turn was a team of goblins working on a hairy beast that made Jennifer look tiny. The creature was no longer in a state that could be described as living. The creature was laid on its side in front of the group.

Woozle said with amazement, "That's a mammoth,"

"I call dibs on the bones." Jennifer's hand shot like a rocket into the air.

"Goblin use bones." While his words were not a question, the raised eyebrow on the goblin told her it was.

Both Kevin and Woozle were running around the massive deposit of meat and bones. They would approach the fallen animal, sniff it, then run.

Jennifer took in a deep breath and closed her eyes. She was used to the power by now, but it was still not one she would have chosen.

"Summon Undead." When she opened her eyes, undead Kevin sat on his hind legs in front of Jennifer wagging his tail.

"Goblin willing to make deal," his words came slowly.

She looked around the group. The goblins working on the mammoth were slicing off portions of meat. They were collecting the cut portions in baskets. This mammoth had four tusks but was missing the crystal fur she remembered seeing on the mural. The elderly goblin, who protected their goblin guide's heart, was speaking in a way that said he was in charge.

"What kind of deal?" Jennifer asked the goblin.

"You no do that to Goblin. Goblin give giant the fur and bones.

One time." His words came out at a slow, deliberate pace.

She thought this offer over. Reviewing the situation, the goblin did not want her to use summon undead on any goblins. If she agreed she would be limiting herself, but she had a supply of human bones. It was only a day trip at most for her to get more. Jennifer dropped to one knee in order to shake the elder's hand. "I will never use the bones of goblins."

After finishing the shake, the old one shouted to the other goblins. They shouted back. Sarah shrugged in Jennifer's direction. Jennifer found a very interesting tree to look at. Not looking at the goblins working on the remains of the animal.

Before leaving the area, the only remains of the mammoth were its fur and bones.

Jennifer never paid much attention to her inventory space, which had never been full. After pulling out many flowers, some moss, a few interesting rocks, and several other things she had forgotten were in her inventory, she had freed up enough space for the Mammoth, leaving her space registered as full.

She tried to use Summon Large Undead, but the mammoth was listed as enormous.

She promised herself she would find a place to store it when she returned home. It took up too much space in her inventory to carry it around everywhere.

The group returned to town and received some experience points for an unmarked quest to bring back meat. Coming back to town they passed groups of four to ten goblins.

The goblins were coming into town in small groups with grim looks on their faces. No one challenged the goblins as they came in. Jennifer watched the goblins with curiosity. The goblins were never idle. They were either helping the wounded who came across the bridge, building defensive emplacements, or working on weapons.

Jennifer's group disbanded with each going back to their own tasks. She returned to her café. She wished it was not empty, but it could not run without her. Her blue skeleton was at a table. He was flipping a set of five separate coins, which was something he made a habit of. Her other skeleton stood idle next to a doorway. She had not de-summoned the undead Kevin, who was acting more and more like the living Kevin with every summons. She decided to let him stay out and do his own thing.

Her eyes fell on their new addition, and she moved a chair so she could sit by it. Woozle was sniffing the treasure chest when she asked, "So, you're a mimic?" Woozle moved into an attack pose with his fur raised. But after a glance at Jennifer, he returned to sniffing.

"What are you going to do with me?" The sadness in the mimic's voice broke Jennifer's heart. Sadness was not something anyone should have to add to their words. The amount of sadness the mimic spoke with could break some peoples' spirits from hearing it.

"What do you want to do?"

"I do not want to fight."

Woozle rubbed his head on the newcomer. "Well, mimic, you are lucky. This kid avoids fights. She is a good one, too. She will help you find a new partner, or she will let you stay here." Woozle moved to circle the Mimic. "Wait, I thought mimics were sticky?"

Jennifer watched as the mimic answered the question. "If I'm stressed or hungry, I am sticky. I am able to control it to a degree or else your head would be attached to me. Whatever gets stuck to me I'm able to capture with my tongue. The barbarian used me to lure enemies too big for him to handle."

"This is a pet café. You can stay here for as long as you like. If you get stressed or hungry, you come into the back. If you are out here, you may get a few people trying to give you pets. If you need something, let me know. The chickens are not food. I'm sure they will be back soon"

"Okay."

Jennifer was unsure how to take the mimic response. "It's been a day. I am going to go up to bed. Before I go, is there anything you need or want?"

"No, I will be okay."

She gave the mimic a hug, before she went up to her room. She had a large bed to sleep in, that was delivered days ago. Woozle also had a large bed to sleep in. Woozle never slept in his own bed.

As she started to drift off to sleep, he asked, "What are you going to do with the mammoth, kid?"

"I have no idea. If you have one, go for it." Her last words as she entered her dreams.

CHAPTER 19

A TIME FOR BATTLE

WHEN SHE WOKE UP, she was greeted with a new notification. People were selecting their starting points for the raid. Someone in Jennifer's team had chosen one for them. They were near the town center. Jennifer moved her marker from the town center to outside the town gate on the path to Bishop's University.

She was not going to take part in this.

When she went downstairs to begin her day, the mayor was knocking on her door. She waved at the mayor to come in.

The mayor walked with a stiffness and small jerky movements. "You're not joining the raid?" Jennifer could tell the mayor was under stress. He normally used more words.

"Nope, I will have the healing potions you need, but I will not fight." She raised a finger to signal Blue. He took the hint, stopped flipping his set of coins, and went into the kitchen.

Jim's face was red, his eyes glaring at Jennifer.

"I know you are going to ask why, but I do not like fighting. I want to be a Sociologist, someone who studies societies, peoples, and that they do. I want to change the world but not by using my mop to smash people." Jennifer took a seat at the closest empty table, extending her hand to the chair across from her and inviting the mayor to sit down. He took the seat but looked like he wanted to smash the table.

Blue came out of the kitchen with cups of cold tea. He placed the mugs on the table, before returning to the kitchen.

Jennifer took her drink and took her first morning sip. She closed her eyes, half savoring the cool beverage and half waiting for the mayor to speak.

She was daydreaming of what it would be like to get her first class's books at the campus bookstore when the mayor broke the silence. "Stay at the café. It's protected, and you will still be able to make the healing tea. I can have goblins running to get the tea and deliver it to those who could use the help."

Jennifer weighed her options. Staying in town and not being in the fight was good enough for her. "Okay, I would like experience for each of the teas being used rather than money."

"Fine." The mayor may as well have spat the word.

There were stress lines on his face, his hair was not as well kept as normal, and there were specks of debris on his top hat. There were signs of stress. She knew he was on the line, fighting more worry than anything and getting ready for a danger that was coming to his town.

He downed the tea before he left the café, saying no more.

Goblins and townspeople formed a line outside of the undead café. All of them brought healing moss. They handed her the moss, and she crafted them. Half the moss was used for the one who brought it in. The other half went to the town's supply.

The day went by so quickly she lost track of how many she made before closing the doors. The timer for the raid was below ten hours when she went to bed. After six hours of trying to sleep, she gave up. "Hey, Woozle, want to go for a walk?"

He was scratching at the door before Jennifer left the bed.

In the first few days when she arrived here, he was overprotective and overcompensating. Now he acted more like a pet and a friend. He could tear off people's limbs if they threatened her in any way, but would rather get head scratches.

The town square was filled with more tents. A goblin sat on a chair playing an accordion with a slow melancholy tone. A goblin came riding up on the back of an armoured spider. The arachnid was not as large as Rover's grandmother, and it was too small for Jennifer to ride. But it was a good size for the goblin.

The goblin rider waved a greeting in Jennifer's direction, adding, "Soary."

Jennifer waved back, a smile touching her lips.

Woozle was hunting rabbits, and she promised herself that hunting rabbits would be the next quest she went on. But she had stopped questing. Instead, she opened a café and waited for her acceptance letter.

A rabbit darted out from some nearby bushes, Woozle following after. She felt a pleasant, cold breeze this night. The sky was clear with the two moons showing. If not for the impending raid, it would have been a good night for a stroll.

"You can't sleep either?" The voice came from behind, causing her to have a little jump.

"Why does everyone use stealth? Jim." Jennifer did not bother turning around.

"Most people do not have force-fields," the mayor's words came out slowly, and were not accompanied with his normal upbeat demeanor.

Jim walked beside Jennifer in silence for some time. She was fine with the lack of conversation. The goblin playing his music and night air helped to improve her mood.

The two moved through the night, each on their own journey, but together through timing. Eventually, the mayor said, "Have you heard of Lord Dexx's theory?"

"I knew that was going to be on a test. Yes, Woozle told me about it when I first got here." She had forgotten most of it but remembered the name.

"I heard it years ago. It didn't make sense to me. It was just backstory for some game. I wanted to be a mayor and build a town. Now, I'm going to be defending it with goblins."

"Why do you hate the goblins so much?"

The mayor took off his top hat and looked down. "The part

that always bothered me about Dexx's theory was, what happens when this world's timeline and my world's timeline are merged? One timeline overwriting another, and you get lost in the crack. The world after two timelines gets merged, and you no longer exist."

Jennifer shrugged. "This place is supposed to exist outside of the normal flow of time. So if you were here before you were deleted, I guess you get to stay here. Sure, it's a bit odd. Raids kinda suck, but you always have more to do."

"To answer your question, I don't hate the goblins. The world and its system hates them. Sometimes it is hard to fight the system. It gets in your head, pushing the way you think, or do things. It is not just playing a role in a game. The system changes you to fit in what it wants you to be. Sometimes you forget the system is even there. The only thing that reminds me of what this place is, is the logout button. With the rules coming in, and respawns for true parallels only came in."

The last three words hurt Jennifer's ears, but she knew what they meant. That was their way of coming and going from this world into their own. "So, you're scared that there's no other world for you, and you're just a fragment?"

A soft chuckle came from the mayor. "Dexx's theory was for functionaries, fragments, and parallels. Then he met me and coined the term echo. Someone who was once a parallel but is unable to log out. An echo of a parallel. I am walking around as someone who is unsure where they will be tomorrow. I am following a tradition of, if one expects a loss, one should inspect the place they command. Between that and the tune the goblin is playing, I'm in far too sober of a mood tonight. Try and get some rest. Tomorrow is always the first day of the rest of your time."

The mayor turned away, continuing his walkabout. Jennifer did the same, she would inspect the place she commanded. Her café was much smaller than the town.

CHAPTER 20

ALONG CAME A RAID

THE NOISE BOTHERED JENNIFER the most: the yelling, the screaming, and the sound of combat. When it started, it never seemed to end.

She had runners coming in and out, getting more potions and returning the empty bottles. The worst thing was how easy it was to tell a fragment from a parallel. Fragments had grim expressions, parallels had smiles.

Minutes turned into hours. Although the runners stopped coming for her potions, she still saw them. Goblins would return to the town square, gather throwing spears, and take the weapons back to the sounds of combat. They were attacking fast, but they were coming back to the town square faster.

The battle was getting closer.

Through the front glass of the shop, Jennifer saw the monster's head above the roofs of the nearby buildings. The big bad's skin was the color of fresh blood. Its sharp teeth looked like they were meant to shred the meat off its victims. The monster had no eyes, only metal rods that came out where the eye sockets would be. The noise that came from the creature's throat was not that of roars or growls but of laughter.

The laughter chilled Jennifer to her soul. She had a flicker of hope that between the goblins, townspeople, and dinosaur people that they would bring an end to the laughing one.

The tail of the beast smashed through the side of the town hall. When the beast came into full view. Spears stuck out of the brute like the quills of a porcupine. The dinosaur raid boss was one that stood on two legs with short front arms, a tyrannosaurus rex, king of the dinosaurs.

The town force was attacking with all the strength they had using range attacks, like Jennifer's dark pulse, and all the colors of the rainbow hitting from all directions. She knew there were those that use much less flashy attacks.

The melee people were attacking with swords, maces, and laser sticks. Kevin tried to bite into a massive leg, but nothing fit into his mouth.

A line of roses crossed the tail of being. It was the attack of one of her hand-fed chickens that was out there fighting. The black rooster with the domino mask used his wing to shield the white chicken as the monster's tail came down on the pair. After the dust settled, they were no more. They had fought and died, as she was only a spectator.

Jennifer watched in silence from a chair in her café. Woozle laying on the floor beside her. The idea of fighting again scared her. She was no hero. Now many of those who went out to save the town lay still. She felt ashamed, but she did not move from her spot. In her mind, she repeated, "if he gets any closer. I will run." With every step he took, she remained in place.

The large, brown rooster came into the café, making frantic noises. Jennifer let her head sink, unsure what to do. Was it too late to join the fight? Even if she did, what more could she do. That thing out there was an unstoppable force.

Duncan McCluken of the clan McCluken, has sent a group invite.

The words on the screen made her turn to the irate rooster. "You too? I'm sorry. What more can I do? I just have a mop. I am scared."

"Mops are used to clean up messes. That looks like a mess out there. I gave you a quest to save the town, and you're just going to sit there?" A small man in a white lab coat and a hair line that had given up holding the line a long time ago stood in the doorway to the kitchen.

Tears began to form in her eyes. "I'm just a girl."

"You're a half giant. Someone who came from a long line of strong people. Are you really going to let the world tell you that you're not enough. Or are you going to dive into the deep end and see if you can swim."

"But . . ." She was trying to hold his gaze. They were warm and inviting.

"I want you to be in one of my classes at bishops. Don't tell anyone about this but take this and save the town." He put something cold and hard into her hand, smiled, waved, and walked out the front door.

Woozle was smelling the thing in her hand. "Is it another egg?"

She looked at the object in her hand. "Lightning in a bottle, just like the one in the first room." The memory of that place filtering through her mind. The bottle had the label, Limit Breaker.

"It's a power up. Maybe we can use it to power up the school. [AP2] If we run, maybe some of the survivors will—"

"Woozle, Destroyer of Worlds, Bringer of Doom, The One Who Is The Storm, Defeater of The Moon, Slayer of All Before Him."

Her words hung in the air, she smiled, she was sure what her next actions would be. She filled her inventory.

"Let's fight."

At first, Woozle titled his head. After a heartbeat, his engine began to spin and glow.

Jennifer accepted the invite from the rooster. Rover appeared from a trap door on Jennifer's shoulder.

Her legs carried her straight into the thick of battle.

She could not stand to look at the monitor in the raid boss's chest. It was a last century, curved monitor, not as old as the dinosaur body, but it was an old monitor that was curved, with inputs on the front. He was part machine, part dinosaur. A green smiley face displayed on the screen.

"Force field." She let the words flow out from her and used the ability on everyone she could. With her mop, she smashed the side of the cybernetic dinosaur as hard as she could. She let her anger and frustration out as she wailed on the beast with her mop.

The beast's every movement struck a defender or a building. Whatever it hit would not be getting up any time soon.

"Why are you doing this," she screamed at the top of her lungs at the beast.

At Jennifer's question, it stopped laughing for a moment. "Because it is fun."

A powerful shout came from behind the invader. "Token of Cowthulhu." A black and white monster the size of the raid boss smashed into the red scaled dinosaur. The black and white newcomer looked like it was made out of rubber with many tentacles coming from where its mouth should have been. Bat-like wings clapped into the side of the head of the invader. It let out a terrifying moo so deep the ground rumbled.

You have resisted Mad Cow. Sanity is wasted on the sane.

The jaws of the cybernetic dinosaur clamped onto Cowthulu's shoulder. Tearing the flesh out, bloody bits hanging from the commodore's jaw.

The resulting scream forming from her monstrous ally caused Jennifer to fall to her knees.

The black and white monster turned into Sarah.

The screen on its chest spoke. "That did not taste like chicken," as its rampage resumed.

Jennifer rushed to her friend's side with a potion. Jennifer saw her friend's eyes for the first time. The large black orbs carried both kindness and pain.

"The cows are watching," were her last words. The body of her friend slowly vanished.

Tears clouded Jennifer's eyes. She smashed the lightning in a bottle against her chest, unleashing the potential. "You want fun? Fun comes with friends, and I can make friends. Summon Undead."

The mammoth skeleton she had been keeping in her inventory rose out of the ground beneath her. The bones were covered in shiny metal. The protective coating covers each bone. The four tusks were replaced with chain saws that whirred to life.

The skeleton could not roar, so it stomped its feet. As the feet of her mount met the ground, the sound was like thunder. The shock wave that reverberated through the ground made the remaining defenders stumble or fall.

The red beast took a step backwards. The green smile on the monitor flickered into a yellow frown for a moment before the laughter returned.

Jennifer urged the mammoth forward in a charge.

The dinosaur returned the charge.

The mammoth was half the height of the invader. But where the invader was tall with tech and flesh, the mammoth was thick with metal and bones.

At that moment, they were both the unstoppable force. When two unstoppable forces meet. They stop and everything around them moves.

When they collided, buildings shook and fell. The town's defenders had at best, slowed the destroyer, but the mammoth stopped it in its tracks. Each of them strained and grunted to push the other back.

It used its mass and legs to push against the chain saw tusks of the mammoth. It was hurting itself trying to hurt the metal bound defender.

As her mount was pushed back an inch, she used the only power she could think of that might help. "Mend." It was the only card she had left. She had used the limit break on her summon undead. The rest of her powers remained the same. She could not think of a way that the spider's webbing could help.

A great axe smashed the dinosaur's monitor followed by a flash of lightning then another and a third. All of the strikes hit the destroyer before Jennifer heard the thunder.

The mayor appeared next to Jennifer. He wore black and gold armor the armor of a legionary a thousand years out of date. His breath was heavy and sweat covered him.

Her mammoth was pushed backward. The monster was taking huge damage for every inch it was pushed.

An unseen choir singing in an ancient language serenaded the town. She had heard the music once before, and she hoped it was signaling the same thing.

The great green-gray forest wolf and a jet-powered lynx-shark each attacked an arm of the menace with their teeth.

A cannonball met the head of the one they were all trying to stop.

Jennifer smiled. She was not alone.

The smoke cleared as he roared. "I am Comadorous Sixtyfourous. I will not be stopped by the likes of you."

It wasn't enough. The machine king of the dinosaurs kept pushing forward.

The mayor took Jennifer's hand, transferring something from his inventory to hers. She looked up from her hand to his face. His mouth was moving, but she could not hear what he was saying. The noise of the battlefield was too much.

The mayor transformed into a being of living lightning, leaped onto the dinosaur's jaws, and called down more lightning strikes than she could count. Each strike louder, thicker, and brighter than the last.

Cannon balls rained down on the beast.

Everyone still on the battlefield attacked with everything they had.

The commodore fell.

They won.

Jennifer won.

The town was saved.

CHAPTER 21

ADMISSIONS

JENNIFER SMILED AT THE dean. He was sitting at his desk, looking over a pile of paperwork and occasionally looking up at her.

"So, you saved the town. Was that once or twice?" A bit of wonderment laced the dean's voice.

"Mayor Jim Gigawatts thinks I saved it twice. I had a quest to save the town, and it was only marked completed the second time." She met the dean's question unflinchingly.

"And you want goblins to be accepted as well?"

"Yes, and as a business owner, I signed all of their letters of recommendation."

"I think I can do that, but you are going to need to do a quest line first."

Jennifer's smile dropped, her eyes narrowed. "You got to be f—"

EPILOGUE

LAST NIGHT'S BATTLE WAS the most intense thing Kevin had ever taken part in. Commadorous Sixtyfourous was part machine and part dinosaur, all monster. It was just the beta version. The upgraded game is being released next month. If that was just the beginning, what more did this game have in store for the players?

The pod he used to enter the game world looked so simple from the outside. Everything he experienced while in the pod, and by extension the turtle planet, felt so real. He had been interviewed so many times because he was one of only a paw full of players that were given pods and access to the game. In every interview, they asked him what it was like playing the game. The only way he could verbalize his experience was by saying, "It felt as if I was really there. It was so real." No other headset, or VR setup compared to this. His mind was transported into another world, while his body remained here.

He turned the pod on. Being a beta player, everything he did in the game was live streamed to millions of canines. He was proud when his human joined the fight and turned the battle. That video had been watched so many times it almost broke the internet. The reaction videos had their own reaction videos. With every view, his company logo was always on the screen as he played.

He entered the pod, waiting for the game to load. Normally the process was smooth, this time it was different. It was like someone slowing down a car. The typically empty space of the loading area, a human with the head of an orca sat in a fine chair and greeted him.

"I am in a bind, I am a byte behind, and I am willing to make a deal. Do you want to be a beast, a monster, a man or even a mix? In exchange for a favor, how about I remake you something more in your own right. A werewolf?"

"Sure, it is only just a game."